Prince de Talleyrand

Memoirs of the Prince de Talleyrand

Volume II

Prince de Talleyrand

Memoirs of the Prince de Talleyrand
Volume II

ISBN/EAN: 9783337172510

Printed in Europe, USA, Canada, Australia, Japan

Cover: Foto ©Raphael Reischuk / pixelio.de

More available books at **www.hansebooks.com**

MEMOIRS

OF THE

PRINCE DE TALLEYRAND

EDITED, WITH A PREFACE AND NOTES, BY

THE DUC DE BROGLIE

Of the French Academy

TRANSLATED BY

RAPHAËL LEDOS DE BEAUFORT, F.R. Hist. S.

VOLUME II

WITH A PORTRAIT

GRIFFITH FARRAN OKEDEN AND WELSH
NEWBERY HOUSE, CHARING CROSS ROAD, LONDON
AND SYDNEY

1891

CONTENTS.

PART VI.

NAPOLEON'S MARRIAGE—HIS BROTHERS—HIS STRUGGLE WITH PIUS VII.

1809—1813.

PART VII.

THE FALL OF THE EMPIRE—THE RESTORATION.

1813—1814.

PART VIII.

CONGRESS OF VIENNA.

1814—1815.

MEMOIRS

<small>OF THE</small>

PRINCE DE TALLEYRAND

MEMOIRS

OF THE

PRINCE DE TALLEYRAND.

PART VI.

NAPOLEON'S MARRIAGE—HIS BROTHERS—HIS STRUGGLE WITH PIUS VII.

1809—1813.

Talleyrand marries his nephew with the daughter of the Duchess of Courland—Napoleon's marriage with the Archduchess Marie-Louise—Napoleon's dream of universal domination—His brothers and his sisters' husbands—Why he gave them thrones—Joseph in Naples—Murat succeeds him—Murat endeavours to shake off the yoke of Napoleon—Murat's ambition—Napoleon and his brother Louis—Westphalia—King Jérôme and the Germans—Joseph in Spain—Lord Wellington—The French driven from Spain—Blunder of Napoleon in Spain—Differences between Napoleon and the Pope—Persecution of Pius VII.—Negotiations between the First Consul and Pius VII.—Some bishops decline to resign their sees—The *Concordat*—*La petite Eglise*—Home regulations concerning Public Worship—Cardinal Caprara—Coronation of Napoleon—Pius VII. at Paris—Napoleon crowned King of Italy at Milan—Refusal of the Pope to recognize Joseph as King of Naples—Occupation of Rome by General Miollis—Annexation of the *legations* of Urbino, Ancona, Macerata, and Camerino—Imprisonment of several cardinals—Disarming of the Papal guards—Annexation of the Papal States to France—Protest of Pius VII.—The bull of excommunication—Arrest of the Pope—The King of Rome—Meeting of an ecclesiastical commission—Had the Pope any right to refuse the bull of confirmation to the French bishops?—Did the French Government infringe the clauses of the *Concordat* by invading Rome?—The Church in Germany and Italy—Measures to be taken to thwart the effect of the bull of excommunication—Considerations on the Commission—Cardinal

ON leaving a position long stirred by the illusions and excitement of power, I had to think of creating one which, though affording me needed rest, might offer interesting and pleasant occupations. Home-life alone can replace all chimera ; but, at the time of which I speak, home-life, sweet and calm, existed for but very few people. Napoleon did not allow any one to grow fond of it ; he believed that, to serve him, people should have no proper home. Carried away by the rapidity of events, by ambition, by the interest of each day ; placed in that mist of war and of political activity which hovered over all Europe, everybody was prevented from paying any attention to his own situation ; public life held too much room in his mind to allow of his giving a single thought to private life. People went home but accidentally, because it was necessary to take rest somewhere ; but no one was prepared to make his home an habitual abiding-place.

I was, like anybody else placed in that position which explains the indifference everybody displayed in all the acts of his life, and that I regret having displayed in several of my own. It was then that I sought to marry my nephew, Edmond de Périgord.[1] It was important that the choice of the wife I should give him should not awaken the susceptibility of Napoleon, who did not wish to have the destiny of a young man, who bore one of the great names of France, escape his jealous influence. He believed that, a few years before, I had influenced the refusal of my niece, the Comtesse Just de Noailles,[2] whom he had demanded from me for Eugène de Beauharnais, his adopted son. Whatever choice I might make for my nephew, I should still find the emperor dissatisfied. He would not have allowed me to choose in France, for he reserved for his devoted generals all the good matches to be found there. I bent my looks elsewhere. I had often, in Germany and Poland, heard much said of the Duchess of Courland.[3] I knew that she was distinguished by the nobleness of her sentiments, by the elevation of her character and by the most amiable and brilliant qualities. The youngest of her daughters was then marriageable. This choice could but please Napoleon. It did not take away a match for his generals, who would have been refused, and it must even have flattered the vanity he displayed in trying to attract to France great foreign families. This vanity had, some time before, led him to have Marshal Berthier marry a princess of Bavaria. I resolved therefore to demand for my nephew the Princess Dorothée of Courland, and in order that the Emperor Napoleon should not, by reflection or by caprice, withdraw his approbation once given, I solicited from the Emperor Alexander, a particular friend of the Duchess of Courland, the favour of asking himself the hand of her daughter for my nephew. I had the

---

[1] Alexandre-Edmond de Talleyrand-Périgord, born August 2, 1787, afterwards Duc de Dino, and later, Duc de Talleyrand-Périgord.

[2] Françoise de Talleyrand-Périgord, daughter of Archambauld Joseph, Comte, then Duc de Talleyrand-Périgord, brother of the author. Born in 1785, she married in 1803 Just, Comte de Noailles, and later Duc de Poix, who was chamberlain of the emperor. She died in 1863.

[3] Charlotte-Dorothée, Countess of Medem, widow of Pierre, last Duke of Courland and of Semigalle, born February 3, 1761, married November 6, 1779. Widowed January 13, 1800. Died August 20, 1821.

[4] Dorothée, Princess of Courland, born August 20, 1793. Died in 1862.

happiness of obtaining it, and the marriage took place at Frank-
fort-on-Main, April 22, 1809.

While determining no longer to take part in anything done
by Napoleon, I remained sufficiently acquainted with current
affairs to be able to judge well of the general situation, to
calculate what must be the date and veritable nature of the
catastrophe which appeared inevitable, and to seek means for
warding off from France the evils this must produce. All my
antecedents, all my former relations with the influential men of
the different courts, assured to me facilities for being informed
of all that took place. But I must at the same time give to my
manner of living an air of indifference and of inaction, which
should not offer the least ground for the continual suspicions of
Napoleon. I had the proof that one already ran risks by no
longer serving him, for, on different occasions, he showed
great animosity towards me, and several times publicly gave
way to violent temper. This did not annoy me, for fear has
never entered my nature ; and I might even say that the hatred
he manifested against me was more harmful to him than to me.
If it were not for anticipating the order of time, I would say
that this hatred maintained me in my independence and decided
me to refuse the portfolio of Foreign Affairs, which the emperor
offered me later with much insistence. But at the time this offer
was made to me, I already regarded his fine *rôle* as finished, for
he no longer seemed to apply himself to anything but destroying
the good he had done. There was no longer any possible transaction for him with the interests of Europe. He had outraged
at one and the same time kings and nations.

Whatever need people in France felt of deluding themselves,
they were forced to recognize in the continental blockade, in the
natural although dissimulated irritation of the deeply-wounded
foreign cabinets, in the sufferings of industry bound by the pro-
hibitive system, the impossibility for a state of things, which
offered no guarantee of tranquillity for the future, to endure.
Each victory, that of Wagram even, was only an obstacle the
more to the strengthening of the emperor, and the hand of an
archduchess which he obtained soon after, was only a sacrifice
made by Austria to the necessities of the moment. Napoleon

might well attempt to represent his divorce as a duty he fulfilled solely to assure the stability of the Empire ; no one was deceived, and it was plainly seen that, in marrying the archduchess, he only sought one more satisfaction for his vanity.

The details of the council where the emperor put in deliberation the choice of his new empress are not without a certain historic interest ; I will give them a place here. For a long time Napoleon had caused it to be circulated in his court and in public that the Empress Josephine could not have any more children, and that Joseph Bonaparte, his brother, who had neither glory nor intellect, was incapable of succeeding him. This was circulated abroad, and from there brought back to France. Fouché took care to spread these reports by his police ; the Duc de Bassano instructed in the same manner the literary men : Berthier took the military in hand ; as has been seen at the interview at Erfurt, the Emperor Napoleon unbosomed himself in that respect to the Emperor Alexander ; finally all was ready, when in the month of January, 1810, the emperor summoned an extraordinary council, composed of great dignitaries, ministers, the Grand Master of Public Instruction, and two or three other non-military eminent personages. The number and quality of the persons who composed this council, the silence observed as to the object of the meeting, the silence still lasting for some minutes even in the hall of assembly, all proclaimed the importance of what was going to take place.

The emperor, with a certain embarrassment and an emotion which appeared to me sincere, spoke mainly in these terms :—

" I have not renounced without regret, assuredly, a union which shed so much sweetness over my domestic life. If, to satisfy the hopes that the Empire places in the new ties that I must contract, I consulted only my personal feeling, it is from the midst of the young pupils of the Legion of Honour, among the daughters of the brave soldiers of France, that I would choose a companion, and I would give to the French for empress the one whose qualities and virtues would render her most worthy of the throne. But it is necessary to make concessions to the customs of the times one lives in, to the usages of other States, and above all to the propriety which policy makes it a

duty to observe. Some sovereigns have desired the alliance of
my relations, and I believe there is now not one to whom I could
not with confidence offer my personal alliance. Three reigning
families could give an empress to France; those of Russia,
Austria, and Saxony. I have summoned you in order to
examine with you which of these three alliances is that to which,
in the interest of the Empire, preference should be given."

This discourse was followed by a long silence which the
emperor broke by these words: "Monsieur the Arch-Chancellor,
what is your opinion?"

Cambacères, who appeared to me to have prepared what he
was going to say, had raked up from his recollections as member
of the committee of public safety, that Austria was and always
would be our enemy. After having developed this idea at some
length, supporting it by many facts and precedents, he finished
by expressing the wish that the emperor should marry a grand-
duchess of Russia.

Lebrun,[1] putting aside policy, employed plainly all the
motives drawn from habits, education, and simplicity, to give
the preference to the court of Saxony, and voted for that
alliance. Murat and Fouché thought the revolutionary interests
more in safety by a Russian alliance; it appears that both found
themselves more at ease with the descendants of the Czars than
with those of Rudolph of Hapsburg.

My turn came; there I was in my element; I discharged
my task tolerably well. I was able to sustain by excellent reasons
that an Austrian alliance would be preferable for France. My
secret motive was that the security of Austria depended on the
resolution the emperor was going to take, but that was not the
place to say it. After having briefly set forth the advantages
and the inconveniences of a Russian match and of an Austrian

---

[1] Charles Lebrun, born in 1739, was in 1768 revenue officer, and inspector-general
of the royal domain. He was the friend and devoted assistant of Chancellor Maupeou.
He was dismissed in 1774. Deputy of the Third to the States-General, then administrator of the department of Seine-et-Oise, he was arrested in 1794, and not released
until after the 9th Thermidor. He was named deputy to the Council of the Elders in
1796. After the 18th Brumaire, he became Third Consul, arch-treasurer in 1804,
Prince and Duc de Plaisance (Piacenza) in 1808, lieutenant of the emperor in Holland
in 1810. In 1814, he was appointed Royal Commissioner at Caen and peer of France.
During the Hundred Days, he accepted both the imperial peerage and the functions
of Grand Master of the University. He died in 1824.

marriage, I gave my voice for the latter. I addressed myself to the emperor, and as a Frenchman, begged of him that an Austrian princess might appear in our midst, in order to absolve France in the eyes of Europe and in her own eyes, of a crime that was not her own, and which belonged entirely to a faction. The term "European reconciliation" that I employed several times, pleased several members of the council, who had had enough of war. In spite of some objections the emperor made to me, I saw well that my advice suited him.

M. Mollien [1] spoke after me, and sustained the same opinion with the shrewd and brilliant powers that distinguished him.

The emperor, after having heard every one, thanked the council, declared the sitting closed, and retired. On the same evening, he sent a messenger to Vienna, and at the end of a few days, the French ambassador wrote that the Emperor Francis granted the hand of his daughter, the Archduchess Marie-Louise to the Emperor Napoleon.

To connect this union with the glory of a conquest made by his army, Napoleon sent the Prince de Wagram (Berthier) to wed the Archduchess by proxy, and gave to the Maréchale Lannes, Duchesse de Montebello (her husband had been killed at Wagram) [2] the place of lady of honour. As it would not do to omit the oddities of these times, I must call attention to the fact that, at the moment when the cannon announced to Paris the betrothal at Vienna, the letters from the French ambassador brought the news that the last treaty with Austria was faithfully executed, and that the cannon was blowing up the fortifications of Vienna. This remark shows with what strictness Napoleon treated his new father-in-law, and proves well that peace was then for him only a truce employed in preparing new conquests. Thus all nations were fretting; all the sovereigns were uneasy and anxious. Everywhere Napoleon caused the growth of hatred, and invented difficulties, which, in the long

---

[1] Comte Mollien, born at Rouen in 1758, was first clerk of the comptroller-general in 1789. He was arrested in 1794 as an accomplice of the *fermiers-généraux*, but was saved by the 9th Thermidor. On the 18th Brumaire, he became Director of the Sinking Fund, Counsellor of State in 1804, Minister of the Treasury in 1806; he remained at this post until 1814, and resumed it during the Hundred Days. He was created a peer of France in 1819. He died in 1850.

[2] Marshal Lannes was killed at Esling, and not at Wagram.

run, must become insurmountable. And, as if Europe did not furnish him enough, he created himself new ones, by authorizing the ambitions of his own family. The fatal words that he had uttered one day, that before his death his dynasty would be the most ancient in Europe, made him distribute to his brothers and to the husbands of his sisters the thrones and principalities that victory and perfidy put into his hands. It was thus he disposed of Naples, Westphalia, Holland, Spain, Lucca, even Sweden, seeing that it was the desire to please him that had caused Bernadotte to be elected Prince Royal of Sweden.

A puerile vanity urged him on that path bristling with so many dangers. For, either these newly-created sovereigns remained in his great policy, and became its satellites, and then it was impossible for them to take root in the country confided to them ; or they must reject it more quickly than Philip V. had discarded that of Louis XIV. The inevitable divergence existing between nations soon alters the family ties of sovereigns. Thus each of these new creations became a principle of dissolution in the fortune of Napoleon. It is found everywhere in the last years of his reign. When Napoleon gave a crown, he desired that the new king should remain bound to the system of this universal domination, of this *grand Empire* of which I have already spoken. The one, on the contrary, who mounted the throne, had no sooner seized the sceptre, than he wished for undivided power, and resisted with more or less audacity the hand which sought to subject him. Each of these improvised princes believed himself placed on a level with the most ancient sovereigns of Europe, by the sole fact of a decree and a solemn entry into his capital occupied by a corps of the French army. The vanity which led him to show independence made him a more dangerous obstacle to the projects of Napoleon than would have been a natural enemy. Let us follow them a moment in their royal career.

The kingdom of Naples, with which I will begin, had been conferred, these were then the official terms, March 30, 1806, upon Joseph Bonaparte, the eldest brother of the emperor. It was desired to give his entry into this kingdom the appearance of a conquest, but the fact is, he must have read with some astonishment in the *Moniteur* the recital of the so-called resistance with which he met.

At the end of four months the new king was already in quarrel with his brother. Joseph resided but a short time at Naples ; circumstances led him soon to Spain. Power, during his sojourn at Naples, had been for him only a means of amusement ; and, as if he had been the fifteenth of his race, he looked on to see how his ministers would extricate themselves, according to the expression of Louis XV., from the daily embarrassments of government. On the throne, he sought only the sweetness of private life and facile libertinage which great names rendered brilliant.

To Joseph succeeded Murat, whose grand duchy of Berg no longer contented him. He had no sooner set foot beyond the Alps, than his imagination presented to him already the whole of Italy as destined to be his own one day. By the treaty which secured to him the crown of Naples, he was bound to maintain the constitution given by his predecessor, Joseph. But as this constitution was not yet executed except in its administrative part, he left to one side the changes in the civil and criminal laws that he had promised to make, and did not show himself in any haste to terminate the financial organization of the country. In order to facilitate the receipts and increase the revenues, he commenced to abolish all the feudal rights. Incited by his minister Lerlo,[1] he desired that this operation, which he only considered from the fiscal point, should be immediately carried out. And the commission instituted to this effect pronounced on all the litigations existing between the lords and the parishes in a manner to favour the parish only ; and this was being done at the very time when Napoleon was seeking to found again an aristocracy in France and to create entailed estates. The result of this operation was not only to despoil the Neapolitan barons of all the feudal rights and of all the payments in kind to which

[1] Giuseppe, Count Lerlo, born in 1759 at Naples, was Director of the Finances in 1798. In 1806, he accompanied King Ferdinand to Palermo, but joined Murat in 1809, became Counsellor of State, Minister of Justice and of Worship, and Minister of the Interior. In 1815, he took refuge in Rome, returned to Naples in 1820, was appointed Minister of the Interior, but was obliged to retire the same year. He died in 1828.

they were entitled, but also to take from them, to the profit of the parishes, the greater part of their lands, which had been jointly held for several centuries.

This measure was very detrimental to the fortunes of the nobles, but it rendered very much easier the assessment of the taxes, and made the latter more productive. Thus, in the space of five years the Neapolitan government raised its public revenues from forty-four millions of francs to more than eighty. Some real ameliorations in the administration, which were the result of the prosperity of the treasury, directed by the skilful hands of M. Agar, since created Comte de Mosbourg,[1] appeased the first discontent of the country, and prevented its reaching Napoleon, who besides, was disposed to indulgence for Murat. The latter was still so weak that the emperor felt flattered at being constantly reminded that Murat was also one of his creatures. He allowed a thousand improper, and sometimes even very grave things to pass unnoticed before making any reproaches to him. He was bound however to break forth, when Murat ordered that the French who, on the authority of Napoleon, were at Naples, should take the oath of fidelity to him, and be naturalized in the country. All were indignant at this demand ; and Napoleon, driven to extremes, manifested his displeasure with his customary violence. He gave orders for the French troops who were in that kingdom to be mustered in a camp a dozen leagues from Naples ; and from this camp he had it declared that every French citizen was by right a citizen of the kingdom of Naples, because by the terms of the decree of its foundation, this kingdom formed a part of the *Grand Empire.*

Murat, who, in a moment of impetuosity, had allowed himself to take so imprudent a step, persuaded himself that the emperor would never pardon him, and that there was no other course for him to follow than to seek safety in an increase of power ; from that time his sole aim was to obtain means to invade all

---

[1] Michel Agar, Comte de Mosbourg, born in 1771 near Cahors, was at first a barrister, and then professor in that city. In 1801, he entered the Legislative Body, became in 1806 Minister of Finances of Murat, his fellow-countryman, who had just been created Grand Duc de Berg, and accompanied him in the same quality to Naples. He lived in retirement under the Restoration, was elected Deputy of Lot in 1830, and peer of France in 1837. He died in 1844.

Italy.   The annexation of Tuscany, Rome, Holland and the Hanseatic cities to the French Empire had already caused him much uneasiness.   The employment, not defined, of this term *Grand Empire*, that he had just heard in the midst of his States, increased his perplexity, and he commenced to disclose his ulterior views.

The queen, who partook to a certain extent of the fears of Murat, was not however of the same opinion as he as to the manner of escaping the projects which might be planned by her brother.   She believed that it was a poor way of preserving a rule but feebly established, to seek to extend it.

The arrival of Marshal Pérignon,[1] at Naples to take the government of the city, justified, in the eyes of Murat, the extremities to which he might be carried.   And soon, the events of Europe, in reviving his hopes of ambition and of vengeance, gave more activity to his combinations.   In his twofold idea of escaping French influence and extending his domination in Italy, he only thought of increasing his army and of seeking to open negotiations with Austria, which was more and more affrighted at the invading policy of the French government. The queen took it upon herself to write to Prince Metternich, over whom she believed she still retained some influence, and whose discretion she had tested.   The king, on the other hand, conducted secretly a negotiation with the English authorities, and particularly with Lord William Bentinck,[2] who was in Sicily. The interests of commerce were the pretext of it.   Murat, believing he had grounds for complaint against Napoleon, and for throwing upon him the odium of the prohibitions, indicated

---

[1] Dominique, Comte, then Marquis Pérignon, was an officer under the old *régime*, deputy to the Legislative Assembly, then commander of a legion of the army of the Pyrenees, he succeeded Dugommier as commander-in-chief.   Member of the Council of the Five Hundred in 1795, ambassador at Madrid in 1796, he was afterwards placed at the head of a corps of the army of Italy, but was wounded and taken prisoner at Novi.   He entered the senate in 1801, was appointed marshal of France in 1804, Governor of Parma and of Piacenza, and finally commander-in-chief of the armies of the kingdom of Naples.   He was created peer of France in 1814, and died in 1818.

[2] Lord William Cavendish Bentinck (1774–1839), son of the Duke of Portland, entered the army, became Governor of Madras in 1803, and major-general in 1808. In this capacity, he made the campaigns of Portugal and Spain.   In 1811, he was appointed commander-in-chief of the English troops in Sicily.   In 1827, Bentinck was named Governor of Bengal, then Governor-General of India.   He was recalled in 1835.

his disposition to separate from him; but time for rupture had not yet come. The Russian campaign had just opened, and Murat could not refuse to go there with his contingent, as to the number of which, he, as well as the other allies of the emperor, was not allowed to decide. The queen remained in charge of the government. A combination of reason, delicacy, and gallantry gave her more influence and power than her husband had ever had. While Murat was fighting for and serving in person, the French cause, all his policy was then directed on a contrary side. This double part rather pleased him; on one hand he fulfilled his duty towards France and the emperor; and, on the other, he believed he was acting as a king, as an independent prince called to the highest destiny.

When Austria declared against France, and the battle of Leipzig had marked the limit of the fortune of Napoleon, Murat hurried to Naples, and from that moment he used all his endeavours to render his defection useful, for the support of his crown, and to enter the great European league. He found it very easy; the desire of all the Allied Powers to isolate Napoleon, and the refusal of Eugène de Beauharnais to enter this combination, rendered the defection of Murat very useful to the united powers. Napoleon, informed of all that was passing, was not enlightened in these circumstances either by his genius or by his counsellors. He should, in his interest, have recalled Eugène de Beauharnais to Lyons, with all that remained of the French troops, and have abandoned Italy to the ambitious dreams of Murat. It was the only means left for preventing his junction with the Allied Powers, and to provoke, in Italy, a national rising, which, in this campaign, would have been of great importance to Napoleon. But his eyes were blinded, and the treason was consummated at the moment when he believed it useful to speak still of the fidelity of him who, for several months already, had signed his treaty with Austria. The intrigues of Murat for arriving at a general domination in Italy continued none the less; one could follow the exact traces of them, until they became, at the Congress of Vienna, a motive of rupture with him on the part of the Powers. His ruin was the result of his intrigues.

My object was to point out here as a fact that there was in the power of Napoleon, up to the point it had now reached, and in his political creations, a radical defect, which, it appeared to me, must injure his consolidation and even prepare his fall. Napoleon delighted in annoying, humiliating, and tormenting those whom he had elevated ; they, placed in a perpetual state of mistrust and irritation, worked secretly to injure the power which had created them, and that they already regarded as their principal enemy.

Under one form or another, the same principle of destruction of which I have just given details to show the condition of affairs at Naples, is found in all the establishments of the same kind that Napoleon had made.

In Holland, he had begun by placing the power, which was hitherto in the hands of a revocable directory, into those of a president. He had decided that Count Schimmelpenninck[1] should accept the sovereign power under the title of Grand Pensioner. Schimmelpenninck was a man of too much sense to believe that the part he was called upon to play could be anything but temporary. But the exactions of the French agents, and the dilapidations of all kinds which were the result, naturally irritated public opinion in Holland. Schimmelpenninck had hoped to be of real service to his country by the momentary credit which was to be the price of his deference for Napoleon, and to obtain by it better conditions for Holland. His illusion in this respect could not be of long duration. The emperor, who always wished to give the appearance of a national movement to the crises which he brought on for the purpose of annihilating the independence of conquered countries, encouraged secretly, from the beginning of the accession of Schimmelpenninck, the complaints of the ancient privileged orders, of the magistracy of the cities, and of the nobility

---

[1] Roger Jean, Count Schimmelpenninck, born in 1761, a Dutch statesman, was associated with the revolutionary movements which disturbed Holland in 1795. He was appointed ambassador at Paris in 1798, then at London in 1802. In 1805, the Dutch Constitution having been transformed at the instigation of Napoleon, he had to accept the charge of Grand Pensioner. Under the reign of Louis Bonaparte, Schimmelpenninck lived in retirement. After the union of Holland with France, he was appointed senator. He resigned in 1814, and again become a Hollander ; he was a member of the first Chamber of the States-General. He died in 1825.

of Holland against the Pensioner, who had sprung from the middle-class ; he sought, at the same time, to rouse the revolutionary spirit of the people, in order to incite them to rise against the authority that the new order of things accorded to a single man.   But the moderation, the wisdom of the Grand Pensioner, the profound good sense of the Hollanders, and the conviction that any attempt at rising would lead immediately to the peremptory intervention of France, decided the nation to submit quietly to its new government.

The emperor, who saw that his underhand dealings did not lead to the end he had in view, and that it had no effect upon the country, followed another plan.   He got Admiral Verhuell[1] to inform Schimmelpenninck himself, and several prominent persons of the country, that this state of things could not last, and that it was indispensable for Holland to form with France a more intimate union, by demanding for sovereign a French prince.   Some explanations made it clear to Napoleon that union with France was what the country dreaded most, and he skilfully made use of this disposition to make them almost desire one of his brothers.   He not only promised to preserve the integrity of the territory, but he added to it Ost-Frise, and held out to the notable families hopes of all kinds.   Schimmelpenninck was in a state of painful irresolution ; he neither dared to consult the nation nor to consent to what was exacted. The step of naming a deputation to go to Paris, and judge there upon the spot just how far resistance might go, appeared to him what was most prudent and wise to do.   He composed this deputation of MM. Goldberg, Gogel,[2] Six and Van Styrum. Their instructions, like those of Admiral Verhuell, were to

[1] Charles-Henri Verhuell, Count of Sevenaar, born in 1764, entered the navy in 1779.   Rear-Admiral in 1803, he commanded the fleet destined to act against England, and was named Minister of Marine of Holland.   In 1806, he presided over the commission charged to offer the crown of Holland to Louis Bonaparte.   He became marshal and ambassador at Paris in 1807.   In 1811, after the annexation of Holland to France, he entered the Legislative Body ; he commanded the armies of the Texel and of the Helder in 1813, and remained faithful to the emperor even to the last minute.   Naturalized Frenchman in 1814, he was created peer of France in 1819, and died in 1855.

[2] Alexander Gogel, born in 1765, a Dutch manufacturer and statesman.   He was Minister of Finances of the Batavian Republic.   He was also minister of King Louis, and became member of the Council of State of France, after the union of Holland with the Empire.   He died in 1821.

demur, under any pretext, to the union, and to dismiss all propositions tending to establish a monarchy, by sustaining that
the forms of it were opposed to the customs and habits of the
country.

The emperor knew all that as well as the Dutch deputies;
but his will was so positive, his vanity was so bound, that no
consideration, of whatever kind it might be, could prevent these
unhappy negotiators from being led to demand formally that
Louis Bonaparte should accept the crown of Holland. Louis
on his side was constrained to accept it; thus they erected a
kingdom in Holland. From such an order of things difficulties
could not fail to crop up for Napoleon. And so they did soon,
in endless numbers.

Prince Louis, on arriving at the Hague, received a very cold
greeting. He remained there at first but a short time; called
by the declaration of war against Prussia, to march at the head
of the Dutch army into Westphalia, he commenced the siege
of Hameln, when this fortress was included in the capitulation
of Magdeburg; his campaign finished there. Having returned
to Amsterdam, he devoted himself to give Holland an independent existence; hence arose interminable discussions between
the two brothers. A treaty very hard for Holland was the result.

The emperor had it drawn up in a manner to offend his
brother enough to decide him to abdicate. But the irritation
of Louis Bonaparte carried him to extremities of another kind.
He submitted in appearance, signed what was desired, and
immediately opened negotiations with the courts of St. Petersburg and of London. His overtures to those two courts however failed. Then, decided that he was not to carry out the
treaty he had signed with his brother, he prepared for open
resistance; he excited all Holland to war, had fortifications
raised against France, and would not cede even to the force
that Napoleon was obliged to employ against him. When he
saw his kingdom invaded by the army commanded by Marshal
Oudinot, he furtively left the country, and retired to I do
not know what corner of Germany, bequeathing to Holland
all the hatred he bore his brother.[1]

[1] Napoleon had only placed his brother on the throne of Holland to bind that

The union of this country with France was the result of his departure.   The emperor enlarged his empire by that, but diminished his forces ; for he had to employ constantly a portion of his army to assure himself of the fidelity of his new subjects. The latter were in much greater fear of the rigorous levies of the conscription, and of the guards of honour, than they were flattered to see the fort of Helder become one of the maritime bulwarks of the French Empire, and the Zuyder Zee furnish a great school of navigation where might be drilled the crews of the fleets that France was building at Antwerp.   The different governments through which Napoleon made Holland pass completely destroyed the confidence of the people, and made them detest the name of Frenchman ; but the greatest difficulties that he had to experience in that country arose, as has just been seen, there as elsewhere, from his own creatures, from his own family.

The aggregation of twenty little states, erected by decree into the Kingdom of Westphalia, in favour of Joseph Bonaparte his brother, brought new embarrassments to his ambition· This kingdom, whose population was about two millions of inhabitants, comprised the whole of the states of the Elector of Hesse-Cassel.   It must be remembered that in Hesse the will of the sovereign replaced very nearly all institutions, and that the people, who were not over-burdened with taxes, did not yet wish for any other form of government.

Jérôme, a short time after his nomination (this was the term

country to the continental system.   His task was difficult, for the interests and sympathies of the Hollanders reconciled them more to England, while the policy of Napoleon ruined them.   King Louis did not wish to, or could not, carry out the intentions of the emperor in his kingdom, and allowed English smuggling to organize on his sea-board.   Napoleon complained bitterly, and neglected nothing to constrain his brother to enter into his views.   By the treaty of November 11, 1807, he took away from him Flushing, one of the best ports of Holland, in exchange for some enlargements of no consequence.   The situation remaining the same, he went still further, and announced to the Legislative Body that the exigencies of his policy might force him to annex Holland (Speech of December 3, 1809).   Nevertheless, this extreme measure was repugnant to him : he attempted to avoid it by signing with King Louis a second treaty (March 16, 1810), by which the latter ceded to him Zealand and Dutch Brabant ; at the same time, it was stipulated that the coasts of Holland should be guarded by French customs officers assisted by a body of troops. Louis came to Paris to sign this treaty, but, returning to his States, he avoided applying it.   Napoleon soon sent twenty thousand men into Holland.   The king, for an instant, had the thought of resisting, but no one having wished to follow him, he abdicated and took refuge abroad.   Holland was annexed to the Empire by a decree dated July 1, 1810.

which the emperor desired to have used), went to Cassel, the capital of his States. His brother had given him a kind of council of regency, composed of M. Beugnot,[1] a man of much intelligence, and of MM. Simeon[2] and Jolivet,[3] whose directions he was to follow.

Their portfolios were full of organic decrees of all kinds. They at first had brought from Paris with them a constitution ; they were afterwards to adapt to it a judiciary, a military, and a financial system. Their first operation was to divide the territory, and to change thus, in a moment, without the aid of revolutionary spirit, all the traditions, all the customs and all the relations that time had established. They then created prefectures and sub-prefectures, and appointed mayors everywhere. They thus transferred into Germany all the machinery of French administration, and pretended to have set it in motion. Their task being over, M. Beugnot and M. Jollivet returned to France. Jérôme Bonaparte hastened to facilitate their going. He retained M. Simeon as his Minister of Justice, and then he

---

[1] Jacques Claude, Comte Beugnot, born in 1761, advocate to the *Parlement* in 1782, *procureur-syndic* for the department of the Aube in 1790, deputy to the Legislative Assembly in 1791. He was arrested in 1793, but was set free by the 9th Thermidor. After the 18th Brumaire, he was named Prefect of the Lower Seine, and Councillor of State in 1806. In 1807, he was one of the administrators of the Kingdom of Westphalia ; Imperial Commissioner and Minister of Finances of the Grand Duchy of Berg in 1800. In 1814, he was named by the government Provisory Commissioner of the Interior, and Director-General of the Police. He afterwards entered the navy. The second Restoration made him Director-General of Post Offices, Minister of State, and Member of the Privy Council. He was elected Deputy of the Marne. He died in 1835.

[2] Joseph Jérôme, Comte Simeon, born at Aix in 1749, was Professor of Law in that city in 1789. In 1792, he was one of the leaders of the federalist movement provoked in the south by the Girondists. He was obliged to flee in 1793, returned to France in 1795, entered the Council of the Five Hundred, and became its president. Proscribed on the 18th Fructidor, he was confined in the island of Oleron until the 18th Brumaire. He was elected Member of the Tribunate of 1800, Councillor of State in 1804, Minister of the Interior and of Justice, and President of the Council of State in Westphalia, Minister of Westphalia at Berlin, and to the Confederation of the Rhine. In 1814, he became Prefect of the Nord. Under the Second Restoration, he was Councillor of State (1815), Under-Secretary of State of the Department of Justice, peer of France, Minister of State and Member of the Privy Council (1821). He was President of the Court of Accounts under the monarchy of July, and died in 1842.

[3] Jean-Baptiste, Comte Jolivet, born in 1754, was a barrister at Melun in 1789. Administrator of the department of Seine-et-Marne, then Deputy to the Legislative Assembly, he sided with the constitutional party, was arrested under the Terror, and only recovered his freedom after the 9th Thermidor. He became Curator-General of Mortgages in 1795, and Councillor of State after the 18th Brumaire. Liquidator-General of the debt of the Departments of the left bank of the Rhine, and Minister of Finances of Westphalia (1807). He retired in 1815, and died in 1818.

reigned alone, that is to say he had a court and a budget, or rather some women and some money.

The court formed spontaneously; but the budget, raised to the point where Napoleon's subsidies which were composed of half the freehold wealth, forced them to swell it, was for the first years very difficult to establish. This dynasty commenced as others finish. Jérôme was reduced to expedients from the second year of his reign. He did not seek those expedients in economies, that might have been made, but in the creation of new taxes. It became necessary, instead of thirty-seven millions of revenue, which would have been sufficient to furnish the necessary expenses of the state, to find more than fifty. For that, they had recourse to a means which displeases most people; they issued a forced loan, which, according to the ordinary result of this kind of tax, caused many exactions and was not half covered. From thirty-seven millions the needs and expenses eventually rose to sixty. The court of Cassel had the pretension to rival the splendour of that of the Tuileries. The young sovereign so gave way to all his inclinations, that I have heard it said by the grave and truthful M. Reinhard,[1] then minister of France at Cassel, that, with the exception of three or four women, respectable by their age, there was scarcely one at the palace over the fidelity of whom His Majesty had not acquired some rights, great though the vigilance was of the beautiful Frau von Truchsess and of Madame de la Flèche, who had also to watch over the doings of the young Prince of Würtemberg.[2]

The luxury of the court, its disorders, and the uneasy state of the country caused the detestation of France and of the

---

[1] Charles-Frederic, Comte Reinhard, born in 1761, entered diplomacy as First Secretary at London in 1791. It was there he made the acquaintance of M. de Talleyrand. He went to Naples in 1793; became, in 1794, head of a section of the department of Foreign Affairs. In 1795, he was appointed Minister Plenipotentiary in the Hanseatic cities and afterwards in Tuscany (1798). In July, 1799, he succeeded Talleyrand as Minister of Foreign Affairs, then was named successively minister to Helvetia (1800), at Milan (1801), to Saxony (1802), to Moldavia (1805), to Westphalia (1805-1814). In 1815, he entered the Council of State, and was afterwards minister to the German Confederation (1815-1829). The Government of July appointed him minister at Dresden (1830), and peer of France (1832). He died in 1837. M. de Talleyrand pronounced his eulogy at the Academy of Moral and Political Sciences.

[2] The Prince Royal of Würtemberg, having quarrelled with the king, his father, had taken refuge at that time with his brother-in-law, Jérôme Bonaparte, married to the Princess Catherine of Würtemberg.

emperor, to whom all was attributed, and if this uneasiness did not produce an immediate outbreak, it was because the natural submissiveness of the Germans was increased by the terror caused by the close alliance of the King of Westphalia with the colossus of French power. How must the grave universities of Göttingen and Halle, of which Jérôme was sovereign, have looked upon this unbridled luxury, this recklessness, so foreign to the simplicity, the decency and the good sense for which this part of Germany was noted? So, when in 1813, the Russian troops entered Westphalia, Jérôme's subjects regarded that moment as that of their deliverance. And yet the country fell again under the domination of that Elector of Hesse, who, thirty years before, sold his soldiers to England.[1]

The luxury of these courts founded by Napoleon, we may remark here, was absurd. The luxury of Bonaparte was neither German nor French ; it was a mixture, a species of learned luxury ; it was copied from everywhere. It had some of the gravity of that of Austria, with something European and Asiatic belonging to St. Petersburg. It paraded some of the mantles taken from the Cæsars at Rome ; but, in return, it showed very little of the ancient court of France where the magnificence of dress was so happily concealed under the spell of all the arts of taste. That which this kind of luxury set off above all, was the absolute lack of propriety ; and, in France, when propriety is too much lacking, mockery is near at hand.

This Bonaparte family, which came from an obscure island, hardly French, where its members lived in a state of parsimony, having as head a man of genius, whose elevation was due to military glory acquired as leader of republican armies, themselves the issue of a democracy in ebullition, ought indeed to have discarded former luxury, and have adopted, even for the frivolous side of life, an entirely new route. Would it not have been more imposing by displaying a noble simplicity which would have inspired confidence in its strength and in its duration? Instead of that, the Bonapartes were mistaken enough to believe that, to imitate in a puerile manner the

---

[1] William IX., Landgrave of Hesse-Cassel, Elector in 1803, despoiled of his states in 1806. He recovered his possessions in 1814. He died in 1821.

kings whose thrones they had taken, was one way of succeeding them.

I wish to avoid all that has a libellous appearance, and I have besides no need of citing proper names to prove that, by their morals also, these new dynasties have injured the moral power of the Emperor Napoleon. The morals of a people in times of trouble are often bad ; but even when the mob has all sorts of vices, its morality is severe. " Men," said Montesquieu, " corrupt in detail, are very honest men in the main." And these honest people are they who pronounce upon kings and queens. When their judgment is unfavourable, it is very difficult for a power, above all a new one, not to be shaken by it.

Spanish pride did not allow that great and generous people to concentrate its hatred so long as that of Westphalia had done. The perfidy of Napoleon gave it birth, and Joseph from his arrival in Spain fed it each day. He was persuaded that to speak ill of his brother, was to separate from him ; and that to separate from his brother was to take root in Spain. Hence he adopted a conduct and a language always in strict opposition to the will of the emperor. He never ceased saying that Napoleon despised the Spaniards. He spoke of the army that attacked Spain as being the refuse of the French army. He related all that could most injure his brother. He even went so far as to reveal the shameful secrets of his family, and that sometimes in full council. " My brother is acquainted with only one kind of government," said he, " and that is a government of iron ; to accomplish that all means are good to him ; " and he stupidly added, " I am the only honest man in my family, and if the Spaniards were to rally around me, they would soon learn to fear nothing from France." As for the emperor, he spoke with the same impropriety of Joseph ; he covered him with scorn, and that also before Spaniards, who, led away by their own exasperation, ended by believing them both, when they spoke of one another. The irritation of Napoleon against his brother made him act always on the first impulse in the affairs of Spain, and made him commit, incessantly, grave mistakes. The two brothers counteracted each other in all their operations ; it was never possible for them to agree together upon any plan of political action, any financial plan, or military arrangement.

It was important to establish a supreme command, to have an invading army and an army of operations, to agree as to the means of nourishing, clothing, and paying the troops. All that could lead to this result failed successively, either through Napoleon's consideration for his generals, on whom he was known to rely, and who ever alleged, often in their personal interest, this trite pretext : *the safety of the army I have the honour to command demands such or such a thing;* or else, everything failed on account of the private policy of Joseph, which tended constantly, in opposition to his brother, to make all the expenses of the war fall upon France. The emperor, in order to avoid the obstacles that Joseph opposed constantly to the execution of his designs, ordered his generals to correspond directly with the Prince de Neufchâtel, his major-general. They all did so, but without mutual agreement, solely guided by their interests ; in nearly all their correspondence, they desired the emperor to renounce his project of securing Spain, there to establish a prince of his family, but rather to parcel it out like Italy, and to distribute its principalities, duchies, and entailed estates, as rewards amongst *his brave lieutenants.* I have been told that the Duc d'Albufera,[1] who was rather a wit, added that this would be going back to the times of the Moorish princes, vassals of the Calif of the West.

What was going on at the quarters of the French generals was known week by week at Cadiz, and from there all over the kingdom ; and one can judge of the intensity that the fear of such prospects gave to Spanish resistance. So, the French generals might conquer indeed, they always found new enemies before them, and there were no points really subdued, except those covered by French troops ; and even their communications were constantly cut off by guerillas.

[1] Louis-Gabriel Suchet, born at Lyons in 1772, enlisted in 1791, became general in 1796, and head of the staff of the army in Italy in 1799. He played a brilliant part in the wars of the Empire until 1808, when he was sent to Spain, where his gallant conduct won for him the staff of marshal of France, and subsequently the title of Duc d'Albufera (1812). He became peer of France in 1814, and died in 1826.

As for Joseph, he only accorded his favours to a few French-men discontented with the emperor, who had embraced his cause; these new Castilians slipped into all the offices of the court, civil and military; they had penetrated into the Council of State; treated the Spaniards with insupportable haughtiness; flattered the vanity of the king in every way, and never failed to revile his brother. The hatred for the emperor was manifested as much in the palace of the king as in the hall of the Junta at Cadiz.

What could be the fate of an undertaking the leaders of which were in open opposition to each other, and whose means were enfeebled by the successive recall of troops already acclimatized, but who were wanted, perhaps against Austria, or against Russia, and who were replaced by wretched recruits?

The emperor having again met at Wagram the good fortune which, for a time, had abandoned him at Lobau, had persuaded himself that the submission of Spain would follow the peace he had dictated at Vienna; but it was not so at all. This peace exercised no influence over the affairs of the Peninsula; resist-ance had had time to organize, and it had done so everywhere. Napoleon then believed that he must make a great effort and he made it, but in the wrong direction. He started with a false idea; he believed he would make a good bargain with the Spaniards by driving Lord Wellington from Portugal. Marshal Massena displayed wondrous ability in, and brought enormous resources to bear on, this operation, which proved fruitless, and the success of which would, in any case, have been of insignificant influence on the point at issue. It was the whole Spanish people which had risen, which was armed, and which must be subdued. And supposing even the emperor to have succeeded in destroying armed resistance, would there not have remained for many years a secret opposition, the most difficult of all to destroy?

Joseph, whom the other enterprises of his brother left a little more to himself and to his own methods, recognized at last that it was the people who were his veritable enemy. He then did his best to win them; his ministers spread pamphlets

filled with promises of all kinds; it was the liberty of the
Spaniards that Joseph desired—it was a constitution adapted
to the customs of the country, the project for which he was
going to submit to the most enlightened men ; he announced
great economies and a considerable reduction of the taxes. In
his proclamations all the revolutionary methods were put in
motion. The Cortes of Cadiz, in order to destroy the effect
of it, immediately vied in liberalism with Joseph, and went
on all points farther than he had done. It was nothing but
decrees from Cadiz, suppressing the Inquisition ; suppressing
feudal rights, privileges, fiscal obstacles between provinces, the
censure of the press, &c. . . . . And from the midst of these
ruins they brought forth a constitution all democratic ; in which,
however, in order not to frighten too much the friends of monarchy, they had placed an hereditary king. But no king would
have been able with dignity, nor even with safety, to occupy
such a throne. The Cortes of Cadiz should have been more
circumspect in re-establishing the fundamental laws of Spain,
so skilfully undermined and finally destroyed by the house of
Austria.

Through all these intrigues, Lord Wellington penetrated
into Spain ; he captured Badajoz from the Duc de Dalmatie,[1]
and Ciudad Rodrigo from the Duc de Raguse.[2] Once master of
these two keys of Spain at the northern and southern extremities of the frontier of Portugal, the English general
skilfully deceived the Duc de Dalmatie, in making him believe
he wished to fall upon Andalusia, while he bore towards
Valladolid on the Douro. As for the Duc de Raguse, without
waiting for a reinforcement of 15,000 men which was within
reach, he permitted the Battle of Arapiles[3] to be fought, at
the beginning of which he received a serious wound. The
army, having lost its leader at the outset, was cruelly beaten.
Lord Wellington who, following his successes, had advanced
too far towards the north, did not hesitate, as a prudent man,
to take retrograde steps ; he re-entered Portugal, whence the
famous disasters of the campaign of Russia, which obliged

---

[1] Marshal Soult.   [2] Marshal Marmont.
[3] Village of Spain, near Salamanca. The battle was July 21, 1812.

Napoleon to recall the best troops that remained in Spain, induced him to dart out again in 1812.

The first news of those disasters had increased the disorder which too numerous and unsubmissive leaders fomented around Joseph; it culminated in the loss of the fatal battle of Vittoria.[1] The Duc de Dalmatie, sent with all speed to Spain, tried to re-organize the remnants of the army. He made well-planned and rapid marches, but they answered no other purpose than to dispute with his skilful adversary the possession of the southern provinces of France. Thus terminated this great conquest of Spain, as badly conducted as it was badly conceived; and I say not only conducted by Napoleon's generals, but by himself; for he, also, had committed grave military faults in Spain. If, at the end of 1808, after the capitulation of Madrid, instead of rushing in pursuit of an English corps which was hastening to embark at Corunna, and to which he did little harm, he had marched on Andalusia and had there struck a great blow, he would have disorganized the resistance of the Spanish generals, who would have had no other resource than to retire into Portugal.

The emperor, having once lost sight of the true interests of France, gave himself up, with the irreflection and ardour of passion, to the ambition of still placing a member of his family on one of the first thrones of Europe, and, to accomplish that, he attacked Spain without shame, and without the least pretext to justify himself; this is what the sense of justice in nations never allows them to forgive. When one studies all the actions or rather all the impulses of Napoleon at this all-important period of his life, one is inclined to believe that he was carried away by a sort of fatality which blinded his high intellect.

If the emperor had only seen in Spain a ground on which he could force England to peace, where all the great political questions then pending in Europe could have been decided, and each sovereign ensured the safe possession of his dominions, his venture would not have been more justifiable; but, at least, it would have been more consonant with the bold policy of conquerors. I have met a few persons who did not know him, and whose

---

[1] City of Spain, chief place of the province of Alava. The battle was fought June 21, 1813.

minds, like those of our old diplomatists, being inclined to judge of events theoretically, supposed he had this intention. And, the fact is that the Bayonne transaction being revocable at will, might be regarded as a sacrifice good to make if need were for the general pacification of Europe ; but from the month of April, 1812, all makers of political combinations were obliged to dismiss this hypothesis; for, at that time, Napoleon refused the overtures of the British Cabinet, which declared it did not see any insurmountable difficulty to arrange with him, on all the points in litigation, if he himself admitted first of all the restoration of Ferdinand VII. on the throne of Spain, and that of Victor Amadeus on the throne of Sardinia. If he had accepted those propositions, he could easily have derived enormous moral advantages from his sacrifices, and all the cabinets could have believed that he had only invaded Spain in the hope of securing a lasting peace for France and of strengthening his dynasty.

But, for a long time, Napoleon was but little concerned with the policy of France, hardly with his own. He did not think of maintaining, but only of extending. It seemed as if the idea of preserving never entered his mind, and as if it were opposed to his nature.

Nevertheless, that which he did not do in proper time, he was forced to do when it was too late, and without any profit to his power or to his glory. Sending back the Spanish princes to Madrid in the month of January, 1814, and the pope to Rome at the same time, were only expedients inspired by distress ; and the sudden and even stealthy manner in which those measures were taken and executed, deprived them of every vestige of grandeur and generosity. But I notice that I am speaking of the return of the pope to his States, without our quarrels with the court of Rome having found room in this recital. It was, however, too remarkable an event of our times for me not to give here some of its details.

The differences which arose between Napoleon and the court of Rome, shortly after the *Concordat* of 1801, grew still more acute after the coronation—though these two events ought to have prevented that contest. Those differences were for a long time only known by the rumour of the violence of the emperor towards the pope, and by the noble complaints of the Holy Father, which only reached the public with great difficulty and great confusion. Their origin and their causes might have been better appreciated, for all that concerned the purely theological part of those discussions, when Napoleon summoned at Paris an ecclesiastical commission, of which I will speak soon. But the deliberations of that commission, composed of very enlightened men, had been kept secret.

By what sequence of events did the pope find himself tormented and persecuted for nearly ten years, so odiously, with such want of policy and in so many ways?

Let us run over the facts and their dates, looking at them from a distance. Several of these dates will explain the great misfortunes of Pius VII., supported with such heroic courage, that one hardly dares to note in the Holy Father some slight wrongs of improvidence.

Pius VI., his predecessor, removed from Rome by order of the Directory, February 10, 1798, died at Valence, August 9, 1799. Pius VII. was elected March 14, 1800, at Venice, which belonged then to the Emperor of Germany, according to one of the stipulations of the treaty of Campo-Formio; and, on July 13 of the same year, he made his entry into Rome which had been re-conquered with the Roman States by the allies, while Bonaparte was in Egypt.

I have already said somewhere that Bonaparte, on his return from Egypt, had arrived suddenly in Paris, October 16, 1799, and that as a result of the *coup d'état* of the 18th Brumaire (November 9, 1799), he had been placed at the head of the government as First Consul, December 13, 1799. The conclave was opened at Venice, on the first of this same month of December, and while Pius VII., elected in the month of March following, was going from Venice to Rome, Bonaparte had just marked his taking possession of power by two acts which had the greatest influence over Italy. On June 2, 1800, he entered Milan where he had re-established the Cisalpine Republic, and twelve days later, on June 14, he gained the famous battle of Marengo, which gave France so large a portion of Italy, and reduced the States of the Church to what had been fixed upon by the treaty of Tolentino.

Thus the pope, entering Rome after these two events, July 3, 1800, must have felt how important it was for him to conciliate so powerful and so formidable a protector as Napoleon, and how important also it was for the religion of which he was the head, and which had experienced so many vicissitudes and persecutions in France, to bring to an end the schism which for so long a time obtained in that unhappy country.

Bonaparte also experienced this same need, and, on his passage through Milan, he heard with the greatest interest the first overtures which were made to him very secretly and very skilfully on the part of the court of Rome. Is it not a remarkable thing, that, raised at the head of the government by his military exploits and by the philosophical and liberal ideas which prevailed then, Bonaparte should have felt immediately the necessity of being reconciled with the court of Rome? It is perhaps in this circumstance that he displayed the greatest proof of the force of his character, for he braved then all the mockery of the army, and the opposition even of the two consuls, his colleagues. He remained firmly attached to the idea that, in order to sustain either the civil constitution of the clergy, or theo-philanthropy, which were equally discredited, he would have to play the part of persecutor of the Catholic religion, and to arm, against her and against her ministers, the laws with severity, whereas in discarding the religious innovations of the Revolution, it would be easy for him to make a friend of our ancient religion and even to find support in all the Catholic consciences of France.

He then resolved, and it was one of the strokes of his great genius, to come to an understanding with the head of the Church, who, alone, could reconcile, lead back, pronounce as judge or as arbiter, and re-establish finally by his authority, to which no other was comparable, unity of worship and of doctrine.

To this authority was added, in the person of the pope, the influence of a great and sincere piety, of an enlightened mind, and of an attractive meekness.

The *Concordat* could not appear under better auspices ; it was greatly desired, above all in the provinces. It was converted into a law, April 8, 1801. It was composed of seventeen articles drawn up with remarkable wisdom and foresight. All was clear, without equivocation ; there was not a word which could offend or displease. Transferred ecclesiastical estates could no longer be claimed back, and it was declared that the acquirers of such property must be fully reassured in this respect. It was an immense point obtained from the condescension of a pope full of piety.

But one point presented prodigious difficulties. To reestablish religion in France there must be obtained the resignation of all the old bishops, or do without them. They had all offered and even sent it to Pius VI. in 1791, after the civil constitution of the clergy. Pius VI. thought he ought to refuse to accept it. Pope Pius VII. demanded it in 1801, by his brief of August 24, *Tam multa*, &c. . . . as an indispensable preliminary to all negotiation, declaring, nevertheless, to the bishops, with sweet, confiding, but firm expressions, that if they refused, which he presumed they would not, he should see himself with regret compelled to appoint new men to the government of the bishoprics of the new circumscription.

Of the eighty-one bishops who were still alive and who had not renounced the episcopacy, forty-five sent in their resignations, thirty-six refused to do so ; the greater number, I think, less from theological conviction, although they were encouraged in their refusal by the learned theologian Asseline,[1] than from attachment to the House of Bourbon, and hatred for the present government. It has been pretended that the refusal of some of them was rather dilatory than absolute, but all persevered in it, and their resistance even seemed to increase from day to day ; for, after their canonical claims of 1803, signed by all the bishops who had not resigned,[2] there appeared in April, 1804,

---

[1] Jean-René Asseline, born in 1742, entered the Church and became grand-vicar of M. de Beaumont, Archbishop of Paris. In 1790, he was named Bishop of Boulogne, refused to swear allegiance to the civil constitution, and emigrated in 1791. He retired to Munster, whence he protested against the *Concordat*, in 1802. In 1807, he complied with the request of Louis XVIII. and lived on intimacy with the royal family until his death (1813). He has left numerous works on theology.

[2] It was in 1801 that the bishops, having refused to resign, assembled in London,

with a list of still stronger claims, a *declaration on the rights of the king*,[1] signed by the thirteen bishops residing in England.

And, finally, anticipating events, I will say here that in 1814, on the accession of Louis XVIII., these bishops pretended even with the pope, to derive credit for having resisted him, and, to this effect, wrote him a haughty letter in which each of them had taken the title of his old bishopric. The pope refused to receive it, and compelled them, by his perseverance in refusing, to address him a letter of apology, in which they abandoned their pretensions, and which they signed only as *late* bishops. In order that there should not remain the slightest doubt in this respect, the pope desired that not one of them should be replaced in the see he had previously occupied, not even the Archbishop of Reims,[2] in spite of all the propriety there would have been in making an exception in his favour.

I revert to what took place in 1801 and the following years. The pope saw the *Concordat* in full working order, without any trouble resulting for France; in spite of the diversity of

---

to protest against the *Concordat*, and sent to the pope a long memorial in which they set forth the motives of their refusal. This memorial was published in London in 1801. It is signed by fourteen prelates : Arthur Dillon, Archbishop of Narbonne ; Louis de Conzié, Bishop of Arras ; Joseph de Malide, Bishop of Montpellier ; Louis de Grimaldi, Bishop-Comte of Noyon, peer of France ; Jean Lamarche, Bishop of Léon ; Pierre de Belboeuf, Bishop of Avranches ; Sébastien Amelot, Bishop of Vannes ; Henry de Bethisy, Bishop of Uzes ; Seignelai Colbert, Bishop of Rodez ; Charles de La Laurencie, Bishop of Nantes ; Philippe d'Albignac, Bishop of Angoulême ; Alexandre de Chauvigny de Blot, Bishop of Lombez ; Emmanuel de Grossoles de Flammarens, Bishop of Périgueux ; Étienne de Galois de la Tour, Bishop (nominated) of Moulins.

[1] On April 15, 1804, M. de Dillon, Archbishop of Narbonne, wrote to the pope to protest anew against the *Concordat*. This letter was accompanied by a *declaration on the rights of the king*, signed by the same bishops as above, with the exception of the Bishop of Périgueux. This declaration conveyed that the inviolable fidelity of the people to their sovereign is recommended by the Gospel ; *that the prince is minister of God ;* that every rebel to his king is guilty towards God ; *that the present government of France, where the legitimate prince does not occupy the place due to him, though it may alleviate the burden of the calamities under which anarchy is causing the people to groan, does not satisfy either God or Cæsar.* . . . . it constitutes a power of fact and not a power of right ; *it has only possession or rather usurpation ;* but the legitimate prince continues to preserve all his rights, although he is forced to suspend their application. In consequence, the undersigned *to fulfil their duty as bishops and as subjects, declare:* 1°, *That their very honoured lord and legitimate king, Louis XVIII., preserves, in all their integrity, the rights which he holds from God to the crown of France ;* 2°, *That nothing has been able to deprive the French, his subjects, of the fidelity they owe to this prince, in virtue of the law of God.*

[2] M. de Talleyrand-Périgord, afterward Cardinal and Archbishop of Paris.

opinions, the opposition was trifling, seldom offered, and without result.

It must, however, be said here that Pius VII. had displayed in this circumstance an authority which transcended the ordinary rules, and which would not have been recognized in any other time, if a pope had tried to exercise it—that of deposing bishops without trial, as also that of suppressing more than half the bishoprics of France without formality. At another epoch, nothing would have appeared in France more opposed to the liberties of the Gallican Church. But the case was here out of all comparison with ordinary times; it was impossible and almost ridiculous to invoke and to wish to apply here the exercise of those liberties. The pope had vainly exhausted the most powerful entreaties with this minority, composed of thirty-six bishops, and then, supporting himself on the majority of the French Episcopacy, he employed the *only* means possible of destroying the schism which it was so urgent to have cease. What other means, in effect, could the pope have employed? Let any one search, he cannot even imagine one. Abbé Fleury,[1] ardent Gallican though he was, and certainly very little disposed to extend the authority of the pope, said none the less in his discourse on *the liberties of the Gallican Church*, that, "the authority of the pope is sovereign, and rises above all," when it is a question of maintaining the rules or causing the canons to be observed. Bossuet makes use of similar language: "It must be said, consequently and with much reason," adds M. Emery,[2] in one of his works, "that the authority of the pope is sovereign, and takes precedence of all, even of the canons, when there is a question as to the preser-

---

[1] Abbé Claude Fleury, born in 1640, was at first preceptor of the sons of the Prince de Condé, then under-governor of the Dukes of Burgundy, Anjou and Berry. In 1716, he came again to the court as confessor of Louis XV. He resigned this appointment soon after, and died in 1723. Abbé Fleury has left a large number of works on ecclesiastical history and religious controversies.

[2] Jacques-André Emery, born in 1732, took orders, in 1756, was Professor of Theology at Orleans, was named in 1776 Grand-Vicar of the Diocese of Angers, Superior of the Seminary of that city, and, shortly after, Superior-General of the Order of Saint Sulpice. Under the Terror, he was imprisoned for eighteen months. After the 9th Thermidor, he was charged with the functions of Grand-Vicar of the Diocese of Paris. Under the Consulate, he reorganized his congregation. He took part in the ecclesiastical commissions assembled by the emperor, and died in 1811.

vation of the Church, since it is only for the *maintenance* of these great interests that these rules and these canons have been made." Father Thomassin, in his great and celebrated work on the discipline of the Church, says also: "Nothing is more consonant with the canons than to violate these canons, when from this violation, there must result a much greater good than from even their observance."

Pius VII. then, in these difficult circumstances, showed himself to be possessed both of a strong will and of a profound knowledge of true principles. In acting as he did, he destroyed the schism without irritating, without humiliating the constitutional bishops, and yet without yielding to them any point, and order was restored everywhere.

There were, nevertheless, some people whose consciences felt uneasy in the dioceses where the former incumbents had not given in their resignation. Some among them, while reserving their jurisdiction, had consented nevertheless, to the exercise of the powers of the bishop who replaced them, and supplied by that the insufficiency of his title. But the most active in their resistance, those who, from political opinions had shown themselves most inimical to the principle of the Revolution, and who were imperturbably ruled by this sentiment, were careful not to do it. This persistent opposition did not produce, however, either the effect, or the results that they anticipated, and that might have been feared. Those of the parishioners of their dioceses whose consciences were more particularly timorous, though uneasy perhaps for a while, were not slow in comprehending that their former bishop, not having wished either to come into their midst, or to give in his resignation at the demand of the pope, they were assuredly protected from all reproach in according, under such circumstances, their confidence to the new bishop sent to them by the Holy Father.

The bishops remaining in London saw surely with grief that men imbued with their doctrines, such as Abbé Blanchard[1] and

---

[1] Abbé Pierre-Louis Blanchard, born in 1762, was Professor of Philosophy in 1789. Having refused the oath, he emigrated to England, where he remained until 1814. From his retreat, he published a great number of statements and of libels, in which he speaks with extreme violence of those who hurt the interests of religion. He attacks the *Concordat*, and does not spare even the pope, principally on the occasion

Abbé Gaschet, pushing to extremes the consequences (quite well deduced however) of these doctrines, published in England, and introduced as much as they could into France, a host of libels against the pope, in which, in a fanatical style which seemed copied from Luther's, they declared him heretical, schismatic, fallen from papacy, even from priesthood; they said it was a blasphemy to pronounce his name at the canon of mass, that he was as much a stranger to the Church as if he were a Jew or a Pagan. They spoke of his outrages, of his scandals, &c. . . . I do not alter a syllable. Let us believe for the honour of those bishops who constituted what was then called *la petite Eglise* that, however contrary they were, they did not approve of these mad fits, although they appeared to have been instigated by them. They were, however, solemnly condemned by twenty-nine Catholic bishops of Ireland, and by the apostolic vicars who resided in London. What must be added is, that in France, where they spread these libels, universal scorn treated them as they deserved. I believe that the police denounced them or wished to denounce them one day to the tribunals, but even that could not remove them from obscurity.

Bonaparte had caused to be decreed, under form of law, at the same time as the *Concordat*, *organic articles*, concerning as much the Catholic as the Protestant clergy. Several of these articles displeased the pope, in as much as they appeared to put the Church of France in too great a dependence on the government, even in minor details. He complained with moderation, and demanded modification; he obtained gradually, and even without much difficulty, essential alterations. Some of these articles were besides transitory; their effects were to cease with the circumstances which had called them forth. There were others which proceeded naturally from old Gallican liberties; modifications could not be introduced in those, and the pope could not expect it. In order to draw up the *Concordat*, they had been obliged to renounce those liberties momentarily; the *Concordat* once made, it was urgent to resume our privileges. All that was really necessary had been granted, if not at once, at least

of the consecration of the emperor. His numerous writings have been published in London.

in time. The pope was perfectly seconded in his desires by
the Bishop of Nantes, as will be seen farther on, and by his
legate, Cardinal Caprara. The latter, knowing the passionate
temper of the First Consul, put great wisdom and extreme cir-
cumspection in all his conduct, knowing how to wait, fearing to
irritate, and deeming himself too happy for what had been
obtained, to seek to compromise it.

Cardinal Caprara, appointed legate *a latere* to Bonaparte,
had been invested with the most extensive powers by the bull
Dextera. . . . of the month of August, 1801, and by the bull
Quoniam. . . . of November 29, of the same year, to enable
him to carry out the *Concordat*, to confirm the new bishops,
. . . and to solve all the difficulties which might arise. But,
although the *Concordat* had been concluded and signed at Paris,
July 15, 1801, and ratified at Rome by Pius VII. in the month
of August following, it had not been converted into a law (on
account of the absence of the legislative body) until April 8,
1802 ; and it was not until that day that the legate could
exercise his functions and confirm the new bishops, after having
taken oath the same day (April 8) at the hands of the First
Consul. His oath, in the terms which he used, though only to
trained eyes, is slightly different from that which had been
settled by the decree of the consuls. The decree bore these
few words, " He shall, according to the usual formula, take
the oath and promise to conform to the laws of the State,
and to the liberties of the Gallican Church."   But the cardinal
took the oath and *promised* (in Latin) " to observe the constitution, laws, statutes and usages of the French Republic," and at
the same time, " not to derogate in any way from the authority
and jurisdiction of the government of the Republic, nor from
the rights, liberties and privileges of the Gallican Church."
The whole was preceded by a compliment to the First Consul,
such as was never paid, perhaps, to any sovereign. It can be
seen, on close examination, that instead of promising *to conform*
to the liberties of the Gallican Church (which implies a sort of
adherence to, or, at least, of recognition of these liberties), he
promised only not to derogate from them, which is purely
negative. The difference, at any rate, is very small or even

insignificant in its result, and very likely passed unnoticed. Besides, he promised, in the other part of the oath, more than had been demanded of him, for they wished him to swear to conform *to the laws of the state*, and he took the positive oath *to observe the Constitution, the laws, the statutes and the usages* of the Republic, which expresses more.

As to the liberties of the Gallican Church, which rouse the fears of the court of Rome, to engage by oath not to derogate from them is assuredly all that could be expected of a legate, above all if we consider that no pope has ever recognized them. Innocent XI.[1] (Odescalchi) disturbed for eight years the Church of France on account of these same liberties consecrated in the Assembly of the Clergy of 1682, and repeatedly refused to grant bulls to the ecclesiastics of the second order, members of that assembly (where, however, they had no vote). His successor, Alexander VIII.[2] (Ottoboni) was more opinionate still in his refusals, since two days before his death, he published a bull against the four articles of 1682, which, for that matter, had no effect, because he was dying. Innocent XII.[3] (Pignatelli), good man as he was, could not make up his mind to grant bulls to the bishops appointed between 1682 and 1693, until they had each written him a letter of apology and of regret for what had taken place in that assembly. This letter was truly humiliating, and that which made it more so was that Louis XIV. added one in his own hand, in which he bound himself to give no sequel to his edict of March 22, 1682. The letter of the king must have seemed as a retractation, though, however, he withdrew it before his death, since finally the edict was not revoked, and after him it continued to be executed.

It is almost useless to recall here that Bonaparte, proclaimed emperor by the senate, May 20, 1804, put a great price, and that is easily conceived, upon being consecrated by the pope. It is a wondrous feature of his destiny that he was able to obtain it, and at the time, I thought myself very happy in having con-

[1] Innocent XI. (Benedict Odescalchi), born at Como in 1611, Pope in 1671, died in 1689.

[2] Alexander VIII., born at Venice in 1610, pope in 1689. He quashed the articles of the declaration of 1682 by the bull *Inter multiplices*, and died in 1691.

[3] Innocent XII. (Antoni Pignatelli), born in Naples in 1615, pope from 1691 to 1700.

tributed to it, because I thought that thereby the ties of France with the court of Rome would become closer. Pius VII. having already recognized the consular government, since it was with that government he had treated for the *Concordat*, could not be stayed by the consideration of rights which might some day be brought forth by the House of Bourbon, if the new government, being itself overthrown, the nation should recall the former. He had then nothing to object against the title of emperor that Bonaparte had given himself, or that had been awarded him in France, with more solemnity, although perhaps with less sincerity, than that of First Consul. Therefore the pope had only to consider a single point, viz., whether, in the sole interest of religion, to which the new emperor might do, by his immense power, so much good or so much harm, he ought to consent to come to consecrate him, as Saint Boniface, the legate of Pope Stephen III., had come to consecrate Pepin, during the life of the legitimate king, Childeric III.; as Leo III. crowned Charlemagne emperor at Rome in 800, and as another pope, Stephen V., came afterwards to consecrate Louis le Debonnaire at Reims, after the death of Charlemagne.

The pope decided to come to perform this consecration at Paris, and this memorable ceremony took place December 2, 1804. Pius VII. was not influenced in this circumstance by temporal views, like Pope Stephen III., who had implored the assistance of Pepin against the Lombards, but very evidently and solely by purely religious motives, since he abstained from allowing even a glimpse to be seen of his desire, a very natural one, to recover his three legations of Bologna, Ferrara, and Ravenna, which the emperor besides was careful not to offer to return him, nor even to give him the hope of it. All the demands of the pope, without any exception, were in the interest of religion. None concerned himself personally, and he refused the presents that were offered him for his family.

He quitted Paris April 4, 1805, leaving everywhere on his passage the profound impression of his virtues, and of his benevolence. Napoleon had left Paris some days before him; he was bent on something else than on showing his gratitude to the Holy Father. On the 16th of May, the pope arrived in Rome, and on the 26th of May the emperor had himself crowned at Milan as King of Italy. A short time after his troops occupied Ancona, on Roman territory.[1] The pope complained; Napoleon did not reply; but, after the battle of Austerlitz, on Dec. 2, 1805, and the peace of Presburg, on the 26th, he wrote to the pope, Jan. 6, 1806, that he did not wish to appropriate Ancona, but simply to occupy it as protector of the Holy See, and in order that that city should not be defiled by the Mussulmans.

Three months after, March 30, 1806, Napoleon places his brother Joseph on the throne of Naples, and asks the pope to recognize him. He asks him at the same time to make with him an offensive and defensive league; to embrace the continental system—to close consequently his ports to the English, that is to say, to declare war against them. Such propositions, at a time above all when the emperor was trampling under foot the *Concordat* that he had concluded with the pope in 1803, for Italy; when he was despoiling the bishoprics and the monasteries of their wealth, suppressing both at his will; when he was plaguing the bishops and the curés with new oaths, &c. . . . , such propositions could not be accepted, and they were not. They gave rise to that correspondence with the French authorities in which there is displayed so much force, reason, and propriety on the side of the court of Rome.

Such a refusal and so much wisdom could not fail to irritate the emperor. On February 2, 1808, he had Rome occupied by his troops under the command of General Miollis.[2] They took possession of the Castello S. Angelo. The general tried to oblige the pope to subscribe to all the demands that were made to him, under the menace of losing his states; he

[1] Ancona had at that time great importance. Some Russian troops were concentrated at Corfu, whence they were awaiting an occasion to pass into Italy and join the English. Ancona was then exposed to a *coup de main*, so much the more that its garrison was almost a cipher, and its fortifications falling to ruins. Napoleon begged the pontifical government to put the city into a state of defence. His request was unheeded. Soon General Gouvion Saint-Cyr, who was at that moment crossing the States of the Church to go to the kingdom of Naples, received the order to take possession of the city. He entered it by surprise and established himself there November 6, 1805.

[2] François, Comte Miollis, born in 1759, was captain of infantry in 1789. He served in the armies of the Republic, became general in 1794, and distinguished himself in the campaign of Italy. He was for a long time Governor of Mantua. In 1807, he was appointed Governor of Rome and of the States of the Church. He retired in 1815, and died in 1828.

multiplied vexations, seized the mail and the press ; had twenty cardinals, among whom were several ministers carried off, &c. . . . . . The pope protested in vain against such violence· Napoleon paid no attention. On the 2nd of April following, he united the legations of Urbino, Ancona, Macerata and Camerino with the kingdom of Italy to make three departments of them. He confiscated the wealth of the cardinals who did not return to the place of their birth. He disarmed nearly all the guards of the Holy Father—the nobles of this guard were imprisoned. Finally, Miollis had Cardinal Gabrielle,[1] pro-Secretary of State, carried off, and put seals upon his papers.

On May 17, 1809, a decree was issued by Napoleon, dated from Vienna, proclaiming the union (in his quality of successor to Charlemagne) of the States of the pope with the French Empire, ordaining that the city of Rome should be a free and imperial city; that the pope should continue to have his seat there, and that he should enjoy a revenue of two millions of francs. On June 10, he had this decree promulgated at Rome. On this same June 10, the pope protested against all these spoliations, refused all pensions, and recapitulating all the outrages of which he had cause to complain, issued the famous and imprudent bull of excommunication against the authors, abettors, and executors of the acts of violence against him and the Holy See, but without naming any one.

Napoleon was incensed at it, and on the first impulse he wrote to the bishops of France a letter in which he spoke in almost revolutionary terms " of him who wished," said he, " to make dependent upon a perishable temporal power the eternal interest of consciences, and that of all spiritual affairs."

On the 6th of July, 1809, Pius VII., taken from Rome, after he had been asked if he would renounce the temporal sovereignty of Rome and of the States of the Church, was conducted by General Radet[2] as far as Savona, where he arrived alone,

---

[1] Jules Gabrielle, issue of an old Roman family, born in 1748, was Bishop of Sinigaglia, then cardinal in 1801. On March 27, 1808, he became pro-Secretary of State. He protested energetically against all the unlawful measures ordered by the emperor against the rights of the pope, and was arrested in June of the same year. He was sent to France, where he was confined, and in 1813 repaired to Fontainebleau to stay with the pope. He died in 1822.

[2] Etienne, Baron Radet, born in 1762, had been non-commissioned officer under

August 10, the cardinals having all been previously transported to Paris. And to complete the spoliation of the pope, Napoleon issued, on the 17th of February, 1810, a *senatus-consultum*, which bestowed upon the eldest son of the emperor the title of King of Rome, and even ordained that the emperor should be consecrated a second time at Rome, in the first ten years of his reign.

It was while oppressed, captive and deprived of all counsel, that the pope refused the bulls to all the bishops nominated by the emperor, and then it was that all the discussions relative to the proper measures to put an end to the viduity of the churches were commenced.

ECCLESIASTICAL COMMISSION.

Formed in 1809.

This commission was composed of Cardinal Fesch, Cardinal Maury,[1] the Archbishop of Tours,[2] the Bishop of Nantes,[3] the

---

the old *régime.* In 1792, he was sub-lieutenant in the National Guard at Varennes. Accused of having favoured the flight of Louis XVI., he was acquitted by the Revolutionary Tribunal. He became brigadier-general in 1799, and commander-in-chief of the *gendarmerie.* It was in this capacity that he received the order, July 6, 1809, to arrest the pope. In 1813, he was appointed Grand Provost of the Grand Army and general of division. Sentenced in 1816 to nine years' imprisonment, he was pardoned in 1818, and died in 1825.

[1] Jean Maury, born in 1746, at Valréas (Vaucluse), was the son of a shoemaker. He took orders in 1771, and soon made himself famous by his eloquence ; he entered the Academy in 1784. Deputy for the clergy of Péronne to the States-General, he became the leader of the Conservative side. He emigrated in 1791, went to Rome, was nominated archbishop *in partibus*, cardinal and Bishop of Montefiascone. Shortly after, Louis XVIII. accredited him as ambassador to the Holy See. He rallied, however, to the side of the emperor in 1807, and became senator and chaplain to Prince Jérôme. In 1810, he was called to the archiepiscopal see of Paris, which caused his condemnation by the pope, and later his disgrace with Louis XVIII. In 1815, he had to leave his archbishopric and fled to Italy. He was momentarily confined at the Castello S. Angelo, but released soon after. He re-entered the good graces of Pius VII., and died in 1817.

[2] Louis, Comte de Barral, born in 1746, had been general agent of the clergy in 1785, then coadjutor of the Bishop of Troyes and bishop *in partibus*. He refused the oath and emigrated. In 1801, he sent his resignation to the pope, and was soon after named Bishop of Meaux, and, later, Archbishop of Tours. In 1805, he accepted the office of chaplain to the empress, and later the dignity of senator. Mgr. de Barral pronounced, in 1814, the funeral oration of the Empress Josephine. It was he also, who, on June 1, 1815, officiated pontifically on the Champs-de-Mars. On the return of Louis XVIII. he was forced to resign. He died in 1818.

[3] M. Duvoisin.

Bishop of Evreux,[1] the Bishop of Treves,[2] the Bishop of Verceil,[3] Abbé Emery, superior of Saint-Sulpice, and Father Fontana [4] General of the Barnabites. The government proposed to it three series of questions. The first on the interests of Christianity in general. The second on the interests of France especially. The third on the interests of the Churches of Germany, Italy, and the bull of excommunication.

Each of these series is divided into several questions. I am going to give them all with the answers, which I have abridged without altering, taking care to underline the expressions of the commission as well as the citations they invoke.

In the preamble heading the answers made by the commission to the questions put by the government, the following passage may be noticed : " *We do not separate from the homage we render to your Majesty, the tribute of interest, zeal and love commanded by the actual situation of the Sovereign Pontiff. . . . All the spiritual good we can expect as the result of our deliberations is then solely in the hands of your Majesty . . . . and we dare to hope that you will enjoy soon this glory, if you deign to grant our wishes in accelerating so desirable a good harmony between your Majesty and the Sovereign Pontiff, by restoring entire freedom to the pope, surrounded by his natural counsellors, without whom he can neither communicate with the Churches confided to his solicitude, nor solve any question of importance, nor provide for the needs of Catholicism.*"

FIRST SERIES.

Question I.—Is the government of the Church arbitrary ?

Answer.—No ; it belongs, it is true, especially to the successor of Saint Peter, who is the head of it, enjoying supre-

---

[1] M. Bourlier.   [2] M. Mannay.

[3] Jean-Baptiste Canaveri, born in 1753, entered the order of the Oratorians in 1771, became Bishop of Bielle in 1797, then of Verceil in 1808. He was soon after appointed first chaplain of Madame Lætitia Bonaparte.* He died in 1818.

[4] François-Louis Fontana, born in 1750, entered the congregation of the Barnabites in 1767, and was elected superior of his order in the province of Milan. In 1804 he accompanied the pope to Paris, and became afterwards procurator-general of his order, Counsellor of Rites, and finally general of his congregation. After the removal of the pope, he was confined at Arcis-sur-Aube, was a member of the Ecclesiastical Commission of 1809, but only attended its first sittings. He was arrested and imprisoned in the following year. He only recovered his liberty in 1814, returned to Rome, was named cardinal in 1819, and died in 1822.

* The Emperor's mother—(*Translator*).

macy of honours and jurisdiction in all the Church ; but it belongs also to the bishops, successors for the apostles ; and, however eminent may be the authority of the apostolic chair *it is regulated in its exercise by the canons, that is to say by the laws common to the whole Church. Pope St. Martin wrote to a bishop : " We are the defenders and the depositaries, but not the transgressors of the holy canons." " It is in observing them and causing them to be observed by others," said Bossuet, "that the Church of Rome raised itself prominently above all others."*

The commission adds that the usages in the possession of particular Churches, and which take their source *in the ancient discipline, make the law for these Churches. They constitute in some way their common law and must be respected.* It quotes Pope Saint Gregory, who says expressly, in speaking of the Church of Africa, " *The usages that do not injure the Catholic faith ought to remain intact.*"

Question 2.—Can the pope from motives of temporal welfare refuse his intervention in spiritual affairs ?

Answer.—The supremacy, by which the pope enjoys divine right, being all for the spiritual advantage of the Church, we believe we here pay him homage in replying that when temporal affairs have no necessary connection with spiritual ones, when they do not prevent the head of the Church fulfilling freely the functions of apostolic nuncio, the pope cannot, from the sole motive of temporal affairs, refuse his intervention in spiritual affairs.

Question 3.—It is beyond doubt that, since a certain time, the court of Rome is confined to a small number of families, that the affairs of the Church are there examined and treated by a small number of prelates and theologians, taken from the small localities in the neighbourhood. . . . . In this state of things, would it be proper to convene a council ?

Answer.—If it is a question of a general council, it could not be held without the head of the Church, otherwise it would not represent the Universal Church. . . . . If it is of a national council, its authority would be insufficient to rule upon any matter which would interest all Catholicism.

Question 4.—Should not the Consistory or Privy Council of the pope be composed of prelates of all nations in order to enlighten his Holiness?

Answer.—The Council of Basel had decided (with some limiting clauses) that the cardinals should be taken from all the Catholic states. The orators of the King of France at the Council of Trent renewed the propositions that the Council of Basel had adopted, and the former limited itself to deciding *that the pope should take cardinals from all nations as much as could be conveniently done, and according as he should find them worthy of that dignity.*

The commission said it could only formulate wishes for the execution of the measure which meets the desire of his Majesty.

Question 5.—Supposing that it should be recognized that there is no necessity for changes in the present organization of the Church, does not the emperor continue in his person the rights which were those of the Kings of France, the Dukes of Brabant, and other sovereigns of the Low Countries, the Kings of Sardinia, the Dukes of Tuscany, &c.—whether for the nomination of cardinals or for all other prerogatives?

Answer.—The commission thinks that the emperor is warranted in claiming the prerogatives of the sovereignties comprised in the empire.

SECOND SERIES.

Questions which concern France especially.

Question 1.—Have his Majesty or his ministers infringed the *Concordat?*

Answer.—The commission thinks the pope has no cause to complain *of any essential infringement* of the *Concordat.* As to the *organic articles* added to the *Concordat,* the commission agrees that the pope, during his sojourn in Paris, laid before the emperor representations as to a certain number of these articles *that he judged contrary to the free exercise of the Catholic religion. But several of the articles of which his Holiness complained are only applications or consequences of maxims and usages received in the*

Gallican Church, from which neither the emperor nor the clergy of France can depart.

Some others, in truth, it adds, *comprise dispositions which would be very detrimental to the Church if they were strictly enforced. There is every reason to believe that they were added to the Concordat as regulations dictated by circumstances, as considerations necessary for paving the way for the restoration of the Catholic religion; and we expect from the justice and piety of his Majesty, that he will deign to revoke or modify them in such a manner as to dissipate the annoyance to which they have given rise.*

The commission indicates three of them : The first on the bulls, briefs, ... which were not to be received nor put into execution without the authorization of the government. It desires that the *penitentiary's briefs*, which were formally excepted by the *parlements*, be excepted. The twenty-sixth, on the fixation at three hundred francs of the title or revenue exacted from ecclesiastics in order to be ordained by the bishop, while it was only one hundred and fifty francs before the Revolution, when the candidates, belonging for the greater part to the higher classes, were very much richer. The thirty-sixth, on the vicars-general who were, according to this article, to continue their functions even after the death of the bishop ; while it is a principle that the powers of the grand vicar expire with him who has given them, that the chapter is *ipso facto* invested with episcopal jurisdiction, and that it is this chapter which appoints the vicars-general who govern during the vacancy in the see.

It is but right to observe that these three demands were granted by decree, February 28, 1810.

Question 2.—Is the state of the clergy in France ameliorated on the whole or made worse since the *Concordat* has been in force ?

The answer is here most affirmative, most detailed, richest in facts. Besides the liberty of the Catholic religion, which is in itself alone the greatest of the benefits due to the *Concordat*, what new benefits did not accrue from it since that time ? The endowment of chapters ; thirty thousand supplementary chapels pensioned ; four hundred scholarships and three hundred half-scholarships for the training-schools of the clergy ; exemption from conscription for students presented by the bishop ; invitation to the general councils of departments to increase the endowments of bishops and chapters, and to provide for the needs of religion ; re-establishment of religious congregations devoted to gratuitous teaching, to the relief of the poor, sick, &c. . . . . All these facts are evident.

Question 3.—If the French government has not violated the *Concordat,* can the pope arbitrarily refuse confirmation to appointed archbishops and bishops, and destroy religion in France as he has destroyed it in Germany, where, for the last ten years, no bishop has been appointed ?

Answer.—The Concordat is a synallagmatic compact between the Head of the State and the Head of the Church, by which each of them is under obligation to the other. IT IS ALSO a public treaty by which each of the contracting parties acquires rights and takes obligations upon himself. The right reserved by the pope cannot be exercised arbitrarily. By the Compact between King Francis I. and Leo X.[1] *(*1515*), the pope was held to grant bulls of confirmation to subjects named by the sovereign, or to allege canonical motives for his refusal. Pius VII. is equally bound towards the emperor and France by the Compact that he has solemnly ratified.*

The Holy Father having written from Savona, August 28, 1809, a letter to Cardinal Caprara, to set forth the motives of *his refusal, the commission does not think it is departing from the profound respect with which it is penetrated for the person and the supreme dignity of the Head of the Church, in putting under the eyes of the emperor the reflections that it would dare to present to his Holiness himself, if it were admitted to the honour of conferring with him.*

The pope gave three motives for refusal in his letter. 1. The religious innovations introduced into France since the

---

[1] This Compact, the preliminaries of which were agreed upon December 10, 1515, at an interview between the two sovereigns, was only signed August 18, 1516. It provided for the abolition of the " Pragmatic sanction," gave up to the pope the income derived from sees left vacant a year or more, and acknowledged the supremacy of the pope over the councils. As compensation, it gave the king the right of nomination to all the prelacies of France.

Concordat, and yet he did not enumerate one which was an essential breach of this Compact. The known innovations had been in France of service to religion. The government had met the remonstrances relative to the organic articles, and besides, this complaint, already an old one concerning France, had not been followed, hitherto, by a refusal of bulls on the part of the pope. 2. The second motive was founded on political events and measures which it did not belong to him to judge. *The principal event,* said the commission, *is the decree of* 1809, *bearing upon the union of the Roman States with the French Empire. Is this motive canonical? Is it founded on the principles and on the spirit of religion?* The commission replies: *Religion teaches us not to confound the spiritual order and the temporal order; the jurisdiction that the pope exercises essentially by divine right is that which Saint Peter received from Christ, the only one he has been able to transmit to his successors; and that is purely spiritual. The temporal sovereignty is for the popes only an accessory foreign to their authority. The first will last as long as the Church, as long as the world; and the other, a human institution, not being comprised in the Divine promises that have been made to the Church, can be taken away, as it has been given, by men and events. In all suppositions in this respect, and whatever may be the political position of the pope, his authority in the universal Church and his relations with individual churches ought always to be the same, and as he has only received his powers for the advantage of the faithful and for the government of the Church, the commission is persuaded that the Holy Father would put an end to his refusals, if he were convinced, like those who see things closely, that this refusal can only be very detrimental to the Church.*

According to the commission, *the invasion of Rome cannot then be a motive for the refusal of the canonical confirmation of the bishops nominated. This invasion is not a breach of the Concordat. The Concordat stipulated nothing, guaranteed nothing temporal; and so long as the jurisdiction of the pope over the Church of France is recognized, the ties which attach this Church to the chair of St. Peter are not relaxed, and the Concordat subsists in its integrity.*

The pope recognizes this distinction in his letter, but he could not, he said, sacrifice the defence of the patrimony of the Church. That is not contested ; he might reclaim it with all the means at his disposal. But how could the refusal of the bulls be one of those means ? If the emperor exacted and obtained from the nominated bishops some declaration contrary to the authority of the Holy Father, or relative to the invasion of the Roman States, the pope would be in the right in refusing them canonical confirmation ; but there is nothing like it in the present circumstances. How then could he wish or could he believe he had the power to punish them for an event which could not be imputed to them ? When Rome was stormed by the troops of Charles V., did Clement VII., to avenge himself on this prince, abandon all the churches to anarchy ? 3. The third motive of refusal in the letter from the Holy Father is taken from the actual situation. God knows, says the pope, if we desire ardently to give to the vacant churches of France their pastors, and if we desire to find an expedient for doing it in a proper manner ; but ought we to act in so important a juncture without consulting our natural counsellors ? Then, how could we consult them, when, separated from them by violence, we have been deprived of all free communication with them, and besides, from all the necessary means for the expedition of such affairs, not even having, up to the present, obtained permission to have near us one of our secretaries ?

The objection was a strong one, and the commission saw itself compelled to make the following reply : *To these last complaints, we have no other reply to make than to place them ourselves under the eyes of his Majesty, who will feel all the force and all the justice of them.*

This phrase was not perhaps lacking in courage, for it was to justify the refusal of the pope and to show clearly to the emperor his injustice and his inconsistency.

Question 4.—The French government not having broken the Concordat, if, on the other hand, the pope refuses to execute it, the intention of his Majesty is to regard the Concordat as abrogated ; but, in this case, what would it be proper to do for the good of religion ?

Answer.—If the pope persisted in the refusal to execute the Concordat, it is certain, strictly speaking, that the emperor would no longer be held to observe it, and that he could regard it as abrogated. These are the first words of the reply ; they appear to decide everything, but, nevertheless, this was not the case, and the commission soon adds : *But this compact is not a purely personal transaction. . . . . It is a treaty which forms a part of our public right. . . . and it is important to demand its execution, even in the supposition that the Holy Father should persist in refusing it as far as he is concerned.*

This reasoning is subtle and even singular ; for the commission seems to put forward with assurance a principle, only to recoil the more quickly before its consequence ; it seems even to have endeavoured to give rise again to the difficulty, at the moment when it appeared quite clearly solved.

The commission says afterwards that the Concordat should be considered not as abrogated, but as *suspended*, and that it would be necessary to protest always against the refusal of the pope, and to appeal either to the pope himself, better informed, or to his successor.

But whether the Concordat be regarded as abrogated, or remain suspended, adds the commission, *what is it proper to do for the good of religion ?* (These are the last words of the question.) Here the commission establishes clearly the principles and does not spare any argument. *All the powers of the ministers of the Church being of a spiritual order, it is for the Church alone to confer them. The bishops have powers of order and powers of jurisdiction. In the three first centuries of persecutions, the Church was obliged alone to invest its pastors with these powers, and she did not lose this right when kings became her children. The Church has never recognized any bishops but those she has confirmed ; but the manner of proceeding with the election, and then of conferring the confirmation, have not always been the same. In the first centuries, the simple nomination, election, or presentation belonged to the co-provincial bishops, to the clergy and to the people of the church that was to be supplied ; and this election was confirmed by the archbishop who consecrated the bishop ; or, if it was the archbishop himself who was to be confirmed, by the council of the province that conferred the institution or the mission, for the particular church to which he had just been elected. Afterwards, the emperors and other Christian princes had a great share in the nomination, that is to say, the election, and gradually the people and the clergy of the country ceased to be called upon. The election passed then to the chapter of the metropolitan church, but always with the requirement of the consent of the prince (representing the people) and of the confirmation or metropolitan institution or of that of the council of the province.*

The ecclesiastical commission forgot to add that, up to the thirteenth century, the popes had had no share either in the election or the confirmation. Since, by reservations and other principles inserted in the *fausses décrétales*,[1] they assumed sometimes both the election and the confirmation. It was this state of things, so foreign to the ancient discipline, since there were no traces of it in the first twelve centuries of the Church, that the Council of Basel as well as the Pragmatic Sanction wished to remedy. After the Council of Basel and the Pragmatic Sanction published at Bourges in 1438[2] conformably to the decrees of that council, it was decided that the election by the people and by the chapter should be confirmed by the archbishop or by the provincial council. In 1516, this Pragmatic Sanction was replaced by the compact between François I. and Leo X., in virtue of which the right of election passed entirely to the king in the place of the people or of the chapter, and the confirmation or institution to the pope, instead of to the archbishops and provincial councils.

The ecclesiastical commission says, with reference to these modifications : *these two modifications to the right of election have been regarded as made with the expressed or tacit consent of the Church. We might even say that this approbation (of the Church) would still be indispensable, even if it were proposed to return to one of the methods adopted in the preceding centuries ; for a law*

---

[1] The name of *fausses décrétales* is applied to a collection of canonical rights of the sixth century, attributed to the monk Denys le Petit, which tended to considerably increase the power of the popes.

[2] The Pragmatic Sanction of Bourges is the name given to the ordinance that King Charles VII. issued, in 1438, on the affairs of the Church of France. This article said in substance that God had given neither to St. Peter nor to his successors any direct power over temporal matters.

once abrogated is no longer a law, and it can only resume that character by an act of the authority that abrogated it. This is one of the capital vices of the civil constitution of the clergy, adopted by the Constituent Assembly . . . for, beyond the fact that the elections decreed by this Constitution resembled in no manner those of the first centuries, the Constituent Assembly which had only political powers was essentially incompetent to re-establish without the concurrence and consent of the Church these rules of discipline that the Church had abolished.

Thus, in the supposition that by persevering in the refusal of the bulls the Concordat should be regarded as suspended or as abrogated, there would be no authority for reviving the Pragmatic Sanction, unless the ecclesiastical authority intervened for its revival. Except in that case, it would become the source of troubles similar to those excited throughout all France by the civil constitution of the clergy in 1791.

What is it proper, then, to do for the good of religion ? For this question recurs constantly.

The commission has not the necessary authority to indicate measures suitable to replace the intervention of the pope in the confirmation of the bishops. (Is this answer really accurate ? Would the suggesting of these measures presuppose an authority ?)

The commission thinks that the emperor can do nothing wiser and more conformable to the rules than to convoke a national council which shall examine the question proposed and suggest the proper means for preventing the inconvenience of the refusal of the bulls. In 1688, *on the occasion of a like refusal of bulls by Pope Innocent XI. to the bishops, as a sequel to the assembly of the clergy in* 1682, *the Parlement of Paris, in the opinion of the attorney-general Du Harlay, rendered a decree to the effect that the king should be prayed to summon the provincial councils or even a national council.*

The emperor, in a note which he dictated to the Bishop of Nantes, M. Duvoisin, found that this answer was not sufficiently clear upon the question. He had thought, he said in this note, that, the Concordat failing, France was *ipso facto* in the situation which existed before. But the commission had caused him to alter his opinion, and he thought now that, the Concordat

having abrogated the law which existed at the time of its conclusion, the former could no longer be re-established except by
the power that had abrogated it, but he differed from the
opinion of the council in that he thought the Gallican Church
was sufficient to pronounce the re-establishment of the ancient
law, without which there would be a gap in the legislation of the
Church. The emperor did not explain his thought further,
having been interrupted by other business.

The ecclesiastical commission, however, on the simple observation contained in the note, discussed the question anew without
entering too much into the idea of the emperor, for it commences
by saying : *that it persists in believing that the convocation of a
national council is the only canonical way that can lead to the
desired end.* It supposes that : *the council will address at first to
the pope respectful remonstrances on the results likely to be entailed
by a refusal prolonged any further, on the necessity in which the
emperor and the clergy would find themselves to provide by some other
means for the preservation of religion and for the perpetuity of the
episcopacy, and that they would propose afterwards all the means
of conciliation, &c. . . . and if the pope refused these prayers and
these conciliations of the assembled clergy of France, the council
would examine* (which we did not believe we ought to do) *if it
be competent to re-establish a mode of canonical confirmation which
could replace the mode established by the Concordat. If it judged
itself competent, it would decree, under the good pleasure of his
Majesty, a regulation of discipline on this matter, but declaring
that this regulation is only provisory, and that the Church of France
would not cease to demand the observation of the Concordat, being
at all times ready to return to it. . . . And if the national council
did not judge itself competent, it would appeal to a general council,
the only authority in the Church which is above the pope.*

*And if this resource became impossible because the pope would
not recognize the council nor preside over it, or if in the political
circumstances its convocation should present too many difficulties to
assemble it—what would it be proper to do for the good of
religion ?—Seeing the impossibility of having recourse to the general
council, and seeing the imminent danger with which the Church is
menaced, the national council could declare that the confirmation*

given by the archbishop to his suffragans, or by the oldest bishop of the province next to the archbishop, should take the place of the pontifical bulls until the pope or his successors consented to the full execution of the Concordat. This is a law of necessity, a law that the pope himself believed he had power to recognize, when, rising above all ordinary rules and by an act of authority without example, he suppressed all the old bishoprics of France in order to create new ones.

Is it not astonishing that the ecclesiastical commission, having arrived at such a solution, did not repeat here that, in order to put an end to the principal motive of opposition of the pope (the motive enunciated by him in his letter to Cardinal Caprara, where he declares that his refusal to give bulls is founded particularly on the fact that, in his prison at Savona, he is deprived of all liberty) the emperor was begged to render to the pope at least the liberty necessary for the expedition of the bulls in order to constitute him in the wrong if he then still persisted in his refusal ? In place of that, the commission was ever dwelling upon the supposition that the pope only refused the bulls from purely temporal motives, and above all on account of the invasion of Rome, whilst the pope had formally declared that it was because he had been deprived of his liberty, of his counsellors, and even of his secretary, that he refused to have the bulls expedited.

The commission, which had felt all the force of this claim, which had already recognized the justice of it, should have renewed its instances in this respect. The liberty claimed here by the pope was not a purely temporal object ; it was an indispensable condition to validate the acts of any private citizen, and with much greater reason, those of the Head of the Church. The commission, in this long and conclusive part of the discussion, has too much the appearance of believing that all the wrongs are on the side of the pope. Is this complacency or pusillanimity ? That it did not counsel the emperor to return Rome may be conceived ; it was not called upon to treat this political question, which besides, was altogether independent of that of the delivery of the bulls, which had been submitted to it ; but not to repeat each day that, before thinking of a council or of any other extraordinary remedy, to which they could have recourse, in case, without any reason, the pope should persist in his refusal to execute the Concordat, it was necessary to allow him enough liberty in order that he could not complain that they did him violence by such a demand, was not only pusillanimity towards the emperor, but also inconsistence ; it was appearing to wish to prolong the rupture, when perhaps only a word could have remedied it.

THIRD SERIES.

Questions which concern the Churches of Germany, of Italy, and the Bull of Excommunication.

Question 1.—His Majesty, who can justly consider himself as the most powerful Christian, would feel his conscience disturbed if he paid no attention to the complaints of the Churches of Germany as to the state of helplessness in which the pope had left them for ten years. He desires, as *suzerain of Germany*, as *heir of Charlemagne*, as *veritable Emperor of the West*, as *eldest son of the Church*, to know what course he ought to take to restore the benefits of religion to the people of Germany.

Answer.—The one the commission gives to this question could not be more vague. The protractor believes he ought to recall here the ancient compact of the Germanic nation of 1447, and the treaty of Munster of 1648 ; he then enters into long details on the Diet of Ratisbon of 1803, which overthrew by so many secularizations the political and religious state of Germany, and transferred the see of Mayence to Ratisbon ; on the preparatory conferences of 1804, between the nuncio of the pope, and the referendary of the Empire ; on the act of the Confederation of the Rhine, July 12, 1806 ; on the abdication of the imperial crown of Germany by the Emperor Francis II. (August 6, 1806), which effected the dissolution of the Germanic body ; on the divers pretensions of a multitude of princes in regard to the Catholic clergy, religious instruction, matrimonial dispensations . . . . on the subjection of the bishops, curates, and prebendaries to all these princes, and finally on the new difficulties caused in any arrangement whatever by the situation of the Holy Father.

The commission does not see, since the abdication of the Emperor Francis II., any one but the Protector of the Confederation of the Rhine (Napoleon), who can, in conjunction with the Sovereign Pontiff, remedy these evils, and it limits itself to expressing wishes.

It must be agreed that there had been much bad grace, and above all much bad faith on the part of the Emperor Napoleon, in imputing at this time the religious troubles of Germany to the state of abandonment in which the pope left for ten years the Church of Germany, and the argument of the commission on this point is very feeble and very insignificant.

Question 2.—Is it indispensable to make a new circumscription of bishoprics in Tuscany, and in other parts of the Empire? If the pope refuses to co-operate in these arrangements, what course ought his Majesty to follow in order to make them regular?

Answer.—The commission thinks that the churches of Tuscany are not suffering like those of Germany; that they are regularly organized and administered; that thus a new circumscription, although useful, is not urgent. *All leads to the belief,* it adds, *that when the pope shall be surrounded by his counsellors, his Holiness will give them an active and sustained attention.* Finally, the commission believes that his Majesty can suspend the ameliorations he is planning for the churches of Tuscany until the general affairs of the Church are terminated, since the case of necessity is not here applicable.

Question 3.—The Bull of Excommunication of June 10, 1809, being contrary to Christian charity as well as to the independence and honour of the throne, what course must be taken so that, in times of trouble and calamity, the popes may not arrive at such an excess of power?.

Answer.—The commission cites at first the extract from this bull which declares that the *authors, abettors, counsellors and perpetrators of the outrages (that is to say the invasion of Rome and of the provinces of the Roman States, as well as the other persecutions) in virtue of book xvii., chapter xi., which it calls attention*

*to, have incurred the excommunication pronounced by the Council
of Trent, and the Holy Father excommunicates and anathematizes
them anew, without, nevertheless, naming any special person. His
Holiness forbids even the detracting from the rights and privileges
of the persons comprised in this category.*

The commission says afterwards:—*That the bulls of Boniface
VIII. against Philippe the Fair, of Julius II. against Louis
XII., of Sixtus V. against Henry IV. have never taken effect
in France, because the bishops of France refused to admit or to publish them. For the same reason, the bull* In Cœna Domini, *so
long published in Rome, was always regarded in France as
null and void.*

If the bull of June 10, 1809, *had been addressed to the bishops
of France,* the commission thinks *that they would have declared
them contrary to the discipline of the Gallican Church, to the
authority of the sovereign, and capable, contrary to the intention of
the pope, of troubling public tranquillity.*

It states *that Gregory XIV., successor of Sixtus V., issued,
in* 1591, *MONITORY letters against Henry IV., and that the
bishops at Chartres declared that the censures and excommunica-
tions conveyed by the aforesaid letters were void, as much in
form as in matter, and that they could not bind nor constrain the
conscience.*

The commission limits itself then to declaring : *That it does
not doubt that the National Council, if it be assembled, remembering
the true principles regarding this, and the spirit of the Church, in
the application of censures, will declare also its nullity, and will
lodge an appeal as much against this bull as against all similar
bulls to the General Council, or to the pope better informed,
as has always taken place in the Church.*

The commission might have added that the monitory letters
against King Henry IV. were consigned to the fire by the
parlements sitting at Tours and at Châlons.

As to Henry IV. himself, then King of Navarre, excom-
municated by Sixtus V. in 1588, it is known that, following his
natural bent, he had this act of appeal posted at the Vatican,
and that the pope only esteemed him the more for that.

The ecclesiastical commission concluded, in its general answer, by citing the first article of the declaration of the clergy, in 1682.[1]

It was by the delivery of these, January 11, 1810, that the commission ended its labours, begun on November 16, 1809.

I forgot to say that the work of the commission on the first series of questions is attributed to the Bishop of Trèves; that on the second series to the Bishop of Nantes, and that on the third to the Archbishop of Tours. It is affirmed that Father Fontana only attended the first sitting, and that M. Emery was not very punctual at the meetings, and did not sign the answers of the commission, alleging that it was not proper for him to put his signature beside those of cardinals and of bishops.

REFLECTIONS ON THIS ECCLESIASTICAL COMMISSION.

I can quite conceive the consideration the members of this commission must have had for the emperor, for fear of irritating him and driving him to still more violent measures, that is to say, to a complete rupture with the pope, which would have revived the schism in the Church of France. But I cannot conceive why they did not try with more persistence to convince him, that, in order to be justified in imputing wrongs to the pope, he must, at least, accord him the kind of liberty that he himself judged necessary in order to give bulls, and to ask him, consequently, what liberty he deemed indispensable for that. The pope would not have dared to say that he needed above all Rome and the patrimony of St. Peter; that would have been too evidently false, natural though it might be that he should much desire this restitution, and that he should not cease to protest against the violence which had deprived him of his States. He would have been satisfied, without doubt, to demand a certain number of cardinals, his secretary, and his papers. If he had demanded more, or having obtained the objects of his first demand, he had continued to refuse the bulls, then the answers of the commission, which we have just analyzed, would have offered to the public the

---

[1] This article said in substance that God had not given either to Saint Peter or to his successors any direct or indirect power over temporal matters.

expression of just and suitable opinions, but as long as this indispensable point was not accorded, to press the pope (in the situation in which he was placed) by arguments which would have no value except in case it had been shown that his refusal proceeded from ill-will, was greatly to enfeeble the reasoning, very good in other suppositions, but which, outside of that, must only appear sophistry mingled with a little bad faith and even with disloyalty.

Before the meeting and deliberations of the ecclesiastical commission, the emperor had made several advances to the pope in order to conquer his repugnance to give the bulls. He had had Cardinal Caprara say, in a letter, that this cardinal (who was no longer a legate, but who was, however, at Paris) wrote to the pope then at Savona, July 20, 1809, that the emperor consented to his own name (the emperor's), and even his right of nomination not being mentioned in the bulls which would then be delivered on the simple demand of the Council of State or of the Minister of Public Worship. To which the pope replied, August 26, that this Council of State, or this minister, being the organs of the emperor, it would be equivalent to recognizing in the emperor the right of nomination and the faculty of exercising it, which he did not wish to do.

And why did he not wish to recognize this right? Was it then on account of the excommunication? If so, that was showing an unreasonable temper and beginning to place himself in the wrong. Why, too, should the emperor have made this sacrifice? Would it not have been better not to have made any, and to have tried upon the Holy Father the effect of what sufficient liberty he might grant him?

The year 1810, far from bringing any alleviation to the situation of the pope and giving him, according to the wishes and prayers of the ecclesiastical commission, a little more liberty, aggravated, on the contrary, this situation, and rendered his captivity harder.

In effect, on February 17, 1810, appeared the *senatus-consultum* pronouncing the union of the Roman States with the French Empire; the independence of the imperial throne of all authority on earth, and annulling the temporal existence of the popes. This *senatus-consultum* assured a pension to the pope, but it ordained also that the pope should take oath to do nothing in opposition to the four articles of 1682. On the same day another *senatus-consultum*, which awards to the eldest son of the emperor the title of King of Rome, and enacts that the emperor shall be consecrated a second time at Rome, was passed.[1]

All these dispositions were hostile and irritating. The pope was not accorded even the right and liberty of complaining. How could he consider he had enough liberty for the rest? To order by a *senatus-consultum* an oath from a captive pope, and an oath to do nothing against the four articles of 1682, were two points irritating in the highest degree, and very evidently inadmissible, above all when they were imposed with such imperiousness.

The pope must have consoled himself, besides, even to rejoicing, that they made the insulting pension they offered him depend upon the taking of such an oath, and it is that which furnished him with a reply so nobly apostolic : *that he had no need of this pension, and that he would live on the charity of the faithful.*

All must be told. In spite of his captivity at Savona, the Holy Father had, however, replied in 1809 to each of the letters of nineteen bishops who had demanded of him *extraordinary powers* for marriage dispensations, and had granted the latter. On November 5, 1810, he made public, at least as much as he could, his brief against Cardinal Maury, and addressed it to him in response to the communication the cardinal had made to him on his nomination to the archbishopric of Paris. The

---

[1] The *senatus-consultum* of February 17, 1820, stipulated besides :

That the papal States should form two departments : that of Rome and that of Trasmania ;

That a prince of the blood or a high dignitary should keep the imperial court at Rome ;

That all foreign sovereignty was incompatible with the exercise of any spiritual authority in France ;

That palaces should be prepared for the Sovereign Pontiff in all the various portions of the Empire where he might be pleased to reside ; that at all events a palace should always be at his disposal in Paris, and another in Rome ;

That his Holiness should enjoy an income of two millions of francs, derived from capital invested in country estates ;

That the expenses of the Sacred College and those of the Propaganda should be provided for by the State.

cardinal, while waiting for the bulls of confirmation, had taken the administration of the diocese which had been conferred upon him by the metropolitan chapter. The pope, in his brief, reproaches him with having abandoned the holy cause, which he had so well defended hitherto ; with having violated his oath, with having left his see of Montefiascone, and taken the administration of a see with which he could not be charged. He *orders* him to renounce it, and not force him to proceed against him conformably to the canons of the Church. This brief made a great noise, and caused, January 1, 1811, the public disgrace of Abbé d'Astros who had made it known, and soon after of his relation, M. Portalis the younger, who had learned it from him.[1]

There was here, it cannot be denied, a little contradiction on the part of the pope. To be able to issue a brief against Cardinal Maury ; to be able to reply to nineteen letters from bishops who demanded powers, and accord them ;—and not to be able, for want of liberty, to deliver the bulls of confirmation and put a stop to the long viduity of the churches ; was that very consistent ?

Two other facts come in support of this reflection.

Towards the end of the year 1810, the emperor had named for the archbishopric of Florence M. d'Osmond,[2] Bishop of Nancy. Pius VII., by a brief of December 2, 1810, declared that this bishop could not administer the diocese of Florence, supporting himself for that on the decisions of the second Council of Lyons, and on those of the Council of Trent, which were not really applicable to this circumstance. The chapter of Florence deferred to the order of the pope, which caused trouble in that

---

[1] This brief had been addressed by Pius VII. to Abbé d'Astros, vicar-general of the diocese of Paris. The latter communicated it to his cousin, Comte Portalis, then councillor of state and director of the section of the Ministry of the Interior, entrusted with the supervision of all publications. Both kept the secret and the brief was published. Napoleon had knowledge of these facts ; his anger was very great. At the sitting of the Council of State of January 4, 1811, he vehemently reproached Comte Portalis for his conduct, deprived him of all his functions and exiled him to Provence. As to Abbé d'Astros, he was arrested and confined at Vincennes, whence he was not released until 1814.

[2] Antoine, Baron d'Osmond, born in 1754, was at first vicar-general of M. de Brienne, Archbishop of Toulouse. On May 1, 1785, he was consecrated Bishop of Comminge to succeed his uncle. He emigrated at the Revolution, resigned his seat in 1801, and was named Bishop of Nancy in 1802. In 1810, he was named Archbishop of Florence, but the pope refused to confirm him, and he was obliged, in 1814, to resume his see at Nancy. He died in 1823.

city.   Napoleon had also named for the bishopric of Asti a M.
Dejean ;[1] this brought forth another brief from the pope en-
joining the chapter to abstain from confiding to him the power
of administration.   The emperor, who saw that the pope wished
to put limits to his power, then gave way to great violence.

On January 1, 1811, occurred the affair of Abbé d'Astros,
who was arrested as he went out of the Tuileries.   The chapter
of Paris deprived him of his powers as grand vicar, and profited
by this occasion to write, probably under the eyes of Cardinal
Maury, a letter to the emperor, in which they established the
right of the chapter to provide for the vacant see, and to confer
upon a nominated bishop all the capitulary powers, that is to say,
all the episcopal jurisdiction, basing this on what had been
practised in the time of Louis XIV., and even by the advice of
Bossuet, they said, though without being able to prove it.   This
letter, sent to all the dioceses of France and Italy, drew to them
the adhesion of a multitude of bishops and chapters, both in
Italy and in France, who confirmed this doctrine.

The publication of all the briefs of which I have just spoken,
far from disposing the emperor to grant more liberty to the pope,
persuaded him that he had too much, since he thus abused it.
The order was given January 7, 1811, to make a strict perqui-
sition in his apartment.   Everything was ransacked, even his
writing-desk ; and his papers and those of the members of his
household were sent to Paris.   There was found, it is said, a
brief which conferred extraordinary powers on Cardinal di
Pietro.[2]   The pope was then deprived of pens, ink, and paper.
His master of the chamber and the prelate Doria, his confessor,
were sent away.   He was not allowed to communicate with the
Bishop of Savona ;[3] the papers of the latter were seized and

[1] François André, Baron Dejean, born at Castelnaudary in 1745, nominated Bishop
of Asti, February 9, 1809.
[2] Michel di Pietro, born in 1747, had been instituted apostolic delegate by Pius
VI. in 1798, when that pope was carried away from Rome by order of the Directory.
Pius VII. named him Patriarch of Jerusalem, cardinal and prefect of the Propaganda.
He was compelled to come to Paris after the arrest of the pope, and was exiled to
Semur for having refused to assist at the marriage of Napoleon and Marie-Louise.
He returned to Rome in 1815, and became Grand Penitentiary and Bishop of Albano.
He died in 1821.
[3] Here is the order signified to the Holy Father by the prefect of Montenotte, M.
de Chabrol, according to the instructions sent him from Paris :—"The undersigned,
according to the orders emanating from his sovereign, His Imperial and Royal

himself even removed to Paris. There remained to the pope a few servants, to whom were assigned about forty sous per day for their expenses. It was at the moment when the emperor gave way to such unworthy violence, and when the pope continued his noble and legitimate refusal, for that which concerned him personally, that Napoleon decided to appoint a second ecclesiastical commission.

SECOND ECCLESIASTICAL COMMISSION.

Formed in January, 1811, this Commission ended its labours at the end of March. It was composed of Cardinals Fesch, Maury, and Caselli ; of the Archbishop of Tours, the Bishops of Ghent,[1] Evreux, Nantes, and Trèves, and of the Abbé Emery.

It had to reply only to these two questions :

Question I.—All communication between the pope and the subjects of the emperor, being interrupted for the present, to whom is it necessary to apply to obtain the dispensations that would be accorded by the Holy See ?

Question II.—When the pope persistently refuses to accord the bulls to the bishops nominated by the emperor, to fill the vacant seats, what is the legitimate means of giving them canonical confirmation ?

The Commission, before responding, expresses first *its profound grief that all communication between the pope and the subjects of the emperor has just been broken. It can only foresee days of mourning and affliction for the Church, if these communications remain long suspended.*

Majesty Napoleon, Emperor of the French, King of Italy, Protector of the Confederation of the Rhine . . . . is charged to notify Pope Pius VII. that he is forbidden to communicate with any church of the empire, and with any subject of the emperor under pain of disobedience on his part and on theirs, that he who preaches rebellion and whose soul is full of gall ceases to be the organ of the Church ; that since nothing can render him wise, he shall see that his Majesty is powerful enough to do what his predecessors have done and depose a pope.—SAVONA, *January* 14, 1811."—(*M. de Bacourt.*)

[1] Maurice-Madeleine de Broglie (1766-1821), third son of Marshal de Broglie, Bishop of Acqui and chaplain of the emperor in 1805, promoted to the bishopric of Ghent in 1809 ; was imprisoned on account of his resistance to the wishes of the emperor at the council of 1811. On his return to his episcopal see in 1814, he protested against various dispositions of the constitution of the Kingdom of the Low Countries, was exiled anew, and came to die in Paris.

It was well to demand the liberty of the pope. But the Commission should not have limited itself to placing that in the preamble. It ought to have returned to it in its replies, otherwise it had the appearance of wishing to get rid, in a preliminary formula, not to return to it any more, of this objection which so strongly accused Napoleon.

Answer to the first question.—The Commission thinks that the power of reserving dispensations attributed to the pope in the Church of the West is very suitable in all that regards the general discipline of the clergy, and that, without examining whether it is of divine right or not, it has become, by this same suitability and by a very long exercise, a sort of common law, from which one ought not to seek exemption. But as to the reserve of the dispensations relative to the daily needs of the faithful, which is found also with many local diversities in his powers, the Commission affirms, without hesitation, *that the bishops have, each in his diocese, entirely in their power to grant to the faithful the dispensations and absolutions belonging thereto ; that this power has never been withdrawn by any law, nor by any canon ; that it is even untransferable, and that they recover this power very naturally, above all when, as in the present circumstances, recourse to the pope is almost impossible.*

Answer to the second question.—This question had already been proposed to the Commission of 1809, and solved in some fashion by it. It had been reproduced here because the emperor presumed that he would have a more precise reply and more nearly like the note he had dictated, at the time, to M. Duvoisin ; in this he was not entirely deceived. The new Commission first laid stress on the fact that the pope had continued to refuse the bulls, without alleging any canonical reason for his refusal, in spite of the supplications of the churches of France, and notwithstanding that the results of this refusal became every day more fatal. It recalled what passed in the time of Innocent XI., when the bishops nominated by the king could govern their dioceses in virtue of the powers given to them by the chapter. Fléchier, thus appointed successively at Lavaur and at Nîmes, afforded a proof of this. It proceeded to say that the pope, in proscribing, by briefs addressed to the chapters of

Paris, Florence, and Asti, this mode adopted in all times by the Church of France, openly attacked the ancient discipline of this Church, which was *a sad proof of the prejudices that had been inspired in him.*

But the emperor, adds the Commission, *does not wish longer to make the existence of episcopacy in France depend on the canonical confirmation of the pope, who would thus be master of the episcopacy. What must be done? It agrees that the Concordat gives a very marked advantage to the pope over the sovereign of France. The prince loses the right to nominate if in a fixed time he does not present a suitable nominee.* (The Commission is entirely mistaken here : he never loses it ; if so, to whom would it pass ?) *In order that there should be equality, it would be necessary that the pope, on his side, should be obliged to give the confirmation, or to produce a canonical motive for refusing, in a determinate time, in default of which he would lose his right of confirmation, which would devolve upon whoever had the right. This clause is lacking in the Concordat. It ought to be added to it; it is the simplest measure and the most conformed to the principles. The emperor,* said the Commission, *is right in exacting it, and the pope ought to consent to it* (these are the terms employed) ; *and if he did not consent, it would justify, in the eyes of Europe, the entire abolition of the Concordat, and the recourse to another means of conferring canonical confirmation.* (The Commission of 1809 had not used such strong and decided language.)

However just might be, under the circumstances, the entire abolition of the Concordat, however legitimate might be the re-establishment of the Pragmatic Sanction or of any other method of canonical confirmation, the Commission thought, however, *that it would be necessary to prepare the minds, and to have the faithful convinced that there remained no other resource for giving bishops to the Church of France, without which the position of the bishops confirmed according to the new forms would be untenable. This change would be likened to the civil constitution of the clergy of* 1791, *and would produce the same troubles. Enlightened persons would clearly see that it cannot be compared with an ecclesiastical constitution decreed by a purely political authority, against the sentiment of the Sovereign Pontiff*

*and of nearly all the bishops of France. But others would
probably not grasp the difference well, chiefly seeing the authority
of the emperor displayed with so much ardour against the Holy
Father. The one side in this struggle would take part for the
pope against the French episcopacy; the others would be separated
too much from the Holy See, and the schism would thus revive
with all its disorders. It was barely stamped out in 1801, by
means of the perfect accord between the pope and the majority of
the bishops. How much cause should we not have to fear its
revival, if the bishops should declare themselves separated from the
pope by so grave a decision?*

*However, things cannot be left in their present state. The
jurisdiction accorded by the chapters to the nominated bishops,
besides its having also the grave inconvenience of being disapproved by the pope, does not really give to the dioceses the possession of a complete episcopacy. If then the pope persists in his
refusal without a canonical motive, we permit ourselves to express
the desire that it be declared to His Holiness, either that the Concordat already broken by his own action shall be publicly abolished
by the emperor, or that it will only be preserved by favour of a
clause appropriate for insuring against arbitrary refusals, which
render those rights illusory which the Concordat assures to our
sovereign.*

These are the exact words of the Commission. It recognized
then that the emperor had, in the present case, the right to
declare the Concordat abolished, under the condition of seeking
afterwards some means of doing without it. Then what other
means were there, if not to recur to the ancient law, according
to which bulls were not necessary (I make use of the expression
of the Commission), or, if it was desired to retain the Concordat,
to add to it a clause by which the right of the pope would pass
to another authority, in default of being exercised by him within
a determined time.

Thus, either the Concordat will be declared abolished, or it
will be modified by the aid of a clause accepted by both parties,
and which will prevent all abuses.

I remark that in the first case, they could do without the
pope entirely, if he persisted in his refusal, and seek elsewhere

some canonical authority different from his. This is said by the Commission without the least restriction. The emperor does not wish, it says, that the episcopacy in France should depend upon the confirmation by the pope, who would thus be master of the episcopacy, and it proves that it is right, that it is just, and entirely within the powers of the emperor, that the Concordat should be abolished by him, since it is no longer executed except by him. It expresses in this respect neither doubt nor regret ; it is the fault of the pope. But, from that to say that the emperor could do the rest, or advise means by which the rest could be done, was hardly a step. For if the emperor had not in himself or at his disposition all that was necessary in order to secure the substitution of another confirmation than that by the pope, of what use would it be for him to abolish the Concordat ? He might find himself as embarrassed then in abolishing it, as he was before.

The Commission, however, did not wish to take this step. It thought, it declared, that, by principle as by prudence, it was necessary that a national council should determine or find this confirmation. But was it sure that the council, influenced by party spirit and by intrigues of all kinds, would believe itself to possess such a right ? Would it not raise new difficulties, instead of solving those it was called to settle ? Would it consent to seek whence the confirmation of the bishops might proceed ? The solution might then remain incomplete.

The Commission ought not to have dwelt so much upon the right of the emperor to abolish the Concordat, and to have proclaimed it so loudly, since it could not acquaint him with a means of doing without it. It was a mistake, I believe, and an inconsistency on the part of the Commission.

I have thought sometimes that if the emperor had made the Bishop of Nantes Minister of Public Worship, they might have been able to do without a council which could only involve matters. That bishop, so honest, so skilful, so versed in theological knowledge, acting with the threefold authority of minister, bishop, and finished theologian, over each of the other bishops separately, would have much more easily obtained their consent to substitute another canonical confirmation for that of the pope, than he could in a council where each bishop feared to appear governed by one more skilful than himself, and where the united bishops had no longer the same fear of the emperor that each of them had in private. Perhaps even the pope himself would have released them all from embarrassment by. giving the confirmation this time for fear of losing the right of conferring it in the future.

Be it as it may with this idea which is purely conjectural, there was another supposition to be discussed besides that of the abolition of the Concordat; it was that of its modification by a clause which would for ever prevent abuses, and this· was incontestably everything that was most desirable and the step most conformable to the principles, and the most suitable, even in the opinion of the Commission, to reassure all consciences.

By that, in fact, both the contracting parties could be satisfied. The pope, in the drafting of it, could have reconciled this clause with even his most ultramontane views, by declaring that, after the expiration of the three or six months, he would authorize the archbishop to replace him; thus it was he who was still the source of power; he would be compromising nothing, even in the eyes of the most fastidious, and I think that this concession on the part of the pope might have been obtained, had the negotiation been well conducted. The emperor, in his turn, would have had all that he wished, more even than he wished up to that time; for, up to the existence of the Commission, he had only desired that the pope should give the bulls to the bishops nominated by him, consenting even that the pope should not insert the name of the emperor in these bulls; and in following the course I propose, Napoleon would have obtained, moreover, even with the consent of the pope, that they should no longer be refused by him in the future, without the confirmation he refused being at once replaced by an act none the less canonical. To obtain that from the pope, without returning to him Rome and his states, would have been a triumph worthy of the fabulous destiny of Napoleon, a triumph a thousand times more important in its results than if he had secured it by means of a national council.

But the commission itself had, in the first place, put an obstacle in the way of obtaining such a clause. While agreeing that this clause in the Concordat was all that could most be desired, it had always insisted that to obtain it, or to do without it, it would be necessary to have recourse to a national council, which was not putting an end to the difficulty, for if the council eluded the question instead of solving it, what would become of it? It had been careful, however, not to do away with the idea of a negotiation : only it did not believe itself qualified to make the proposition, not having been assembled for that.

What the commission did not believe it had the right to do, the Bishop of Nantes ventured to attempt directly with the emperor, out of fear, no doubt, of the scandal that would accrue from the sudden rupture of the Concordat, which in the preambles of the decree, would surely be accompanied by hard expressions, and consequently of injurious effect. M. Duvoisin was also perhaps uneasy as to the disposition in which the council might ,be, or as to that which might be suggested to it when it was once assembled. He therefore pressed the emperor not to send, if that did not suit him, the members of the commission to make a last effort with the pope, but merely to authorize them to go.

The emperor resisted for a long time, and M. Duvoisin had much difficulty in inducing him to yield. In a moment of passion he had resolved to destroy the Concordat ; he had said it, and he did not wish to retract ; I believe, in truth, he rather gloried in it, although there was not much occasion to do so. He wished, he said, to have done with the pope. The Concordat once destroyed, he believed all would be finished. He had consented, it is true, to summon a council, but he thought he had nothing to fear from it. "The Concordat once abolished by a decree," said he, "the council would of course be required, if it wished to preserve the episcopacy, to propose another mode of confirmation for the bishops, since they could not have recourse to a Compact which would exist no longer."

M. Duvoisin did not give himself up as conquered, but insisted still ; finally he decided the emperor, who, while yielding did it with such a bad grace, that he applied himself in the instructions he gave more to increase the difficulties than to level them ; he seemed anxious to make the negotiation fail. It was known that the instructions given by the Minister of Public Worship[1] to the bishops leaving for Savona had been dictated by the emperor. The minister, who did not wish to be held responsible for them, had told it to several influential members of the clergy.

Instead of confining himself to the important point he would have been so happy to obtain, Napoleon desired the bishops to make the most inadmissible demands, as if it were a favour he was according to the pope to maintain the Concordat, even with the clause that he claimed. He wished them to inform him before all, that a national council was convened for June 9 following, and to explain to him the measures that the Church of France would be likely to take after former precedents. He would consent to maintain the Concordat, he said, in these same instructions, only provided the pope would first confirm all the nominated bishops, and agree that, in future, the confirmations should be made by the archbishop, in case he should not have confirmed them himself in the term of three months. He wished, and *this was a strict order*, that the negotiators should declare to the pope that he should never re-enter Rome as a sovereign ; but that he would be permitted to return there simply as head of the Catholic religion, if he consented to ratify the modifications to be introduced in the Concordat. In case it should no longer suit him to go to Rome, he could reside at Avignon, where he would enjoy sovereign honours, and where he would have the liberty of administering to the spiritual interests of the other countries of Christendom. Finally, they were to offer him two millions, all this on condition that he would promise to do nothing in the Empire contrary to the four articles of 1682.

[1] The Minister of Public Worship was then Jean Bigot de Preameneu. Born in 1747, he had been an advocate in the *Parlement*. In 1791, he was elected deputy from Paris to the Legislative Assembly, and became its president in 1792. He lived in retirement during the Revolution. After the 18th Brumaire, he was named commissioner of the government at the Tribunal of Cassation, then councillor of state and president of the Legislative Section. He took part in the commission appointed with drawing up the civil code. In 1808, he became Minister of Public Worship. The first restoration retained him in his office, and created him peer of France. He lived in retirement under the second, and died in 1825.

The three negotiating deputies were : the Archbishop of Tours, the Bishop of Nantes and the Bishop of Treves, to whom were added the Bishop of Faenza [1] nominated Patriarch of Venice, who was himself to repair to Savona. They were deputed by all the cardinals and bishops who were then in Paris, and who had given to them seventeen letters addressed to the Holy Father ; the longest and most pressing was that of Cardinal Fesch.

Furnished with these letters, instructions and powers for concluding and signing an arrangement, the three deputies started at the end of April, 1811. They arrived at Savona on the 9th of May. It had been strongly recommended to them to return to Paris eight days before the opening of the council, that is before June 9; they left Savona, in fact, May 19.

The contents of the letters, nine in number, they wrote from Savona to the Minister of Public Worship, and of the more detailed one they wrote to him afterwards from Paris, on their return, show with what wisdom and what propriety they conducted this negotiation, and how they led the pope, while disguising nothing from him, to show each day to them a sweeter and more conciliating disposition, and to cause him to consent at last, with a few slight modifications, to the principal demands they were charged to submit to him, or if one prefers, to impose upon him.

It is worthy of remark that on the day after their arrival, the pope, on seeing them, showed at first some uneasiness lest they came to announce to him that the future council was going to constitute itself a judge of his conduct. They dismissed most forcibly this idea, and made use of forms of the greatest respect in order to calm him. It was pretended at the time, that the fear he had allowed himself to manifest might well have had some influence on his benevolent dispositions. He resisted during the first days without bitterness, with an extreme moderation and even with some words of affection for the emperor ; but what they demanded of him was so important, that it necessitated his conferring with his customary counsellors, and he complained of

[1] Monsignor Buonsignori, appointed by Napoleon, Patriarch Archbishop of Venice.

being deprived of them. The three negotiators could not return them to him, but they neglected nothing to persuade him that he would no longer be deprived of them, when he should have entered into the conciliatory and pacific ideas of which they were the agents with him ; they added that for that which concerned the bulls, there was no need of much deliberation nor of counsellors ; that in the main the demand was just and that he must see clearly how important it was for the good of the faithful, of the dioceses and of religion, that he should grant the bulls to the nominated bishops ; and, in his own interest, as sovereign pontiff, that he should preserve, in adopting the new clause in the Concordat, this precious tie with the episcopacy of France, which would be broken if that Compact were once abolished.

The pope made new objections, but each day less strong ; he expressed regret, never the appearance of ill-will. The bishops made no haste to speak to him of the sovereignty of Rome, for fear of injuring the principal negotiation. They believed, besides, that they could perceive that the Holy Father, no longer expecting to recover this sovereignty, would doubtless always protest upon this point, since he had not the right to make the sacrifice of it ; but that he would engage not to return to Rome rather than consent to take the oath by which he would recognize the emperor as sovereign ; finally, that he felt that the deprivation of this sovereignty ought not to prevent him from governing the Church, as soon as his counsellors should have been returned to him. The pope was then resigned ; it was all that the negotiating deputies wanted.

There was no real discussion on the subject of the Bull of Excommunication, on which, however, the bishops had had occasion to express their views. The Holy Father did not seem to them to hold to it, but rather to consent to regard it as not having been issued.

The pope resisted gently but constantly, to make the promise to regard as a disciplinary regulation for the clergy of France the four articles of 1682. He showed himself well disposed in favour of the first of these articles, which recognized the independence of the temporal sovereignty, But why, he added,

exact from him a declaration on the three other articles? He
gave his word of honour to do nothing against them; they could
rely upon him.   How could they demand of him what had
never been demanded of any pope, a written promise to this
effect? There was a question here on one side and on the other
as to free opinions. Bossuet himself did not ask anything else.
He had taken care not to express his to the theologians of
Italy and above all to the pope. The Holy Father referred
often to the bull of Alexander VIII. (Ottoboni) successor to
Innocent XI., who far from relaxing from the inflexibility of his
predecessor, had issued a bull against the declaration of 1682,
three days before his death. He agreed that this bull had had
no results; he did not seek to justify it, but was it for him to
judge his predecessor and to condemn him? Would it not be
said in Italy and in all Christendom, that he had consented to give this promise from weariness of his captivity?
His memory would be tarnished by such suspicion. These
questions were, besides, complicated and difficult; there were
none on which he stood more in need of counsel. . . . .

As to the bulls, we have not been able, wrote the three bishops,
after seven or eight interviews, to obtain from the pope, the
promise to accord them to the bishops already nominated; he
does not believe he can decide anything for the future without
his council, and consequently, to consent to the new and important clause, which would be inserted in the Concordat. We
exhausted, on this point, all possible arguments and considerations, and we announced with regret that we would start
on the morrow. This prompt departure appeared to affect him;
he expressed to us the desire to see us again; we yielded to his
desire, and it seemed to us that he no longer held to any point,
except obtaining the substitution of the term of six months for
that of three in which to exercise his right of confirmation. We
presumed that that would not make any real difficulty; we
therefore expressed all our confidence in regard to this. Finally
we led him, little by little, to agree to the following articles,
drawn up, in a measure, under his dictation, and of which he
wished to retain a copy as a witness to his own concessions, and
of his ardent desire to restore peace in the Church.

ARTICLES TO WHICH THE POPE CONSENTED.

His Holiness, taking into consideration the needs and the wish of the Churches of France and of Italy, which have been presented to him by the Archbishop of Tours and by the Bishops of Nantes, Treves, and Faenza, and wishing to give to these Churches a new proof of his paternal affection, has declared to the above-named archbishop and bishops

1. That he will accord canonical confirmation to the bishops and archbishops nominated by His Imperial and Royal Majesty, in the form agreed upon, at the time of the Concordats of France and Italy.

2. His Holiness will hold himself ready to extend the same dispositions to the Churches of Tuscany, Parma, and Plaisance, by a new Concordat.

3. His Holiness consents that there should be inserted in the Concordats a clause by which he agrees to expedite the bulls of confirmation to the bishops nominated by His Majesty, in a fixed time which His Holiness esteems should not be less than six months ; and, in case he should defer longer than six months for other reasons than the personal unworthiness of the candidates, he would invest with the power of giving the bulls in his name, after the expiration of the six months, the archbishop of the vacant see, and in default of him, the oldest bishop of the province.

4. His Holiness only determines upon these concessions in the hope which has arisen from the interviews he has had with the deputy-bishops, that they would prepare the way for arrangements which would re-establish order and peace in the Church, and would restore to the Holy See the liberty, independence and dignity which are befitting to it.

SAVONA, *May 19th*, 1811.

The declaration they obtained thus from the pope was a grand thing which closed so to say, for the future, all debate between the French government and the court of Rome. How could it in future trouble order in France ? The canonical confirmation of the bishops was the only arm by which the refusal of a pope and his inaction could bring trouble ; his action could never bring it ; for it could only be produced by briefs of bulls . . . . and France would always keep up the custom of not permitting their publication until she had had them examined and judged as containing nothing contrary to the laws of the country. All hostile will of a pope and even all dissidence which would displease, would be paralyzed by this. It mattered little what the pope thought of Gallican liberties, since it would not be in his power to arrest the effect of them. To wish to make him sign in advance some promise to this effect, was then entirely useless. The pope himself had said so ; and besides, it was only a petty tyranny they exercised over him. They had the word of honour of the Holy Father ; that was indeed something ; it was even much more than any pope had ever done : and if he had not given it, there would have resulted no danger, not even the slightest inconvenience.

I forgot to say that there was another point on which he had shown in his conversation that he would never yield : it was that by which the emperor had the pretension to reserve to himself the nomination to all the bishops of Italy, leaving to the pope only the *confirmation.* " What ! " said he with emotion, " to recompense subjects, even cardinals who shall have served with zeal and talent the pontifical administration, the pope could not even nominate a single bishop in all Christendom, even in the churches which, from time immemorial, have formed part of the diocese of Rome, and whose titles would become annulled by a simple compact ? That would indeed be *terrible. . . . .* " This was his expression, the only one of the kind which escaped him in his interviews with the French bishops. They had nothing to reply to him on this point, the wish of the Holy Father appearing to them so natural.

They had occasion to speak to him of the two millions of income in rural property, fixed by the decree of February 17, 1810, for the maintenance of the pope. Pius VII. began by an absolute refusal, being pleased to repeat what he had said from the outset, that he wished to live on very little and on the assistance that might be procured from the charity of the faithful. But the bishops combated this resolution, noble as it was, by showing him that he might deprive his successors of the temporal advantages accorded by the emperor, of the sovereign honours, and of means of communicating with Catholic princes ; and also of the resources necessary for the maintenance of the Sacred College, which, by virtue of the decree of February 17, 1810, was charged to the imperial treasury.

These considerations appeared to shake him; he did not insist; but nothing was decided on this point.

The bishops returned to France convinced that with more liberty and good advice the Holy Father, if his susceptibilities were not offended, might still make new concessions on several points of some importance. But they had obtained the principal one.

Such a negotiation, so well commenced, ought to have removed all contest in the end.

What was necessary for that? A single thing, it seems to me: not to allow the council to open, and to adjourn it for a month. During this time, Napoleon would have treated with the pope on the article of the bulls and on the new clause to be added to the Concordat, without interfering with anything else. He might have returned to him a few counsellors and sufficient liberty, and the pope would have held himself in honour bound to ratify what he had promised, as the result of an intimate conviction, at least in appearance.

This treaty once signed, the emperor would no longer have need of the council, and he might be all the more inclined to adjourn it indefinitely, because its convocation had already thrown upon him some ridicule, which he could hardly ignore. Besides, would it not be better for him to agree to terminate with the pope himself, all of whose prejudices he had been able to conquer through his negotiators, than to have to do with an assembly which would surely be tumultuous, and probably, for him, ungovernable? With the promise of the pope, what was there to be done by a council which had only been convoked on the supposition that the pope would never consent to give confirmation to the nominated bishops, and still less to bind himself for the future in such a manner that he could no longer refuse this confirmation? Then all this had been granted and could be embodied in the treaty. Should the council wish anything different on this point? So much the worse! and if it wished only that, of what use would be its intervention? It was not at all agreeable to the pope ; we have seen that. It could only be so to the emperor in a case which no longer existed. And more, it would have been preferable, in any case, to do without it. Was M. Duvoisin very sure of directing at his will those ninety-five bishops of France and of Italy, who, pliable enough individually, might easily become heated when in a body? And precisely because they would feel that there was nothing to be decided, they would be all the more disposed to create a host of difficulties, to raise incidental and annoying questions, in order that they should not be reproached with not having been able to say or do anything.

The emperor counted without doubt on the influence in his favour Cardinal Fesch would obtain by presiding over the council. Here he was mistaken, as in all that he had done in raising every member of his family, with the thought of making use of him afterwards. His uncle, Cardinal Fesch, had to cause his origin to be forgotten ; and he wished, as did the brothers of Napoleon, to derive consideration from his opposition to the emperor's will and rigour, and not from the credit of his nephew.

Neither the emperor nor the Bishop of Nantes, whom his success at Savona ought to have better enlightened, felt all the gravity of the assembling of the council. Napoleon, who was not disarmed either by the cruel situation of the pope, or by the prodigious concessions which, in spite of this situation, had been obtained from him, had some injurious expressions in store against the pope, and did not wish to lose them. He prized the ridiculous honour of having them heard in the council, without thinking that the assembly, even the most cowardly, could not refuse to show an interest, at least for the sake of propriety, in the misfortunes of the Holy Father, and would not wish to dishonour itself openly.

The Bishop of Nantes perhaps also flattered himself, and in that he was wrong, that he could exercise a paramount influence in the council, by his great ability, and by his brilliant and fluent elocution. He believed he could interest at first, and acquire afterwards a right to, the confidence of the assembly, by relating his conferences with the pope. He only succeeded in creating jealousy. They did not pardon him his success ; they refused to believe in it ; and as the four articles consented to by the pope were not signed by him, they pretended that no account should be taken of them. Besides, they knew that the emperor bore him special good will ; they soon spoke of him as being a favourite, and for this reason all his words were suspected. Thereupon the emperor, in his violence, spoke as severely of the council as of the pope ; and it was supposed that M. Duvoisin was the instigator of this language. Finally, when the latter read one day in the council the project of an address to the emperor in reply to his message, and when, on some objections being offered as to its drafting, he had the inconceivable ill-taste to try to dismiss them, by saying that the project, as he had just read it, had already been submitted to the emperor, he was lost irretrievably.

What remains clear for me, is that there cannot have been an instant when Napoleon must not have repented convoking this assembly, and having permitted it to meet, since he was able to ascertain to what extent, after the return of the deputation from Savona, this council had become useless, and how it might become fatal for him. It is equally true that with the intention of the emperor to cause this assembly to turn to the profit of his power, it was impossible to follow a plan more inconsiderate and more awkward than the one he followed.

I wish only to pass rapidly in review the direction taken by this assembly and some incidents which relate to it.

The council had been convoked for June 9, 1811, but, under the pretext of the baptism of the King of Rome, son of Napoleon, it did not hold its opening sitting until June 17, in the Church of Notre Dame. M. de Boulogne,[1] Bishop of Troyes, preached the sermon. The assembly numbered ninety-five bishops (six were cardinals) and nine bishops nominated by the emperor, but who had not received their confirmation from the pope.

---

[1] Etienne-Antoine de Boulogne, born in 1747, took orders in 1771, was in 1782 grand-vicar of M. de Clermont-Tonnerre at Châlons-sur-Marne. He lived at Paris during all the Revolution, was imprisoned three times under the Terror, and proscribed at the 18th Fructidor ; but he then escaped all researches. Under the Empire, he became grand-vicar of the bishopric of Versailles, then Bishop of Troyes (1807). At the close of the council of 1811, he was arrested and imprisoned at Vincennes. He gave in his resignation, and was exiled to Falaise ; but the pope did not accept his resignation, and M. de Boulogne returned to Troyes in 1814. He was created peer of France in 1822, and died in 1825.

Cardinal Fesch, as we have said, took, at the first onset, the presidency, which no one contested with him, and, in the enumeration of his titles, that of Primate of Gaul, which came to him by right in his quality of Archbishop of Lyons. It will be seen further on, why I make mention of this particular. After the sermon, the president took the customary oath, which all the bishops repeated after him, and which is couched in the following terms:

" I recognize the Holy Catholic Roman, Apostolic Church, Mother and Mistress of all the other Churches ; I swear a true *obedience* to the Roman Pontiff, successor to Saint Peter, Prince of the Apostles, and Vicar of Jesus Christ."

This oath produced much effect, in attracting attention to the unhappy victim to whom it was addressed. Thereupon the council separated for that day.

On the 18th, the very day after the opening, Napoleon invited some of the bishops to Saint Cloud, to one of those evening receptions called *entrées*. The Empress Marie Louise and the ladies who were in attendance upon her were present, as well as a number of other persons, and among them the Prince Eugène, Viceroy of Italy. The emperor, taking some coffee that the empress poured out for him, had Cardinal Fesch, Duvoisin, Bishop of Nantes; Mannay, Bishop of Treves ; de Barral, Archbishop of Tours ; and an Italian prelate introduced. At the moment they entered, Napoleon seized quickly and so that they could see him, the *Moniteur*, placed probably by order on a table. This paper in his hand, he went up to these gentlemen. The excited countenance he assumed, the violence and confusion of his expressions and the attitude of those whom he addressed, made of this singular conference a scene such as he delighted in playing, and in which he displayed his brutal coarseness.

The report of the first sitting of the council was reproduced in the *Moniteur* the emperor was holding ; he creased it in his hands. He first attacked Cardinal Fesch, and, what is curious, he threw himself at the first onset, with singular volubility, into a discussion of ecclesiastical principles and usages, without the slightest previous knowledge, either historical or theological.

"By what right, Monsieur," said he to the cardinal, "do you take the title of Primate of Gaul? What ridiculous pretension! And what is more, without having requested of me the authority! I see your subtlety; it is easy to unravel. Your object was to raise yourself, Monsieur, in order to call attention to 'yourself and to prepare the public for a still higher rank in the future. Profiting by your relationship with my mother, you seek to make it believed that I wish one day to make you the Head of the Church; for it would not enter into any one's mind that you would have the audacity to take, without my authorization, the title of Primate of Gaul. Europe would believe that I wish thus to prepare her to see in you the future pope. . . A fine pope, in truth! . . . With this new title you wish to frighten Pius VII. and render him more intractable still!"

The cardinal, wounded, replied with firmness, and caused one to forget, by his honourable reply, the little dignity of his figure, tone, manners, and even the recollection of his former profession,[1] of which there were habitually seen too many traces in him, for the corsair re-appeared often under the coat of the archbishop. But there, before the emperor, he had all the advantage: he explained that, from all time there had been in France, not only a Primate of Gaul, but a Primate of Aquitania, and a Primate of Neustria. Napoleon, a little astonished, turned towards the Bishop of Nantes and asked him if that was true. "The fact is incontestable," said the bishop. Then the emperor left the cardinal whom alone, until then, he had taken to task. He generalized his anger, and on the word *obédience* in the oath, which he confounded with *obéissance*,[2] he became so heated as even to call the fathers a council of traitors. "For one is a traitor," he added, "when he takes two oaths of fidelity at the same time, and to two sovereigns, enemies."

The Bishop of Nantes spoke a few words to which the emperor did not listen. He paid no attention either to the

---

[1] During the first years of the naval war, that is to say in 1793, 1794 and 1795, Cardinal Fesch commanded a privateer named *l'Aventurier*. He took several prizes that he brought to Genoa, which later were the occasion of a suit against him which he defended warmly before the tribunals of that city, and for which he had several times to my knowledge demanded the support of the government.—(*Talleyrand.*)

[2] *Obéissance* means here allegiance, whereas *obédience* means the homage paid by Roman Catholics to the pope.—(*Translator.*)

sad, discontented and reflective air of M. Duvoisin, to the dejected air of MM. de Barral and Mannay, to the submissive demeanour of the Italian, or to the angry liveliness of Cardinal Fesch, and he continued to talk for an hour with an incoherence, which would have left no recollection other than astonishment at his ignorance and his loquacity, if the phrase which follows, and which he repeated every three or four minutes, had not revealed the depth of his thought. " Messieurs," he exclaimed to them, " you wish to treat me as if I were Louis le Débonnaire. Do not confound the son with the father. You see in me Charlemagne. . . . . I am Charlemagne, I, ... yes, I am Charlemagne ! " This " I am Charlemagne," recurred at each instant. The bishops, after a few vain efforts to make him understand the difference which exists between the word *obédience*, which is only used in a spiritual sense, and that of *obéissance*, whose meaning is more extended, became tired at last of their unfruitful attempts. There was nothing for them to do but to wait, in the most profound silence, until fatigue put an end to this ill-regulated flow of words. The Bishop of Nantes, profiting then by a moment of rest, asked the emperor to speak to him in private. Napoleon went out, and he followed him into his cabinet. It was nearly midnight, and each one went his way, carrying from Saint-Cloud strange impressions.

As a result of this scene the emperor exacted that the two Ministers of Public Worship, M. Bigot de Préameneu for France and M. Bovara for Italy, should attend all the sittings of the council. This was an impropriety added to so many others, these two laymen in the midst of an assembly entirely ecclesiastic, where they had no right to take part in the deliberations, and could only occupy there a position as humiliating for the assembly as for themselves.

The two ministers went, therefore, to the second sitting of the council, which was held on June 20. They produced an imperial decree which ordered that a committee should be formed of the president, three bishops, and of the two ministers, and that this committee should direct the operations of the council. There was some debate on this subject, but they took no notice of it and the committee was composed of Cardinal Fesch, president , the Archbishop of Bordeaux (M. d'Aviau),[1] the Archbishop of Ravenna (Codronchi), the Archbishop of Nantes, and the two ministers. The latter read immediately a message from the emperor, which was nothing more than a long manifesto against Pius VII. and against all popes in general. It was the emperor who had done everything for religion ; it was the pope who did everything against it in France and in Italy ; such was, in short, the sense of this message, the drafting of which was attributed at the time to M. Daunou, a former Oratorian monk. It set forth that the pope had broken the Concordat, that, consequently, this was abolished, and the assembly was called upon to find a new mode of providing for the confirmation of the bishops. This diatribe produced just the contrary effect to that expected by the emperor ; that is to say, increased interest for the calumniated and persecuted Sovereign-pontiff. And at this same sitting, the majority decided to exclude from the deliberations the nine bishops nominated by the emperor and not confirmed by the pope, who, up to that time, had taken part in the proceedings of the council. This was already a grievous omen for the government.

On June 25, the council nominated a commission which was called upon to propose an address to the emperor, in reply to his message. This commission was composed of twelve members, including the president, Cardinal Fesch ; Cardinals Spina[2] and Caselli[3] who had concluded, in the name of Pius VII., the Concordat of 1801 ; the Archbishops of Bordeaux and of Tours ; and the Bishops of Comacchio, Ivrea,[4]

---

[1] Charles-François, Comte d'Aviau de Sanzay, born in 1736, was at first grand-vicar of the diocese of Angers. In 1789, he was nominated Archbishop of Vienna, but refused the oath to the civil constitution and emigrated. In 1802, he became Archbishop of Bordeaux, and died in 1826.

[2] Cardinal Comte Joseph Spina, one of the negotiators of the Concordat of 1801, archbishop *in partibus* of Corinth, chaplain to Princess Pauline Bonaparte, was nominated Archbishop of Genoa, July 5, 1802.

[3] Charles-François Caselli, born in 1740, entered the order of the Servites, and became its procurator-general. After the signing of the Concordat of 1801, he became bishop *in partibus* and cardinal (1802), then Bishop of Parma in 1804. This city having been annexed to the Empire, the cardinal came to Paris, where he lived until 1814. He returned to Parma in 1814, became privy councillor of the Empress Marie Louise, who had become Duchess of Parma, and died in 1828.

[4] Joseph-Marie de Grimaldi, born in 1754, Bishop of Pignerol in 1797, then of Ivrea in 1805. In 1817, he became Archbishop of Verceil. He belonged to the old and powerful family of the Grimaldi, who have long possessed the principality of Monaco.

Tournai,[1] Troyes, Ghent, Nantes and Treves. On the 26th, they discussed the project of the address ; its drafting had been entrusted to the Bishop of Nantes, and it was during this discussion that he had, as I have already said, the awkwardness to let it escape that the project had already been submitted to the emperor, which did not prevent the majority voting against the passage which found fault with the Bull of Excommunication. On the morrow, the 27th, after the adoption of the amended plan of the address, a bishop, I believe it was the one from Chambéry,[2] made the motion and in very touching terms, that the council should go to Saint-Cloud and ask the emperor for the release of the Holy Father. Cardinal Fesch hastened to close the sitting in order to cut this motion short, without which it would certainly have been carried by acclamation.

Napoleon, greatly displeased, refused to receive the address.

It was necessary, now, that, the commission of twelve should report upon the proposition presented by the government, and which consisted in finding a means of supplying the canonical confirmation of bishops refused by the pope. The Bishop of Nantes made a report on the work of the commission of 1810, on the subject of this question ; and M. de Barral, Archbishop of Tours, gave an account of the journey of the three bishops to Savona, and ended by reading the note drawn up in the presence of the Holy Father and approved but not signed by him.

This point was laid aside immediately and a member of the commission moved that, first of all, they should decide the question of the competency of the council. This proposition led to a lively discussion, in which the Bishop of Ghent (M. de Broglie) spoke with much heat against the competency of the council. The question put was : *Is the council competent to ordain another mode of confirming bishops ?* Eight votes were for the negative,[3] and the bishops who had been sent to Savona for the affirmative.[4] Cardinal Fesch did not vote.

---

[1] François-Joseph de Hirn, born at Strasbourg in 1751, Bishop of Tournai in 1802.
[2] Irenée Yves, Baron de Solles, born at Auch in 1744, Bishop of Digne, April 29, 1802 ; Bishop of Chambéry, May 30, 1805.
[3] The Cardinals Spina and Caselli, MM. de Broglie, d'Aviau, Hirn, de Boulogne, de Grimaldi, and the Bishop of Comacchio.
[4] MM. de Barral, Duvoisin and Mannay.

Napoleon became furious when he learned this result ; he exclaimed that he would dismiss the council, that he had no need of it, that he would himself make a decree which the whole world would obey, and which would contain the concessions made at Savona. The Bishop of Nantes succeeded again this time in calming him, and in bringing him to consent to a project of decree being sent to the council, containing, in effect, the Savona concessions, but to which should be added an article thanking the pope for his concessions, and that the assembly should be asked to sanction this project by its vote.

The commission of twelve welcomed the project of decree, but with one restriction, that before having the force of law, it should be submitted to the pope for approbation, which was implicitly declaring the incompetency of the council. On July 10, the plan of the amended decree was communicated, on the same evening, Napoleon sent to Vincennes three members of the commission, the Bishop of Ghent, M. de Broglie ; the Bishop of Troyes, M. de Boulogne ; and the Bishop of Tournai, a German whose name I have forgotten,[1] and an imperial decree announced that the council was dissolved.

This dissolution of the council pronounced *ab irato*, this violence exercised against three of its members, solved nothing and even created new embarrassments, for there was no longer any method of sending to the pope a projected decree in the name of a council which had been dissolved, and above all because it had been so on account of its having sustained that it was necessary that the project should be submitted to the Holy Father. That which could have been so well done before the council and consequently without it, could no longer be done now.

Perplexed by the result of his passion, Napoleon was obliged to retrace his steps ; he had to fall back upon the pitiful means of reconstituting, so to speak, the council after having dissolved it. The bishops who had not left Paris were collected again, as well as those who had been retained there by force. They were each called separately to the residence of the Minister of Public Worship, and a written approbation obtained from them of the plan of decree with a new article nevertheless, which

---

[1] M. Hirn

stated that the decree should be submitted to the pope, and that the emperor should be begged to permit a deputation of six bishops to go to His Holiness to pray him to confirm a decree which alone could put an end to the misfortunes of the Churches of France and of Italy.

This was a double inconsistency, since, on the one hand, they submitted to the pope propositions to which he had already consented, and on the other, they solicited his approbation when the council had been dissolved for having demanded this approbation.

The bishops, more despondent than irritated, signed separately what was proposed to them, and, at a general sitting, August 15, 1811, adopted by rising or remaining seated (a new mode of voting suggested by a *ruse* of Cardinal Maury) the following project :

Art. 1.—Conformably to the spirit of the canons, the archbishoprics and bishoprics could not remain vacant more than a year at the longest. In this space of time the nomination, confirmation, and consecration, must have taken place.

Art. 2.—The emperor will be begged to nominate for the vacant sees, conformably to the Concordats, and the nominees will address themselves to the Holy Father for canonical confirmation.

Art. 3.—In the six months which will follow the notification to the pope in the usual forms, of the aforesaid nomination, the pope shall give the canonical confirmation, conformably to the Concordats.

Art. 4. — The six months expiring without the pope's having accorded the confirmations, the archbishop, or, in default of him, the oldest bishop of the ecclesiastical province, shall proceed to the confirmation of the bishop nominated, and if it be to confirm an archbishop, the oldest bishop of the province shall confer the confirmation.

Art. 5.—The present decree shall be submitted to the approbation of our Holy Father, the pope, and to this effect, his Majesty will be begged to permit a deputation of six bishops to go to His Holiness to pray him to confirm this decree which alone can put an end to the misfortunes of the Churches of France and of Italy.

There was absolutely no difference in reality between what was proposed at first by the council and this which was

adopted by the new assembly.   Article 5 demanded the approbation of the Holy Father, while in the original draught it was
the approbation of the emperor which was to be solicited.   It is
true that this was useless, since the draught was only the literal
expression of the personal demand of the emperor.   Of what
use then to submit it to him?   But to substitute so literally one
expression for the other might have seemed offensive, if they
had submitted this substitution to him ; but I imagine the
assembly would not have dared to ask him, and that it must
have felt very happy when the decree arrived, invested with the
imperial approbation, for it was Napoleon, that is to say his
council, which proposed the wording.   His approbation was
included in the proposition made in his name to the council, in
his sending the deputation to the pope, and in the instructions
that he gave to this deputation.   And as to the approbation to
be conferred by the pope according to the fifth article, and upon
which the council laid such stress, the Bishop of Nantes might
easily persuade the emperor that the first draught which had
been so violently rejected by him, was in reality only a form,
by the aid of which they asked the pope if he recognized fully
his own work.   There was no harm, he added, in according this
petty satisfaction to the council, which he engaged himself to
convince that the imperial severity towards some of its members
did not proceed from their having wished to insert this article
in the decree, but rather from the hostile disposition they had
manifested towards the government.

A few days after, on August 19, eighty-five bishops, among
whom, this time, were the nine unconfirmed ones, signed in common a letter to the pope, in which they asked him to confirm the
decree.   Then they named nine deputies to carry it to him to
Savona.   These deputies were the Archbishops of Malines,[1] of
Pavia and of Tours ; the Bishops of Evreux,[2] Nantes, Trèves,
Piacenza,[3] Faenza and Feltre ; and in order that the pope could

---

[1] M. de Pradt.   [2] M. Bourlier.

[3] Etienne André Fallot de Beaumont, born in 1750, took orders and became
Bishop of Vaison (Comtat Venaissin).   He protested against the annexation of the
comtat to France, was deprived of his see at that time, and took refuge in Rome.   In
1801 he was appointed Bishop of Ghent, then Bishop of Piacenza (1807), and Archbishop of Bourges (1813).   But he did not receive a bull of confirmation for the latter
see, and had to give it up in 1814.   He lived in retirement ever after until his death.

not complain that he was deprived of his council, they sent him
also five cardinals : MM. Doria,[1] Dugnani,[2] Roverella, de Bayanne,[3] and Ruffo,[4] the concurrence of whom I have every reason
to believe was secretly assured. Finally, they sent, at the same
time, the *cameriere segreto* of the pope, Bertazzoli, and his chaplain.

They all arrived in Savona towards the end of the month of
August. The pope did not receive them till the 5th of December.
It was said that he did not welcome them as graciously as he had
the first deputation. He was ignorant of what had passed in the
council ; besides, he did not use that word, for which he continually substituted that of *assembly ;* which proves how easy it would
have been for the first deputation to have come to terms with the
pope on the essential point, viz., that relative to the confirmation
of the bishops, without having recourse to a council, for which the
Holy Father cared nothing. But it was because Napoleon did not
know what to do, and no one had the tact to persuade him. The
evil became irreparable, because the approbation of the decree
that they obtained from the pope, and which was to put an end
to this great quarrel, ended in nothing, on account of the uncon-
querable temper of Napoleon who, having almost concluded
all, sought to embroil everything, and found only too many
means of so doing.

---

[1] Giovanni Pamphili Doria, issue of an old Genoese family of that name. Born
in 1751, he was archbishop at twenty, then nuncio at Paris, cardinal and Secretary of
State (1797). He became afterward camerlingo of the pontifical court.

[2] Antoine Dugnani, born in 1748, took orders and became, in 1785, Archbishop *in
partibus* of Rhodes. He was nuncio at Paris in 1789. On his return from Rome in
1792, he was created cardinal, and in 1800, contributed powerfully to the election of
Pius VII. His attachment to this pontiff was the cause of his exile to Milan in 1808.
He was taken to France in the following year. He returned to Rome in 1814, was
appointed Bishop of Porto and of Santa Ruffina, and died in 1818.

[3] Alphonse-Hubert de Lallier, Duc de Bayanne, born at Valence in 1739, was at
first auditor at *rota* at the Holy See. He was created cardinal in 1802. He returned
to France under the Empire, played rather an active part in the negotiations between
the pope and the emperor, and was appointed senator in 1813. He became peer of
France under the Restoration, and died in 1818.

[4] Fabrice-Denis Ruffo, born in 1744 at Naples. Destined for ecclesiastical
life, he never rose to more than a deacon. Pius VI. nominated him assessor-
general and treasurer of the pontifical chamber. On his return to Naples, he was
appointed by King Ferdinand intendant of the palace, and became his most trusted
counsellor. He was created cardinal in 1794. In 1798, he accompanied the king to
Sicily, was named by him vicar-general with unlimited powers. He aroused the
Calabrians and restored everywhere the royal authority.. In 1805, Ruffo returned
to Rome, then went to France in 1809 ; he could not return to Italy until 1814. In
1821, he was appointed member of the Royal Council by the King of the Two
Sicilies, and died in 1827.

After a few very gentle explanations between the deputations sent to Savona and the pope, explanations which did not bear upon any real difficulty opposed by him, the Holy Father agreed with a good grace to the five articles of the decree. He inserted them literally in a brief, dated September 20, 1811, which he addressed to the bishops with expressions full of paternal tenderness, and without the least retractation. He recalls, in the preamble, with touching gratitude, that God has permitted that, with the consent of his very dear son Napoleon I., Emperor of the French and King of Italy (these two titles are mentioned there), four bishops should come to visit him and to pray him to provide for the Churches of France and Italy . . . . . He speaks of the affection with which he received them, and with real joy of the manner in which they had reported his views and his intentions. He announced that after a new authorization from his very dear son Napoleon I. . . . . five cardinals and the archbishop, his chaplain, had returned to him, and that eight deputies (for one died on the way [1]) while informing him that a general *assembly* of the clergy had been held at Paris, August 5, had delivered to him a letter which related what had passed in this assembly, and which was signed by a large number of cardinals, archbishops, and bishops, and that finally they begged of him, in suitable terms, to approve anew the five articles he had *previously approved.*

The pope after having heard the five cardinals and his *cameriere*, the Archbishop of Edessa, confirmed all the acts they presented to him. He added only in the brief that the archbishop or the oldest bishop, when they should have to proceed with the confirmation, should give the customary information, exact the profession of faith, confirm in the name of the Sovereign Pontiff, and that they should transmit to him the authentic papers stating that these formalities had been faithfully accomplished. This addition was a perfectly simple clause, it was even a consequence of the adoption of the articles, and it does not appear that the emperor himself was offended when he read it.

But it was no longer so, when he had knowledge of the

[1] The Bishop of Feltre.

portions which contained the congratulations and praises that the Holy Father addressed to the bishops for their conduct and sentiments. On reading a phrase which testified that the bishops had shown, as was proper, towards him and towards *the Roman Church, which is the mother and the mistress of all the other Churches, a true obedience—" aliarum omnium matri et magistri veram obedientiam,"* Napoleon could control himself no longer. The words *mistress* and *obedience* excited first his laughter, then his fury, and he resolved to send back the brief with scorn, insisting on another wording. Divers rumours circulated in Paris concerning his changing disposition, growing each day more hostile to the Holy Father. Finally, without any public act, without even anything appearing in the *Moniteur* (at least that I remember), it was spread about, after some little time, that the negotiations with the pope were broken off. The bishops were not called together to be informed of this, but the news was sent to them in their dioceses without telling them anything except that all was broken off with the pope, and by his fault.

The brief, however, was returned. Napoleon, little accustomed to the language of the court of Rome, might find fault with a few expressions and even demand their modification ; but in spite of himself, of his violence and fury, the concessions demanded from the pope and so much desired for three years, were accorded. The execution of the brief had even been commenced at Savona, for the pope had without difficulty confirmed the four bishops nominated by the emperor, and the name of the emperor was in the bulls as formerly, which was plainly a revocation of the Bull of Excommunication. Finally the pope accepted what they had been far from daring to hope, the additional clause of the Concordat ; this was his brief, and the emperor could then in future, when he wished, apply this clause, by a decree or by a *senatus-consultum*, without having need to refer to the pope. Why should he prefer to send back the brief, to reject all that was useful from his point of view, on account of a few expressions which were outside of the principal part of the brief, and against which, in accepting it, he could make all the reservations he desired ? I do not know ; he was capable of every inconsistency.

The Bishop of Nantes, if he had been at Paris, might have been able, I think, to reconcile him to the words *mother* and *mistress* of all the Churches, and to that of *obedience*, by showing them to him repeated several times in the famous discourse of Bossuet, pronounced at the opening of the assembly of the clergy in 1682 ; he might have added that these expressions are reconcilable with the liberties of the Gallican Church, since they merely signify that the pope has the right to speak, as head, to all the Catholic Churches, as is admitted by the Church of France, as well as by the others.   But the Bishop of Nantes was at Savona with the other deputies, where they were all to await new orders.

The emperor sent back the brief ; the pope received it with grief, and was obliged to look upon it as not having been sent. However, with the sweet condescension which he is known to have possessed, he was surely ready, when it was desired, to maintain it, since he had given it unconditionally, and above all since he had demanded nothing for himself.

In reading the instructions given by Napoleon to the bishop-deputies, before their departure for Savona, it is clearly seen that it is not on account of a few expressions scattered through the text of the brief, and which formed no part of its substance, that the emperor rejected the entire brief, but that it is above all because the pope spoke therein in his own name.   (As if he could do otherwise !)

These instructions, besides, were in themselves not concili-ating ; they were of a revolting offensiveness, and revealed at each word the evident desire to break off the negotiation.   Thus the bishop-deputies were ordered to say to the pope that the emperor had instructed them to declare to him that the Con-cordats had ceased to be laws of the Empire and of the kingdom of Italy, and that the pope had warranted him in taking this measure by violating himself, for several years, some portions of these treaties ; that in consequence France and Italy were henceforth to be ruled by common law.   The bishops were charged besides to demand of His Holiness his *pure and simple* approbation of the decree, and they were to exact that this should include not only France and Italy, but Holland,

Hamburg, Münster, the Grand Duchy of Berg, Illyria, in fine, all the countries now annexed, or those which would hereafter be annexed to the French Empire. They were to refuse this approbation, if the pope made it depend upon any modification, restriction or reservation whatever, except respecting the see of Rome. They were to say to him, especially, that the emperor *would accept no constitution or bull from which it should result that the pope had made over in his name what had been done by the council.* Finally they were only to speak to him in menaces. It is probable that Napoleon, not finding in the brief the literal execution of his instructions, sent it back to the deputies, that the pope might have to conform to them; that they proposed, doubtless without menaces, but with respectful and supplicating forms, while acquainting him with the manner in which the brief had been received; and that the Holy Father, seeing plainly that there was no possibility of satisfying the emperor by the only means at his disposal, refused in his turn that which was so harshly and arbitrarily exacted of him.

I forgot to say that it was observed that, in the brief, the word *council* was not employed, but only that of *assembly* of bishops. That ought to have been a matter of indifference to Napoleon: the bishops alone might have felt wounded, and they were far from complaining. The emperor, who had treated this council so lightly, who had dissolved it with so much scorn, who had repented each time it was mentioned to him, that he had convened it, should have had very little jealousy as to its title, above all, when the pope gave it one so perfectly equivalent. His quarrelsome humour however impelled him to draw from this omission of the word *council* a new subject of attack upon the Holy Father, that he repeated often in his conversation, although this was not assuredly, the principal motive of his refusal and of his anger.

The bishops who were at Savona remained there still a long time in spite of themselves. They did not return to Paris until the beginning of the spring of 1812. The emperor wished, he said, to punish them for their want of judgment. He did not even call the council together at Paris to inform them of what had taken place at Savona; he had had them told on October 2,

1811, by the *Minister of Police*, that they were to re-enter their dioceses, and they had done so. Nothing was published regarding the negotiation, the council, or the brief. Each one drew from this imbroglio his own conclusion ; and thought of other things.

The rigorous treatment to which the Holy Father was subjected at Savona was continued during the winter of 1811— 1812, and in the following spring. At this time, it seems there was some fear, on the appearance of an English squadron, that it might carry off the pope ; and the emperor gave the order to transfer him to Fontainebleau. The unhappy old man left Savona, June 10, and was forced to travel day and night. He fell quite ill at the hospital of Mont Cenis ; but they forced him none the less to continue his journey. They had compelled him to wear such clothes, so as not to betray who he was on the way they had to travel. They took great care also to conceal his journey from the public, and the secret was so profoundly kept, that on arriving at Fontainebleau, June 19, the *concierge* who had not been informed of his arrival, and who had made no preparation, was obliged to receive him in his own lodgings. The Holy Father was a long time before recovering from the fatigue of this painful journey, and from the needlessly rigorous treatment to which they had subjected him.

The cardinals who were in favour with Napoleon, and were in Paris, as well as the Archbishop of Tours, the Bishop of Nantes, the Bishop of Evreux, and the Bishop of Trèves, were ordered to go and see the pope. It was said that the latter expressed the wish that Cardinal Maury should abstain from visiting him quite so often. The report was spread that the pope would be brought to Paris, and they made great preparations to receive him at the archiepiscopal palace, to which, nevertheless he never came.

The Russian campaign, marked by so many disasters, was drawing to a close. The emperor on his return to Paris, December 18, 1812, still cherished chimerical hopes, and was meditating without doubt, more gigantic projects. Before carrying them out, he wished to take up again the affairs of the Church, either because he repented of not having finished them at Savona, or because he had the fancy to prove that he could do more in a two hours' *tête-à-tête* with the pope, than had been done by the council, its commissions, and its most able negotiators. He had beforehand, however, taken measures which were to facilitate his personal negotiation. The Holy Father had been surrounded for several months by cardinals and prelates, who, either from conviction or from submission to the emperor, depicted the Church as having arrived at a state of anarchy which put its existence in peril. They repeated incessantly to the pope, that if he did not conciliate the emperor and secure the aid of his power towards arresting the evil, schism would be inevitable. Finally, the Sovereign Pontiff overwhelmed by age, by infirmities, by the anxiety and cares with which his mind was worried, found himself well prepared for the scene Napoleon had planned to play, and which was to secure him what he believed would be a success.

On January 19, 1813, the emperor accompanied by the Empress Marie Louise, entered the apartment of the Holy Father unexpectedly, rushed to him and embraced him with effusion. Pius VII., surprised and affected, allowed himself to be induced, after a few explanations, to give his approbation to the propositions that were imposed, rather than submitted to him. They were drawn up in eleven articles, which were not yet a compact, but which were to serve as the basis of a new act. On January 24, the emperor and the pope affixed their signatures to this strange document, which was lacking in the usual diplomatic forms, since they were two sovereigns who had treated directly together.

It was said in these articles, that the pope would exercise the pontificate in France, and in Italy;—that his ambassadors and those in authority near him, should enjoy all diplomatic privileges;—that such of his domains as were not disposed of should be free from taxes, and that those which were transferred should be replaced by an income of two millions of francs;—that the pope should nominate, whether in France or in Italy, to episcopal sees, which should be subsequently fixed; that the *suburban* sees should be re-established, and depend on the nomination of the pope, and that the unsold lands of these sees should be restored: that the pope should give bishoprics *in partibus* to the Roman bishops absent from their dioceses by force of circumstances, and that he should allow them a pension equal to their former revenue, until such time as they should be appointed to vacant sees ; that the emperor and the pope should agree in due time as to the reduction to be made, if it took place, in the bishoprics of Tuscany and of the country about Geneva, as well as to the institution of bishoprics in Holland, and in the Hanseatic departments ; that the propaganda, the confessional, and the archives should be established in the place of sojourn of the Holy Father ; finally, that His Imperial Majesty should bestow his good graces upon the cardinals, bishops, priests, and laymen, who had incurred his displeasure in connection with actual events. The principal article consented to by the Holy Father at Savona, naturally figured here also, and it was drawn up anew in the following terms : *In the six months which shall follow the usual notification of the nomination by the emperor to the archbishoprics, and bishoprics of the Empire and of the kingdom of Italy, the pope shall give canonical confirmation conformably to the Concordats and in virtue of the present indult. The preliminary information shall be given by the archbishop. The six months having expired without the pope's having accorded the confirmation, the archbishop, and in default of him, or when concerning the confirmation of an archbishop, the oldest bishop of the province, shall proceed to confirm the nominated bishop, so that a see may never be vacant for more than a year.*—Such was Article IV.

In a final article, the Holy Father declared that he had been induced to make the above dispositions by consideration for the actual state of the Church, and in the confident belief with which His Majesty had inspired him, that he would accord his powerful protection for facing the numerous needs of religion at the present time.

The news of the signing of the treaty occasioned great joy among the people, but it appears that that of the pope was of short duration. The sacrifices he had been led to make were hardly consummated, when he experienced bitter grief ; this could but be increased in proportion as the exiled and imprisoned cardinals, Consalvi, Pacca, di Pietro, on obtaining their liberty, received also the authorization to repair to Fontainebleau. What passed then between the Holy Father and these cardinals I do not pretend to know ; but it must be that Napoleon had been warned by some symptoms of what was about to happen ; for, in spite of the agreement he had made with the pope to consider the eleven articles only as preliminaries which were not to be published,[1] he decided nevertheless to make them the object of a message that the arch-chancellor was charged to submit to the senate.

This premature publicity given to an act which the pope so strongly regretted having signed must have hastened his retractation which he addressed to the emperor by a brief, on March 24, 1814. I do not know upon what considerations the Holy Father founded this retractation ; but one can but deplore the weakness which directed his conduct in this circumstance, and which, after so short an interval, made him consent to retract. The best explanation that can be given of this conduct is, that by physical and moral enfeebling, his spirit bent before the exactions of Napoleon, and only regained its strength when he found himself surrounded by his faithful counsellors. One may regret, but can one believe oneself warranted in blaming ?

This time, the emperor, although greatly irritated by the retractation, believed it was to his interest not to make any noise about it, and decided to take outwardly no notice of it. He had two decrees published : one of February 13, and the other of March 25, 1813. By the first, the new Concordat of January 25 was declared state law ; by the second, he declared it obligatory upon archbishops, bishops, and chapters, and ordered, according to Article IV. of this Concordat that the archbishops should confirm the nominated bishops, and in case of refusal, ordained that they should be summoned before the tribunals.

He restricted anew the liberty that had been given momentarily to the Holy Father, and Cardinal di Pietro returned to exile. Thereupon, Napoleon started, soon after, for that campaign

---

[1] Indeed, the preamble of this compact ran as follows : "H.M. the Emperor and King and His Holiness, wishing to terminate the differences which arose between them and remedy consequent difficulties touching the affairs of the Church, agreed upon the following articles, as being likely to furnish a basis for a definite arrangement."

of 1813 in Germany, the prelude to that which was to lead to his downfall.

The decrees issued *ab irato* were not executed, and during the vicissitudes of the campaign of 1813, the imperial government several times attempted to renew with the pope negotiations which failed. Matters dragged along thus, and no one could foresee any issue when, on January 23, 1814, it was suddenly learned that the pope had left Fontainebleau that very day, and returned to Rome.

Napoleon was then hotly pressed by the allied troops who had penetrated into France; but as he counted so confidently on success, it was difficult to comprehend so unexpected and precipitate a resolution. It can be explained, however. Murat, who had abandoned the cause of the emperor, and who, as we have already said, had treated with the coalition, was then occupying the States of the Church, and it is evident that Napoleon in his indignation against Murat, preferred to allow the pope to re-enter his States, to seeing them in the hands of his brother-in-law.

While Pius VII. was *en route* and the emperor was fighting in Champagne, a decree of March 10, 1814, announced that the pope was again taking possession of that part of his States which formed the departments of Rome and Trasimene. The lion, although vanquished, would not yet let go all the prey he so confidently hoped to retake.

The journey of the Holy Father was not made without hindrances and difficulties, so much so that the provisory government, over which I had the honour to preside, was obliged to give orders, April 2, 1814, to facilitate the progress of the Sovereign Pontiff, and render to him all the honours he was entitled to.

It must be said that the viceroy of Italy, Eugène, greeted the pope with respect, and that Murat himself dared not oppose his taking possession of his States, although he was occupying them himself with his troops.

The pope arrived on April 30, at Cesena, on May 12, at Ancona, and made his solemn entry into Rome on May 24, 1814.

In dwelling as long as I have done on the negotiations

between the emperor and the pope, I had a double purpose ; I desired to show how far Napoleon could be carried by passion, even when he encountered before him resistance on the side of right, and to prove that, in the question treated here, he was equally wrong in the main and in form ; which it will be easy for me, I believe, to demonstrate. I have nothing more to add, it seems to me, to prove how odious was all his conduct towards the pope, from the year 1806 ; the facts that I have just exposed with impartiality and with as much coolness as it has been possible for me to employ in relating such unworthy persecutions, these facts speak for themselves ; I should risk enfeebling them by insisting. But I care still more, perhaps, to emphasise the enormous faults from a general political point of view, which were committed by the emperor in his relations with the court of Rome.

When in 1801, Napoleon re-established religion in France, he performed not only an act of justice, but also an act of cleverness ; for he immediately secured, by this single deed, the sympathies of the Catholics of the entire world ; and by the compact with Pius VII. he had re-established on a solid foundation Catholic power which had been shaken for a moment by the French Revolution, and in the development of which every sensible government of France ought to aid, were it only for the annihilation of Protestantism and the Greek Church. For, what are the principal forces of Catholicism, as of all power, if they are not unity and independence ? And these were precisely the two forces Napoleon wished to sap and to destroy, on the day when, urged by the most insensate ambition, he entered upon a struggle with the court of Rome. He attacked the unity of the Catholic Church in wishing to deprive the pope of the right of confirming the bishops ; its independence, in withdrawing from the Holy See its temporal power.

The confirmation of the bishops by the pope is the only real tie which unites all the Catholic Churches of the world with that of Rome. It is that which maintains the uniformity of the doctrines and rules of the Church, in not allowing any to attain the episcopate who are not recognized as capable by the

Sovereign Pontiff of sustaining and defending them. Suppose for a moment that this tie were broken, you fall into schism. Napoleon was so much the more guilty in this respect, that he had been enlightened by the errors of the constituent assembly. I do not hesitate to acknowledge here, whatever share I may have taken in this work, that the civil constitution of the clergy, decreed by the constituent assembly, was perhaps the greatest political error of that assembly, independent of the frightful crimes which were its consequences. It was inexcusable after such an example, to fall into the same error and to recommence against Pius VII., the persecutions of the Convention and of the Directory against Pius VI., which had been so severely and so justly blamed by Napoleon himself. There is no possible excuse, therefore, for his conduct in this matter. It would be vainly objected to me that there have existed turbulent popes, who abused the confirmation of the bishop and turned it into a weapon even against Catholic governments. I would reply to that, that it is exact, but that these governments extricated themselves from these difficulties, and that the same could be done if a similar case happened again, and that it is a bad policy to prevent a possible abuse by creating a real danger. Let us add that Napoleon was less justified than any other in acting as he did, after having met in Pius VII. the most unhoped-for facilities for regulating the affairs of the Church, and a gentleness and meekness which never belied themselves for an instant, in spite of the most odious proceedings ; for the Bull of Excommunication is an incident which had no bearing whatever. And how guilty must Napoleon have been on this occasion, in order that he, who so boasted of creating enemies everywhere for England, even as Mithridates formerly did for the Romans, should have come to make of the pope an ally of the English, and should have experienced some fear that they might carry off his victim from Savona ?

The destruction of the temporal power of the pope by the absorption of the Roman States into the *Grand Empire* was, politically speaking, a fault no less serious. It is obvious to all that the head of a religion so universally spread over the globe as is the Catholic religion, has need of the most perfect independence in order to exercise impartially, its power and influence. In the actual state of the world, in the midst of the territorial divisions created by time, and of political complications resulting from civilization, this independence can only exist if guaranteed by a temporal sovereignty. It would be as absurd to wish to return to the times of the primitive Church, when the pope was only the Bishop of Rome, because Christianity was included within the Roman Empire, as it was insensate in Napoleon to pretend to make a French bishop of the Holy Father. What then would have become of Catholicism in all the countries which were not a part of the French Empire? What would France think if the pope were in the hands of Austria or of any other Catholic power? Would it believe it impartial, or independent? However deluded Napoleon may have been as regards the extent and duration of his power, his person or that of his successors, he ought not to have created so dangerous a precedent, which might, some day, have been fatal to France. 1814 has proved that nothing of this kind was impossible.

I stop. I have said enough to show all the evil the insatiable ambition of the emperor prepared for France in the future. But, perhaps there will be said to me by the Revolutionists of the school of the year 1800, why, then, have re-established religion, and the papacy? It is Napoleon himself who replied to them beforehand by making the Concordat of 1801; but this is the truly great Napoleon, enlightened and guided by his splendid genius, and not ruled by the furious passions which eventually led to his ruin.

END OF THE SIXTH PART.

PART VII.

THE FALL OF THE EMPIRE—THE RESTORATION.

1813—1814.

The political faults of Napoleon—What might have been a masterpiece of policy—No chance for the House of Bourbon—Why Louis XVIII. ascended the throne—Why Napoleon is the first and only man who could have given Europe her true equilibrium—The cause of his ruin—Talleyrand's apology for having left Napoleon's service—Rejects the imputation of having conspired against the Emperor—General Savary and Talleyrand—Napoleon wants Talleyrand to resume office—"*Ah ! si Talleyrand était là !*"—La Besnardière and Napoleon—Wrath of the latter against Murat—Napoleon alone plotted against himself—His obstinacy at the Congress of Châtillon—Lord Wellington—Abbé Juda —The Colossus has feet of clay—Lord Wellington's plan—The Duc d'Angoulême and the Duke of Wellington—Sir Henry Bunbury—The Marquis de la Rochejacquelein—Wellington refuses to support a Bourbon rising—Battle of Orthez—Wellington yields—Viscount Beresford—M. Lynch and the Bourbons—Lord Bathurst's letter to the Duke of Wellington—Battle of Toulouse—Correct attitude of Wellington—Colonels Frederick Ponsonby and H. Cook—The abdication of the Emperor—Charge brought against the Provisory Government—The English Government and Napoleon—Louis XVIII. and the Prince Regent of England—Baron de Vitrolles at the headquarters of the allied sovereigns—Talleyrand and the Baron de Vitrolles—Interview between the latter and Count von Stadion—Prince Metternich and Baron de Vitrolles —Interview between the latter, the Czar Alexander, and the Emperor of Austria—Napoleon's movements—Saint-Dizier—Marshal Macdonald's error—General Wintzingerode—Napoleon's suspicions—Hastens on the rear of the allies—Troyes, Fromenteau and Fontainebleau—The allies were bent on treating with Napoleon—Why they did not—The views of the allies on France—The position of the House of Bourbon —A constitutional Monarchy—Contrast between Spain and France— The security of France under Napoleon—The great need of Europe— The legitimacy of governments—Why Talleyrand supported the claims of the Bourbons—Napoleon's opinion of the Bourbons—Capitulation of Paris—The Czar and the King of Prussia in Paris—March past of the

THE attention of my readers must now direct itself to the time of the reign of Napoleon, when I mentioned that by a clever move in Spain he would have been able to arrive at a general peace, and thus to firmly establish his own rule.

Napoleon had been raised to supreme power by the concourse of united wills against anarchy. The fame of his victories had caused him to be chosen ; it was his sole claim ; defeat revoked it as much as a glorious peace would have justified and affirmed it. But, dupe to his imagination that overruled his judgment, he said emphatically, that he must raise about France a rampart of thrones occupied by members of his family to replace that line of fortresses created previously by Louis XIV. He found among his ministers and among his courtiers, men to approve that extravagance ; and the greater portion of these men were former members of the Convention and of the Council of elders. But the good sense of the masses of France, confined itself to desiring the conservation of the real and useful results of the Revolution, that is to say, to the maintenance of those civil liberties, the forms of which the emperor had scarcely allowed to exist, by ever placing his despotic power above the law.

His success had so blinded him that he did not see that by pushing to extremes the political system he had foolishly embraced, as much at home as abroad, he would tire the French as well as other nations, and compel them to seek with them guarantees for a general peace, outside of himself, as well as for themselves, the enjoyment of their civil rights.

In his enterprise against Spain, everything was unreasonable. Why ruin a country that was attached and devoted to him, in order to seize a portion of it, while he left its rich colonies to the mercy of England whom he intended to destroy or at least to weaken everywhere ? Was it not evident that if all the provinces of the Peninsula were forced to bend under the yoke of France and to submit to the royalty of his brother, the Spanish colonies would rise in rebellion of their own accord, or at the hint of England ? A master stroke of policy at that time would have been to isolate Great Britain, so as to leave her without a link of any description with the Continent, and without fresh intercourse with the colonies. Napoleon, on the contrary, by the war in Spain, threw open to England the Continent of Europe and the American colonies.

When remembering what struck me most among my recollections of the twenty years of which I have just spoken, I often asked myself what would have happened if the emperor at such or such a time in his career had paused, had changed his system, and had only aimed at strengthening his position. Thus, for example, after the peace of Lunéville, after having signed his first treaty with Russia, concluded the peace of Amiens with England, and had all the powers of Europe recognize the position of the empire, was not everything easy for him ? France had then acquired limits to which Europe had been obliged to consent ; internal opposition had vanished, religion had resumed its proper place in the state. That situation evidently left no longer any prospect to the house of Bourbon.

If that same idea sometimes occurs to Louis XVIII. what gratitude ought he not to feel towards Providence, and what attention should he not devote to the happiness and prosperity of France. Let him think a moment of all that has been necessary since 1803, in order to prepare his return.[1]

---

[1] It may be as well to note here that this portion of Prince Talleyrand's *Memoirs* was written during the Restoration, and previous to the death of Louis XVIII.

It was necessary that all sorts of delusions should take possession of Napoleon's mind at the same time ; that he should engage recklessly in the most hazardous expeditions ; that, by caprice, he should raise thrones, and, by other caprices, deprive those thrones of all chance of stability, and make enemies even of those he had placed on them. It was necessary that, in order to destroy the confidence of France and of foreign nations, he should impose upon them institutions, at first republican, then monarchical, and, that he should end by submitting them all to his despotic sway. It was necessary, finally, that he should furnish peoples who, as a rule, very soon understand each other, the sad consolation of successively despising the different forms of government that passed under their eyes, and that he should fail to see that that contempt was to generate a general disposition for rebellion, and, soon after, for vengeance.

But if passing from the date of 1803, we direct our attention to the year 1807, when the emperor had vanquished one after the other, Austria, Prussia and Russia, and held in his hands the destiny of Europe, what a grand and noble part might he not have played?

Napoleon is the first and only man, who could have given Europe the real equilibrium for which she has been searching in vain for several centuries, and from which she is to-day farther off than ever.

It was necessary for that, 1st, to appeal to the unity of Italy in transferring to her the house of Bavaria ; 2nd, to divide Germany among the house of Austria, that would have extended to the mouth of the Danube, and the house of Brandenburg,[1] that would have been enlarged, and 3rd, to resuscitate Poland by giving her to the house of Saxony.

With a real equilibrium, Napoleon would have been able to give to the peoples of Europe an organization consonant with true moral law. A real equilibrium would have rendered war well nigh impossible. A suitable organization would have carried to every household the highest degree of civilization which could possibly be attained.

---

[1] The house of Hohenzollern-Brandenburg, which occupies the throne of Prussia.

Napoleon was able to do all this, and he did not do it. If he had done so, gratitude would have raised statues to him everywhere, and his death would have been mourned in every heart. Instead of that, he has brought about the state of things which we see, and paved the way for the dangers that threaten Europe from the East. It is on these results that he should be, and will be judged. Posterity will say of him, " That man was endowed with very great intellectual force; but he has not understood veritable glory. His moral force was very small or even null. He was not able to enjoy prosperity with moderation, nor to bear misfortune with dignity, and it is because he lacked moral force, that he caused the ruin of Europe and of himself."

Placed for so many years in the very midst of his pro-jects, and so to say in the very *crater* of his policy, a witness to all that he did or that was done against him, there was not much credit in foreseeing that all the countries recently placed under his rule, and all the kingdoms newly created for the benefit of his family, would be the first to deal a blow at his power. Not without bitter grief, I confess, did I witness such a sight. I was fond of Napoleon ; I was attached to his person, not-withstanding his faults—when he first appeared on the scene of the world, I felt attracted towards him by the irresistible spell peculiar to great genius. I was sincerely grateful to him for the favours he had bestowed on me. Besides, why should I fear to say it ? I had shared in his glory, which reflected upon all those who assisted him in his noble work. Thus I can boast of having served him with devotion and, as far as I was able, with enlightened devotion. In the days when he still listened to the truth, I loyally told it to him ; I told it to him even later, when it was necessary to be cautious in letting him know it ; and the disfavour that my candour caused me, justified me, in my conscience, in first leaving his policy, then his person, when he had reached the point of imperilling the destinies of my country.

When Napoleon, casting aside every reasonable transaction, threw himself in 1812, into the fatal Russian expedition, any well-balanced mind could almost fix the date, when, followed up by those powers he had humiliated, and forced to cross the Rhine again, he would lose the prestige with which fortune had hitherto surrounded him. Napoleon vanquished, was doomed to disappear from the world's stage ; that is the destiny of vanquished usurpers. But France once invaded, what odds there would be against her! What means could thwart the evils which threatened her ? What form of government should she adopt, if she resisted such a catastrophe ? Those were serious subjects of meditation for all good Frenchmen. To consider them was a duty for those whom circumstances, or, if one prefers, their ambition, had already called, at other times, to exercise an influence on the future of their country. It is what for several years I believed I had the right to do ; and according as I saw the dreadful issue approaching, I examined and combined with more care and attention, the resources that would remain to us. This was neither to betray nor to conspire against Napoleon, though he had more than once charged me with doing so. I have never conspired in my life, except at those times when I had the majority of France for an accomplice, and when I sought with her, the salvation of the country. Napoleon's mistrust of and insults to me cannot change the truth of the facts, and I proclaim it loudly, he never had a dangerous conspirator against him, but himself. He, nevertheless, had the most rigid watch kept over me during the last years of his reign. I could almost cite that constant watch as a witness to the inability I should have experienced to conspire, had I been so inclined.

I shall perhaps be excused for recalling an incident of that supervision, that comes to my mind, and that will show how the emperor's police construed the most insignificant events of private life. One evening in the month of February, 1814, I had some guests in my drawing-room, among whom were the Baron Louis, the Archbishop of Malines, M. de Pradt, M. de Dalberg and many others. We were speaking of every subject, but particularly of the serious events of the time, which, naturally, engrossed all minds. The door opened with a great bustle, and without giving time to the footman to announce him, General Savary, minister of the general police,

rushed into the middle of the drawing-room exclaiming :
" Ah ! I find you all in the very act of conspiring against the
government ! " Notwithstanding the serious tone of his ex-
clamation, we saw at once that his intention was to joke, though
trying at the same time to discover, if possible, indications
likely to supply him with a police-report to Napoleon. He
did not succeed, however, in disconcerting us, and the state of
things justified only too well the anxiety which each one expressed as to the perilous situation of the emperor and the
consequences that might result from it. I am rather inclined to
believe, that but for the fall of Napoleon, General Savary would
not have failed to turn to account for his own advancement
the boldness, and what he believed to be the cleverness, with
which he acted on that occasion. It is decidedly a villanous
calling, that of Minister of Police.

What was most peculiar in the conduct of Napoleon towards me, even at the time when he suspected me most, was,
that he was always seeking to reconcile me to him. Thus
in the month of December, 1813, he asked me to again accept
the portfolio of foreign affairs, which I plainly refused, understanding thoroughly that we could never agree as to the sole
manner of extricating himself from the maze into which his
folly had driven him. Some weeks later, in the month of
January, 1814, before his departure for the army, and when M.
de Caulaincourt had already gone to the Congress of Châtillon,[1]
the emperor worked nearly every evening with M. de la
Besnardière,[2] who, in the absence of M. de Caulaincourt, held
the portfolio of foreign affairs. In these conversations that were
prolonged far into the night, he grew strangely confidential.
For example, he repeated several times, after having read the

---

[1] As early as the month of November, 1813, the negotiations had begun. The
allies then offered the frontiers of the Alps and of the Rhine. Napoleon consented
to the assembling of a congress at Manheim. But events rushed on, and the congress only met on the 7th of February at Châtillon-sur-Seine. M. de Caulaincourt,
Minister of Foreign Affairs, represented the emperor. This time, the allies offered
only the limits of 1789. Congress separated March 19, without having accomplished
anything.
[2] Jean-Baptiste de Gouey, Comte de la Besnardière, born in 1765, entered in the
congregation of Oratorians under the old *régime*. In 1796, he entered the ministry of
Foreign Affairs as a simple clerk. He became in 1807, director of the first political
section, and discharged those important functions until 1814. He became councillor
of state in 1826, retired from public affairs in 1830, and died in 1843.

despatches in which the Duc de Vicence gave an account of the progress of the negotiations at Châtillon, "Ah! if Talleyrand were here, he would help me out of the difficulty." He was mistaken, for I could only have helped him out of it, by taking upon myself, which I should probably have done, to accept the conditions of the enemy; and if that day, he had had the slightest military success, he would have disowned my signature. M. de la Besnardière related to me also another scene at which he was present, and which is too characteristic to be omitted. Murat, to remain faithful to his brother-in-law's cause, demanded that Italy should be given up to him, as far as the right bank of the Po. He had written several letters to Napoleon, who did not reply, of which he bitterly complained, as being a proof of contempt. "Why," said Besnardière to the emperor, "does your Majesty leave him this pretext, and what inconvenience would you find, in according him not exactly what he wishes, but in holding out some hope to him?" Napoleon then answered, "Can I reply to an insane man? Why does he not feel that my extreme preponderance alone prevented the pope from being in Rome? It is to the interest of all the powers that he should return there, and now that interest is also mine. Murat is a man who is ruining himself; I shall be obliged to do him a charity, but I shall shut him up in a good dungeon finally, in order that so black an ingratitude may not remain unpunished." How could one so well realize the follies of others and fail to grasp one's own?

I said above, that Napoleon alone had conspired against himself, and I can support the perfect exactitude of that fact, for it is true, that until the last minute which preceded his ruin, it depended only upon him to save himself. Not only could he, in 1812, as I have already said, consolidate his power for ever by a general peace, but in 1813 at Prague,[1] he could have obtained conditions if not as brilliant as in 1812,

---

[1] After the victories of Lutzen, of Bautzen, and of Wurtschen, Napoleon victorious had consented to an armistice that was signed at Pleiswitz on the 5th of June. Austria interposed as mediator, and a congress was opened at Prague on the 12th of July. Napoleon would cede nothing. The negotiations were broken off on the 10th of August, and Austria joined in the coalition.

at least still advantageous, and finally, even at the congress
of Châtillon, in 1814, if he had ceded when necessary, he could
have arranged a peace beneficial to France thus driven to
bay, which, even in the interest of his reckless ambition,
would have offered him opportunities for recovering later
some glory; the terror he had inspired in all the cabinets
maintained them until the last moment in their resolution to
treat with him. This claims certain developments, and I will
state here some facts which are perfectly known to me, and
which will prove the exactitude of what I advance. We must
first transport ourselves to the frontier of the Pyrenees, where
the French army had sustained so bravely an unequal struggle
against the combined English, Spanish and Portuguese troops.
We shall return afterwards to the plains of Champagne.

San Sebastian had been taken at the end of August, 1813,
and Pampeluna had just surrendered towards the end of
October, when the Duke of Wellington, who saw Spain
rid of her enemies on that side, and was informed of the
battle of Leipzig and of the important results that followed it,
decided to carry the war into French territory, in order to contribute as much as possible to the success of the general cause
of Europe; that of Spain was only secondary. He crossed
the Bidassoa towards the middle of November, notwithstanding
the sharp resistance of the French army commanded by Marshal
Soult, and established his head-quarters on the first day at
Saint Pé, a little village on the frontier.

The weather was fearful; the rain fell in torrents, which forced
the Anglo-Portuguese army to halt and its head-quarters to
remain at St. Pé. It so happened that there was in the
village a *curé*, full of intelligence and activity, who was in
every way devoted to the Bourbons and to the royal cause.
He had emigrated to Spain at the beginning of the Revolution, and returned to France only after the Concordat. His
name was Abbé Juda; he was very popular among the Basques,
and much esteemed among the Spaniards, and as the bad
weather did not permit the Duke of Wellington to go out,
weariness and leisure caused him to seek the society of the
curé, at whose house he was residing.

The conversation naturally turned on the state of France and on the spirit that reigned there. The *curé* did not hesitate to affirm that they were tired of the war to which they could see no termination, that they were especially very much annoyed at the conscription, and that people complained very much of the increasing burden of the taxes ; finally, that they desired a change whatever it might be, just as an invalid desires to change his position in bed, with the hope of obtaining relief. "The colossus has feet of clay," said the Abbé Juda. "Attack it vigorously and with resolution and you will see it fall to pieces more easily than you think."

Those conversations convinced the Duke of Wellington of the necessity of attacking France simultaneously on all her frontiers, if it were wished to obtain from the head of the government a durable and honourable peace, and he suggested that plan to his own government.

There was no question of the Bourbons, for it was easily seen that they were forgotten and entirely unknown to the new generation. However, it was thought advisable to make a trial of the effect that would be produced by the sudden appearance of one of those princes on any portion whatever of French territory, and to ascertain what would be the result. That was the pretext for the arrival of the Duc d'Angoulême at the head-quarters of Saint-Jean-de-Luz, about the beginning of January, 1814.

The Duc d'Angoulême [1] was very well received by the general-in-chief, which was quite natural ; by the mayor of the village of Saint-Jean, and by the clergy ; but his presence had no other effect upon the people than to rouse their curiosity. They ran in his path when he went to church, without testifying any special sentiment, nor giving any proof of approbation or dis-approbation. If there were any offers of service, or protestations of fidelity they remained quite secret and had not the least outward effect.

Time was thus expected to bring the only solution to the situation, when towards the middle of January, Sir Henry

---

[1] Louis-Antoine de Bourbon, Duc d'Angoulême, eldest son of the Comte d'Artois (1775–1844). He had married in 1799 the Princess Marie-Thérèse, daughter of Louis XVI.

Bunbury [1] coming from London, landed at Saint-Jean-de-Luz. He was Under Secretary to the War Office and, besides other important messages, was instructed to inform the Duke of Wellington of the acceptance by England of the basis proposed at Frankfort by the allied sovereigns to settle the general peace, and of the necessity of taking every precaution to prevent that, under English protection, the people should be incited to rebellion against the government with which they were negotiating. The English government, in accordance with very honourable principles, did not wish to countenance an uprising of people, whom at the conclusion of the peace they would have been obliged to leave unprotected to the resentment of Napoleon's government, and they insisted so much on this point that the situation of the Duc d'Angoulême at head-quarters became very unpleasant for him as well as embarrassing for the general-in-chief. In consequence, he was no longer invited to take part in the operations that were about to be undertaken, as was at first intended; and when, in the beginning of February, it was contemplated to cross the Adour in order to attack the French army and lay siege to Bayonne, the Duc d'Angoulême was left at Saint-Jean-de-Luz, far from the scene of operations.

Just at the moment of crossing, different persons from Bordeaux presented themselves to the general-in-chief, among them being M. de la Rochejacquelein,[2] who greatly insisted on the necessity of making a movement in favour of the Bourbons, and laid special stress on the good disposition of the town of Bordeaux. They saw the prince at Saint-Jean-de-Luz, and the Duke of Wellington, who was then in the neighbourhood of Saint-Palais, several times. They tried to induce him to favour and foster this movement, but he was immovable in his

---

[1] Sir Henry Edward Bunbury, born in 1778, lieutenant-general in the English army. In 1809 he became Under Secretary of State in the War department. In 1815, he was charged, with Admiral Keith, to notify to the Emperor Napoleon his exile at St. Helena. He entered the House of Commons in 1830, and refused a short time after, the post of Secretary of War. He died in 1860.

[2] Louis du Vergier, Marquis de la Rochejacquelein, brother of the celebrated Vendean General, killed in 1794. He was born in 1777, followed his father in his emigration and returned to France in 1801. In 1814 he came to meet the Duc d'Angoulême at Saint-Jean-de-Luz, and was, a short time after, appointed brigadier-general by Louis XVIII. During the Hundred Days, he sought to raise Vendée, but was killed on the 4th of June in the fight of Pont-de-Mathes. He had married the widow of the Marquis de Lescure.

refusal, according to the instructions he had just received from his government.

On the 27th of February the French lost the battle of Orthez, which left open all the country of Landes as far as Bordeaux, and the Duke of Wellington, who desired to have a communication more easy, open, and direct with his country, decided to occupy that town with troops, and sent thither the 7th division of his army, under the command of Lord Dalhousie.

The entreaties and the motions in favour of a Bourbon rising became more pressing than ever, and many other people came from Bordeaux, to urge that movement on the occasion of the military occupation of the town.

The Duke of Wellington did not believe it right to oppose it ; but wishing to enlighten the people of Bordeaux and to inform them of the state of affairs between his government and those of his allies, he appointed General Beresford,[1] general marshal of the Portuguese troops, and second in command of the army, to fulfil that task. He gave him the most positive instructions to declare before entering the town, and after the occupation, " that they treated for peace with the Emperor Napoleon ; that it was now probably signed, and that as soon as it became known, the allied army would retire from the country without being able to lend assistance to any one. It was then for the inhabitants of Bordeaux to decide themselves if they wished to run the risk of their enterprise." Letters couched in similar terms were sent to both governments of the Peninsula, and the night before entering Bordeaux, Marshal Beresford declared what has just been read to the mayor, M. Lynch,[2] who, with several other people, had come to meet the Duc d'Angoulême, the latter having followed the head-quarters of Lord Beresford.

---

[1] William Carr, Viscount Beresford, descended from an Irish family, was born in 1768. He entered the army and fought in the campaigns of 1793 and 1794, against France. In 1795 he went to the West Indies, and afterwards to India (1797) ; to Egypt (1800), to the Cape (1803). In 1806 he attacked Buenos Ayres, then a Spanish colony, but was beaten and made prisoner. On his return to England he commanded an expedition against Madeira, landed in Portugal, in 1808, and was appointed Governor of Lisbon. He then became major-general and general-in-chief of the Portuguese troops. In that capacity he made the campaign of Spain until 1814. After the peace, he entered the House of Lords. He retired from public life in 1830, and died in 1854.

[2] Jean-Baptiste Comte Lynch was born at Bordeaux in 1749. His family, of Irish origin, had emigrated after the Revolution of 1688 and established itself in that town.

That declaration spread discouragement among the greater portion of those who were in the plot, and to neutralize the bad effect that it might produce on the public, M. Lynch ventured to say in a proclamation that the rising was taking place with the agreement of the English army, which gave rise to a very energetic contradiction from the Duke of Wellington, who exacted a retractation and who obtained it finally, notwithstanding the steps taken by M. Ravez,[1] sent by the Duc d'Angoulême to the duke's head-quarters to give explanations. These did not satisfy Wellington, for he insisted upon the retractation of M. Lynch's expressions, and it was made.

The rest of the month of March passed without any decisive event. The French still retreated before the English army, and, in the end, they were obliged to cross the Garonne in the beginning of April, in order to take up a stronger position before the city of Toulouse, on the Languedoc canal.

On April 6, the English head-quarters were at Grenade, on the left bank of the Garonne, and the same day, the Duke of Wellington received an official letter from Lord Bathurst, Secretary of War, which announced, that "at the reception of his letter, peace would probably be made with the Emperor Napoleon, but that he should still continue his military operations until he received the official notification of peace from the English plenipotentiaries who were at Châtillon."

Lynch was received in 1771 as counsellor at the *parlement* of Bordeaux. He was a long time imprisoned under the Reign of Terror. Under the Empire, he became General Councillor of Gironde, and Mayor of Bordeaux in 1808. In 1814, he called for English aid and proclaimed the restoration of the Bourbons, as early as the 12th of March. In 1815, he endeavoured, with the Duchesse d'Angoulême to organize the resistance, but he failed and fled to England. At the second restoration, he was created peer of France. He died in 1835.

[1] Simon Ravez, born in 1770, was in 1791 barrister at Lyons. He took an active part in the revolt of that town against the Convention, and was afterwards able to take refuge at Bordeaux, after the defeat of Lyons. He declined every public function under the Empire, and in 1814 was one of the first to proclaim the restoration of the Bourbons. In 1816, he was elected deputy of Gironde, and became in 1819, president of the House. In 1817, he was appointed Under-Secretary of State to the Minister of Justice. He retired in 1840. In 1848, he was chosen as deputy to the legislative assembly, but died in 1849.

[2] Lord Henry, third Earl Bathurst, born May 22, 1762; died July 26, 1834. Famous for his hatred towards Napoleon and France, and for his entire Liberal opinions. In 1815, he insisted in Parliament on the detention of Napoleon, and appointed Sir Hudson Lowe his *gaoler* at St. Helena. In 1812, he was appointed Colonial Secretary in Lord Liverpool's Cabinet, and resigned his post, with Lord Wellington and Peel, on the accession of Canning's Liberal Cabinet in 1827.— (*Translator.*)

In consequence, the Garonne was crossed on the 8th of April, and on the 10th was fought the battle of Toulouse, without either party knowing what was going on in Paris, beyond the entrance of the allies into the capital, the news of which the Toulouse authorities had had posted at the crossings.

After the battle, the French evacuated the town during the night from the 11th to the 12th, and so persuaded was the Duke of Wellington of the signing of the peace with Napoleon, that when about ten o'clock in the morning at the moment of mounting his horse to enter the city on the 12th, people came to communicate to him officially that there had been a proclamation in favour of the Bourbons, and that they had hoisted the white flag at the *Capitole*, after having thrown down the bust of Napoleon, he could not conceal his disapprobation, nor his desire to have been consulted by the town authorities before they had taken such a step. He then repeated what he had said to the Bordeaux people. He employed the same language before the municipality of Toulouse, when after having been received by the national guard with the Bourbon colours, he alighted from his horse at the *Capitole*. The duke's expressions were clear and precise, and admitted of no misinterpretation.

But, at about three o'clock in the afternoon, the English Colonel Frederick Ponsonby, arrived from Bordeaux, preceding M. de Saint-Simon and Colonel H. Cook, instructed by the provisory government to inform the two armies of the events of Paris : the emperor's abdication, and the restoration of the Bourbons.

The provisory government was then accused of having delayed acquainting the armies with those important events, and of having thus neglected to prevent the bloodshed resulting from the battle of Toulouse. But this accusation was groundless, for the government lost no time in despatching M. de Saint-Simon and Colonel H. Cook, with instructions to acquaint the two armies with the abdication of the Emperor and the restoration of the Bourbons, and, certainly on examining the dates of their instructions, it is obvious that they would have arrived in time to save the lives of many a poor wretch, if, after being arrested at Orleans, and taken to Blois, where was the Empress Marie Louise, they had been sent to their destination, instead of being directed to Bordeaux, where the Duc d'Angoulême was at that time.

When one examines the dates of those past events, and sees that one whole month after the declaration of the town of Bordeaux, not only did Wellington continue to treat for peace with Napoleon, but that he believed that a treaty had been made and signed with the emperor, until after the letter from Lord Bathurst was received at Grenade, one may well appreciate the importance of that declaration, and the little influence it would have had upon the overthrow of the imperial government and on the restoration of the Bourbons, had not events at Paris decided the question otherwise.

The result of all those incontestable facts is, that the English government remained convinced until the last moment that peace had been signed at Châtillon with Napoleon, which, it may be here said, diminishes somewhat the credit which, they say, Louis XVIII. ascribed to the Prince Regent of England, when he affirmed that it was to him, after God, that he was indebted for the recovery of his throne.

Let us return now to the events that were taking place at Paris and in Champagne ; and here it is as well to speak of M. de Vitrolles' mission to the head-quarters of the allied sovereigns. The results of that mission will serve to elucidate the main point of the question of which I treat, and as to the mission itself, I will say what truth there is in the part that has been ascribed to me in it.

Thus, as I have already said, no conspiracy was carried on at Paris against the emperor ; but there reigned there a general and very marked anxiety as to the consequences that his reckless conduct and his resolution not to conclude peace were likely to produce. It became of the highest importance to know the part which the united powers would take, when the day, clearly inevitable for those who watched the state of things, came, when they would overthrow the power of Napoleon. Would they continue to treat with him ? Would another government be imposed on France, or, by leaving her at liberty to choose herself, would they deliver her up to an anarchy of which it was impossible to calculate the results?

I was informed of some conversations held by the Czar Alexander with the Grand Duchess Stephanie of Baden; as also of the insinuations made by that sovereign regarding Eugène de Beauharnais, and of the pretensions of Bernadotte; M. Fouché was intriguing with Queen Caroline, Murat's wife. Finally, the English newspapers informed me that the Duc d'Angoulême was at the head-quarters of Lord Wellington, and that the Comte d'Artois had taken up a position in Switzerland near the frontier of France. There existed there so many diverging elements that it was impossible to arrive at a reasonable notion, so long as the real intentions of the allied powers should not be known, seeing that those powers, definitely speaking, would be the masters of the situation if they triumphed over Napoleon. It was then their opinion that must be known. It was necessary for that that some reliable person should be sent to their head-quarters. The Baron de Vitrolles was chosen for that delicate and difficult mission. I did not know him, but he was acquainted with M. Mollien and M. d'Hauterive.[1] He was spoken of to me as a distinguished, energetic man, a royalist at heart, but having, however, recognized the necessity of establishing in France a constitutional monarchy. I even believe I remember that he wrote a pamphlet [2] to that effect, which he published after the restoration of the Bourbons.

The instructions given to M. de Vitrolles bore only on these two points. Supposing (which is inevitable) that Napoleon succumbed in the struggle, what course would the allied cabinets take? Would they still treat with the emperor? or would they leave France free to choose another government?

M. de Vitrolles must have employed a very long and indirect

---

[1] Alexander-Maurice Blanc, Comte d'Hauterive, was born in 1754, entered the diplomatic service as secretary to M. de Choiseul-Gouffier at Constantinople. In 1792, he was chosen consul to the United States, but was dismissed in the following year. He returned to France after Fructidor 18, and was appointed *chef de division* at the ministry of Foreign Affairs. After the 18th of Brumaire he entered the council of state. On several occasions, he was *ad interim* Minister of Foreign Affairs. He remained in office under the Restoration and died in 1830.

[2] *Du Ministère dans le Gouvernement Représentatif.* (The Part of Ministries in Representative Governments.) By a Member of the Chamber of Deputies (Paris, Dentu, 1815.)—M. de Vitrolles was then deputy of the Lower Alps.

route to reach the head-quarters of the allies, where he arrived only on March 10, 1814. It was precisely the day fixed when Napoleon should have given a definite reply as to the acceptance or the non-acceptance of the *ultimatum* of the allied powers. That reply having been found dilatory and unsatisfactory, the plenipotentiaries wished to break off,[1] but M. de Caulaincourt, by his personal influence, obtained a new delay until March 15. I make this remark to show that M. de Vitrolles' mission had no influence whatever on the decision of the allied governments,[2]

---

[1] The allies offered the frontiers of 1790. Napoleon, in his counter-project, submitted March 15 by M. de Caulaincourt, insisted on the Alps and the Rhine as limits. Besides, he claimed some sovereignty in Italy for Prince Beauharnais, and one for the Princess Elisa.

[2] We have thought it advisable to add further explanations at this important point of the memoirs of M. de Talleyrand, and we have asked Count von Nesselrode, to-day chancellor of the Russian Empire, to communicate to us such information as he could possibly give us regarding it. Here are those he has been good enough to give us:—

"During the campaign of 1814, and the second entrance that the troops were about to make into the town of Troyes, the sovereigns established their head-quarters in that town. I was there, when I saw a gentleman who was completely unknown to me, and who was announced under the name of M. de St. Georges, enter my house. Then this gentleman made himself very soon known as the Baron de Vitrolles, declaring that he had been sent from Paris by several personages to deliver certain important communications to the allied sovereigns: he mentioned among those personages MM. de Talleyrand and de Dalberg. To secure my confidence, as it was to me he had been particularly sent, he drew from his pocket a sheet of white paper, and asked for a light. By the aid of the light I was able to recognize the writing of one of my friends and relatives—M. de —— who wrote as follows: 'Receive the person whom I send to you, with every confidence, listen to him and be grateful to me. It is time to be more explicit. You are walking on crutches. Make use of your legs and be willing to do what you can.' Then M. de Vitrolles entered into all the details on the situation of Napoleon, and on the lassitude the French nation felt under his yoke, and on the need that it had of guarantees against his despotism. The disposition of the allied sovereigns was not such that immediate action could be taken on these communications, and M. de Vitrolles was obliged to leave with only vague promises.

"Another incident, more serious, followed a short time after. Towards the end of March, 1814, at the time of the battle of Arcis-sur-Aube (March 21 and 22), I attended a conference that was held at Bar-sur-Aube, between the ministers of the allied sovereigns. After the conference, the chancellor Von Hardenberg wished me to stay to dinner. I excused myself, being forced to join the Czar Alexander, and to report to him the deliberations that had just been held. I thus was fortunate enough to meet the Czar at Arcis, whilst the other ministers and the Emperor of Austria were severed from the army by Napoleon's move on St. Dizier, and forced to direct themselves towards Dijon. The same evening, the Russian head-quarters were transferred to the château of Dampierre. It was reached very late. The head-quarters of the Czar Alexander were united with those of the Prince of Schwarzenberg. I lodged in an attic. I was scarcely asleep when an aide-de-camp to Prince Wolkonsky came to wake me and to invite me to go down to Prince Schwarzenberg's rooms to aid him in unravelling a large quantity of letters from the authorities in Paris to the Emperor Napoleon, intercepted from a messenger who had been sent to him.

"I began at once, and I found letters and reports written by the Empress Marie Louise, by the ministers, and among others, by the minister of police, Savary, in which they informed Napoleon that there no longer remained any means of resistance

who, until March 15, 1814, persevered in the determination to treat with the emperor, and it was the latter's wilfulness alone that prevented the negotiations from being successful. On March 15, they again offered him the limits of France in 1789, and the treaty of Chaumont[1] of March 1, 1814, establishes in a most irrefragable manner, that, at that date, the allied powers did not think of any other sovereign for France than Napoleon.

M. de Vitrolles first saw at Troyes Counts Nesselrode and Stadion.[2] He explained to them the state of mind reigning at Paris and in those parts of France not yet invaded : he declared to them that several persons whom he named desired a change and legislative guarantees against the violence and the character of the emperor, and that it had become urgent to take a decision to prevent France from falling into anarchy.

Count von Stadion introduced him to Prince Metternich, who, after listening, replied that he " would with sincerity inform him of the full mind of the powers ; that they recognized that Napoleon was a man with whom it was impossible to continue to treat ; that the day when he had reverses he appeared to yield everything ; but that as soon as he obtained a slight success, he again assumed pretensions as exaggerated as inadmissible. They were then agreed to establish in France another sovereign, and so to regulate things, that Austria, Russia and

and that public opinion was much roused against him, and that it would be very nearly impossible to defend Paris if the enemy approached. Finally, the success of the Duke of Wellington on the frontier of the Pyrenees was announced, and the arrival of the Duc d'Angoulême at Bordeaux.

"I immediately reported this important news to the Czar Alexander. It brought about the project of uniting the grand army with that of Blücher and to march to Paris ; whilst concealing this plan by a corps of six thousand horse that would follow Napoleon near St. Dizier. The Czar Alexander communicated this project to the King of Prussia, with whom he united on the heights before Vitry-le-Français, and it is there that it was decided to march straight on to Paris."—(*M. de Bacourt.*)

[1] The treaty of Chaumont, signed by all the allied powers, prolonged their alliance for a period of twenty years, and declared that peace should not be signed with Napoleon, unless he accepted the ultimatum proposed at the Congress of Châtillon.

[2] Johan-Philip-Joseph-Karl, Count von Stadion, born in 1763, was an Austrian statesman. As early as 1787, he was ambassador at Stockholm, and at London in 1790. He resigned in 1792, and resumed office only in 1804. He was then sent as ambassador to Saint-Petersburg, and greatly contributed to the third coalition. After the peace of Presburg, he was appointed Minister of Foreign Affairs, but was compelled to retire after the campaign of 1809. Since 1812, he played a leading part in the various diplomatic incidents that occurred until the downfall of Napoleon. He was present at the treaty of Töplitz, at the conferences of Frankfort, at the Congress of Châtillon, and signed the treaty of Paris in 1814. In 1815, he was appointed Minister of Finances, and died at Baden in 1824.

France should be, on the Continent, countries of equal power, and to let Prussia remain a power half as strong as any of the others. That regarding the new Sovereign to be established in France, it was not possible to think of the Bourbons, because of the personal character of the princes of that family."

Such was, according to M. de Vitrolles, the opinion expressed by Prince Metternich.

M. de Vitrolles, who was devoted to the Bourbons, and whom that reply satisfied but little, requested Count Nesselrode to manage an interview for him with the Czar Alexander, and obtained it.

The Czar Alexander repeated about the same things as the ministers, but he added, on the question of the choice of a Sovereign for France, that he had thought first to establish Bernadotte, and then Eugène Beauharnais, but that different motives were opposed to it. That, in any way, the intention was especially to consult the wishes of the French themselves, and that, if they wished to constitute a republic, they would not be opposed. The Czar dwelt still more than the ministers on the impossibility of thinking of the Bourbons.

M. de Vitrolles also saw the Emperor of Austria, who told him that he was going to Dijon, that the Czar of Russia and the King of Prussia would act as circumstances indicated at Paris, and that he would come there later.

M. de Vitrolles, instead of returning to Paris, joined the Comte d'Artois, who had come to France from Switzerland, and who was now at Nancy. He saw the prince there, March 23, and did not write to Paris, where he did not arrive till after the entrance of the allies. Later, he returned to the Comte d'Artois at Nancy, with powers from the provisory government to invite the Prince to come to Paris.[1]

What was the Emperor Napoleon doing all this time?

After having been attacked by a considerable force in front of Arcis, March 20, and having acquired the certainty that it was the grand army of the allies, that the Czar Alexander commanded in person, the Emperor Napoleon passed on the right

---

[1] See Appendix I., at the end of Part VII. It contains the account of M. de Vitrolles' mission by the Duc de Dalberg.

bank of the Aube, and set out, by way of Somme-Puis and Olconte, or St. Dizier, where he arrived March 23. From St. Dizier, he decided to march to the rear of the enemy, and went to spend the night at Doulevent. At the time of resuming this plan, he received news (I believe from Marshal Macdonald), that a numerous force, in fact, a whole army, was following his rear-guard. In consequence of that report, the emperor delayed his march, spent the 25th at Doulevent, and Marshal Macdonald, having insisted on the exactitude of the information that he had sent, and which the emperor had doubted, the latter decided to present himself with all his forces at St. Dizier, but instead of the army of which mention had been made to him, he found only a corps of cavalry commanded by General Wintzingerode,[1] who, on arriving at St. Dizier, separated, and retired in three different directions, Bar, Joinville, and Vitry. The main body took the last route.

The Emperor Napoleon held a kind of council to find out if they should follow them ; but as they feared to experience a strong resistance at Vitry, and to find perhaps the bridge on the Marne cut, it was decided that they should set off again towards Doulevent, where they arrived on the 28th, having spent a day at St. Dizier. It was at Doulevent that the Emperor Napoleon obtained the certainty of the enemy's march to Paris, and that he decided to hasten there. He arrived on the 29th at Troyes ; on the 30th at Fromenteau, and on the 31st at Fontainebleau.

The emperor had informed the Empress Marie Louise of his project of coming up on the rear of the armies of the allies, in order to force them to retreat. This letter was written at Arcis, and the pomp with which the messenger who took it proceeded to his destination, was noticed by the enemy, and roused their suspicion of the movement on foot, which determined them probably to march upon Paris.

[1] Ferdinand, Baron von Wintzingerode, born in 1770, at Bodenstein (Wurtemberg), entered at first the service of the Landgrave of Hesse, and afterwards that of the Emperor of Germany. In 1797, he went to Russia, where he obtained the grade of major, became aide-de-camp to Alexander in 1802, and ambassador at Berlin in 1805. He fought in the campaigns of 1805, 1806 and 1807. He was at Essling in 1809, where he was seriously wounded. He was then appointed field-marshal. He took an active share in the campaigns of 1812, 1813, and 1814, and distinguished himself at the head of the Russian cavalry. He died in 1818.

All the facts I have just related without heeding the order in which I stated them, establish, it seems to me, by the clearest and most complete evidence, the three following points :—

(1) That until March 15, 1814, the united powers were firmly decided to treat with Napoleon, and, consequently, to conclude with him a treaty on the basis of the maintenance of his government.

(2) That it is Napoleon alone, who, by his obstinacy, and because of the vain hopes in which he indulged, brought upon himself his own ruin, and exposed France to the misfortune of having to treat, for her existence and safety, with an enemy everywhere victorious and triumphant.

(3) Finally, that the allied sovereigns on entering Paris, had not yet taken any decision as to the choice of government that they should impose on France, or that they should allow her to adopt.

Before continuing this rapid narrative of the facts that I relate briefly and only with the object I have in view, I wish to explain the reasons that decided me to adopt at the time of the Restoration the system which I then followed ; that will be the best explanation of the influence that I was able to exercise at that time, as it is, in my eyes, its best justification.

I have already said that in these last days of the Empire, I had often asked myself the question, what form of government ought France to adopt after the catastrophe that would result from the fall of Napoleon ?

To dream of preserving the family who had pushed him into the abyss, was to increase the depths of his misfortune, by adding humiliation to it. Besides, Austria, who alone could have seen without displeasure the regency of the Empress Marie Louise, had only a feeble voice in the council of the allies. She had come the last among the great powers who had undertaken to avenge the rights of Europe, and Europe certainly had not made surprising efforts to place the throne of France at the disposition of the court of Vienna.

Russia, in her plans, could think of Bernadotte, to rid herself of a troublesome neighbour in Sweden ; but, Bernadotte was only a new phase of the revolution. Eugène de Beauharnais would perhaps have been elected by the army, but the army was beaten.

The Duc d'Orléans had only a few individuals in his favour. His father had, for some, the wrong of having tarnished the word equality; for others, the Duc d'Orléans was but an usurper, of a better family than Bonaparte.

Nevertheless, it became more pressing every hour to prepare a government that could be rapidly substituted for the one that was falling to pieces. One day's hesitation might cause the ideas of division, and of subjection, that secretly threatened our unhappy country, to break forth. No intrigue could now be carried on, all would have been insufficient. What was necessary, was to find just what France wanted, and what would be best for Europe?

France, in the midst of the horror of an invasion, wished to be free and respected. This was equivalent to wishing for the return of the House of Bourbon in the order prescribed by legitimacy. Europe, still anxious, in the midst of France, wished her to disarm, and to resume her former limits, so that peace should no longer need to be constantly guarded. She required for that guarantees : this was also to wish for the return of the House of Bourbon.

Thus the requirements of France and of Europe once recognized, everything would concur to render the restoration of the Bourbons easy, for the reconciliation could thus be sincere.

The House of Bourbon alone could veil, in the eyes of the French nation, so jealous of her military glory, the impression of the reverses which had just befallen her flag.

The House of Bourbon, alone, could in a moment, and without danger to Europe, dismiss the foreign armies that covered her soil.

The House of Bourbon alone could nobly aid France to again take possession of the secure frontiers indicated by policy and by nature. With the House of Bourbon, France would cease to be gigantic, but would become great. Relieved from the weight of her conquests, the House of Bourbon alone, could replace her in the lofty position that she should occupy in the social system. It alone could avert that vengeance that twenty years of violence had heaped up against her.

Every road was open to the Bourbons to reach a throne founded on a free constitution. After having tried all manner of organizations, and submitted to the most arbitrary of them, France could find rest only in a constitutional monarchy. The monarchy with the Bourbons, offered complete legitimacy, for even the most innovating minds; for it combined family legitimacy to that given by institutions, and it was that that France desired.

Strange to say, when the dangers of the community began to vanish, it was not against the doctrines of usurpation, but only against him who had so happily and so long made use of them, that people inveighed, as if peril had come from him alone.

Usurpation, triumphant in France, had not then made on Europe as great an impression as she should have produced. It was more the effect, than the cause, that struck people, as though the one were independent of the other; France, especially, had fallen into no less serious errors. On seeing under Napoleon the country strong and peaceful, enjoying a sort of prosperity, people thought that it little mattered to a nation on what rights the government that ruled it was based. A little more judgment would have shown that that strength was but precarious, that that tranquillity did not rest on any solid basis, and that that prosperity being, after all, the fruit of the devastation of other countries, did not present any element of duration.

What force, in fact, is that which succumbs to the first reverses! Spain, invaded by valiant and numerous armies, before even knowing that she would have a war to face; Spain, without troops, without money, languishing, weakened by the long and disastrous reign of an unworthy favourite under an incapable king; Spain, in short, deprived by treason of her government, struggled for six years, with a gigantic power, and came out victorious from the contest. France, on the contrary, having, under Napoleon, reached, in appearance, the highest degree of strength and power, broke down after three months' invasion. And if her king, an exile for twenty-five years, forgotten, almost unknown, had not come to endow her with a mysterious force and to impart cohesion to her *débris*, ready to be dispersed, perhaps to-day she would be erased from the list of independent nations.

She was peaceful, it is true, under Napoleon, but her tranquillity she owed to the firm hand which oppressed all, and threatened to crush all that would have stirred ; and that hand could not, without danger, have released its grasp even for an instant. Moreover, how is one to believe that this tranquillity could have survived him, whose energy was not too much to maintain it ? Master of France by the right of the strongest, could not his generals after him pretend to possess her by the same right ? The example given by him, taught that cleverness, or chance, were sufficient to secure power. How many would not have wished to tempt fortune, and run the chances of so brilliant a prospect ? France would have had perhaps as many emperors as armies ; and, destroyed by her own hands, she would have perished in the convulsions of civil wars.

Had even her apparent and superficial prosperity taken the deepest root, it would have been, like her strength and tranquillity, limited to the term of a man's life—a term short indeed, and one which might be reached any day.

Thus, nothing is more fatal than usurpation, for nations which rebellion, or conquest, have caused to fall under the yoke of an usurper as well as for neighbouring nations. To the first, it only offers a future with no end of troubles, revolutions, and internal calamities ; and it constantly threatens the others, to oppress and crush them in turn. It is for all an instrument of destruction and death.

The first need of Europe, her greatest interest, was then to banish the doctrines of usurpation, and to revive the principle of legitimacy, the only remedy for all the evils which had overwhelmed her, and the only one which could prevent a relapse into them.

This principle, as may be seen, is not, as thoughtless men suppose, or as the abettors of revolutions would have us believe, solely a means of preservation of the power of kings, and the safety of their persons ; it is especially a necessary element of the tranquillity and happiness of nations, the most solid, or rather, the only guarantee of their strength and duration. The legitimacy of kings, or, to say better, of governments, is the safeguard of nations. That is the reason why it is sacred.

I speak of the legitimacy of governments in general, whatsoever be their form, and not only of those of kings, because it applies to all governments. A lawful government, be it monarchical or republican, hereditary or elective, aristocratic or democratic, is always one whose existence, form, and mode of action, have been consolidated and consecrated by a long succession of years, and I should say almost, by a secular prescription. The legitimacy of the sovereign power results from the ancient status of possession, just as, for private individuals, does the right of property.

But according to the kind of government, the violation of the principle of legitimacy may, in some respects, have various effects. In an hereditary monarchy, this right is indissolubly linked to the person of the members of the reigning family in the established order of succession. It can only die out by the death of all its members, who, themselves, or their descendants, could have been called to the crown by virtue of that order of succession. That is why Machiaveli says in his book of *The Prince*, that the usurper could not firmly establish his power, if he did not take the life of all the members of the family which reigned legitimately. Therefore, this is why the Revolution would have the blood of all the Bourbons. But, in a republic, where the sovereign power exists only in a collective and moral person, as soon as usurpation, by destroying the institutions that gave it existence, destroy, it also, the political body is dissolved, the state is struck to death. There no longer exists any legitimate right ; because there no longer exists any one to whom this right belongs.

Thus, though the principle of legitimacy be not less violated by the overthrow of a republican government than by the usurpation of a crown, it does not require that the former be restored, whereas it does require that the crown be returned to him to whom it belongs. Thus is manifested the excellency of the monarchical government, which, more than any other, guarantees the preservation and the perpetuity of states.

Those were the ideas and the reflections which determined

the resolution I adopted, to insist on the restoration of the House of Bourbon, if the Emperor Napoleon made himself impossible, and if I could exercise some influence on the final decision that would be taken.

I do not pretend that I was alone in having these ideas, I can even cite an authority who shared them with me, it is Napoleon himself. In the interview held with M. de la Besnardière, and of which I speak above, he told him the day he learned of the allies having entered Champagne, " If they reach Paris, they will bring you the Bourbons, and you will not be able to help your-selves."

" But," replied Besnardière, " they are not there yet."

" Ah," replied he, " that is my business to prevent them, and I certainly hope to do so."

Another day, having talked a long time of the impossibility of making peace on the basis of the old limits of France, "a kind of peace," he said, " that the Bourbons alone could make," he said that he would sooner abdicate ; that he would readily re-enter private life, that he had very few needs, that five francs a day would be sufficient, that his only passion had been to make the French the greatest people on earth, that being obliged to re-nounce that, nothing remained for him, and he concluded with these words, " If no one will fight, I cannot carry on a war alone ; if the nation wants peace on the basis of the former limits, I shall say to it, ' Seek another ruler, I am too great for you ! ' "

Being thus obliged to recognize the necessity of the return of the Bourbons, he reconciled his vanity with the misfortunes he had brought upon his country.

But let us return to facts.

I have not the intention of relating the history of the Restoration of 1814, which will be written some day by people more clever than myself. It will be sufficient to recall here a few of the principal events of that epoch.

While Napoleon followed up the rear of the chief army of the allies, the latter had advanced near Paris, where it arrived the 30th of March. After a lively struggle which lasted all the day of the 30th, and that was bravely sustained by Marshals Marmont and Mortier, the latter were obliged to capitulate during the night of the 30th to the 31st, as they had been authorized to do by Joseph Bonaparte, who had retired to Blois with the empress and the King of Rome.[1]

The Emperor Alexander, the King of Prussia, and Prince von Schwarzenberg entered Paris on the 31st of March at the head of their troops, and after having reviewed them in the Champs-Elysées, the Czar Alexander came directly to my hôtel, in the rue St. Florentin[2] where he had been preceded in the morning by Count Nesselrode. It had been arranged that the Czar Alexander should reside at the Elysée palace, but, on some one's advice, I do not know whose, he preferred to stay at my house.[3]

The first point touched upon between the Czar Alexander and myself could naturally only concern the choice of government to be adopted by France. I laid stress on the reasons that

[1] King Joseph, in the capacity of lieutenant-general of the empire had, March 30 at noon, authorised the Duc de Trévise, and the Duc de Raguse to open negotiations with the enemy. In consequence, a convention was signed on the same evening at six o'clock, between the two marshals and Count Nesselrode, which regulated the evacuation of Paris by the French troops.

[2] M. de Talleyrand occupied in the rue St. Florentin a mansion built at the beginning of the eighteenth century by the architect Chalgrin for Louis Phelypeaux, Comte de St.-Florentin, Minister of State. That mansion belonged successively to the Duc de Fitz-James, and to the Duchess of Infantado (1787). In 1793, it was turned into a saltpetre manufactory. The Marquis d'Hervas purchased it afterwards, and sold it to Prince Talleyrand, who died there in 1838.

[3] We also thought it advisable to obtain on this point explanations from Count Nesselrode. This is what he said to us :—

" The head-quarters of the Czar Alexander were situated March 30, under the walls of Paris, which capitulated on the night of the 30th to the 31st. On the 31st, in the morning, the emperor sent me to Paris, escorted by one Cossack. I was thus the first to enter the city by the barrier St. Martin, and followed all the boulevards that were thronged with people. I reported myself at once at rue St. Florentin at M. de Talleyrand's hôtel, who received me extremely well, and who, being in the act of combing his hair, covered me with powder from head to foot in embracing me. While I was at M. de Talleyrand's, the Czar Alexander sent word that he had just been informed that the Elysée Palace, where he was about to reside was undermined, and that he must take care not to reside there. M. de Talleyrand said he did not believe that report, but that if the Czar found it more convenient to reside elsewhere, he would place his own hôtel at his disposal, which he accepted, and it is thus that the emperor came to stay in the rue St. Florentin."

We must add what Count Nesselrode does not say, though history does, that he played a leading part in the great events which took place in that hôtel. It was he, among others, who, conjointly with the Duc de Dalberg, drafted the proclamation addressed by the allied sovereigns to the French nation. However great the service rendered to Louis XVIII. by Count Nesselrode and Prince Metternich, it is absolutely false that they each received a million from that sovereign. It is a calumny invented by libellous writers, and repeated as true by one of the would-be historians of the Restoration, M. de Vaulabelle. These two statesmen received on the occasion of the treaty of Paris, the usual diplomatic present, a box of the value of 18,000 francs. —(*M. de Bacourt.*)

I mentioned above, and I no longer hesitated to declare to him that the House of Bourbon was recalled by those who dreamed of the old monarchy with the principles and virtues of Louis XII., as well as by those who desired a new monarchy with a free constitution, and the latter fully proved it, since the wish expressed by the only body that could speak in the name of the nation, was proclaimed all over France, and found an echo in every heart.

That was the peremptory reply that I made to one of the questions that the Czar of Russia addressed me : " How can I find out that France desires the House of Bourbon ? "

" By a decision, sire, that I shall take upon myself to have adopted by the senate, and of which your Majesty will immediately see the effect."

" You are sure of it ? "

" I will answer for it."

I convened the senate on April 2, and, in the evening at seven o'clock, I carried to the Czar the memorable decision that I had had signed individually by all those who composed the senate. It was that which pronounced the overthrow of Napoleon, and the restoration of the Bourbons with constitutional guarantees.[1]

The Czar Alexander was amazed, I must say, when he saw among the names of the senators who asked for the return of the house of Bourbon, the names of several of the very men who had voted for the death of Louis XVI.

The decree of the senate being rendered, the house of Bourbon could consider itself as seated almost peacefully, not on the throne of Louis XIV., but on a solid throne resting on really monarchical and constitutional foundations, which should render it not only steady but even unassailable.

I know that all I have just said may displease a great many, for I destroy, I believe, the importance of all those little efforts that a number of persons faithfully devoted to the Bourbons, boast of having made to lead to their restoration. But I speak

---

[1] See Appendix II. at the end of Part VII., containing a letter from Benjamin Constant to Prince Talleyrand, congratulating the latter on the part played by him on April 2.

my mind, and my opinion is, that no one has caused the restoration, nor I, nor others. Though I was able to say to the Czar Alexander, whose confidence I had had during many years "Neither you, sire, nor the allied powers, nor I, whom you believe to possess some influence, not one of us, could give a king to France. France is conquered—and by your arms, and yet even to-day, you have not that power. To *force* a king upon France, would require both intrigue and force ; one or the other alone would not be sufficient. In order to establish a durable state of things, and one which could be accepted without protest, one must act upon a principle. With a principle we are strong. We shall experience no resistance ; opposition will, at any rate, vanish soon ; and there is only one principle. Louis XVIII. is a principle : he is the legitimate King of France."

By the political relations I had preserved, and by those which I had newly established, I had the advantage of being able to tell the foreign sovereigns what they could do, and by my long acquaintance with politics I had been enabled to fathom, and fully grasp, the needs and the wishes of my country. The end of my political life would have been too glorious if I had had the happiness of being the principal instrument that served, by restoring the throne of the Bourbons, to ensure for ever to France that wise liberty which a great nation should always enjoy.

I omitted to say that, in its sitting of the 1st of April, the senate, had, on my motion, decreed the formation of a provisory government.[1]

The overthrow once pronounced by the senate in the sitting of the 2nd, Napoleon fully realized that there was nothing left for him to do but to treat with the allied sovereigns respecting the situation that was henceforth to be offered him. M. de Caulaincourt and two of his marshals[2] came to Paris to watch the negotiation. They nobly discharged that painful mission. A few days previously, on April 2, M. de Caulaincourt had already come from Fontainebleau to Paris, to uphold the rights of Napoleon. At the moment when I was leaving on that day

---

[1] It was composed of M. de Talleyrand, president ; of the Duc de Dalberg, the Comte de Jaucourt, Abbé de Montesquiou, and General Beurnonville.
[2] Marshal, Prince de la Moskowa, and Marshal, Duc de Tarente.

to go to the senate, to have that assembly proclaim the emperor's overthrow, M. de Caulaincourt, with whom I had just had a long discussion in the presence of the Czar Alexander, of Count Nesselrode, and of several others, and who had warmly and courageously defended the interests of Napoleon, said to me :

"Very well, if you go to the senate to have the forfeiture of the emperor's rights pronounced, I shall go there to defend them."

I replied in a jesting tone : "You do well to inform me of this ; I am going to give orders to have you detained at my hôtel until my return."

"You may well think," he said, in the same tone, "that if I had had the intention of doing so, I should have been very careful not to inform you. I see only too well that there is no means of saving him, since you are all against me."

As a sequel to the negotiations between the allied powers and the provisory government on the one hand, and the pleni-potentiaries of Napoleon on the other, an arrangement inter-vened, by which the emperor and his family were treated generously, and which even respected their dignity by the very terms employed in the wording. The declaration of the allies ran thus :—

Wishing to prove to the Emperor Napoleon that all animosity ceases on their part, from the moment when there is no longer any need to watch over the rest of Europe, and that they cannot, nor will not, forget the place which belongs to the Emperor Napoleon in the history of his time, the allied powers accord him in full ownership, for himself and family the Island of Elba ;[1] they settle on him an income of six millions a year, of which three millions shall be for himself and the Empress Marie Louise, and three millions for the rest of his family, to wit : his mother, his brothers Joseph, Louis and Jérôme, his sisters Eliza and Pauline, and the Queen Hortense, who shall be considered as a sister, while awaiting the fate of her husband.

There was, a little later, a change made in this apportioning,

---

[1] See Appendix III. at the end of Part VII., concerning Fouché's opinion on this matter (letter of the Duc d'Otrante to Napoleon).

the Empress Marie Louise not having followed the Emperor Napoleon ; it was made in the following manner :—

The emperor, two millions ; his mother, three hundred thousand francs ; Joseph and his wife, five hundred thousand francs ; Louis, two hundred thousand francs ; Hortense and her children, four hundred thousand francs ; Jérôme and his wife, five hundred thousand francs ; Eliza, three hundred thousand francs ; and Pauline, three hundred thousand francs.

The provisory government in its turn adhered to this act by the following declaration :—

The allied powers having concluded a treaty with His Majesty the Emperor Napoleon, and this treaty containing dispositions in the execution of which the French government is in a position to take a part, and mutual explanations having been held on this point, the provisory government of France, with the intention of concurring in all the measures that are adopted to give to the events which have taken place a special character of moderation, grandeur, and generosity, considers it a duty to declare that it will adhere to them as much as possible, and guarantee in everything which concerns France, the execution of the stipulations contained in this treaty which have been signed to-day between the plenipotentiaries of the high allied powers and that of His Majesty the Emperor Napoleon.

I had had the honour to be placed by the senate's decree of the 1st of April at the head of the provisory government, which for a few days conducted the affairs of France. I shall not allow myself to speak here of all the acts of the government ; they are to be seen in print everywhere. The brilliant pen of M. de Fontanes may be seen in several of them, and since I have mentioned him, I am very happy to remember the services that the Duc de Dalberg, and the Marquis de Jaucourt[1] rendered France at that epoch. I think it almost

[1] François Marquis de Jaucourt, born in 1757, was colonel of dragoons in 1789. He was in 1791 elected deputy to the legislative assembly. Having emigrated the following year, he returned to France after Brumaire 18, was named member of the tribunal in 1802, senator in 1803, intendant of the house of Prince Joseph 1804. In 1814 he took a part in the provisory government ; served as *ad interim* Minister of Foreign Affairs during the sojourn of M. de Talleyrand at Vienna, and was appointed peer of France. He became Minister of the Marine in 1815. In 1830 he re-allied himself with the monarchy of July, retained his seat in the House of Peers and died in 1852.

my duty, when I see the widespread disposition to forget those courageous men who so nobly devoted themselves to saving their country.

In one hour the empire of Napoleon was destroyed; the kingdom of France existed, and all was already easy to that weak provisory government. It encountered no obstacles anywhere; the need of police, or of money, did not make itself felt, and everything worked satisfactorily. All the expenditure of the provisory government that lasted seventeen days, and of the entrance of the king into Paris, is entered in the budget of that year as two hundred thousand francs. It is true that every one aided us, and I am persuaded that the expense of the journeys I forced upon the officers of Napoleon's army, from one end of France to the other, is still owing.

On the 12th of April, 1814, the Comte d'Artois, to whom I had sent M. de Vitrolles at Nancy, entered Paris, and took the title of lieutenant-general of the kingdom. I found in him the same kindness as on the night of the 17th of July, 1789, when we separated, he to emigrate, I to fling myself into the exciting events which had finished by conducting me to the head of the provisory government. Strange destinies!

The duties of my position kept me at Paris, and made it impossible for me to go to meet Louis XVIII. I saw him for the first time at Compiègne. He was in his study. M. de Duras[1] conducted me there. The king, on seeing me, held out his hand, and, in the kindest and most affectionate manner, said, "I am exceedingly pleased to see you. Our houses date from the same epoch. My ancestors were the cleverest; if yours had been more so than mine, you would have said to me to-day, 'Take a chair—draw near—let us speak of our affairs;' to-day it is I who say it to you. Let us sit down and talk."

I had, soon after, the pleasure of repeating those words of the king's to my uncle, the Archbishop of Reims, so complimentary to all our family. I repeated them the same evening to the Czar of Russia, who was at Compiègne, and who with

---

[1] Amédée, Duc de Durfort-Duras, was born in 1770, became brigadier-general and first gentleman of the king's chamber. He followed Louis XVIII. into exile, was made a peer of France at the Restoration, and died in 1836.

great interest asked me, " *si j'avais été content du roi.*" I employ
the terms that he used.   I have not been so weak as to speak of
the opening of this interview to other people.

I gave the king an account of the state in which he would
find things.   That first conversation was a very long one.

The king decided, before arriving at Paris, to issue a proclamation, in which his dispositions should be announced ; he
drafted it himself.   It was dated from Saint-Ouen.   During the
night which he passed at Saint-Ouen, the intriguers who
surrounded the king, caused several changes to be added to
that declaration—of which I did not approve.   The address
that I had read him in presenting the senate to him the
evening before his entrance into Paris, will show more than
all I could say, what was my opinion, and what was that which
I sought to give him.   Here is the address :—

SIRE,—

The return of your Majesty restores to France her
natural government, and all the necessary guarantees for her
repose, and for the repose of Europe.   All hearts feel that
this benefit can be due only to yourself ; and therefore rush to
greet you.   There are joys that cannot be controlled.   That
whose transports you now hear, is a joy truly national.   The
senate, profoundly touched by this affecting spectacle, happy
to mingle its sentiments with those of the people, comes, as
they, to place at the foot of the throne its testimony of respect
and love.

Sire, scourges without number have made desolate the
kingdom of your fathers.   Our glory has taken refuge in the
camp ; the armies have saved the honour of the French.   In
ascending the throne you succeed to twenty years' of ruin and
misfortunes ; such an inheritance would frighten an ordinary
mind ; the reparation of so great a disorder requires the
devotion of great courage ; prodigies are necessary to heal the
wounds of a country ; but we are your children, and the
prodigies are reserved for your paternal care.

The more difficult the situation, the more need of power,
and reverence towards the king.   In speaking to the imagination by the brilliant past it recalls, royal authority will know
how to conciliate all the desires of modern reason, by borrowing
from the wisest political theories.

A constitutional charter will link all interests to those of the crown, and strengthen the prince's will by backing it with the will of the whole nation.

You know better than we, sire, how well such institutions—as has been proved lately by a neighbouring people—give support, and not barriers, to the monarchs who are friends of the law, and fathers of their people.

Yes, sire, the nation and the senate, full of confidence in the great enlightenment, and magnanimous sentiments of Your Majesty, desire with you, that France be free and the king powerful.

I returned to Paris to occupy myself with the preparations for the brilliant entrance of Louis XVIII. He was shown on all sides, that France saw in him the guarantee of her peace, the pressrver of her glory, and the restorer of her liberty.

There was gratitude on every face. Madame, the Duchesse d'Angoulême, falling upon her knees in the church of Notre-Dame, appeared to all sublime : every eye was filled with tears.

The first two mornings, the king received nearly all the dignitaries of state ; the addresses were very good, and the king's responses suitable and affectionate. The foreign sovereigns had the delicacy to show themselves but little.

The courts of the Tuileries, the public squares, the theatres, were filled with people. There was a crowd everywhere, but an orderly crowd, for not a soldier was to be seen.

Very soon, it was necessary to set about the drafting of the charter which had been announced, and then, intriguing and incapable persons beset the king, and induced him to intrust to them the drawing up of this important document. I had no part in it ; the king did not even designate me to be one of the members of the commission to whom it had been intrusted. I am forced to leave all the honour of it to Abbé de Montesquiou,[1]

---

[1] François-Xavier-Marc-Antoine, Abbé de Montesquiou-Fezenzac, born in 1757. Having embraced the ecclesiastical profession, he was appointed in 1785, agent-general of the clergy. In 1789 the clergy of Paris sent him to the States-General and he was twice president of the assembly in 1790. He escaped arrest under the Reign of Terror ; was after the 9th Thermidor one of the agents appointed by Louis XVIII. to defend his cause in France. He was also exiled to Mentone under the Consulate. In 1814 he took a part in the provisory government, and, on the 13th of May, was appointed Minister of the Interior. Under the second Restoration he remained minister of state, and was created peer of France. He resigned in 1832 and died the same year.

and M. Dambray,[1] M. Ferrand,[2] and M. de Sémonville. I only name the principal compilers. As for myself, I knew the charter only by the chancellor, M. Dambray, reading it in a council of the ministers on the evening before the opening of the House, and I was ignorant of the names of those persons who were to compose the House of Peers, until the royal sitting, when the Chancellor proclaimed them.

The king had appointed me Minister of Foreign Affairs, and I was supposed, in that capacity, to occupy myself with the treaties of peace. Now is the time to speak of that difficult work, for which I have been so much attacked, and with regard to which it will be very pleasant to defend myself.

From April 23, and before the king's arrival, I had to negotiate, and sign a preliminary convention with the plenipotentiaries of the allied powers.

In order to judge impartially of the transactions of that epoch, it is necessary to take into consideration the state to which the faults of Napoleon had reduced France, drained as she was of men, money, and resources ; invaded on all her frontiers at the same time, on the Pyrenees, the Alps, the Rhine, and Belgium, by innumerable armies, composed, as a rule, not of mercenary soldiers, but of a people completely animated with the spirit of hate and vengeance. During twenty years these people had seen their territories occupied and ravaged by the French armies ; they had been oppressed by every means, insulted, treated with the most profound contempt ; there had been no manner of outrage that one could mention that it was not their lot to avenge ; and yet, if they resolved to wreak their vengeance, what had France to oppose to them ?

[1] Charles Henry, Vicomte Dambray, born in 1760 at Rouen, was first counsellor at law in *parlement.* In 1788 he was appointed general advocate at the Court of Aids. He was not disturbed under the Reign of Terror ; was in 1795 elected deputy to the Council of Five Hundred, but refused to sit. Under the Consulate he became counsellor general to the Lower Seine. In 1814 M. Dambray was appointed chancellor, keeper of the seals, and peer of France. Under the second Restoration he retained only his functions of president of the House of Peers. He died in 1829.

[2] Antoine-François-Claude Comte Ferrand, born in 1751 of an old family of magistrates. He was received as counsellor of *parlement* at the age of eighteen. He emigrated about the month of September, 1789 ; presented himself to the army of the princes and took part in 1793 in the regents' council. He returned to France in 1801, and lived in retreat, busying himself with historical works. In 1814, he was appointed minister of state and postmaster-general. In 1815 he again took up his functions, was elected peer of France, and member of the privy council. He died in 1825.

It was not the last scattered remnants of its armies, dispersed as they were to all the parts of the country without union, and commanded by rival chiefs that had not always submitted, even under the iron hand of Napoleon. There existed still, it is true, a fine and numerous French army ; but it was parcelled out among fifty fortresses, from the banks of the Vistula to those of the Seine ; there also existed the masses of prisoners held by our enemies. But the fortresses were closely blockaded, the days of their resistance numbered, and their garrisons, like the prisoners, could only be given up to France by a treaty.

It was under such circumstances that the French plenipotentiaries had to negotiate with those of the united powers, and that too in the very capital of France. I think I am justified in here recalling with pride the conditions I obtained, no matter how painful and humiliating they were.[1]

Here are the terms of the preliminary convention of April 23, 1814 (*Moniteur* of 1814, No. 114).

CONVENTIONS

BETWEEN H.R.H. *MONSIEUR*, SON OF FRANCE, BROTHER OF THE KING, LIEUTENANT-GENERAL OF THE KINGDOM OF FRANCE, AND EACH OF THE HIGH ALLIED POWERS, NAMELY : GREAT BRITAIN, RUSSIA, AUSTRIA, AND PRUSSIA, SIGNED AT PARIS, APRIL 23, 1814, AND RATIFIED THE SAME DAY BY *MONSIEUR*.

The allied powers are at one in their intention to put an end to the misfortunes of Europe, and to found its peace on a just division of the forces between the states that compose it, and wishing to give to France, now that she has once again a government whose principles guarantee them the maintenance of peace, the proofs of their desire to place themselves in amicable relations with her ; desiring also that France enjoy as much as possible beforehand the benefits of the peace, even before all the provisions of it have been established, have resolved to proceed conjointly with H.R.H. *Monsieur*, son of France, brother of the king, lieutenant-general of the kingdom, towards a suspension of hostilities between the respective forces,

[1] See Appendix IV. at the end of Part VII.

and to the resumption of former friendly relations between them.

H.R.H. *Monsieur*, son of France, &c. on the one hand, and H.M. &c. on the other, have appointed, in consequence, plenipotentiaries to agree upon an act, which, without prejudging the conditions of peace, shall stipulate for a suspension of hostilities, and which shall be followed, as soon as possible, by a treaty of peace, namely (designation of the high contracting parties and of their plenipotentiaries), who, after the exchange of their full powers, have agreed upon the following articles.

Art. I.—All hostilities by land and sea are and shall remain suspended between the allied powers and France, namely : for the land forces as soon as the generals commanding French armies and fortresses, shall have informed the generals commanding the allied troops that are opposed to them, that they recognize the authority of the lieutenant-general of the realm of France ; and as regards naval forces either on the high seas, or in seaports, and naval stations, as soon as the war-vessels and the ports of the kingdom of France, or of other countries occupied by French troops, shall send in similar submissions.

Art. II.—To acknowledge the resumption of friendly relations between the allied powers and France, and to cause her to enjoy beforehand, as much as possible, the advantages of peace, the allied powers agree to have their armies evacuate French territory such as it was on Jan. 1, 1792, according as the places outside of these limits, still occupied by the French troops, shall be evacuated and handed over to the allies. (It will be noticed that, at the Châtillon Congress, it was the limits of France in 1789, that the enemies imposed upon Napoleon. Thus by virtue of that article 2, we retained the Comtat of Avignon, Landau, Savoy, the county of Montbéliard, and other territories annexed to France between 1789 and 1792.[1])

Art. III.—The lieutenant-general of the realm shall, in consequence, give to the commanders of those fortresses, the order of handing them over in the following manner : those situated on the Rhine, not comprised within the limits of France, on Jan. 1, 1792, and those between the Rhine and the same limits, within a delay of ten days, dating from the signing of the present act ; the fortresses of Piedmont and of the other parts of Italy, which belong to France, within fifteen days, those situated in Spain within twenty days, and all other fortresses

---

[1] Montbéliard was formerly the chief town of an independent principality, which, after passing under many different masters, belonged to the Dukes of Wurtemberg, since 1723. France conquered it in 1792, and was allowed to keep it by the peace of Lunéville.

without exception, which are occupied by French troops, in such a manner that the final delivery shall be performed by June 1, next. The garrisons of those fortresses shall take with them, their arms and baggage, as well as the private property of the military men and civilian employés of all grades. They shall take away their field artillery, in the proportion of three pieces for every thousand men, sick and wounded included.

The endowment for fortresses, and all that which is not private property, shall remain and shall be returned in its entirety to the allies, without excepting a single article. In the endowment, are included not only the depots of artillery and of ammunition, but also all other provisions of every kind, as also the archives, inventories, plans, maps, models, &c.

First, after the signing of the present convention, commissioners for France and for the allied powers, shall be appointed and sent into the fortresses to verify the state in which they are, and to superintend together the execution of this article.

The garrisons shall follow, by daily stages, different roads, previously agreed upon, for re-entering France.

The siege and blockade of fortresses in France shall be at once raised by the allied armies. The French troops belonging to the army of Italy, or occupying the strongholds of that country, or fortresses in the Mediterranean, shall be at once recalled by H.R.H. the lieutenant-general of the kingdom. [It must not be forgotten that before the allied powers crossed the Rhine, Napoleon had offered to return to them the fortresses situated on the Vistula and on the Oder, on the conditions indicated in the first two paragraphs of this article.[1]]

Art. IV.—The stipulations of the preceding article shall be equally applied to naval stations ; the contracting powers how-

---

[1] We give the following letter for those who might feel inclined to doubt the assertion of Prince Talleyrand on this point :—

THE MAJOR-GENERAL TO MARSHAL MARMONT.

"PARIS, *November* 18, 1813.

" MONSIEUR LE MARÉCHAL DUC DE RAGUSE,

" The emperor requests me to write to you, to let you know that his intention is, that you send an intelligent officer to the Prince von Schwarzenberg to offer to negotiate for the surrender of Danzig, Moellin, Zamose, Custrin, Stettin, and Glogau. The conditions of the surrender of these places shall be that the garrisons return to France with arms and baggage, without being prisoners of war ; that all the field artillery bearing French arms, as also the storehouses of clothing that are found in those fortresses, shall be left to us ; that means of transportation shall be furnished us ; that the sick shall be nursed, and sent home, as soon as cured. You shall make it known that Danzig can still hold out a year ; that Glogau and Custrin can likewise hold out a year ; and that if the enemy would have those places by a siege, they would spoil the city ; that these conditions are therefore very advantageous to the allies ; moreover that the surrender of these places will pacify the Prussian States. If they talk of the surrender of Hamburg, Magdeburg, Erfurt, Torgau, or of Wittenberg, His Majesty desires you to reply that you will take his orders thereon, but that you have

ever reserve to themselves the right of regulating in the treaty of definite peace, the disposal of the arsenals, and war vessels, armed and not armed, that are found in the said stations.

Art. V.—The fleets and the men of war of France shall remain in their respective situations, except vessels charged with missions, which shall be allowed to pass ; but the immediate effect of the present act regarding the French ports, shall be the raising of all blockades by land or by sea, the right of fishing, of coasting, particularly of that necessary for the victualling of Paris, and the re-opening of commercial intercourse conformable to the internal rules of each country; and the immediate effect as regards the interior, will be the free supply of provisions to the towns, and the free transit of military or commercial transports.

Art. VI.—To prevent all subjects of complaint, and dispute, that might arise on the occasion of captures by sea after the signing of the present convention, it is mutually agreed that the vessels and goods that may be captured in the Channel, and in the North Sea after the space of twelve days, beginning from the date of the ratification of the present act, shall be restored by each side ; that the limit shall be a month for anywhere between the Channel and the North Sea, and the Canary Isles; two months for the Equator ; and finally of five months in all the other parts of the world, without exception or distinction of time or place.

Art. VII.—The prisoners on both sides, officers and privates, army and navy, or whatever they may be, and especially hostages, shall be immediately sent back to their respective countries without ransom or exchange. Commissioners shall be appointed on both sides to proceed with this general liberation.

Art. VIII.—Immediately after the signing of the present act, the administration of the departments or towns actually occupied by their forces, shall be handed over by the co-belligerents, to the magistrates appointed by H.R.H. the lieutenant-general of the realm of France. The royal credit will provide for the subsistence and needs of the troops until such time as they shall

---

received no instructions ; that the only question is now to treat for the fortresses on the Oder and the Vistula. These communications, Monsieur le Maréchal, will also enable you to gauge the dispositions of the allies.

"THE PRINCE VICE-CONSTABLE, MAJOR-GENERAL.*
"ALEXANDER."

Let us add that the convention of April 23, 1814, benefited France by the return of two hundred and fifty thousand men, who had been shut up in fifty-four fortresses, and of a hundred and fifty thousand prisoners of war. Maréchal Davoust alone returned from Hamburg with twenty thousand armed men, a hundred pieces of artillery, and two hundred ammunition waggons ; it was, consequently, five pieces of artillery instead of three per thousand men as stipulated by the convention.—(*M. de Bacourt.*)

* See Mémoires du Duc de Raguse, vol. 6, p. 75-76.

have evacuated French territory, the allied powers agreeing as a result of their friendship for France, to cease the military requisitions, as soon as the handing over of the administration to the legitimate powers shall have been established.

All that bears upon the execution of this article shall be regulated by special agreement. [This Article VIII. was of great importance as putting an end to the requisitions of the hostile generals, which had so exhausted France.]

Art. IX.—It shall also be determined in accordance with the terms of Art. II., as to the routes that the troops of the allied powers shall follow in their march, in order to prepare them means of subsistence, and commissioners shall be appointed to regulate all arrangements of details, and to accompany the troops till the moment of their leaving French territory.

In faith of which . . . . .
Given at Paris, the 23rd of April, 1814.

ADDITIONAL ARTICLE.—The addition of ten days granted by virtue of the stipulations of Art. III., of the convention of that day for the evacuation of the fortresses on the Rhine, and of those between this river and the ancient frontiers of France, is extended to those places, forts, and military establishments, of whatever nature they may be, in the United Provinces of the Low Countries.

By this convention, that which was thought to be most urgent, has been provided for, viz., the liberation of the territory, of prisoners, the return into France of the French garrisons on the Rhine, and the cessation of the ruinous requisitions. The definite treaty which was to regulate the new relations with France and Europe, remains to be negotiated, and it cannot be concluded and signed until the 30th of May.[1] I shall however insert this treaty here :—

TREATY OF PEACE

BETWEEN THE KING AND THE ALLIED POWERS, CONCLUDED AT PARIS, MAY 30th 1814.

In the Name of the most Holy and Indivisible Trinity His Majesty the King of France, and of Navarre, on the one

---

[1] The day after the signing of the treaty, M. de Talleyrand addressed the following letter to the Princess of Courland :

" PARIS, *May* 31, 1814.

" I have concluded peace with the four great powers.   The three accessions * are
    * The accessions of Spain, Portugal, and Sweden.

side, and His Majesty the Emperor of Austria, King of Hungary and Bohemia, and his allies on the other, being animated by an equal desire to put an end to the long agitations of Europe, and to the misfortunes of the people, by a solid peace, founded on a just assessment of the forces of the powers, and bearing in its stipulations the guarantee of its duration ; and His Majesty the Emperor of Austria, King of Hungary and Bohemia, and his allies, wishing to exact no more from France, now that she is placed under the paternal government of her kings, and thus offers to Europe a pledge of security and stability, conditions and guarantees that they regretted having missed under the last government, their said Majesties have appointed plenipotentiaries to discuss, conclude, and sign a treaty of peace and of amity—to wit :

His Majesty the King of France and Navarre, M. Charles Maurice de Talleyrand-Périgord, prince de Bénévent, Grand Eagle of the Legion of Honour. . . . his minister and State Secretary of Foreign Affairs ;

And His Majesty the Emperor of Austria, King of Hungary and Bohemia, MM. Prince Clément-Wenceslas-Lothaire von Metternich-Winneburg-Ochsenhausen, Knight of the Golden Fleece. . . . Chamberlain, Privy Counsellor, and State Minister of the Conferences and Foreign Affairs of His Imperial and Royal Apostolic Majesty, and Count Johan-Philippe von Stadion Thannhausen and Warthausen, Knight of the Golden Fleece, Chamberlain, Privy Counsellor, Minister of State, and of the Conferences of His Imperial and Royal Apostolic Majesty ;

These, after having exchanged their full powers, which were found to be in good and due form, have agreed upon the following articles :

Art I.—There shall be, from this day forth, between His Majesty the King of France and of Navarre on the one side, and His Majesty the Emperor of Austria, King of Hungary and Bohemia and his allies, on the other, between their heirs and successors, and respective states and subjects, peace and friendship for ever.

The high contracting powers shall bring every means to bear to maintain, not only among themselves, but, as much as possible, among all the states of Europe, a perfect harmony and understanding, so essential to her repose.

Art. II.—The kingdom of France preserves the integrity of its limits as they existed on January 1, 1792. It will receive in

---

only trivial. At four o'clock the peace was signed. It is very good, nay, even noble, being based on the standard of the greatest equality, although France is still covered with foreigners. My friends, and you at their head, ought to be content with me."

all an increase of territory comprised by the line of limits fixed by the following article.

Art. III.—On the side of Belgium, of Germany, and of Italy, the former frontier, just as it existed on the first of January 1792 shall be re-established, commencing from the North Sea, between Dunkirk and Newport, to the Mediterranean, between Cannes and Nice, with the following corrections :

1. In the department of Jemmapes, the cantons of Dour, Merbes-le-Château, Beaumont, and Chimay, shall continue to belong to France ; the line of demarkation shall pass there where it touches the canton of Dour, between that canton and those of Boussu and Pâturage, as further on, between that of Merbes-le-Château and those of Binch and Thuin :

2. In the department of Sambre-et-Meuse, the cantons of Valcourt, Florennes, Beauraing and Gédinne shall belong to France ; the line of demarkation, when it reaches that department, shall follow the line which separates the above-mentioned districts from the department of Jemmapes, and the remainder of that of Sambre-et-Meuse.

3. In the department of the Moselle, the new line of demarkation, where it digresses from the old one, shall be formed by a line to extend from Perle to Fremesdorf, and by that which separates the canton of Tholey from the rest of the department of the Moselle.

4. In the department of the Sarre, the cantons of Saarbruck and of Arneval shall remain to France, as well as that portion of Lebach which is situated in the middle of the line extending along the borders of the villages of Herchenbach, Ueberhofen, Hilsbach and Hall (leaving these different places outside the French frontier), to the point where, near Querselle (which belongs to France), the line which separates the districts of Arneval and of Ottweiler, touches that which separates those of Arneval and of Lebach ; the frontier, on this side, shall be formed by the line above designated, and afterwards by that which separates the canton of Arneval from that of Bliecastel.

5. The fortress of Landau having formed before the year 1792 an isolated point in Germany, France preserves on that side of her frontiers a part of the departments of Mont Tonnerre and of the lower Rhine, in order to join the fortress of Landau and its radius to the rest of the kingdom. The new line of demarkation in leaving the point where, near Obersteinbach, which remains out of the limits of France, the frontier between the department of the Moselle and that of Mont Tonnerre, reaches the department of the lower Rhine, shall follow the line which separates the cantons of Weissenbourg and of Bergzabern, on

the side of France, from the cantons of Pirmasens, Dalm, and Anweiler, on the side of Germany, to the point where these limits, near the village of Wolmersheim, touch the old radius of the fortress of Landau. From that radius, which remains as it was in 1792, the new frontier shall follow the branch of the river Queich, which, on leaving the radius near Queichheim (which remains French) passes near the villages of Merlenheim, Knittelsheim and Belheim (remaining equally French) to the Rhine, which shall continue afterwards to form the boundary between France and Germany.

As to the Rhine, the *Thalweg* shall constitute the limit, in such a manner however that the changes which this river shall undergo shall have no effect in the future on the ownership of the islands found there. The status of possession of these islands shall be re-established as it existed at the time of the signing of the treaty of Lunéville.

6. In the department of the Doubs, the frontier shall be rectified in such a manner that it begin above Rançonnière near Locle, and follow the crest of the Jura, between Cerneux-Péquignot and the village of Fontenelles, to a peak in the Jura situated about seven or eight thousand feet to the north-west of the village of Brevine, where it shall again fall into the old French limits;

7. In the department of the Léman, the frontiers between the French territory, the country of Vaud, and the different portions of the territory of the republic of Geneva (which shall form a part of Switzerland) remain the same as they were before the incorporation of Geneva into France. But the canton of Frangy, that of Saint-Julien (with the exception of the part situated to the north of a line extending from the point where the bank of the river Laire enters near Chancy, the Genevan territory, along the confines of Sesequin, Lacouex, and Seseneuve, which shall remain outside the limits of France), the canton of Régnier (with the exception of the portion which is found to the east of a line which follows the confines of Muraz, Bussy, Pers and Cornier, which shall be outside the French limits), and the canton of Roche (with the exception of the places named Roche and Armanoy with their cantons), shall remain French. The frontier shall follow the limits of these different cantons and the lines dividing those portions which remain French, from those which she is not to preserve.

In the department of Mont-Blanc, France acquires the subprefecture of Chambéry (except the cantons of l'Hôpital, of Saint-Pierre d'Albigny, of Rocette and of Montmélian), and the sub-prefecture of Annecy (except the portion of the canton of Faverge, situated to the east of a line which passes between

Ourechaise and Marlens on the French side, and Marthod and Ugine from the opposite side, and which afterwards follows the mountain crests to the frontier of the canton of Thones) : this line with the boundary of the cantons mentioned shall, on that side, form the new frontier.

On the Pyrenees side, the frontiers shall remain as they were between the two kingdoms of France and Spain on January 1, 1792, and a joint commission shall at once be appointed by the sovereigns of the two realms, in order to fix the final line of demarkation.

France renounces all rights of sovereignty, suzerainty and possession of all the countries and districts, villages and places of every description, situated outside the frontier designated above, the principality of Monaco, nevertheless, re-assuming the position it occupied on the 1st of January, 1792.[1]

The allied courts insure to France the possession of the principality of Avignon, of the Comtat Venaissin, of the county of Montbéliard, and of all the districts situated in French territory and formerly belonging to Germany, and comprised in the above-mentioned frontier, whether they were annexed to France before or after January 1, 1792.

The powers reserve to themselves reciprocally the entire right of fortifying such parts of their dominions as they shall deem fit for their security.

In order to avoid all damage to private property, and to protect, after the most liberal principles, the estates of individuals living on the frontiers, there shall be appointed by each of the states adjacent to France commissioners, to proceed conjointly with the French commissioners in the demarkations of the frontiers of the respective countries.

As soon as the commissioners' work shall be finished, maps shall be drawn and signed by the respective commissioners, and frontier posts put up to indicate the respective limits.

Art. IV.—In order to insure the communications of the city of Geneva with the other parts of Switzerland situated on the lake, France consents to the Versoy road being used by the inhabitants of both countries. The respective governments shall come to some amicable agreement as to the means of preventing smuggling, and of regulating the postal service, and the keeping of the Versoy road in repair.

Art. V.—Navigation on the Rhine from the point where it

---

[1] The principality of Monaco was, before the Revolution, under the protectorate of France (treaty of Péronne, 1641). In 1793, it had been annexed by France. The treaty of 1814 re-established her independence, whilst maintaining the French protectorate ; but in 1815, France lost that right, which was attributed to Sardinia, who kept it until 1860.

becomes navigable, to the sea, as well as from the sea to that point, shall be free, so that no one shall be forbidden to use it ; and, at the future congress, the principles by which the tolls to be raised by the bordering states may be arranged in a manner most equitable and favourable for the commerce of all nations shall be decided.

It shall likewise be examined and decided at the future congress how, in order that communications may be facilitated between neighbouring nations, and they be rendered less foreign to one another, the above provision may be equally extended to all the other rivers which in their navigable course separate, or cross, different states.

Art. VI.—Holland being placed under the sovereignty of the House of Orange, shall receive an increase of territory. The title and the exercise of sovereignty in that country can in no case belong to a prince wearing a foreign crown.

The States of Germany shall be independent and united by a federal link.

Switzerland, independent, shall continue to govern herself.

Italy, outside the limits which shall become Austrian, shall be composed of sovereign states.

Art. VII.—The island of Malta and its dependencies shall belong to His Britannic Majesty as sole sovereign and possessor.

Art. VIII.—His Britannic Majesty, stipulating for himself and his allies, agrees to restore to His Most Christian Majesty, in a term hereafter to be fixed, the colonies, fisheries, factories, and establishments of every kind that France possessed on January 1, 1792, in the seas and on the continents of America, Africa, and Asia, with the exception of the islands of Tobago and of Saint Lucia, and of the island of France and its dependencies, namely Rodriguez and the Seychelles, which His Most Christian Majesty yields to His Britannic Majesty as sole sovereign and owner, as also the portion of San-Domingo, ceded to France by the treaty of Basel, and which His Most Christian Majesty returns to His Catholic Majesty as sole sovereign and owner.

Art. IX.—His Majesty the King of Sweden and Norway, in consequence of arrangements made with his allies, and to further the execution of the preceding article, agrees that the island of Guadaloupe be restored to His Most Christian Majesty, and foregoes all the rights he possesses to that island.[1]

Art. X.—His Most Faithful Majesty, in consequence of arrangements made with his allies, and in view of facilitating

---

[1] The English had taken Guadaloupe and ceded it to Sweden (Art. IV. of the treaty of March 3, 1813).

the execution of Art. VIII., binds himself to restore to His Most Christian Majesty, in the terms hereafter fixed, French Guiana, as it existed on Jan. 1, 1792.[1]

The effect of the above stipulation being to revive the contest, existing at that time, as to the limits of the adjacent territories, it is agreed that this contest shall be settled by amicable arrangement between the two courts, under the mediation of His Britannic Majesty.[2]

Art. XI.—The strongholds and forts existing in the colonies, and the establishments which are to be returned to His Most Christian Majesty by virtue of the Articles VIII., IX., and X., shall be handed over in the state in which they shall be at the time of the signing of the present treaty.

Art. XII.—His Britannic Majesty binds himself to take all necessary measures that the subjects of His Most Christian Majesty may enjoy, as regards their commercial pursuits, and the safety of their persons and property within the limits of British sovereignty on the continent of India, the same facilities, privileges, and protection which exist at present, or which shall hereafter be accorded to the most favoured nations. On his part, His Most Christian Majesty, having nothing more at heart than to insure lasting peace between the two crowns of France and England, and wishing to contribute, as much as possible, henceforward, towards the removal from the intercourse of the inhabitants of the two kingdoms, of all that might some day alter the mutual good understanding now happily existing between them, binds himself to raise no fortifications in the settlements which shall be restored to him, and which are situated in the limits of British Sovereignty on the continent of India, and to place in those settlements only such troops as shall be necessary as police forces.

Art. XIII.—As to the fishing rights of France on the great bank of Newfoundland, on the coasts of the island of that name, and of the adjacent islands, and in the Gulf of St. Lawrence, all shall be put again on the same footing as in 1792.

Art. XIV.—The colonies, factories, and settlements which are to be restored to His Most Christian Majesty, by His Britannic Majesty, or his allies, shall be returned, viz.: those which are situated in the North Sea, or on the oceans, or on the continent of America and of Africa, within three months, and those that are beyond the Cape of Good Hope, within six months, from the ratification of the present treaty.

[1] The Portuguese had taken French Guiana at the beginning of hostilities, in 1809.

[2] It is well known that this question of boundaries has never been definitely settled ; to this day it is in suspense between France and Brazil.

Art. XV.—The high contracting powers having reserved to themselves, by Art. IV. of the convention of last April 23rd, to settle, in the present definite treaty of peace, the ownership of the arsenals and vessels of war, armed or unarmed, which may be found in the seaports returned by France in execution of Art. II. of the said convention, it is agreed that the said men of war and ships, armed or unarmed, as also the naval artillery and naval ammunition, and all the shipbuilding materials and arms, shall be divided between France and the countries in which the above-mentioned seaports are situated, in the proportion of two-thirds for France, and of one-third for the powers to which the said seaports are to be ceded.

Shall be considered, six weeks after the signing of the present treaty, as naval materials and divided as such, in the above-mentioned proportion, after having been previously demolished, all unfinished war-vessels and ships in dock, which shall not be in a sufficiently forward state to be sent to sea.

Commissioners shall be appointed on either side to proceed with the division, and to draw up a statement thereof; passports, or safe conducts, shall also be given by the allied powers to enable to return to France all French workmen, sailors, and others employed in her service.

Shall not be comprised in the above stipulations, the vessels and arsenals existing in the seaports which shall have been captured by the allies prior to the 23rd of April, nor the vessels and arsenals which belong to Holland, not excepting the fleet of the Texel.

The government of France binds itself to remove, or to have sold, within the delay of three months after the division shall have taken place, everything which may be awarded to it, by reason of the aforesaid stipulations.

Henceforth the port of Antwerp shall be solely a commercial port.

Art. XVI.—The high contracting powers wishing to consign to oblivion and to destroy all records of the quarrels which have disturbed Europe, hereby declare and promise, that in the countries restored and ceded by the present treaty, no individual of any class or condition shall be prosecuted, disturbed, or interfered with, in his person or his property, under any pretext, nor on account of any conduct or political opinion, nor of any attachment, either to any of the contracting powers, or to governments that have ceased to exist, nor for any other reason, except for debts to private individuals, or for deeds committed subsequently to the present treaty.

Art. XVII.—In all countries which will now, or in the

future, change masters, either in accordance with the present treaty, or by reason of the arrangements which are to be made in consequence of it, all foreign and native residents of whatever condition or nation, shall be allowed a delay of six years, to be reckoned from the exchange of ratifications, wherein to dispose, if they deem fit, of whatever property they may have acquired either before, or since, the breaking out of the present war, and wherein to go to whatever country they please.

Art. XVIII.—The allied powers being anxious to give to His Most Christian Majesty a new testimony of their desire to obliterate as far as lies in their power, the consequences of the period of calamity so happily ended by the present peace, forego all claims to whatever sums their various governments may be entitled to by reason of contracts, supplies, or advances of any description, made to the French government in the course of the various wars which have taken place since 1792.

In his turn, His Most Christian Majesty foregoes all claims France might bring forward for similar reasons against the allied powers. In execution of this article the high contracting powers promise to mutually return to each other all bonds, deeds, and documents relative to the debts and claims which they have each and all foregone.

Art. XIX.—The French government undertakes to discharge, and pay, the sums which it may owe in addition in countries situated beyond French territory by reason of contracts or other agreements, passed expressly between individuals, or private establishments, and the French authorities, representing the price of supplies or any other legal claims.

Art. XX.—The high contracting powers shall, immediately after the exchange of the ratifications of the present treaty, appoint commissioners to regulate and assist in the execution of the whole of the provisions contained in Articles XVIII. and XIX. These commissioners shall examine the claims which have been mentioned in the preceding article, draw up the statements of the amounts claimed, and indicate the means by which the French government shall propose to settle its debts. They shall also be empowered to hand over all bonds, deeds, and documents relative to the claims mutually foregone by the high contracting powers, in such a way that the ratification of the results of their work shall complete the mutual renunciation.

Art. XXI.—The debts originally mortgaged on countries which now cease to belong to France, or which were contracted by her for their internal administration, shall be chargeable to those countries. The French government therefore shall be indemnified from Dec. 22, 1813, for all such debts, if they have been registered in the grand ledger of the public debt of France. The deeds of all those which have been prepared for registration, and have not yet been registered, shall be handed over to the governments of the respective countries to which they belong. The statements of all these debts shall be drawn up by a commission composed of plenipotentiaries appointed by all the states concerned.

Art. XXII.—The French government shall, on the other hand, be called upon to refund all sums deposited by the subjects of the above-mentioned countries in the French treasury, whether as security, deposit, or guarantee. French subjects in the service of the said countries, who have deposited sums as security, deposits, or consignments in the respective treasuries of those countries, shall likewise be faithfully repaid.

Art. XXIII.—Holders of official appointments subject to security, but who do not have the management of public moneys, shall be reimbursed with interest, until repaid in full at Paris, a fifth of the whole sum due to them being paid to them every year, the first of such payments to begin from the date of the present treaty. As regards officials entrusted with the management of public moneys, reimbursement shall begin at the latest, six months after the presentation of their accounts, the case of embezzlement being excepted. A copy of the last account shall be laid before the government of their country, to serve as information and as a point of departure.

Art. XXIV.—The judiciary deposits and consignments, placed in the sinking funds, in execution of the law of the 28th of Nivôse xiii. (18th of January, 1805), and which belong to the inhabitants of the countries which France has ceased to possess, shall be replaced, within the term of one year, counting from the exchange of the ratifications of the present treaty, in the hands of the authorities of the said countries, with the exception of those deposits and consignments that may interest French subjects ; in which case, they shall remain in the sinking fund, to be replaced only on authorizations, resulting from the decisions of competent authorities.

Art. XXV.—The funds deposited by parishes and public establishments with the government cashiers, and in the sinking fund, or in any other bank of the government, shall be reimbursed to them by a fifth, year by year, from the time of the present treaty, with the deduction of the advances that may have been made them, and with the exception of the legal attachments made on the funds by the said creditors, that is to say the parishes and the public establishments.

Art. XXVI.—Dating from January 1, 1814, the French

government ceases to be responsible for the payment of all civil pensions, whether military or ecclesiastical, for the balance of pensions, and for the half-pay of officers, to all individuals who are no longer French subjects.

Art. XXVII.—National estates acquired by purchase by French subjects in the departments formerly belonging to Belgium, on the left bank of the Rhine, and in the Alps, outside the old French limits, are, and shall, remain the property of the purchasers.

Art. XXVIII.—The abolition of the rights of escheatage, of detraction, and others of the same nature, in the countries which have mutually stipulated for it with France, or which have been previously united to her, is expressly maintained.[1]

Art. XXIX.—The French government promises to restore the bonds and other deeds that may have been seized in provinces occupied by French armies or French administrations, and, in the case in which this restitution cannot be effected, these bonds and deeds are, and shall remain null and void.

Art. XXX.—The sums which may be due for all public works, not yet terminated, or that were terminated since December 31, 1812, on the Rhine, and in the departments detached from France by the present treaty, shall pass to the charge of the future possessors of the territory, and shall be liquidated by the commission charged with the liquidation of the countries' debts.

Art. XXXI.—The archives, maps, and documents of every description appertaining to the ceded countries, or referring to their administration, shall be faithfully restored at the same time as the countries, or, if this be impossible, within a delay that shall not exceed six months after the restitution of the countries themselves.

This stipulation is applicable to the archives, maps, and plans, that may have been taken into countries temporarily occupied by the different armies.

Art. XXXII.—Within the delay of two months, all the powers that have been engaged, on either side, in the present war, shall send plenipotentiaries to Vienna, to regulate, in

---

[1] The right of escheatage, as it existed under old French law constituted the sovereign the heir of all foreigners who died in France. But numerous treaties concluded with almost all the powers of Europe had, more especially during the eighteenth century, simply and solely abolished this right in all cases of reciprocity; or replaced it by one of simple detraction, which only left the king a part of the inheritance (from a quarter to a twentieth.) The National Assembly entirely abolished both rights (by the decree of August 6, 1790, and April 15, and 28, 1791). A law of July 14, 1819, confirmed and completed this reform, which certain provisions of the *Code Civil* (Art. 726 and 912) seemed to modify.

a general congress the arrangements that are necessary to complete the dispositions of the present treaty.

Art. XXXIII.—The present treaty shall be ratified, and the ratifications shall be exchanged, within the delay of fifteen days, or sooner if possible.

In witness whereof . . . .

THE PRINCE DE BÉNEVENT.
THE PRINCE VON METTERNICH.
THE COUNT VON STADION.

PARIS, *May* 30, 1814.

ADDITIONAL ARTICLE.—The high contracting parties, wishing to eradicate all traces of the unhappy events which have weighed upon their peoples, have agreed to annul all effects of the treaties of 1805 and 1809, in so far as they are not already annulled by the present treaty; in consequence of this determination, His Most Christian Majesty, promises that the decrees existing against French subjects, or those reported to be so, who either are, or have been, in the service of His Imperial and Royal Apostolic Majesty, shall remain without effect, as well as the decisions that may have been put into execution in consequence of these decrees.

The present additional article shall have the same force and value as though it were inserted word for word in the open treaty of this day. . . .

The same day, in the same place, and at the same time, the same treaty of definite peace, was concluded

Between France and Russia,

Between France and Great Britain,

Between France and Prussia,

with the following additional articles :—

ADDITIONAL ARTICLE TO THE TREATY WITH RUSSIA.

The Duchy of Warsaw, being under the administration of a provisory council, established by Russia, since that country has been occupied by her armies, the two high contracting parties have agreed to name a special commission immediately, composed on both sides of an equal number of commissioners, who shall be employed with the examination, liquidation, and all other arrangements relative to the reciprocal claims.

ADDITIONAL ARTICLES TO THE TREATY WITH GREAT BRITAIN.

Art. I.—His Most Christian Majesty, sharing without reserve all the sentiments of His Britannic Majesty, relative to a class of commerce which is repugnant, both to the principles of justice, and the enlightenment of the times in which we live, promises to unite in a future congress all his efforts with those of His Britannic Majesty, to induce all the Christian powers to pronounce the abolition of the slave-trade, in such a manner that the said trade shall universally cease, as it shall cease, in any case, on the part of France, within five years; and that, moreover, during this interval, no trader shall import or sell slaves anywhere, except in the colonies of the state of which he is a subject.

Art. II.—The French and British governments shall immediately appoint commissioners to ascertain their respective expenses for the maintenance of their prisoners, in order to agree as to the best means of settling the balance which may occur in favour of the one or other of the two powers.

Art. III.—The respective prisoners of war shall be bound down to pay, before their departure from the place of their detention, any private debts they may have contracted there, or to give at least satisfactory security.

Art. IV.—Both sides shall, immediately after the ratification of the present treaty of peace, agree to the replevin of the escheatment which may have been applied since the year 1792, to the funds, revenues, credits, and other effects whatsoever, of the high contracting parties, or their subjects. The same commissioners, of whom mention is made in Article II., shall occupy themselves with the examination, and settlement of the claims of the subjects of His Britannic Majesty on the French government, for the value of goods, movable or not, that may have been unduly confiscated by the French authorities, as well as for the total or partial loss of their credits or other property unduly retained by the escheatment since the year 1792.

France engages to treat, in this respect, all English subjects with the same justice that French subjects have experienced in England, and the English government, desirous to concur for its part in the fresh token that the allied powers have determined to give His Most Christian Majesty of their desire to blot out the consequences of that troubled epoch, so happily terminated by the present peace, promises on its side to renounce, from the time complete justice shall have been rendered to its subjects, any excess which shall be found in its favour, relative to the maintenance of the war prisoners, in such a manner that the ratification of the result of the work of the commissioners herein mentioned, and the acquittal of the sums, as well as the restitution of the effects which shall be pronounced belong to subjects of His Britannic Majesty, shall complete its renunciation.

Art. V.—The two high contracting parties, desiring to establish the most amicable relations between their respective subjects, promise to agree as soon as possible upon an arrangement for their commercial interests, with the intention of encouraging and increasing the prosperity of their respective states.

The present additional articles shall have the same force and value. . . . .

Additional Article to the Treaty with Prussia.

Though the treaty of peace concluded at Basel, April 5, 1795, that of Tilsit, July 9, 1807, the Paris Convention, September 20, 1808, as well as all conventions and acts whatsoever concluded since the peace of Basel between Prussia and France, be already annulled according to the present treaty, the high contracting powers have nevertheless thought fit to expressly declare that the said treaties cease to be obligatory in all their articles, open as well as secret, and that they mutually renounce all rights, and hold themselves free from any obligation that can result from them.

His Most Christian Majesty promises that the decrees aimed at French subjects, or those reported as such, who either are, or have been, in the service of His Prussian Majesty, shall remain without effect, as well as any decisions which may have been given in the execution of these decrees.

The present additional article shall have the same force and value. . . . .

The enumeration of all that relates to the open treaty of May 30, 1814, would not be complete, if I did not also insert here the separate and secret articles of that treaty, to which I was obliged to consent, and which formed perhaps the most unfortunate part of the negotiations that the French plenipotentiaries would have to follow at the future congress. Those articles were only communicated to me, and I did not put my signature to them.

SEPARATE AND SECRET ARTICLES OF THE TREATY OF PARIS
OF MAY 30, 1814.

The disposition of the territories which His Most Christian Majesty foregoes, by Art. III. of the open treaty of this day, and the future relations of the various states from which there is to result a system of real and durable equilibrium in Europe, shall be regulated at the congress on a basis agreed upon between the allied powers, and in compliance with the general provisions contained in the following article :—

Art. I.—The establishment of a just equilibrium in Europe, demanding that Holland be strong enough to be able to maintain her independence by her own means, therefore the countries included between the sea, the frontiers of France, such as they are determined by the present treaty, and the Meuse, shall be united to Holland for ever.

Art. II.—The frontiers of the right bank of the Meuse shall be determined according to the military convenience of Holland and her neighbours.

Art. III.—The right of navigation on the Scheldt shall be established on the same principle as that of navigation on the Rhine, as stipulated for in Art. V. of the open treaty of to-day.

Art. IV.—The German countries on the left bank of the Rhine which have been united to France since 1792 shall serve for the aggrandisement of Holland and for the compensation of Prussia and other German states.

When I think of the date of these treaties of 1814, of the difficulties of every kind that I experienced, and of the spirit of vengeance that I encountered in some of the negotiators with whom I treated, and whom I had to thwart, I await with confidence the judgment that posterity shall pass upon me. I shall simply call attention to the fact that, six weeks after the king's entrance into Paris, France's territory was secured, the foreign soldiers had quitted French soil, and, by the return of the garrisons of foreign fortresses and of the prisoners, she possessed a superb army, and finally that we had preserved all the admirable works of art carried off by our armies from nearly all the museums of Europe.

If new disasters overwhelmed France in 1815, and caused her to lose the benefits of the treaties of 1814, it is again Napoleon alone who was guilty, and who deserved the execration of his country for drawing upon it irretrievable calamities.

The treaty of Paris, by depriving France of those immense countries that conquest had previously placed in her hands, rendered ulterior arrangements for disposing of those territories, indispensable. Several sovereigns, for instance, the King of Sardinia,[1] the Elector of Hanover,[2] that of Hesse-Cassel,[3] had resumed possession of the states that had been taken from them in the war, as soon as those states were evacuated. But the fate of many of the countries released from France remained to be decided. That of the King of Saxony, towards whom the allied powers displayed implacable hatred because of his fidelity to the cause of Napoleon, had also to be pronounced upon, and that of the Duchy of Warsaw, taken, not by France, but by her ally, the King of Saxony, and finally, that of the realm of Naples, that the policy of France, as well as the will of Louis XVIII., unmovable on that point, could evidently not leave in the hands of Murat.

It has been noticed, that by the treaty, it had been agreed that all the measures to be taken should be arranged at a congress, to meet at Vienna. One of the stipulations of the treaty was that Holland, placed under the sovereignty of the House of Orange, should receive an increase of territory that could be taken only from Belgium ; it was the result of a promise made by England, who wished to have the port of Antwerp under her control, and to prevent its becoming a military port. The King of Sardinia was also to receive an increase of territory taken from the former state of Genoa, for Napoleon, like the allied cabinets, no longer thought of re-establishing the old republics, shaken, or already destroyed, by the French Republic.

The states of Germany which had survived the dissolution of

---

[1] Victor-Emanuel I., second son of Victor Amadeus III., was born in 1759 ; he succeeded, 1802, his brother Charles-Emmanuel, who had abdicated. Until 1814, he reigned only on the island of Sardinia. Having then recovered his states, he reigned until 1821, was then obliged to abdicate in consequence of an insurrection, ceded the throne to his brother Charles-Felix, and died in 1824.

[2] George III. King of England, recovered, in 1814, his electorship of Hanover, which was formed into a kingdom and increased by various territories.

[3] William IX., Landgrave of Hesse-Cassel and Elector in 1801, was dispossesed in 1806 ; in 1814 his estates and his title of elector were returned to him. He died in 1821.

the German Empire, and those of Italy (with the exception of the countries which belonged to the Emperor of Austria), which had become independent, were to continue so. For the rest, the treaty determined nothing as to the other divisions and apportioning of territories. It simply stipulated that territorial and other arrangements should be made to secure a *real* and *durable equilibrium*. These words *real* and *durable equilibrium* were very vague, and could not fail to open up a vast field for discussion, the issue of which it was impossible to foresee. For neither the direction that the negotiations were to take at the Congress, nor the spirit that would preside over its deliberations, had been determined beforehand in accordance with fixed principles. Whatever points had been decided, were so, by clauses relative to particular cases.

In such a state of things, the part France had to play was singularly difficult. It was very tempting and very easy for cabinets embittered for such a long time to refuse to admit her to a council discussing the great interests of Europe. By the treaty of Paris, France had escaped destruction ; but she had not resumed, in the system of general politics, the rank she is called upon to occupy. Experienced eyes could easily discover in several of the principal plenipotentiaries, the secret desire to reduce her to playing a secondary part ; and the secret articles of the treaty provided that the territories re-taken from France should be divided *between the powers*, that is to say, to the exclusion of France. If then France did not herself point out, at the very opening of the congress, the place ascribed to her by the recollection of her power, and by the transitory generosity of some of the allied sovereigns, she would have to submit to remaining for a long time to come, a stranger to the transactions of Europe, and to being exposed to the effect of the alliances which her success, which she had so much abused, had brought about and which jealousy could renew. In a word, she would lose the hope of tracing, between the empire of Napoleon and the Restoration, that deep line of demarkation which would prevent the cabinets of Europe from requiring regenerated France to account for the violence and the excesses of revolutionary France.

It required a negotiator well convinced of the importance

of the circumstances, well penetrated with the means that had contributed to the changes brought about in France, and in a position to speak a firm and true language to the cabinets, whom it was difficult to induce to forget the fact of their being victorious. It required, above all, of the French plenipotentiary that he be impressed with, and impress the fact, that France desired only what she possessed ; that she had frankly repudiated the heritage of conquest ; that she thought herself strong enough in her old boundaries ; that she had no intention of extending them ; that, finally, she to-day placed her glory in her moderation ; but that, if she wished her voice to be heeded in Europe, it was in order to be able to defend the rights of others, against all kinds of trespass.

I did not see among all the men who had held office any who seemed to me to possess the conditions necessary to suitably fill that mission. The *émigrés* who had returned with the king had remained strangers to general politics ; the men who were partisans of the fallen government could not yet understand the interests and position of the newly revived monarchy. I looked upon the post of French plenipotentiary at Vienna, as a very difficult one to fill. I have never known one more honourable.

It was in fact, the duty of the plenipotentiary to complete the work of the restoration, by ensuring the solidity of the edifice that Providence had permitted to be reconstructed. I believed I possessed the right, and I regarded it as a duty to claim that post. The king did not allow me to finish the request that I was about to put to him, and he interrupted me by saying, " Draw me up a project for your instructions." I thanked him, and begged him to appoint with me the Duc de Dalberg, whom I wished to distinguish, and for whom I had a friendship, and whom moreover, by his birth, by his family relations in Germany, and by his ability, would be, for me a useful co-operator.

At the end of a few days, I was able to place before the king, the project of instructions, that he had asked me for. He approved of it, and I believe that when the instructions, that I give farther on, are known, France will take a pride in the sovereign who signed them.

To accompany me, I chose from the Department of Foreign Affairs, the faithful and clever La Besnardière, whom I regard as the most distinguished man who has appeared in the ministry of Foreign Affairs for a great many years. I gave him as assistants MM. Challaye, Formond[1] and Perrey, all three young, and possessing aptitudes that would enable them to profit by the lessons that could be learned in such great circumstances.

I afterwards sought in society for two more persons whom I could attach to the French Legation at Vienna. In my choice, I studied Paris, that is to say, the Tuileries, more than Vienna, because, at Paris, I had to check all the would-be diplomats who surrounded the princes, and whom I wished to believe that they were (without my being aware of it, though without any risk to my mission) acquainted with my movements ; for, as to Vienna, and France, I depended upon myself. It is thus, that the Comte Alexis de Noailles[2] and the Marquis de la Tour du Pin Gouvernet[3] were associated with the Duc de Dalberg and myself as plenipotentiaries at the congress at Vienna.

It appeared to me also, that it was necessary to shake off the hostile prejudice with which imperial France had inspired the high and influential society of Vienna. For that it was necessary to make the French embassy attractive. I then asked my niece, the Comtesse de Périgord, to accompany me

---

[1] M. de Formond was employed in the cipher department of the Seal office. He became consul afterwards and resided in that capacity at Bucharest (1815), at Cagliari (1817), at Livorna (1830). He retired on a pension in 1840.

[2] Alexis, Comte de Noailles, son of Louis-Marie, Viscomte de Noailles, was born in 1783. In 1809, he was arrested as guilty of having given publicity to the pope's bull of excommunication against the emperor. Having been set at liberty a short time after, he emigrated in 1811, went to Switzerland, afterwards to Stockholm, and finally to England, where he joined Louis XVIII. He fought in the campaign of 1813 as Bernadotte's aide-de-camp, and served likewise in the enemy's ranks in 1814. He then became aide-de-camp to the Comte d'Artois and followed Prince Talleyrand to Vienna. In 1815, he was elected deputy of the Oise and of the Rhône, and appointed state minister and member of the privy council. He was always elected until 1830, when he retired into private life. He died in 1835.

[3] Frederic, Marquis de la Tour du Pin Gouvernet, born in 1758, was the son of the Comte de la Tour du Pin, who was a deputy at the States-General, Minister of War in 1789, and guillotined in 1794. The former was colonel at the outbreak of the Revolution, and was appointed Minister at the Hague. Having been recalled in 1792, he emigrated, returned to France under the Consulate, and became *préfet* of Amiens and of Brussels. He accompanied M. de Talleyrand to Vienna, was afterwards appointed again Minister at the Hague, and sent later in that capacity to the King of Sardinia. He retired in 1830, and died in 1837.

and do the honours of my house. By her superior intellect and tact, she knew how to attract and please, and proved very useful to me.

At Vienna, it was necessary to have France use different language from that which people had been accustomed to hear from her for the last twenty years. Nor was it less necessary that the dignity that she should display should be expressed with nobleness, even with brilliancy. The part of self-resignation, so new to her, and that had been imposed upon her by Napoleon's faults, could, in my opinion, scarcely be deprived of grandeur, and should even give weight to the observations that I might be called upon to make in the interest of right and justice. It was therefore, because of the aid which she could afford in supporting weak powers, that I endeavoured to place her, from the outset, in a worthy and honourable situation.

It is thus easy to guess that difficulties sufficiently serious awaited me at Vienna, for no other answer to be needed to the reproach made me for having left Paris at the time when the government, being badly advised, might follow an imprudent course, delay thereby its consolidation, and damp the sentiments that had been displayed on the king's arrival. And besides, one must first do that which one knows how to do, and in this I undertook a task, in which I felt confident of success. And, I would ask of all honest people, was it natural to believe that, instead of exerting every effort not to revive recollections which it was necessary to consign to oblivion, and of banishing all appearances of an arbitrary will, the new government would apply itself only to do the reverse? The truth is, I confess, that I had not expected such blindness. I should never have believed that Abbé de Montesquiou, who had most influence, would have employed it so badly.

The Czar Alexander very soon showed how astonished he was at the course being followed in the internal affairs of France. It was one more obstacle. He received his impressions from the most ardent Liberals, whom he was accustomed to see. After his departure for England, from whence he intended to return to Paris, I believed it my duty to write him the following letter. It probably caused him to make certain reflections, if he found it again in his pocket-book [1] in 1823 :—

FROM THE PRINCE DE BENÉVENT TO THE CZAR ALEXANDER.

PARIS, *June* 13, 1814.

SIRE,

I did not see your Majesty before your departure, and I take the liberty of reproaching you for it with the sincere respect of my most affectionate attachment.

Sire, important relations disclosed to you my most secret sentiments a long time ago. Your esteem was the result of such disclosure. It comforted me for many years, and enabled me to bear painful ordeals. I foresaw your destiny, and felt that I could, Frenchman though I am, associate myself some day with your projects, because they would never cease to be magnanimous. You have completely accomplished that grand destiny ; seeing that I followed you in your noble career, do not deprive me of my recompense. I ask it from the hero of my fancy, and, dare I add, of my heart.

You have saved France. Your entrance into Paris has been the signal for the end of despotism ; whatever be your secret observations, if you were again called there, what you have already done you would do again, for you could not fail in your glory, even if you were to believe the monarchy disposed to assume a little more authority than you think necessary, and the French people to neglect to look to their independence. After all, what are we yet ? And who can flatter himself, after such a catastrophe, that he understands in a short time the character of the French ? Do not doubt it, sire, the king whom you have brought back to us, shall be obliged, if he would give us useful institutions, to take certain precautions, and to seek in his faithful memory what we were formerly, in order to judge what will really suit us. Having swerved from our national customs owing to a gloomy oppression, we shall for long seem foreign to the government that shall be given us.

The French in general, were, and will be, somewhat fickle in their impressions ; they will always be ready to make them known because a secret instinct tells them that they are not to last long. This versatility will lead them very soon to place an unlimited confidence in their sovereign, and ours will not abuse that confidence.

In France, the king has always come before the country. It

---

[1] I have ascertained that the original of this letter is still (1857) to be found in the imperial archives at Saint Petersburg.—(*M. de Bacourt.*)

seems to us that the country is represented by the one man. We have no national pride, but a vast amount of vanity, which, well regulated, produces a deep sentiment of individual honour. Our opinions, or rather our tastes, have often directed our kings (Bonaparte would have shed French blood with more impunity, if he had not tried to oppress us by his gloomy manners). The forms and manners of our sovereigns have in turn fascinated our own, and from that mutual action there shall result for us a method of governing and of obeying which, after all, might eventually deserve the name of constitution. The king has long studied our history. He knows us, he knows how to give a royal character to all that proceeds from him ; and when we shall have become ourselves again, we shall resume that truly French custom of adapting to ourselves the actions and qualities of our king. Besides, liberal principles are keeping pace with the spirit of the age. We cannot fail to reach that point ; and if your Majesty will place confidence in my word, I will promise you that we shall have a monarchy blended with liberty; that you shall witness men of merit welcomed and honoured in France; and it will be your glory to have made the happiness of our country.

Sire, I confess that you saw many discontented persons in Paris ; but if we put aside the quickness of the past revolution, and the surprise of so many passions all stirred at the same time, what is Paris after all but a city of officials ? The cessation of official appointments alone warned the Parisians of the despotism of Napoleon. If the government had continued paying people in places, it is in vain that the provinces would have groaned under tyranny. The provinces really constitute France ; there they really hail the return of the House of Bourbon, and proclaim your happy victory.

Your Majesty will pardon the length of my letter. It was indispensable in order to reply to the greatest portion of your generous anxieties ; it will replace a verbal explanation that I should so much like to have given you. General Pozzo,[1] whom

---

[1] Charles-André, Comte Pozzo di Borgo, born near Ajaccio, in 1764. Was at first intimate with Napoleon in his youth ; but they fell out in the course of the civil outbreaks of Corsica, and this was the beginning of an enmity which continued during their lives. In 1791, Pozzo was elected deputy of Corsica at the legislative assembly. Having returned to Corsica in 1792, he was in the following year called to office with Paoli, by his fellow citizens. Corsica having momentarily submitted to England, Pozzo was president of the State Council and Secretary of State. He was obliged to emigrate in 1796, went to London, then to Vienna, and, in 1803, entered the Russian service as a diplomat. He returned to Austria after Tilsit, went from there to England (1809), and negotiated a reconciliation between London and St. Petersburg. He had a considerable influence over the events of 1812 and 1813. In 1814, he accompanied the Czar Alexander to Paris, was appointed Russian ambassador to France, entrusted with numerous diplomatic missions, and attended

I see every day, and whom I cannot thank you enough, sire, for having left with us, shall look to our interests and warn us, for we sometimes need to be warned. I shall discuss with him our national interests ; and if, as I hope, your Majesty honours France with a short visit, upon his return, he will tell you, and you will yourself see, that I have not deceived you.

Another confidant, one only, has received the secret of my grief, I mean the Duchess of Courland, whom you honour with your kindness and who so well understands my anxiety. When we shall have the happiness of seeing you again, I shall leave it to her to tell you how grieved I have been, and she will also tell you that I did not deserve to be so.

May, sire, your generous soul have a little patience ! A really good Frenchman as I am, permit me to ask of you, in the old French language, to allow us to resume the former *accoutumance*[1] of love for our kings ; it is certainly not yours to refuse to understand the influence of that sentiment on a great nation.

Please deign to accept, sire, with your usual kindness, the homage of the profound respect with which I am, sire, your Majesty's most humble, obedient servant,

PRINCE DE BÉNÉVENT.

INSTRUCTIONS FOR THE KING'S AMBASSADORS AT THE CONGRESS.

No assembly invested with powers can do anything legitimate unless it be legitimately constituted, and consequently, unless none of those who have a right to be there be excluded therefrom, and none of those who have not such right be admitted. Let it confine itself scrupulously to its province, and proceed according to prescribed rules, or failing such rules, according to those which may be drawn from the purpose for which it was constituted, and from the nature of things. It is the nature of things to fix the order in which it is indispensable to regulate them, by the various degrees of connection of dependence that it places between different objects, seeing that a subordinate question cannot be treated and decided before that upon which it depends. Finally the most legitimate and wisest acts would be useless and fail in their object if, for want of means of execution, they were not enforced.

all the congresses of the Holy Alliance. In 1835 he became ambassador at London, resigned in 1839, and died in 1843.

[1] An old French expression, now obsolete, meaning what one is wont to do.—(*Translator.*)

It is then most necessary that the congress should determine first of all,

1. Which are the states which may send plenipotentiaries.

2. What subjects should or might be settled there.

3. By what means they can be settled, if by decision or arbitration, or by means of negotiations, or again partly by both these means, and the cases in which each of those means should be employed.

4. In cases in which the means of decision shall be employed, in what manner the votes are to be taken.

5. The order in which the subjects are to be treated.

6. The form to be given to the decision.

7. The modes and manners of execution in case obstacles of any description should be met with.

According to Article XXXII. of the treaty of May 30th, the congress should be general, and all the powers engaged in the war that that treaty terminated should send their plenipotentiaries there. Although the term *powers* carries with itself an indeterminate idea of greatness and of strength which seems to render it inapplicable to many states deprived of the one and the other, employed as it is in Article XXXII. in an abstract and general sense, restrained only by the expression of a connection entirely independent of the comparative strength of states and common to the smallest and the largest, it comprises incontestably all those between which that connection exists, that is to say, that have been in one way or another engaged in the war that the treaty of May 30th terminated. If one excepts Turkey and Switzerland, for the republic of San-Marino cannot be reckoned, all the states of Europe, great and small, have been engaged in that war. The right of the smallest to send a plenipotentiary to the congress results then from the provision of the treaty of May 30th. France has not thought of excluding them, and the other contracting powers have not been able to do so, since stipulating for them and in their name they were not able to stipulate against them. The smallest states, being those which would most readily be excluded because of their weakness, are all, or nearly all, in Germany. Now Germany intends to form a confederation of which they are members ; the organization of this consequently interests them in the highest degree. It could not be done without them without violating their natural independence, and Article VI. of the treaty of May 30, which by implication lays great stress upon it, by saying that the states of Germany should be independent and united by a federal link. That organization will be made at the congress, it would then be unjust to exclude them from it.

To these motives of justice a more practical motive of utility to France must be added. All that is of interest to the small states is of interest to her also. All wish to preserve their existence, and she should wish that they preserve it. Some of them might desire to be enlarged, and that would suit her, inasmuch as it would diminish the growth of the large states. Her policy would be to protect and favour them, but without any one being able to take umbrage on that account, which would be less easy if they did not attend the congress, and, instead of having to support their requests, she should even be obliged to make their requests for them, while, from another point of view, the need they would have of her assistance would give her an influence over them. Thus the question of their votes being or not being counted, is not indifferent to her.

In pursuance of which, if it should occur that, under the pretext of the smallness of any state engaged in the last war, the plenipotentiaries of the sovereign of that state be excluded from the congress, the king's ambassadors shall oppose, and shall insist on their being admitted.

The nations of Europe do not yet acknowledge in their mutual intercourse the moral law alone, nor yet that of nature alone, but are still under a law that they have made for themselves, and which gives to the first a sanction which it otherwise lacks ; it is a law established by written conventions, or by usage constantly, universally, and reciprocally followed, which is always founded on mutual consent, whether tacit or expressed, and which is obligatory for all; this law is the law of public right.

Now there are in this right two fundamental principles : the one that the sovereignty cannot be acquired by the simple fact of conquest, nor pass to the conqueror if the sovereign does not cede it ; the other, that any title of sovereignty, and consequently the right that it supposes, are binding for the other states only in so far as they may recognize it.

Whenever a conquered country has a sovereign, cession is possible, and it follows from the first of the principles cited, that it cannot be replaced, or supplied by anything.

But a conquered country can be without a sovereign, either because he who was sovereign has for himself and his heirs renounced his right simply, without ceding it to another ; or because the reigning family has just died out without any one being legally called to reign after it. The moment a republic is conquered, the sovereign ceases to exist, because his nature is such that liberty is a necessary condition of his existence, and because it is an absolute impossibility for him to have one moment of liberty so long as the conquest lasts.

The cession by the sovereign is then impossible.

Does it therefore follow that in this case the right of conquest can prolong itself indefinitely, or convert itself into the right of sovereignty? By no means.

Sovereignty is, in the general society of Europe, what private property is in civil society. A country or state under conquest and without a sovereign, and a property without a master, are unclaimed goods ; but forming both the one and the other a portion of a territory which is not unclaimed, and consequently subject to the law of that territory, and can be acquired only in conformity with that law ; for example, private property, in conformity with the public law of the special state in which it is situated, and the country or state only in conformity with the European public law, which is the general law of the territory forming the common domain of Europe. Now it is one of the principles of this law that the sovereignty cannot be transferred by the mere act of conquest. Therefore, when the cession by the sovereign is impossible, it is of the fullest necessity that it be supplied. And this can only be done by the sanction of Europe. A sovereign whose states are under conquest (if he be an hereditary sovereign) does not cease to be sovereign, unless he has ceded his right or has renounced it, nor does he lose by the conquest anything beyond actual possession, and consequently preserves the right to do all that does not presuppose this possession. The sending of plenipotentiaries to the congress presupposes it so little, that it could even have for object to demand it.

Thus the King of Saxony and the prince-primate, as legitimate sovereign of Aschaffenburg [1] (at least if he has not abdicated in the meantime), could send theirs there, and not only could they do so, but it is even necessary that they should, for in case, which is more than probable, one wished to dispose entirely, or in part of their possessions, since it would be impossible to legitimately dispose of them, without a cession or renunciation on their part, it is necessary that some one, invested with their power, cede or renounce them in their name ; and as it is a third principle of the public law of Europe, that a cession or renunciation is null, if it has not been freely made, that is, by a sovereign at liberty, the king's ambassadors

---

[1] The prince-primate had been created sovereign Prince of Aschaffenburg, Frankfort and Wetzlar, by the emperor, at the time of the formation of the Rhine Confederation.

shall take the necessary steps that one of the plenipotentiaries claim, in conformity with this principle, for the King of Saxony, the authorization to repair immediately wherever he may deem fit, and they shall personally second that request, and if needed, shall themselves make it.

The Duke of Oldenburg,[1] the Duke of Arenberg,[2] and the Princes of Salm,[3] possessed in sovereignty countries that were seized in open peace by him who named himself, and who should have been, their protector, and they were annexed to France, but their sovereigns did not yield. The allies do not appear to have, up to the present, recognized the rights of the houses of Arenberg and Salm ; but those rights exist, as well as those of the Prince of Isenburg, who, absent from home and in the service of France, was treated like an enemy, and whose estates are under conquest.

The princes and counts of the old German empire who have become subjects of the members of the Rhine Confederation by virtue of the act which constituted it, cannot be considered as dispossessed sovereigns, seeing that they were not sovereigns, but simply vassals and subjects of the emperor and of the Empire, whose sovereignty over them has been transferred to their new masters. The attempts that they might make to have themselves recognized as dispossessed sovereigns, and that certain powers might be willing to support, ought to be rejected as illegitimate and even dangerous. Mere hesitation on that point would suffice to agitate, and perhaps, to set on fire, the whole of Southern Germany.

The order of St. John of Jerusalem might desire to send representatives to the congress, but, considering that the island of Malta and its dependencies were the only territories that it

---

[1] The grand-duchy of Oldenburg had been annexed by Napoleon, December 13, 1820.

[2] The states of the dukes of Arenberg had been partially annexed to France by the treaty of Lunéville. They had received in exchange, the county of Meppen and the Fort of Rechlinghausen. In 1803, the reigning duke, Louis-Angilbert, abdicated in favour of his son Prosper-Louis, born in 1785. The latter became in 1806, senator of the French Empire, entered the Rhine Confederation in 1807, raised, in 1808, a regiment of Chasseurs with which he was sent to Spain. He was made prisoner and taken to England. In 1810, Napoleon disposed of his states that were partially annexed to France and partially united to the Grand Duchy of Berg. In 1815, the states of the Duke d'Arenberg were divided between Hanover and Prussia, and that prince himself became a member of the Upper Chamber of Hanover.

[3] Constantine-Alexander, Prince of Salm-Salm, and Frederick IV., Prince of Salm-Kyrburg. The principality of Salm was united with France in 1802. In exchange, the Prince Salm-Kyrburg, who served in the French army as superior officer of cavalry, obtained the bishopric of Münster and entered the Rhine Confederation. In 1812, Napoleon annexed that territory on condition of the payment of an income of 400,000 francs which was made to the prince. In 1814, his ancient principality was united to Prussia.

possessed ; that it yielded them, and that there can be no sovereign without territory, as there can be no property without an owner, it has ceased to be sovereign and can only become one by acquiring a territory.

The deliverance of a conquered country, in whatever manner it be done, returns immediate possession to the sovereign who has only lost that, and to the republic its existence. They can only retake possession, the one and the other, of that which belonged to them, and not to any one else.

The Electors of Hanover and of Hesse, the prince of Nassau-Orange as prince of Germany, the Dukes of Brunswick[1] and of Oldenburg, who all, in consequence of the dissolution of the German Empire were independent when their countries were invaded, or disposed of, possess them to-day as legitimately as formerly.

The cities of Lübeck, Bremen, and Hamburg, had become independent by reason of the dissolution of the German Empire : that of Danzig, by the peace of Tilsit.[2]   The republics of Valais, of Genoa, Lucca, and Ragusa, were independent for centuries. All have fallen under conquest, unless the documents by which Genoa and Lucca seemed to give up their own sovereignty, be regarded as valid.

Countries that are not now occupied by any foreign force, nor governed by any foreign authority, have again become what they were, and can have ministers at the congress.   The others cannot.

Geneva has recovered her former independence ; but she has not been engaged, as a state, in the war that the treaty of May 30 has terminated ; and she is to be included in the Helvetic confederation, which was not engaged therein either.

The island of Elba forms an independent state only since the war has ceased.[3]

Conquest being unable by itself to give sovereignty, cannot return it.   The sovereign who enters by conquest into a country which he has ceded, cannot again become sovereign of that country, any more than a private owner can seize upon property he has already disposed of.

That which conquest cannot give to one it cannot give to

---

[1] Frederick-William, Duke of Brunswick-Œls, born in 1771, had succeeded his father in 1806. But he was deposed at the peace of Tilsit and his dukedom annexed to the kingdom of Westphalia. After vain efforts to reconquer his patrimony, he took refuge in England. He took up arms again in 1813, was reinstated in his states, December 22 of the same year, and was killed at Waterloo.

[2] Napoleon had then taken Danzig from Prussia, and declared it a free city, but it was to be occupied by a French garrison.

[3] Napoleon had been recognized as sovereign prince of the island of Elba.

several. If then several fellow-conquerors attribute to themselves, or give to themselves reciprocally, a sovereignty over the country which they have conquered, they commit an act which public law disapproves and annuls.

The Prince of Orange [1] ceded all his rights to Holland, but the treaty of May 30, signed by eight of the principal powers of Europe, and agreed to in the names of all, returns him that country (Open Treaty, Art. 6).

That treaty on laying down the bases of several dispositions to be made by the congress, says that the former states of the King of Sardinia, a portion only of which he had ceded, shall be returned him (Art. 2, Secret), and that Austria shall have as limits beyond the Alps, the Po, Lago Maggiore, and the Tessin, which will be returning to her countries that belonged to her, and that she had yielded on the Adriatic Gulf and in Italy (Art. 6, Open, and 2, Secret).

The Prince of Orange possesses therefore a legitimate and actual right, and the King of Sardinia, and Austria an almost actual right of sovereignty over the countries which had ceased to belong to them because they had ceded them.

But the treaty has not returned to Prussia any of the countries that she ceded at various times on this side of the Elbe. She has then no real right of sovereignty over those countries, if we except the principality of Neufchâtel, for which the last and legitimate possessor has made with her an arrangement that may be considered as a cession. The treaty has not given Tuscany and Modena back to the Archdukes Ferdinand [2] and Francis,[3]

---

[1] William, Prince of Orange-Nassau, afterwards King of the Netherlands, was born in 1772 ; he was the son of the Stadtholder, William V. He was in command of the Dutch forces in 1794 and 1795. At the time of the French invasion his father abdicated and took refuge in England, and Prince William himself entered the service of Austria. In 1803, he obtained, in exchange for all his rights on Holland, the abbey of Fulda, which had just been secularized. But having, in 1806, embraced the cause of Prussia, he was despoiled of that principality as well as of his paternal estates. He then took up service again in Austria. He re-entered Holland in 1813, and took the title of sovereign prince of the United Provinces. The Congress of Vienna bestowed on him the title of King of the Netherlands, and united Belgium to Holland. In the following year King William I. again joined the coalition and was wounded at Waterloo. He reigned peacefully until 1830, when Belgium rose against him, and proclaimed her independence. He abdicated in 1840, and died three years later in Berlin.

[2] Ferdinand, Archduke of Austria, son of the Emperor Leopold and of Marie-Louise infanta of Spain. He became Grand-Duke of Tuscany in 1791. He retained his states until 1799, when he was deposed, and regained possession of his states in the same year. But the victory of Marengo again deprived him of his states, which were transformed in 1801 into the kingdom of Etruria, and given to the duke Louis of Parma. Ferdinand retired to Vienna, received in 1803 the archbishopric of Salzburg, with the title of elector, and in 1805, the bishopric of Wurtzburg, and in 1806 joined the Rhine Confederation with the title of grand-duke. Ferdinand re-entered Tuscany in 1814 and reigned until 1824.

[3] Francis IV., son of the Archduke Ferdinand and of Marie-Beatrix d'Este, by his mother grandson of Hercules III. Duke of Modena. In 1797, Hercules was

who consequently have not, nor can have, any legitimate right as sovereigns over them.

A prince who attributes to himself the sovereignty of a conquered country that has not been ceded to him, usurps it.   If the country previously belonged to him, and if it be vacant, the usurpation is less odious ; but it is still usurpation, which cannot confer legal right.

The country about Modena having been yielded, and having become an integral portion of another state, before the war which the treaty of May 30 terminated, was not engaged in that war as a state.   Thus, if it possessed now a legitimate sovereign, that sovereign could not have a minister at the congress.

The country about Parma, which was likewise ceded, had likewise ceased before the war to form a separate state, and became one only after the war was over.[1]

Tuscany is not a vacant country, though France, to whom it has been ceded and united, has renounced it, because it was ceded under a condition which has not been fulfilled, namely, that of furnishing a determinate equivalent, which has not been furnished, and which caused the Queen of Etruria to recover her right of sovereignty over that country.[2]

The most legitimate right çan be contested, it then becomes, and remains, doubtful, as long as the dispute is not terminated ; and the effect of that right is suspended for all cases, and everywhere when it is necessary for it to be unchallenged.   A sovereign who is such only for the states which acknowledge him, cannot send an envoy where representatives of all states meet, a portion of which do not recognize his rights.

Ferdinand IV. can therefore have representatives at the congress only as King of Sicily.   It is not necessary to add that he who reigns at Naples cannot have any.

From all that precedes, the following general rule can be drawn :

That every prince possessing over states engaged in the last

deposed by the French, and his states were incorporated in the Cisalpine republic, where they formed the departments of Crostolo, chief-town Reggio, and of Panaro, chief-town Modena, in 1814.   He reigned until 1846.   By his marriage with Marie-Beatrix, daughter of the King of Sardinia, Victor Emmanuel, he had several children, among whom was the princess Maria-Theresa, who married the Comte de Chambord.

[1] The duchy of Parma had been annexed to the Cisalpine republic in 1802.   Under the Empire it was annexed to France, and formed the department of Taro, chief-town, Parma.

[2] It will be remembered that the secret treaty of Fontainebleau of October 27, 1807, promised to the Queen Regent of Etruria, in exchange for her states in Italy, the kingdom of Lusitania that was to be formed of a part of Portugal.   That agreement had not been kept.

war, a right of sovereignty which has been universally recognized, which he has not ceded, and which is not recognized as belonging to any other person (be those states under conquest or not), can, as well as all states that the war found free, which have been engaged in it, and are now actually free, have a plenipotentiary at the congress ; all other princes or states cannot.

The king's ambassadors shall abide by this rule, and arrange that it be adopted and followed.

The treaty of May 30 mentions as the points to be regulated at the congress only the following :

1. The disposal of the territories which France had renounced (Art. I. Secret) ;

2. The establishment of relations from which should result a real and durable system of equilibrium in Europe (Same Article);

3. The organization of the confederation of the German States (Art. VI. Open) ;

4. The guarantee of the organization that Switzerland has, or shall have, given herself since the treaty (Art. II. Secret) ;

5. The duties to be levied on the navigation of the Rhine by the bordering states (Art. V. Open) ;

6. The application, (if it be judged practicable,) to the rivers that separate or cross different states, of the clause which provides for the free navigation of the Rhine (Same Article) ;

7. The universal abolition of the slave trade (Treaty with England, 1st additional Article).

But the territories which France has renounced are not the only ones to be disposed of. There are yet those to dispose of which belonged to Napoleon, in another capacity than that of ruler of France, or to members of his family, and over which as well for the latter as for himself, he has renounced all pretensions.

Besides these territories, there are many others which are under conquest. If the congress should not regulate their fate, how could it establish that equilibrium which ought to be the main and final object of its operations ? Is not a determined ratio between the forces, and consequently between the possessions, of all the states, a necessary condition of it ? Can certain proportions exist between the possessions of all, if the right of possession be uncertain for some ? It is not a momentary equilibrium that should be established, but a durable one. It can endure only so long as the proportions upon which it is founded exist ; and these proportions can themselves endure only as long as the right of possession shall be transmitted in such a way that they shall not be changed. The order of succession in each state ought then to enter as a necessary element in the calculation of the equilibrium, not so as to be changed, if it is certain, but in such a manner as to be rendered certain, if it is not that. There is all the more reason for fixing it, if the state where it is doubtful is a state that is about to be aggrandized ; for, by giving to its present possessor, one gives to his heir after him, and it is necessary to know to whom one gives. The ordinary, and almost inevitable, effect of a right of uncertain succession is to produce civil and foreign wars, and often the one and the other at the same time, which is not only a just motive for removing, but even makes it a necessity to remove all uncertainty on that point.

The King of Sardinia added to his former titles that of prince and perpetual vicar of the Holy Roman Empire. Savoy, Montferrat,[1] and some districts of Piedmont were the feoffs of it. The right to succeed to them was regulated by the law of the Empire, and that law excluded women for ever.

The King of Sardinia possessed his other states as independent prince. The right to succeed to them could not then be regulated by the law of the Empire to which they were not subjected. Was the order of succession there established by an express law which might be applied to a circumstance which could not be replaced by the tacit law of usage, because that circumstance never offered before ? namely that in which the house of Savoy being divided into two lines, there would only remain women in the reigning line, a circumstance which, to say the truth, still belongs to the future, but to a future so certain and so near that, in the eyes of Europe, and with respect to the points which the congress should settle, it ought to be considered as present. The reigning line counts only three princes, all three of an advanced age— the old king, who is a widower,[2] the present king,[3] who has only daughters, and the Duc de Genevois,[4] who has been married seven years and who has no children.

In 1445, Piedmont being already for four centuries in the house of Savoy, Duke Louis, considering that the ruin of sovereign houses is the result of a division of their

---

[1] Montferrat was an ancient marquisate situated between Piedmont and the republic of Genoa. Its capital was Casal. That state was conceded to the kingdom of Sardinia by the emperor in 1708, and the kings of Sardinia took the title of vicar of the emperor, a title which had been conferred upon the Marquis of Montferrat by the emperor Charles IV.

[2] Charles-Emmanuel II. who abdicated in 1802. He died at Rome in 1819, where he was a Jesuit. His wife was Marie-Adélaïde-Xavière-Clotilde, daughter of the Dauphin Louis, and thus sister of Louis XVIII.

[3] Victor-Emmanuel I. brother of the above.

[4] Charles-Felix, born in 1765, brother of the two above-mentioned, ascended the throne in 1804, and died without children in 1824. The Duke of Carignan (Charles-Albert) issue of the collateral line, succeeded him.

possessions, declared the domain of Savoy untransferable, that is to say, all that his house possessed then or was thereafter to possess. All the acquisitions made or to be made, were thus annexed to the ducal crown of Savoy. That is why we see that, in the course of several centuries, the heir of Savoy has always been heir to the possessions of his house, which certainly would not have occurred if there had been a different order of succession for the one and the other. To say that that which was common to them should exist only in the reigning line, and that the women of that line, if alone remaining, should be preferred to the males of another line for all that which was not imperial fief, would be to advance a proposition impossible to admit without proving it, and impossible of proving otherwise than by a legal act, authentic and solemn, which should have established such a distinction between the two lines. An act of that nature if it existed would not have remained ignored, it would have been found, cited, or transcribed in more than one record, and no trace of it is found anywhere. It can then be looked upon as certain that it never existed, and that thus the totality of the inheritance of the house of Sardinia, and not only a portion of that inheritance which depended on the empire, ought, by virtue of the law of inheritance in force, to pass immediately from the last prince of the reigning branch to those of the second branch; in other terms, that all the possessions of the house of Sardinia are hereditary from male to male by right of primogeniture, and to the exclusion of women. It is then, probable, that no doubt would arise in that respect, if Austria, who aspires to possess, by herself, or by the princes of her house, all the north of Italy had no interest in raising some, and if the marriage of the Archduke Francis with the princess, eldest daughter of the king, did not offer him a pretext, which it is to be feared that power will seize. It would suffice Austria to give to the pretensions, that of himself or incited by her, the archduke should form in his wife's behalf, the qualification of rights, to assume that of upholding them by the force of arms. It is these pretensions and the fatal results that they cannot fail to bring about, that it is not only wise but even necessary to obviate, by establishing the right of the house of Carignan by a recognition that would prevent all litigation.[1]

The same principle of public law which renders all claim to

---

[1] The house of Carignan descended from Charles-Emmanuel I., Duke of Savoy, who died in 1630. It was then represented by Charles-Amadeus-Albert, Prince of Carignan, born in 1798, cousin of king Victor-Emmanuel. He was called to the throne in 1831, at the death of king Charles-Felix.

sovereignty null for the states which have not recognized it, applies, as a necessary consequence, to every means of acquiring sovereignty, and, therefore, to the laws of inheritance that transmit it. It is known what happened when the last prince of each of the two branches of the first house of Austria substituted (Charles II. by his testament, and Charles VI. by his pragmatic) a new order of succession to that which should have ended with his person. Recognized by some, rejected by others, the new law of inheritance became the cause of a bloody contest, that did not and could not terminate except when all the states were of one accord on the right that the disposition made by each prince tended to establish. To terminate a contest being only to acknowledge a right, those without whose recognition a right should be reputed not to exist, can proclaim it, and are indeed the only ones who can do so. And by the same means (and because it is not with Europe as with particular states, where disputes relative to the right of property cannot have very serious results, nor ones which may not easily and quickly be terminated, and where those who can terminate them are always present) to the power of terminating the present disputes relative to the right of sovereignty, is added for the congress, not only the right but even the power of preventing them, as much as the nature of things will permit, by removing that of all causes that could most infallibly produce them, namely : uncertainty regarding the right of succession.

Switzerland enjoyed, during several centuries, amidst the wars of Europe, and though situated between two great rival powers, a neutrality constantly respected, and not less profitable to others than to herself. Not only by that neutrality the arena of war was restrained, but again many causes of war were prevented, and France found herself dispensed with devoting a portion of her means and forces to defend that portion of her frontiers, the most vulnerable, which Switzerland, always neutral, protected. If, in the future, Switzerland was no longer to be free to remain neutral, or, what amounts to the same thing, if her neutrality should not be respected, such a state of things, by the influence that it would necessarily have on the relative power of the neighbouring states, would disturb and perhaps even destroy that equilibrium which it is to establish. The treaty of May 30 only speaks of guaranteeing the organization of Switzerland ; but it is necessary that her future neutrality be also guaranteed.

The Ottoman Porte was not engaged in the last war, but it is an European power, whose preservation is important for the European equilibrium. It is then useful that its existence should also be assured.

Thus the Congress should decide :—

1. The fate of the states under conquest and not vacant, of which there are two classes, including : the first, the states in litigation, that is to say, the states over which the same right of sovereignty is recognized to several persons, by different powers.

To this class belong the realms of Naples and Tuscany.

The second, the states or countries, the possession of which the sovereign has lost, without having ceded them and without another person claiming sovereignty over them.

The kingdom of Saxony, the duchy of Warsaw, the provinces of the Holy See situated on the Adriatic, the principalities of Arenberg, Isenberg, and Salm, to which must be added that of Aschaffenburg (if the prince primate has not abdicated) compose the second class.

2. Doubtful rights of succession.

3. The disposal to be made of those states or vacant countries, that is to say, the states which the legitimate sovereign has renounced, without ceding them, or those over which no actual right of sovereignty has been conferred upon any one with the consent of Europe.

They form also two classes ; in the first of which are included those which have not been actually assigned, but destined by the treaty of May 30, namely :—

To the King of Sardinia, the portion of his old states ceded to France, that is to say, Savoy and the county of Nice, (his other possessions not having been ceded, he remained lawful sovereign of them), and an indeterminate portion of the state of Genoa.

To Austria, the Illyrian provinces and the portion of the realm of Italy to the left of the Po, and to the east of Lago Maggiore and of Tessin.

To Holland, Belgium, with a frontier to fix to the left side of the Meuse.

Finally, to Prussia and other German states that have not been mentioned, the countries situated between the Meuse, the frontiers of France and the Rhine, to serve them as compensation and to be divided among them in a proportion that has not been indicated.

To the other class belongs the rest of the vacant countries, namely :—

The undetermined part of the state of Genoa which has not been destined to the King of Sardinia; the part of the former realm of Italy not destined to Austria ; Lucca ; Piombino ; the Ionian Isles ; the Grand Duchy of Berg, such as it existed before January 1, 1811 ; Ost-Frise ; all the provinces formerly Prussian, which formed a portion of the kingdom of Westphalia ; the principality of Erfurt and the town of Danzig.

4. The future destiny of the Island of Elba, which, given to him who possesses it for life only, shall, at his death, become a vacant country.

5. The organization of the German Confederation :—

All those points should be so settled as to bring about a real equilibrium, into the composition of which shall enter as necessary elements the organization of Switzerland, its future neutrality, and the integrity of the recognized and guaranteed Ottoman possessions in Europe.

6. The toll dues on the Rhine, the Scheldt, and the other rivers, the navigation of which is to be made free.

7. The universal abolition of the slave-trade.

An obligation can neither be created, nor a certain right of a state removed, without its consent.

In every case where it is necessary to do the one or the other, all the powers together have no more power than one alone. The consent of the party interested being necessary, it must be obtained, or that which, without it, would not be just must be renounced. Means of negotiation is then the only one permitted.

The means of decision is, on the contrary, the only one that can be taken when the competence, having been established (and that of the congress is an obvious consequence of the principles set forth above), the question at issue is either to proclaim a disputed right of sovereignty or to dispose of territories which belong to no one, or to regulate the exercise of a right common to several states, which, by explicit consent made it subordinate to the interest of all. For if it were necessary to secure, in the first case, the consent of him whose right is declared null, in the second, the consent of all those who pretend to a vacant territory, and, in the third, that of all concerned, never could a litigation be terminated, a vacant territory could never cease to be so, never could a right the exercise of which should have to be regulated according to the interest of all, be discharged.

The fate of states in litigation.

The doubtful rights of succession ;

The disposal of vacant states ;

And to establish the toll dues on the Rhine ;

Should be settled by means of decision, with this difference, which arises from the disparity of objects, namely that, in the first case, the litigation cannot be terminated only in so far as the right of one of those between which it exists, is unanimously recognized; that in the second case, the decision ought to be likewise unanimous; and that it should be so again, in the third, with the exception of the votes of the co-claimants, which ought not to be counted; finally that, in the fourth case, the majority should suffice.

The other points can only be settled by means of negotiation.

The fate of the countries that are neither vacant, nor in litigation, because for disposing of them otherwise than by returning them to their respective sovereigns, the consent of the latter is necessary.

The organization of the German Confederation, because that organization shall become, for the German states, a law which cannot be imposed upon them without their consent.

The abolition of the slave-trade, because it has been hitherto a matter foreign to the public law of Europe, under which the English wish to bring it now.

Out of about one hundred and seventy millions of inhabitants that Christian Europe contains, more than two-thirds of them belong to France and to the seven states that signed with her the treaty of May 30, and the half of the other third to countries under conquest, which not having been engaged in the war, have no ministers at the congress; the surplus forms the population of more than forty states, of which some would be scarcely the hundredth part of the smallest of those which signed the treaty of May 30, and which all united would not constitute a power equal to one of the great powers of Europe. What part shall they play in the deliberations? What share in the right of voting? Shall each one have a share equal to that of the largest states? This indeed would be unwarrantable. Shall they have but one vote in common? They would never succeed in coming to an agreement. Shall they have none? It would be better, then, not to admit them. But which shall be excluded? The ministers of the pope, of Sicily, of Sardinia? or that of Holland, or that of Saxony, or only those who are not ministers of crowned heads? But who would cede on behalf of those princes if they should have to cede? Who would, on their behalf, give to the obligation, that was about to be imposed upon them, the consent that they should give? Shall their states be disposed of without their ceding them? Shall their consent be passed over when public law renders it necessary? Shall Europe thus have met to violate the principles of the law which governs her? It is on the contrary most important to enforce them more strictly, now that they have been so long ignored and so ruthlessly violated. A simple means of conciliating at the same time, law and propriety would be to value the share that the states of the third or fourth order should take in the arrangements about to be made, not by the scale of power, but by that of their interest.

The general equilibrium of Europe cannot be composed of simple elements. It can only be a system of partial equilibrium The small or medium states should be allowed a vote only in the questions concerning the particular system to which they belong—the states of Italy in the arrangements relative to Italy, and the German states in the arrangements relative to Germany. The great powers alone, being interested in the whole, should co-ordinate each part with regard to the whole.

The order which appears the most natural and suitable for treating those points, is that in which they have been presented above. That which each one has, and that which he ought to keep, must first be determined so as to know if it is necessary and what is necessary to add to it ; not to dispose of vacant countries except when having good grounds for doing so; to divide afterwards that which is to be divided, and thus to fix the general state of possession which is the first principle of all equilibrium. The organization of Germany can only come afterwards, for it is necessary that it be relative to the reciprocal power of the German States, and consequently that that power be previously fixed. Finally, the guarantees should follow and not precede the arrangements on which they bear.

A protocol should be kept of the deliberations, acts and decisions of the congress. These decisions ought not to be expressed in other language than that of ordinary treaties. To return the realm of Naples to Ferdinand IV., it will suffice that the treaty recognize that prince as King of Naples, or simply name him with that title in the following style, " His Majesty Ferdinand IV., King of Naples and Sicily."

In like manner, to proclaim the right of the house of Carignan, the treaty has only to say, " Such part of the state of Genoa is for ever united to the states of his Majesty the King of Sardinia, to be. like them, possessed in full ownership and sovereignty, and to be inherited from male to male, by order of primogeniture, in both branches of his house."

For that which concerns the manner and means of execution a guarantee common to all the recognized rights, will be sufficient, since it forces the guarantees to uphold those rights, and that it deprives from all external support the pretensions opposed to them.

After having indicated what points the congress can and should decide, and pointed out that its competence results from the very principles of law that are to serve to decide those points, it remains to consider them in the light of the interest of France, and to show that fortunately for France she sees no reason why justice and utility should be antagonistic, and does not seek her own utility save in that justice which is the utility of all.

An absolute equality of power between all the states, not only can never exist, but is not necessary to the political equilibrium, and would perhaps, in some respects, be hurtful to it. That equilibrium consists in a relation between the reciprocal power of resistance and forces of aggression of the various political bodies. If Europe were composed of states being so related to one another that the minimum of the resisting power of the smallest was equal to the maximum of the aggressive force of the largest, there would then be a real equilibrium, that is to say resulting from the very nature of things. But the situation of Europe is not and will never become such. Contiguous to large territories belonging to one single power there are territories of a greater or less size divided in a greater or less number of states, often of diverse natures. To unite these states by a federal link is often impossible, and it is always impossible to give those which are thus united the same unity of will and the same power of action as though they were a simple body. Therefore, they only contribute to the formation of the general equilibrium as imperfect elements ; in their capacity of composite bodies, they have their own equilibrium, subject to a thousand modifications, which necessarily affect that of which they form a part.

Such a situation admits solely of an equilibrium quite artificial and precarious, that can endure only so long as certain large states are animated with a spirit of moderation and justice which will preserve that equilibrium.

The policy of preservation was that of France, during the whole of the past century, until the outbreak of the events which produced the last war ; and it is that policy which the king wishes constantly to follow. But before preserving, one must establish.

If Austria were to ask for the possession of all Italy, there would be no one perhaps who would not denounce such a demand, think it monstrous, and regard the union of Italy to Austria as fatal to the independence and safety of Europe. Nevertheless, by giving all Italy to Austria, the independence of the former would simply be assured. Once united in one body, Italy, by whatever right she belonged to Austria, would escape her, not sooner or later, but in a very few years, perhaps in a few months, and Austria would have acquired her only to lose

her. On the other hand, let Italy be divided into seven territories, of which the two principal shall be at the extremities and
the four smallest contiguous to the largest ; give the latter to
Austria, and three of the smallest to the princes of her house,
this would offer her a pretext by the aid of which she would
cause the fourth one to fall to the share of one of those princes.
Let the territory at the other extremity be occupied by a man,
who because of his personal position towards a number of the
sovereigns of Europe, can have no hope except in Austria nor
any support but hers ; let the seventh territory belong to a prince
whose sole strength rests in the respect due to his character, is it
not manifest that in appearing to give but a portion of Italy to
Austria she will really have been given the whole ? and that her
apparent division into different states would be, in reality, but a
means given to Austria to possess that country in the only
manner in which she can possess it, without losing it. Such,
indeed, would be the state of Italy, if Austria were to have the
Po, Lago Maggiore, and Tessin as limits, if Modena, Parma and
Piacenza, if the grand-duchy of Tuscany had princes of her
house for sovereigns, if the right of succession in the house of
Sardinia remained doubtful, if he who reigns at Naples continued
to reign there.

Italy, divided into non-confederate states, is not susceptible
of a real but only of a relative independence, which consists in
being submitted not to one influence only, but to several. The
relation which causes those influences to balance each other is
that which constitutes her equilibrium.

That the existence of this equilibrium is of importance to
Europe is a thing so obvious that it is unnecessary to question it ;
and it is no less obvious that, were Italy situated as has just been
surmised, all kind of equilibrium would cease for her.

What is necessary, and what can be done to establish it ?
Nothing except what justice requires or authorizes.

Naples must be restored to her legitimate sovereign, Tuscany
to the Queen of Etruria, not only the provinces on the Adriatic
that have not yet been ceded, but also the legations of Ravenna
and of Bologna, now vacant, must be returned to the Holy See.
Piombino, as well as the mines of the Island of Elba, under the
suzerainty of the crown of Naples, must go back to the prince of
that name to whom it belonged, and who, having been deprived
of both properties without indemnity, has been reduced to a
state bordering upon indigence.[1] To remove all doubts con-

---

[1] The principality of Piombino included in Tuscany, was about ten miles long and
contained an area of above fifty thousand acres. It belonged formerly to the family
Buoncompagni, who had bought it in 1634. The prince of Piombino was deposed

cerning the rights of the house of Carignan, and to aggrandize Sardinia.

If it were proposed to assembled Europe to declare :

That the sovereignty is acquired by the sole fact of conquest ; and that the patrimony of a prince who only lost it through his unswerving fidelity to the cause of Europe, should with the consent of Europe, belong to him into whose hands the misfortunes of Europe have alone caused it to fall, it is impossible to suppose that such a proposition would not be at once received with an unanimous cry of reprobation. All would feel that it tended to nothing less than to the overthrowing of the only barrier that the natural independence of peoples has permitted reason to raise between the right of sovereignty, and force, in order to restrain the one and preserve the other, and to the undermining of the very foundations of morality itself.

This is nevertheless what would be implied if it were possible for the congress to recognize as sovereign of the country him who reigns in Naples, and it is again what it will be reputed to have declared if it does not recognize Ferdinand IV. as king. For peoples would never understand that it should have consecrated by its silence the violation of a principle so important to all sovereigns, and yet have held it for true. They will conclude from it that this principle does not exist, and that force alone constitutes right.

Austria might object that she has given guarantees to him who reigns at Naples.[1] But the act by which one guarantees the possession of a thing which does not belong to him, though necessity may excuse that act, is, to say the least, null and void. That guarantee moreover was not given against a judgment of Europe, but against the man with whom all Europe was then at war.

It would undoubtedly be better that he who reigns at Naples should obtain no sovereignty. But the services he has rendered to the cause of Europe have been much talked of; if he has really rendered them, and if it be necessary to recompense him on that account, the king's ambassadors will not oppose something being given to him, but it must not belong to others ; it

---

in 1801. Bonaparte took possession of the principality and gave it to his sister Princess Eliza Baciocchi. The treaty of Vienna restored it to the family Buoncompagni, and the latter ceded it to the Grand-Duke of Tuscany for a sum of four millions seven hundred and four thousand francs.

[1] Murat had signed two treaties of January 6 and 11, 1814, the one with Austria, the other with England, by which those two powers guaranteed him his states, and even promised him an increase of territory at the expense of the States of the Church, in regard to which he undertook to add to the allied armies, thirty thousand men from his own troops.

may be anything which is unoccupied, such as a portion of the Ionian Isles.

No right was ever more legitimate than that of the Queen of Etruria to Tuscany. That country had been ceded by the grand-duke, and Charles IV. had acquired it for his daughter, giving in exchange the duchies of Parma, Piacenza, Guastalla, and Louisiana, with a certain number of vessels and millions. If, however, the restitution of Tuscany offered too many difficulties, and if, in its place, the duchies of Parma, Piacenza, and Guastalla should be offered, the king's ambassadors shall persuade those of Spain to content themselves with that offer, and accept it.

Austria had not only guaranteed to him who reigns at Naples the possession of that kingdom ; she had even engaged to procure him an aggrandizement to the extent of a territory of from four to six hundred thousand souls. The provinces of the Holy See on the Adriatic, of which three departments of the kingdom of Italy had been formed, have been intended to serve for the accomplishment of that promise, and continue for that reason to be occupied by the Neapolitan troops. If, as must be hoped, he who reigns at Naples, ceases to reign there, there will no longer be question of that promise, and the difficulty that Austria would have in keeping it might become a very good motive for her abandonment of him to whom she made it. But in any case, the king's ambassadors will second, by all the means in their power, the opposition that His Holiness will undoubtedly offer to the provinces being separated from the pontifical domain. They will in like manner, as far as depends upon them, contribute to the legations of Ravenna and of Bologna being restored to the Holy See. That of Ferrara being comprised in the territory which, according to the treaty of May 30, is destined to Austria, its restitution might cause great, and even insurmountable, difficulties. But if any arrangement can facilitate it, provided it be not of a nature to increase Austrian influence in Italy, the king's ambassadors shall give their support to it.

The Prince of Piombino, though a simple feudatory of the crown of Naples, having been deposed as though he had been a sovereign prince, shall be re-established in all the rights of which he has been deprived by violence.

The rights of the House of Carignan have been set forth with sufficient details, so that it is not necessary to speak of them again. It is only on the supposition that these rights be placed beyond all doubt, that Sardinia can be aggrandized, but in that case it is to be hoped that she will be as much aggrandized as the quantity of vacant territories will allow, in order to increase thereby, and ensure her independence.

In Italy, it is Austria who must be prevented from acquiring paramount power, by opposing other influences to hers. In Germany, it is Prussia. The exiguity of her monarchy makes ambition a sort of necessity to her. Any pretext seems good to. her. No scruples stop her. Her convenience forms her right. It is thus that, in the course of sixty-three years, she has raised her population from less than four millions of subjects to ten millions, and that she has been able to form for herself, if I may so term it, the frame of an immense monarchy, by acquiring here and there scattered territories, which she aims at uniting by incorporating in herself those that separate them. The terrible fall that her ambition brought upon her has not yet cured her of it. At this very moment, her emissaries and partisans are agitating Germany, by representing France as bent on invading her again, and Prussia, as the only power in a condition to defend her, and are asking that Germany be delivered up to Prussia that the latter may save her. She would have liked to have had Belgium. She would like to have all that lies between the present frontiers of France, the Meuse, and the Rhine. She wants Luxembourg. All is lost if Mayence is not given her. She can have no security, if she does not possess Saxony. It is said that the allies have arranged to re-establish her in the same degree of power in which she was before her fall, that is to say, with ten million subjects. If that were permitted, she would very soon have twenty, and the whole of Germany would be subjected to her. It is necessary, then, to put a rein to her ambition, by first restraining as much as possible, her status of possession in Germany, and afterwards by cutting short her influence by a federal organization.

Her status of possession shall be checked by the preservation of all the small states, and the aggrandisement of the medium ones.

All the small states should be preserved for the sole reason that they exist, with the single exception of the ecclesiastical principality of Aschaffenburg, whose preservation seems incompatible with the general plan of the distribution of territories; but a sufficient income ought to be assured to the former possessor.

If all the small states ought to be preserved, far more does this hold good of the kingdom of Saxony. The King of Saxony has governed his subjects for forty years like a father, giving an example of the virtues of both the man and the prince. Assailed for the first time by the tempest, at an advanced age, which should have brought him repose, and raised again forthwith by the hand that had vanquished him, and had crushed so many others, if he made mistakes, they should be imputed to an excusable fear, or to a sentiment that is always honourable to him who experiences it, whatever be its object. Those who reproach him for those mistakes have made far greater ones themselves, without having the same excuse. That which was given him, was given without his asking, or desiring it, or even knowing that he had it. He enjoyed prosperity with moderation, and now bears misfortune with dignity. To these motives, which are alone sufficient to guarantee him against being abandoned by the king, are joined the links of relationship,[1] and the necessity of preventing Saxony from falling a prey to Prussia, who, by such an acquisition, would take a long and decided step towards the absolute dominion of Germany.

This necessity is so great, that if, on a supposition hereafter to be mentioned, the King of Saxony should find himself called upon to take possession of another kingdom, that of Saxony must all the same not cease to exist, and must be given to the ducal branch, which ought to be especially agreeable to the Emperor of Russia, since his brother-in-law, the hereditary Prince of Weimar, would then find himself presumptive heir.

The king's ambassadors shall, consequently, support, by every means in their power, the cause of the King of Saxony, and, in every case, do all that is possible in order that Saxony may not become a Prussian province.

Important as it is that Prussia should not acquire Saxony, it is equally important that she be prevented from acquiring Mayence, or any portion whatever of the territory on the left bank of the Moselle ; that Holland be enabled to carry, as far as possible to the right bank of the river Meuse, the frontier that she is to have on that river ; as it is important that the requests for increase of territory which Bavaria, Hesse, Brunswick, and particularly Hanover, shall make (with the understanding that these demands shall bear only upon vacant territories), should be seconded, in order to render as small as possible the portion of vacant countries that shall remain for Prussia.

It is said that the allies have a plan, according to which Luxemburg and Mayence would belong to the confederation, and be occupied by federal troops. That plan would seem to suit the personal interests of France, and, for that reason, the king's ambassadors should, when supporting it, avoid doing so in a manner likely to give rise to suspicion.

Every confederation is a republic, and, to be well constituted, should have the spirit of one. Therefore, a confederation of princes could never be well constituted, for the spirit of the

[1] Louis XVIII. was by his mother, Marie-Josephe of Saxony, first cousin of the king Frederick-Augustus.

republic tends towards equality, and that of the monarch towards independence. But the question is not to give a perfect organization to the German confederation ; it suffices to give her such a one as will have the effect of preventing :

1. The oppression of subjects in the small states;
2. The oppression of the small states by the larger ones ;
3. The influence of the latter from changing themselves into domination, in such a manner that one or several of them could, for the furtherance of their own views, dispose of the power of all.

But these results can only be obtained by dividing power both in the small states, and in the confederation ; if it be concentrated in the latter, by having it change hands, and pass successively through as many hands as possible.

This is all that can be said here on the future federal organization of Germany. The king's ambassadors will not need to draw the plan of it. It will be sufficient for them to know in what spirit it should be made, and after what standard they are to judge the projects on which they shall be called upon to decide.

The re-establishment of the realm of Poland would be a good and very great improvement, but only under the three following conditions :

1. That it be independent ;
2. That it have a strong constitution ;
3. That it be not necessary to compensate Prussia and Austria for the portion that has respectively fallen to them.

Those conditions are all impossible, and the second more so than the two others.

In the first place, Russia does not wish for the re-establishment of Poland, in order to lose what she has acquired of it ; she wishes it so as to acquire what she does not possess of it. Thus, to re-establish Poland in order to give it entirely to Russia, and carry the population of the latter, in Europe, to forty-four millions of subjects, and extend her frontiers to the Oder, would mean creating so great and imminent a danger for Europe, that, although we must do everything to preserve peace, if the execution of such a plan could only be stopped by force of arms, not a single moment should be lost in taking them up. It would be vainly hoped that Poland, thus united to Russia, would detach herself from her of her own accord. It is not certain that she would wish to do so, it is less certain still that she could, and it is certain that, if she could, and would do so at a given time, she would escape one yoke, only to carry a new one ; for Poland, restored to independence, would infallibly be delivered up to anarchy. The size of the country excludes the existence of an aristocracy properly speaking, and there can exist no monarchy where the people are without civil liberty, and where the nobles possess political liberty or are independent, and where anarchy does not reign. Reason alone tells it and the history of all Europe proves it. Thus, how, on re-establishing Poland can political liberty be taken from the nobles, or civil liberty be given to the people ? That civil liberty could not be given by a declaration, or by a law. It is but a vain word, if the people, to whom it is given, have no independent means of existence, no property, no industry, and no arts, all of which no declaration nor law can give, and which can only be the work of time. Anarchy was a condition from which Poland could emerge only by the aid of an absolute power ; and as there did not exist in her the elements of that power, it was necessary that it come to her from outside, that is to say, that she fall under conquest. And she fell under it as soon as her neighbours wished, and the progress that has been made by those portions of her that have been allotted to nations more advanced in civilization, proves that it was fortunate for them to have fallen into their power. Let her be restored to independence and be given a king, no longer elective, but heredi- tary ; let there be added all imaginable institutions ; the less free the latter shall be, the more will they be opposed to the genius, customs, and recollections of the nobles, who will have to be subjected to them by force—and where is that force to come from ? And, on the other hand, the more liberty is given to those institutions, the more inevitably will Poland be plunged anew into anarchy, to end anew by being conquered. All this is because there is in that country, as it were, two peoples, for whom there must be two institutions each of which excludes the other. Being neither able to arrange that these two peoples be as one, nor to create the one power that could conciliate all ; being, on the other hand, unable, without evident peril to Europe, to give all Poland to Russia (and the mere addition of the duchy of Warsaw to that which she already possesses would mean giving her all Poland), what better can be done than to replace things in the same state in which they were before the last division ? That would be all the more advisable, that it would put an end to the pretensions of Prussia on the realm of Saxony ; for it is only as compensation, for what she should not recover, in the event of the re-establish- ment of Poland, that she dares to ask for Saxony.

Austria would also surely demand compensation for the five millions of subjects that the two Gallicias contain, or if she did not ask for it, she would become all the more exacting in all questions relative to Italy.

If nevertheless, contrary to all probability, the Czar of Russia consented to renounce that which he possesses of Poland (and it is clear that he could not do so without exposing himself to personal dangers on the part of the Russians), and if it were wished to make an experiment, the king, without expecting any favourable result from it, would not oppose it. In that case, it would be desirable that the King of Saxony, already sovereign of the duchy of Warsaw, whose father and ancestors have occupied the throne of Poland, and whose daughter was to bring the Polish crown as a dowry to her husband, should be made King of Poland.

But, with the exception of the case in which Poland could be re-established in complete independence of each of the three co-possessing courts, the only admissible proposition, and the only one to which the king could consent, is (save several rectifications of frontiers) to restore everything in Poland to the footing of the last division.

By remaining divided, Poland will not be annihilated for ever : the Poles no longer forming a political society, will continue to form a family. They will no longer have the same country, but they will have the same language, they will thus remain united by the strongest and most durable of all links. They will arrive, under foreign dominations, at the virile age which they have not been able to reach during nine centuries of independence, and the moment when they attain it will not be far from that of their emancipation, when they will all converge to the same centre.

Danzig must follow the destiny of Poland, of which she was only the emporium ; she will have to be free, if Poland recover her independence, or to submit again to the domination of Prussia, if the old division be maintained.

A disposition which could be made of the Ionian Islands, has already been indicated ; it is important that those islands, and especially that of Corfu, should belong neither to England nor to Russia, who both covet them, nor to Austria. Corfu is the key of the Adriatic Gulf. If, to the possession of Gibraltar and Malta, England added that of Corfu, she would be absolute mistress of the Mediterranean. Those islands would furnish Russia with a point of aggression against the Ottoman Empire, and with a point of support for fomenting an uprising among the Greeks. In the hands of Austria, Corfu would serve to establish and consolidate her dominion over Italy.

The order of Saint John of Jerusalem is without a capital, and it might be said, without asylum, since it lost Malta. The Catholic powers have an interest in its being restored and resuscitated from its ruins.   It is true that it ceded Malta, but it is equally true that it did so only in consequence of an invasion, that no motive of right, or even of utility, could justify or excuse.   It would be to the honour of England, who, by the way, profits by that injustice, to contribute towards a reparation, by uniting with the Catholic powers in order to obtain a compensation for the order.   Corfu could be given her without compromising the interests of any Christian state.   It shall ask the possession of it, and the king's ambassadors shall support this claim.

The island of Elba, being a possession which, at the death of him who occupies it, will become vacant, and only at the time when it shall become so, could be restored to its former masters, Tuscany and Naples, or given to Tuscany alone.

The future of all countries under conquest, of those which are not vacant, of those which are, and of those which will become so, shall thus be completely settled.

In some of those countries, certain Frenchmen possessed, by right of endowment, estates which the treaty of May 30 caused them to lose.   That harsh measure, which might be considered as unjust, concerning endowments situated in those countries that had been ceded, has been aggravated by the retro-active effect that was given it, by applying it to rents and revenues fallen due.   The king's ambassadors shall protest against such injustice, and shall do all in their power to get it repaired.   The allied sovereigns having given occasion to hope that they will make, and several having already made, exceptions to the clause which deprived the donees of their endowments, the king's ambassadors shall again do all in their power to effect that that favour be extended and accorded to as many donees as possible.

As to the right of navigation on the Rhine and on the Scheldt, as they are to be the same for all, France has nothing to desire, except that they be very moderate.   Owing to the free navigation of the Rhine and of the Scheldt, France will have the advantages that the possession of the countries crossed by those rivers would have given her, and which she has renounced, and she will not have the charges of their possession.   She cannot thus reasonably regret it.

The question of the abolition of the slave-trade is decided as regards France, who, on that point, has no more concessions to make ; for, if it were asked simply to remove, or merely shorten the agreed delay, she could not consent.   But the king has promised to unite all his efforts to those of England so as to effect that the universal abolition of slavery be pronounced. That promise must be discharged, because it has been made, and because it is of importance to France to have England on her side in the questions that interest her the most.

England, who has given herself up to conquest outside of Europe, brings a conservative spirit to the affairs of Europe. That proceeds, perhaps, simply from her insular position, that does not permit of any territory being added to her own, and from her relative weakness, that would not enable her to retain on the Continent any conquests she might already have made there. But, be it with her a necessity or a virtue, she has shown herself to be animated with a conservative spirit, even towards France, her rival, under the reign of Henry VIII., of Elizabeth, of Queen Anne, and perhaps also at a much more recent period.

France, bringing before the congress only thoroughly conservative views, has then occasion to hope that England will second her, provided that she herself satisfy England on the points she has most at heart, and England has nothing more at heart than the abolition of slavery. That which was, in its origin, but a matter of interest and speculation, has become for the English people, a passion carried to fanaticism, and one which the ministry is no longer at liberty to check ; that is why the king's ambassadors shall give every satisfaction to England on that point, by pronouncing themselves frankly and energetically for the abolition of slavery. But if Spain and Portugal, which are the only powers that have not yet bound themselves in that direction, consented only to give up the slave-trade after the expiration of a delay of more than five years, and if that delay were granted, the king's ambassadors should arrange that France be admitted to take advantage of it.

The present instructions are not given to the king's ambassadors as an absolute rule from which they must not deviate in any degree. They can relinquish that which is of a less interest to obtain that which is of a greater one. The points that are most important to France are classified according to their relative importance as follows—

1. That no opportunity be left to Austria to obtain possession for the princes of her house, or rather for herself, of the estates of the King of Sardinia ;

2. That Naples be restored to Ferdinand IV. ;

3. That the whole of Poland should not be placed in a position eventually to pass under the sovereignty of Russia.

4. That Prussia neither acquire the realm of Saxony, at least in totality, nor Mayence.

In making concessions on the other points, the king's ambassadors will make them bear only on matters of simple utility and not of obligation ; in the first place, because, for nearly all the various points to be decided by the congress, the rights result from one and the same principle, and that to forego that principle with regard to one point, would be to forego it with regard to all ; in the second place, because recent times have left impressions that it is of importance to efface. France is such a powerful state, that other nations can be tranquillized only by the idea of her moderation—an idea which they will accept all the more easily, that she will have given them a greater one of her justice.

The king having decided on having at the congress several representatives of his will, which must be one, his intention is, that no overture, proposal, or concession be made except with the consent of his Minister of Foreign Affairs, who shall himself go to Vienna, and then only in so far as he shall have decided what overtures, proposals, and concessions should be made.

PARIS, *August*, 1814.

Approved : signed, LOUIS.

And below : signed : PRINCE DE TALLEYRAND.

SUPPLEMENTARY INSTRUCTIONS
FROM THE KING TO HIS AMBASSADORS AND PLENIPOTEN-
TIARY MINISTERS AT THE CONGRESS OF VIENNA.

The king, conformably to the instructions given to his plenipotentiary ministers before their departure for the Vienna Congress, and informed by their correspondence of an agreement formed between Russia and Prussia to establish the semblance of Poland under Russian dependence, and to aggrandize Prussia by Saxony, has judged it advisable to address to his plenipotentiaries the following supplementary instructions :—

It appearing that, the same reasons that induced his Majesty to think that the aggrandizement of Russia by Poland's being subjected to her rule, and the union of Saxony to the Prussian monarchy, would be equally contrary to the principles of justice and of public law, and to the establishment of a system of solid and durable equilibrium in Europe, have been taken into consideration by other powers, and that it will be possible perhaps to cause, without disturbing the peace, Russia and Prussia to adopt views more moderate and more consonant with the general interest of Europe, by an agreement formed in opposition to that which now exists between them ; His Majesty authorizes his plenipotentiaries to declare to the Austrian and Bavarian plenipotentiaries that their courts can count on the most active military co-operation, on his part, in opposing the views of Russia and Prussia, as well on Poland, as on Saxony. The king's plenipotentiary ministers can confide the contents of the present instructions to the English plenipotentiaries, if they be of opinion that that might determine the cabinet of St. James's to act in concert with France, Austria, and Bavaria, or at least, to remain neutral. It would especially be well to confide these instructions to Count von Münster,[1] the Hanoverian plenipotentiary.

PARIS, *October* 25, 1814.

(Signed) LOUIS.

And underneath :—

The State-minister, charged *ad interim* with the portfolio of Foreign Affairs.

Signed, COMTE FRANÇOIS DE JAUCOURT.

---

[1] Ernest-Frederick, Count von Münster, born at Osnabrück (Hanover) ; in 1766, he became intimate counsellor of the Elector of Hanover, King of England. He was appointed minister at St. Petersburg. When Hanover fell into Napoleon's hands, Münster took refuge in London. King George entrusted him with various important diplomatic missions. In 1814, he represented the Elector of Hanover at the Congress of Vienna, and in the following year he was placed at the head of the Hanoverian government. He remained in charge of it until 1830, and died in 1841.

END OF THE SEVENTH PART.

APPENDICES.

APPENDIX I.[1]

We subjoin here an account of the mission of M. de Vitrolles in 1814, drawn up by the Duc de Dalberg. This document, written throughout in the duke's own hand, was found among the papers of the Prince de Talleyrand.

The mission of M. de Vitrolles to the Congress of Châtillon was only undertaken as a means of *obtaining the information* desired at Paris, as to the final intentions of the allies with regard to the Emperor.

There existed in Paris neither plan nor conspiracy against the emperor; but the conviction was unanimous that his power was undermined by his follies and extravagances, and that he would himself be the victim of his foolish resistance and policy of continual deception !

Anxiety as to the future was increasing.

Baron Louis said to M. de Dalberg one day: "The man [meaning the emperor] is a corpse, but he does not stink yet: that's the fact of the matter." The enemy was then thirty leagues from Paris.

Propositions offered by the Emperor Alexander to the Grand Duchess of Baden, and insinuations let fall by him to Bernadotte and Eugène de Beauharnais, were well known at Paris.

The intrigues of Fouché with the family of Murat were suspected; in the south, the Duc d'Angoulême was approaching ; the Duc de Berry was intriguing in Brittany ; the Comte d'Artois had drawn near to the German frontier, and was already at Basel ! Risings had occurred at Vesoul and Troyes ! People were so weary in France of the excessive

[1] See page 114.

military despotism of the emperor, and expected so little concession from him, that it began to be a serious question as to
how far the crisis brought about by him would drag France and
Europe. It was no longer an ordinary war ; all the nations
were involved in the struggle. This situation alarmed every
one ; and its solution was sought on all sides !

The English newspapers were had by M. Martin, commissioner of the police at Boulogne, who sent them to Abbé de
Pradt ! At the Ministries of War and Foreign Affairs it had been
forbidden to communicate them, especially to M. de Talleyrand.

The latter desired to know what the allied powers would do
as a last resource ; he spoke of it to M. de Dalberg ; the advice
of the latter, was to ascertain this by sending some agent to
Counts von Stadion and Nesselrode.

The choice fell on M. de Vitrolles, a friend of M. Mollien
and of M. de Hauterive, at this time a man who had very pronounced opinions on the progress of constitutional ideas, on
which he had written a very good pamphlet, which he published
later.

M. de Vitrolles set out ; his instructions were limited to
this : he was to go to Châtillon to explain to Count von
Stadion or Count Nesselrode, the danger incurred by every
one by arriving at no definite decision ; after which he was to
return to Paris bringing back the reply to the question as to
whether or not the allies intended to maintain the emperor in
power.

M. de Vitrolles, believing that there were more facilities for
reaching Châtillon by the north route, and by skirting the
armies, only arrived at Châtillon on March 10, 1814.

He introduced himself to Count von Stadion, and proved his
identity to him by having him read two names written in his
album by the Duc de Dalberg (they were the names of two
sisters, whom the writer and reader had both known at Vienna).

He declared to Count von Stadion that the state of opinion in
France and the dispositions of *several people* demanded a
change and legislative guarantees against the violence and
character of the emperor, that it was important to enforce a
speedy decision, in order that the war might not take a turn
which should defer peace for a long time.

Count von Stadion promised to return to Troyes, where the
political cabinet of the allies was, and where the emperor and
the King of Prussia were to be found.

Baron de Vitrolles set out with a letter from Count von
Stadion to Prince Metternich. The latter told him— "That he
wished, without unnecessary circumlocution, to inform him of the

unanimous opinion of the powers, viz., that they considered Bonaparte was a man with whom it was impossible to treat any longer ; that on the day that he experienced reverses, he appeared to cede everything ; that when he gained some slight success, he returned to pretensions as exaggerated as inadmissible ; that it was therefore desirable that another sovereign should be appointed in France, and that affairs should be regulated in such a manner as to give Russia, Austria, and France, an equal weight in Europe ; that Prussia should remain a power, half as strong as each of the three others ; that with regard to the new sovereign to be appointed for France, it was impossible to think of the Bourbons, because of the friends and supporters of these princes."

We must here mention that M. de Vitrolles' policy was that peace could only be restored to France and Europe by the re-establishment of the House of Bourbon, with a charter guaranteeing to France the enjoyment of public liberties.

He was on intimate terms with Madame Étienne de Durfort, and from her he had received on setting out, a message for the Comte d'Artois, which would give him access to that prince, and win his confidence.

M. de Vitrolles saw Count Nesselrode after an interview with Prince Metternich. He received almost the same information from him. He was at the same time told that nothing could dissuade the allies from acting unanimously, and in perfect agreement, till the general peace was established on a firm footing ; that no intrigue would gain a hearing.

A few days after, M. de Vitrolles solicited from Count Nesselrode an audience with the Emperor of Russia. That minister told him that he had already thought of this himself, and that he was afraid it would prove rather difficult ; he nevertheless secured this interview, by informing the emperor that M. de Vitrolles was in relation with Prince Talleyrand, Abbé de Pradt, and the Duc de Dalberg. The emperor repeated almost the same things as the ministers. He said that he had thought of placing at first Bernadotte and then Beauharnais on the throne of France ; but that motives of a different nature forbade this plan : that, besides, his intention was above all to consult the wish of the French themselves, and that should they even wish to establish a republic, the allies would perhaps offer no objection.

The emperor expatiated at even greater length than the plenipotentiaries on the impossibility of thinking of the Bourbons, and on the unfavourable opinion the sovereigns had of them.

M. de Vitrolles, according to his own account, had a sudden

inspiration at this point, and invited the emperor, instead of following the ordinary operations of war to march at once on Paris ; for that he could there judge of the state of public opinion.

On the other hand, General *Pozzo di Borgo asserts* that it was he who persuaded the emperor to take this step, and persons who were qualified to know, declare that the emperor refused to decide anything, without having first consulted Prince Talleyrand, and that it was his advice that would have to be followed as to the future of France.

The last words of the emperor to M. de Vitrolles were : " Monsieur, our conversation of to-day will have ominous results for Europe ; I set out to-morrow in person for the general headquarters."

As a matter of fact, he did start on the morrow, in order to confer with Prince von Schwarzenberg.

After the capitulation of Paris, Count Nesselrode called, in the morning, on Prince Talleyrand, to whose residence M. de Dalberg had also been summoned. The emperor entered Paris at mid-day, and lodged at the house of Prince Talleyrand.

M. de Vitrolles also saw the Emperor of Austria, who told him that he was about to return to Dijon, that the Emperor of Russia and the King of Prussia would take at Paris the course that circumstances indicated, and that he would go there himself afterwards.

M. de Vitrolles, instead of returning to Paris, paid a visit to *Monsieur*. He heard, on the way, that Bonaparte had had some fresh successes ; that the negotiations at Châtillon had been affected by that news, and that the Comte d'Artois was at Nancy. He arrived there on March 23.

I give no account of his doings at Paris, where he only arrived several days after the allies, after having written to Prince Talleyrand a letter in the name of *Monsieur*, who found fault with his having allowed the Senate to express wishes for a constitutional regime.

APPENDIX II.[1]

On the day after the sitting of the senate, Prince Talleyrand received the following letter from Benjamin Constant. This letter was found among the papers of Prince Talleyrand.

" You have gloriously solved a long puzzle, and however strange, however inconvenient, this manner of congratulating you may be I cannot resist thanking you for having at once broken

[1] See page 123.

the power of tyranny, and laid down some basis for liberty. Without the one, I should not have been able to thank you for the other. 1789 and 1814 are glorious annals in your life. You resemble Maurice of Saxony in history, and you will not die at the moment of success. You will not accuse me of addressing this homage to your prosperity only. My past life ought to save me from being thus suspected. There is also no personal motive in what I do. I left France to escape a yoke I could not destroy, and although I have endeavoured to be reconciled to her, in order to serve her, bonds that are dear to me detain me elsewhere. But it is pleasant to me to express my admiration, when feeling it for one, who is at once the saviour, and the most courteous, of Frenchmen : I write this after having read the basis of the proposed constitution.

"Pardon me if I add no title to those you already possess : Europe and history will readily award them you : but the finest will always be that of President of the Senate.

"With homage and respect.

" BENJAMIN CONSTANT.

"*April* 3, 1814."

APPENDIX III.[1]

The following letter was addressed by Fouché to the emperor at the moment when he had just accepted the sovereignty of the Island of Elba, which the allied sovereigns had offered him. As the enclosed letter indicates, this note reached the emperor through the hands of Prince Talleyrand, amongst whose papers it was found.

I have the honour to forward to your Highness two letters in place of the one I had promised.

I thought fit to communicate to *Monsieur* the letter I have written to Bonaparte.

I have added some reflections which I thought needful under the circumstances ; your Highness knows that those whose anxieties I do not share suspect me of pusillanimous transactions.

I shall call on your Highness at half-past five, and shall have the honour of dining with you ; your Highness may take it for granted that I shall seize every possible opportunity of seeing you and profiting by your conversation.

(Signed)   THE DUC D'OTRANTE.

April 23, 1814.

P.S.—I beg your Highness to be so good as to forward the letter to Bonaparte, when it has been communicated to *Monsieur.*

[1] See page 125.

" SIRE,

"When France and a part of Europe were at your feet, I ventured, even at the risk of displeasing you, to consistently tell you the truth, for your own interests. To-day you are in misfortune, and, though I fear to wound you yet more if I speak sincerely, it is both useful, and even necessary, to you, that I should do so.

"You have accepted the isle of Elba, and its sovereignty. I am lending an attentive ear to all that is said of this sovereignty and this island. I think I owe it to you, to assure you that its situation in Europe suits yours but little, and that the title of sovereign of some acres of land, still less befits him who possessed an immense empire.

"I beg you to weigh these two considerations, and you will feel how well founded they both are.

"The island of Elba is not very far from Africa, Greece, and Spain. It nearly touches the coasts of Italy and France ; from this island, the sea, the wind, and a felucca, can quickly transport you to all the countries that are most liable to outbreaks, revolts, and revolutions. To-day there is no stability anywhere. In the present uneasy state of Europe, a genius such as yours will always cause uneasiness and suspicion to the powers.

"You will be accused without being guilty, but without being guilty, you will do wrong, for these alarms are bad both for governments and peoples.

"The king now about to reign over France, wishes to reign by justice alone ; but you know how clever hatred can be in giving to slander the colour of truth !

"The titles which you preserve, and which cause you to remember what you have lost, only serve to embitter your recollections : they will seem not the relic, but so many empty badges of vanished grandeurs. I say more : without honouring you, they will bring you more prominently into notice. Men will say that you only retain these titles, because you refuse to let slip any of your pretensions. They will say that the rock of Elba is the fulcrum for placing the levers with which to lift the world. Permit me to tell you what I think about it, after mature reflection. It would be more glorious, and more con-soling for you, to live as a simple citizen ; and to-day, the surest, and the most comfortable, refuge for a man like you, would be the United States of America.

"There you would begin your existence anew, among a new people ; they would admire your genius, without fearing it. You would be under the protection of laws that are just and in-violable towards all that breathes, in the land of the Franklins,

the Washingtons, and the Jeffersons.   You would prove to these
people, that if you had been born amongst them, you would have
had the same thoughts, feelings, and aspirations, as they ; that
you would have preferred their virtues and liberty, to ruling
over all the countries of the earth.

"I have the honour to be your Majesty's most humble and
respectful servant.

"(Signed)   THE DUC D'OTRANTE.

"PARIS, *April* 23, 1814.

"P.S.—I must inform your Majesty that I have asked no
one's advice as to writing this letter, nor have I received any
instructions."

APPENDIX IV.[1]

*At this point a long note in the manuscript is inserted, written
probably by M. de Bacourt, according to a chapter of M. de Cape-
figue's work, "L'Histoire des Traités de 1815." The author
states that the Emperor Napoleon had accepted the ultimatum of
the allies at the Châtillon Congress, and that the conditions obtained
by M. de Talleyrand on the 30th of May, after the fall of the
Empire, were much better.*

On the 17th of February, 1814, the Châtillon Congress
decided the formula of the treaty to be proposed to the Emperor
Napoleon, and Prince Metternich sent it to M. de Caulaincourt.
Here it is :—

"In the name of the Most Holy and Indivisible Trinity.

"Their Imperial Majesties of Austria and Russia, His
Majesty the King of the United Kingdom of Great Britain and
Ireland, and His Majesty the King of Prussia, acting in the
name of all their allies, on the one side, and of His Majesty the
Emperor of the French on the other, wishing to cement the
repose and future welfare of Europe by a solid and lasting peace,
by land and sea ; and having, with a view to this happy result,
assembled their plenipotentiaries at Châtillon to discuss the
conditions of this peace, the said plenipotentiaries have agreed
on the following articles :—

"Article I.—There shall be peace and amnesty between
their Imperial Majesties of Austria and Russia, His Majesty the
King of the United Kingdom of Great Britain and Ireland, and
His Majesty the King of Prussia, acting at the same time in the

[1] See page 131.

name of all their allies, and His Majesty the Emperor of the French, their heirs and successors for ever.

"The high contracting parties bind themselves to employ all their influence in maintaining, for the future happiness of Europe, the good harmony, so happily established among them.

"Article II.—His Majesty the Emperor of the French, renounces for himself and his successors, all acquisitions, alliances, or incorporations, made by France since the commencement of the war in 1792.

"His Majesty equally renounces all constitutional authority, direct or indirect, beyond the ancient limits of France as established before the war of 1792, as well as all titles derived from them, namely, those of King of Italy, King of Rome, Protector of the Rhine Confederation, and Mediator of the Swiss Confederation.

"Article III.—The high contracting parties formally and solemnly recognize the principle of the sovereignty and independence of all the states of Europe, as they shall be definitely constituted in the final treaty of peace.

"Article IV.—His Majesty the Emperor of the French recognizes expressly the following reconstitution of the countries bordering on France :—

"1. Germany, composed of independent states, united by a federal tie.

"2. Italy, divided into independent states, situated between the Austrian possessions and France.

"3. Holland, under the sovereignty of the House of Orange, with an increase of territory.

"4. Switzerland, a free and independent state, replaced in its former limits, and under the protection of all the Great Powers, France included.

"5. Spain, under the dominion of Ferdinand VII., in its former limits.

"His Majesty the Emperor of the French further recognizes the right of all the allied powers to determine, according to the existing treaties between the powers, the limits and relations of the countries ceded by France, as of their own states among themselves, without France having the power to interfere in any way.

"Article V.—On his part, his Britannic Majesty consents to restore to France (with the exception of the Isles called Saintes) all the conquests which have been made by him during the war, and which are at present in the power of his Britannic Majesty, in the West Indies, in Africa, and in America.

"The island of Tobago, in accordance with Article II. of the present treaty, will continue to belong to Great Britain, and the allies promise to do their best to persuade their Majesties of Sweden and Portugal to put no obstacle in the way of the restoration of Guadaloupe and Cayenne to France.

"All the settlements and factories taken by conquest from France to the east of the Cape of Good Hope, with the exception of the isles of Mauritius (Ile de France), of Bourbon, and their dependencies, shall be restored to her. France shall not re-enter those of the above-mentioned settlements and factories which are situated in the continent of India, and within the boundaries of British possessions, unless she recognize them as commercial settlements only, and she promises in consequence to construct no fortifications, and never to settle any garrisons, or military forces of any kind whatever, beyond what may be necessary for maintaining order in the said settlements.

"The restitutions above-mentioned, in Asia, Africa, and America, shall not include any possession which was not completely under the dominion of France, before the commencement of the war of 1792.

"The French government promises to forbid the importation of slaves into all the colonies and possessions restored by the present treaty, and to forbid her subjects, by the most efficacious means, to engage in the traffic of negroes at all.

"The island of Malta, with its dependencies, will remain entirely under the dominion of his Britannic Majesty.

"Article VI.—His Majesty the Emperor of the French will give up, immediately after the ratification of the present preliminary treaty, all fortresses and forts of the countries ceded, as well as those which his troops still occupy in Germany, without exception, Mayence being specially mentioned : those of Hamburg, Antwerp, Bergen-op-Zoom, are to be ceded within a delay of six days ; Mantua, Palma-Nuova, Venice, and Peschiera, and the fortified places of the Oder and the Elbe, in fifteen days ; all other forts and fortresses, with the shortest delay possible, which must not exceed fifteen days. These forts and fortresses are to be given up in the condition in which they now are, with all their artillery, ammunition of war, and various stores, archives &c. . . . . . ; the French garrisons of these forts shall take away their arms, baggage, and all private property.

"His Majesty the Emperor of the French will also give up to the allied armies within the space of four days the fortresses of Besançon, Belfort, and Huningen, which shall remain as pledges till the time of the ratification of the final peace, and which are to be kept in the state in which they shall have been ceded, according as the allied armies evacuate French territory.

"Article VII.—The generals in command shall, without delay, appoint commissioners charged with determining the line of demarcation between the various armies.

"Article VIII.—As soon as the present preliminary treaty shall have been mutually accepted and ratified, hostilities shall cease both by land and sea.

"Article IX.—The present preliminary treaty shall be followed, with the shortest delay possible, by a definite treaty of peace.

"Article X.—The ratifications of the preliminary treaty shall be exchanged within four days, or sooner if possible."

M. de Caulaincourt, according to the orders of Napoleon tried to get better conditions than those enclosed in the projected treaty. His hesitation, which must be attributed to the vicissitudes of the strife which the Emperor Napoleon was undergoing, now victorious, now beaten, in his encounters with the allied armies, provoked from Prince Metternich the following letter, addressed to M. de Caulaincourt:

"March 18, 1814.

"Affairs are taking a very unfavourable turn, Monsieur le Duc. The day that a definite decision for peace shall have been arrived at, with its indispensable sacrifices, come and sign it, but not to be the interpreter of inadmissible projects. The points at issue are too important for it to be possible to add further romances to the Emperor's life without his incurring great dangers. What do the allies risk? At the very worst, after the greatest reverses, they can only be forced to quit the territory of old France. What will the Emperor Napoleon have gained? The people of Belgium are making enormous efforts at the present time. All the left bank of the Rhine is to be put under arms. Savoy, spared hitherto, in order to leave it at the disposal of the first comer, will be forced to revolt, and there will be against the person of the Emperor Napoleon plots which can no longer be prevented.

"You will see that I speak frankly, as to the man of peace. I shall always be of this mind. You, should know our views, principles, and wishes. The first are European, and therefore, French; the second tend to interest Austria in the well-being of France; the third are in favour of a dynasty so closely bound to that of Austria as is that of the emperor Napoleon.

"I have shown you, my dear Duc, the most complete confidence, in order to put an end to the dangers which threaten

France ; it still depends, on your master, as to whether peace is to be made ; very shortly, perhaps, it will no longer be in his power. The throne of Louis XIV. with the additions of Louis XV. is a sufficiently fine one not to be staked on a single trump. I will do all I can to retain Lord Castlereagh a few days. If this minister is once allowed to depart, no chance of peace will be left.

"Be pleased to accept　.　.　.　.　.

"PRINCE VON METTERNICH."

This letter is important : it shows the position of Austria, who can no longer stand aloof, and must go with the allies : the latter are marching on Paris. It was then alone that Napoleon decided to accept the conditions of the allies. The fact of his having accepted them has been denied ; it is said that the emperor refused the humiliating terms proposed by the allies. This is not true : he accepted them, late indeed, but he did accept them.

The following is the letter of M. de Caulaincourt, addressed to Prince Metternich, which was despatched from Doulevent on *the 25th of March* by M. de Gallebois, orderly of Marshal Berthier :—

"DOULEVENT, *March* 25, 1814.

"I only reached the emperor to-night. His Majesty immediately gave me his final orders for the conclusion of the peace. He gave me, at the same time, all the powers necessary for negotiating and signing it with the ministers of the allied courts, this means being, in reality, better than any other for assuring its speedy accomplishment. I therefore hasten to inform you that I am ready to return to headquarters, and await the reply of your Excellency at the outposts. Our zeal will prove to the allied powers how strongly the emperor is bent on peace, and that, on the part of France, no delay will be opposed to the salutary work which is to ensure the peace of the world.

"CAULAINCOURT, DUC DE VICENCE."

This letter is dated the 25th of March, a month after the ultimatum of the allies : a second letter, also from M. de Caulaincourt to Prince Metternich, was sent off on the same day ; it agreed to everything :—

"YOUR HIGHNESS,—

"I have only just arrived, and hasten to execute the commands of the emperor, and to put in my letter all that I owe to the confidence displayed in yours.

"The emperor authorizes me to renew the negotiations in

the frankest and most positive manner. I therefore ask for the facilities that you have led me to expect, that I may arrive as soon as possible. I beg of your Highness not to leave to others the care of restoring peace to the world. There is no reason why it should not be done in four days, if your kindly spirit presides, and if they are as frank as ourselves in their wishes for it. Let us seize the occasion, and many faults and misfortunes will be remedied. Your Highness' task is glorious, mine will be very painful ; but since the tranquillity and welfare of so many peoples will result from it, I shall put no less zeal and devotion into it than yourself.

"CAULAINCOURT, DUC DE VICENCE."

This is what is certain, and is stated in authentic documents ; Napoleon accepted at the end of March the frontier of the old monarchy with all the harsh conditions laid down by the allies ; he gave up the fortresses, and the fleet of Antwerp (for which Prince Talleyrand has been so much blamed) ; as pledges he gave the fortresses of Besançon, Belfort, and Huningen, which the Bourbons did not do in 1814. That is the truth. To deny that Napoleon definitely accepted the ultimatum of the allies at Châtillon, is to ignore all the correspondence of M. de Caulaincourt and his ulterior negotiations at Paris.

Those who have with much simplicity written that, in the two restorations, there were disloyalties and treasons without number, have not sufficiently remarked that the first of all treasons is the suicide of power ; when it gives the blow to itself, is it astonishing that its supporters should desert it ?

The following truths are shown by the clearest evidence :—

1. At Prague, in 1813, Napoleon had it in his power to make peace by giving up Illyria, and the Hanseatic towns, and allowing the independence of Germany and Spain.

2. At Frankfort, he could have made peace (December 1813) by keeping the natural boundaries of the Rhine, the Alps, and the Pyrenees.

3. At Châtillon (March, 1814), in the midst of our misfortunes, he had accepted this peace on most humiliating terms, demanding that the ancient boundaries be kept ; the surrender of almost all our colonies ; the occupation of Besançon, Belfort and Huningen by the enemy ; the surrender of the fleet of Antwerp, and of all the ammunition of the garrisons.

4. By the treaties of April 24 and May 30, 1814, the Bourbons gained a larger frontier for France, and at the Congress of Vienna, Prince Talleyrand succeeded in regaining the preponderance of France in Europe.

PART VIII.

CONGRESS OF VIENNA.

1814—1815.

Talleyrand's arrival at Vienna—Dispositions of the Allies towards France—
The position of the French plenipotentiaries at the Congress—Difficulties to be contended with—Opening of the Congress—The intentions of
the first-class Powers—Talleyrand finds unhoped-for support in Spain
and the second-class Powers—Want of courtesy towards Talleyrand—
Defeats the aim of the Allies—The first meeting of the Congress
attended by Talleyrand—Prince Metternich's speech—Talleyrand's
reply—*Puissances Alliées*—Count de Labrador's motion in support of
Talleyrand's proposals—Embarrassment of the plenipotentiaries of the
Allied Powers—The Congress agrees to the annulling of the protocols of
the preceding sittings—Distribution of the work of the Congress—Change
of disposition towards France—The anniversary service of the death of
Louis XVI.—The Congress at work—The fate of the kingdom of
Saxony and of the Grand Duchy of Warsaw—Prussia's designs—Talleyrand demurs to the recognition of her claims—The sacred principle of
legitimacy—*Suum cuique*—The laxity of the public law of Europe
—Growing tendency to uphold usurpations—Indifference of the Allies as
to the rights of the House of Bourbon—Obstacles encountered by
Talleyrand in enforcing the triumph of legitimacy—Hostile attitude of
Russia towards France—Compromise offered—" I am not here to
strike a bargain ! "—" No compromise with principles ! "—England
backs up the views of Russia and Prussia on Saxony—Her delusion—
Doubtful attitude of Austria—Talleyrand wins her support—He succeeds
in dispelling the prejudices of England—A secret alliance between
France, Austria, and England, against Russia and Prussia—The
prestige of principles—Discord among the Allies—Prussia gives way—
Napoleon's return from Elba—Anxiety of the Congress—The Comtesse
de Brionne—" Politics must wait ! "—Indecision of the King of Saxony—
His interview with Metternich, Wellington, and Talleyrand—A plenipotentiary of Saxony at the Congress—Russia compelled to desist—The
deliberations of the Congress concerning Poland—France disposed to
admit the restoration of independent Poland—Russia's ministers give

in—Ferdinand IV. and Murat—The latter defeated by the Austrians—
Talleyrand created Duc of Dino—Sardinia' and the House of Carignan
—Switzerland's neutrality—The Netherlands—The German Confederation—Louis XVIII. at Ghent—The Congress, at Talleyrand's suggestion,
denounces the *usurper*—The Powers rush to arms—Louis XVIII. admitted into the Alliance of Europe against Napoleon—Correspondence
exchanged between Louis XVIII. and Talleyrand at the Congress—
Text of the Secret Treaty of Defensive Alliance, concluded January 3,
1815, between Austria, France, and Great Britain—Napoleon acquaints
the Czar Alexander with the text of the above-mentioned Treaty—
Interview between Alexander and Prince Metternich—Napoleon's aims
defeated—Indulgence of the Czar for Prince Metternich—The Czar
Alexander incensed at Talleyrand's duplicity.

I ARRIVED at Vienna September 23, 1814. I repaired to the
" Hôtel Kaunitz," which had been hired for the French legation.
On entering, the porter handed me several letters addressed :—
" To Prince Talleyrand, *Hôtel Kaunitz.*" The two names thus
side by side appeared to me a good omen.

The day after my arrival, I presented myself at the houses of
the members of the diplomatic corps. They all seemed to me
rather surprised at the little advantage they had derived from
the capitulation of Paris. They had just traversed countries that
had been ravaged by war for many years, in which they had
heard, they said, but words of hatred and vengeance against
France, for having overwhelmed them with taxes, and treated
them with the arrogance of a victor. My new colleagues assured
me that they had been reproached everywhere for their weakness
in signing the treaty of Paris. I therefore did not find them
very enthusiastic over the satisfaction to be derived from
generosity, but rather disposed to excite each other about the
pretensions they were to advance. Each was perusing the treaty
of Chaumont, which had not only tightened the bonds of an
alliance destined to last for the present war, but had also laid
down conditions for an alliance which should survive it,
and bind the allies together even in the remote future.
And moreover, how could they make up their minds to admit
to the council of Europe the very power against which Europe
had been in arms during twenty years ? The minister of a
country so newly reconciled, they said, ought to think himself

very fortunate in being allowed to give in his assent to the resolutions of the ambassadors of the other powers.

Thus, at the opening of the negotiations, all the cabinets
regarded themselves as being, notwithstanding the peace, in
an attitude which, if not hostile, was at least very equivocal,
with France! They all thought, more or less, that it would
have been to their interest that she should have been more
enfeebled still. Unable to do anything in that direction, they
endeavoured to at least diminish her influence. I saw that they
were all agreed on those various points.

It remained for me to hope that there would be among
the powers some divergence of opinion, when they came to
distribute the numerous territories that the war had put at
their disposal, each one desiring, either to obtain for itself, or
to give to the states dependent upon it, a considerable portion
of the conquered territories. It was specially desired, at the
same time, to exclude from the division those countries which
it was feared would prove too independent. That style of contest, however, offered me but scant opportunity for interfering
with matters ; for previous arrangements, by which the disposal
of the most important territories had been regulated, existed
between the powers. To succeed in modifying those arrangements, or in having them completely renounced, according to the
dictates of justice, there was more than prejudices to remove,
more than pretensions to check, more than ambition to defeat.
It was necessary to annul all that had been done without
France. For, if they consented to admit us to take a share in
the acts of the congress, it was for the sake of form only, and in
order to deprive us of the means of contesting their validity ;
but it was intended that France should have nothing to say
in the resolutions already settled, and that were looked upon as
accomplished facts.

Before giving here, that which, in my opinion, constitutes the
most faithful picture of the Vienna Congress, that is to say, my
official correspondence with the Department of Foreign Affairs
of France, and my private correspondence with King Louis
XVIII., as well as the letters from that sovereign during the
congress, I believe I should furnish a rapid but general glance

on the progress of the deliberations of that great assembly. The details of it will subsequently be better understood.

The opening of the congress had been fixed for the 1st of October. I had been at Vienna since September 23, but I had been preceded there by several days, by the ministers who, having directed the war, and repented of peace, wished to take advantage of their position at the congress. It was not long before I was informed that they had already formed a commission, and were holding among themselves conferences, of which a protocol had been prepared. Their object was to decide alone what ought to be submitted to the deliberations of the congress, and that too, without the assistance of either France, Spain, or any power of the second order ; to these however they would afterwards communicate, in the form of a proposition, what would in reality be a resolution, viz., the different articles they should have determined upon. I made no remonstrances. I continued to see them, without speaking of business. I limited myself to communicating to the ministers of the secondary powers, who had a common interest with me, the dissatisfaction I felt. Discovering also, in the past policy of their countries, traces of confidence in France, they very soon looked upon me as their support, and once assured of their assent in all that I was about to do, I officially pressed the opening of the congress. In my first requests, I acted as though I had no knowledge of the conferences that had been held. The opening of the congress was fixed for a certain day. That day passed ; I entreated that another should be fixed in the near future. I gave it to be understood that it was necessary that I should not remain too long absent from France. A few replies, evasive at first, caused me to repeat my entreaties. I even went so far as to complain a little, but was finally obliged to make use of the personal influence that I had fortunately acquired in the previous negotiations, over the principal personages of the congress. Prince Metternich and Count Nesselrode, not wishing to be disobliging to me, had both invited me to a conference which was to have been held at the office of the minister of foreign affairs. Count de Labrador, minister of Spain, with whom I had the honour to support a common

cause in the deliberations of the congress, received the same
invitation.

I went to the office of the minister of state at the hour
indicated, and found there, Lord Castlereagh,[1] Prince von
Hardenberg,[2] Herr von Humboldt, and Herr von Gentz,[3] a
man of distinguished talents, who fulfilled the functions of
secretary. The protocol of the preceding sittings was on the
table. I mention all the details of that first sitting, because it
decided the position of France at the congress. Prince Metternich opened it by a few sentences on the duty incumbent on the
congress to give solidity to the peace which had just been restored
to Europe. Prince von Hardenberg added, that in order to consolidate the peace it was indispensable that the agreements the
war had caused them to enter into should be religiously kept ;
and that such was the intention of the *allied powers.*

Placed by the side of Prince von Hardenberg, I was naturally
forced to speak after him, and after having said a few words on
the good fortune of France in finding herself in relations of confidence and friendship with all the cabinets of Europe, I remarked
that Prince Metternich and Prince von Hardenberg had let fall an

[1] Robert Stewart, Marquis of Londonderry, Viscount Castlereagh, born in 1769, in
Ireland, was elected at twenty-one to the House of Commons. In 1797, he became Lord of the Privy Seal of Ireland, then secretary of the Lord-Lieutenant
Camden, and member of the Privy Council of Ireland. Strongly attached to Pitt he
was appointed Minister of War, and of the Colonies in 1805. The death of Pitt
brought about the dissolution of the ministry ; but Castlereagh took office again in
1807. He retired in 1809. In 1812, he returned to power as Minister of Foreign
Affairs, and was the moving spirit of the ministry of Lord Liverpool. He had considerable influence over the events of 1814 and 1815 ; he was present at the congresses
of Châtillon and Vienna. He died in 1822. It is known that he committed suicide.

[2] Charles-Augustus, Prince von Hardenberg, a Prussian Statesman, born in 1750,
in Hanover. He was first in the service of the elector, passing afterwards to that
of Brunswick, and became, a short time after, minister of the Margrave of Baireuth
and Anspach. These principalities having been united to Prussia in 1791, Hardenberg
became minister of the king of Prussia. In 1795, he signed the peace of Basel with
France. In 1804, he replaced Count von Haugwitz as Minister of Foreign Affairs,
but resigned after the battle of Austerlitz. He took office again after the battle of Jena,
but was obliged to retire after the peace of Tilsit. In 1810, he was appointed
Chancellor of State. After the campaign of Russia, he actively prosecuted the war
against France, and was one of the signatories of the treaty of Paris. He was
present at the Congress of Vienna. In 1817 he became president of the Council
of State, and died in 1822.

[3] Frederick von Gentz, born in 1764, was first, secretary general of the Minister
of Finance of Prussia, then counsellor at Vienna. A bitter enemy of France, he
played an important part in European diplomacy. In 1813, he drafted the manifesto
of the powers against France, was present at the Congress of Vienna as secretary,
drafted the treaty of Paris in 1815, and attended the different congresses of the
Holy Alliance. He died in 1832.

expression that appeared to me to belong to other times, for that they had both of them spoken of the intentions of the *allied powers*. I declared that *allied powers*, and a *congress* in which powers that were not *allied* were to be found, were in my eyes scarcely likely to arrange affairs loyally together. I repeated with some astonishment and even warmth, the word *allied powers* . . . "*allied*," I said, "and against whom? It is no longer against Napoleon—he is on the isle of Elba . . . it is no longer against France ; for peace has been made . . . it is surely not against the King of France ; he is a guarantee of the duration of that peace. Gentlemen, let us speak frankly; if there are still *allied powers*, I am one too many here."—I perceived that I had produced some impression, and especially on Herr von Gentz. I continued : "And nevertheless if I were not here, I should decidedly be missed. Gentlemen, I am perhaps the only one who asks nothing. Great esteem is all I would have for France. She is sufficiently powerful by her resources, her extent of territory, by the number and intelligence of her inhabitants, by the contiguity of her provinces, by the unity of her administration, by the defences with which nature and art have guaranteed her frontiers. I want nothing, I repeat it, but I bring you a great deal. The presence of a minister of Louis XVIII. consecrates here the principle upon which all social order rests. The first need of Europe is to banish for ever the opinion that right can be acquired by conquest alone, and to cause the revival of that sacred principle of legitimacy from which all order and stability spring. To show to-day that France troubles your deliberations, would be to say that true principles are no longer the only ones that guide you, and that you are unwilling to be just ; but that idea is far from me, for we all equally feel that a simple and straightforward path is alone worthy of the noble mission we have to fulfil. In the words of the treaty of Paris : ' *Toutes les puissances qui ont été engagées de part et d'autre dans la présente guerre, enverront des plénipotentiaires à Vienne, pour régler, dans un congrès général, les arrangements qui doivent compléter les dispositions du traité de Paris.*'[1] When does the

[1] "All the powers who were on either side engaged in the present war, shall send plenipotentiaries to Vienna, there to settle, at a general congress, the arrangements which are to complete the provisions of the treaty of Paris."

general congress open? When do the conferences begin? These are questions asked by all those whose interests bring them here. If, as is already rumoured, some privileged powers would exercise a dictatorial authority over the congress, I must say that, confining myself to the terms of the treaty of Paris, I could not consent to recognize in this assembly any supreme power in questions that the congress is competent to treat, and that I should heed no proposal that proceeded from them."

After a few moments' silence, Count de Labrador made, in his proud and piquant language, a declaration almost identical with my own. Embarrassment was depicted on every face. They denied and explained in the same breath all that had taken place before this meeting. I profited by this moment in order to make a few concessions to the pride that I saw thus hurt. I said that in so numerous an assembly as the congress, where one was obliged to occupy oneself with so many different matters, to regulate questions of the first importance, and to decide a host of secondary interests, it was very difficult, nay, even impossible, to reach any result by treating of all these subjects in general assemblies, but that some means of distributing and classifying all the business could be found without wounding either the interest or the dignity of any of the powers.

This language, though vague, yet pointed out the possibility of a particular direction being given to general business, and thus permitted the assembled ministers to reconsider what they had done, and to regard it all as null; and Herr von Gentz destroyed the protocols of the previous sittings, and arranged one for that day. That protocol constituted the reports of the first sitting, and, in order to officially date our arrival at the congress, I signed it. From that time, there was no conference among the great powers in which France did not take a part. We met on the following days to distribute the work. All the members of the congress divided themselves into commissions that were charged to examine the questions submitted to them. The plenipotentiaries of those states who had a more direct interest in the objects to be examined, joined these commissions. The most important matters and questions of general interest were submitted to a committee formed of the representatives of the eight principal powers of Europe, and in order to form a nucleus, it was arranged that it should be those who had signed the treaty of May 30, 1814. This arrangement was not only useful because it wonderfully abridged and facilitated the work to be done, but it was also very just, since all the members of the congress consented to it, and no one raised objections.

Thus, at the end of the month of October, 1814, I was able to write to Paris, that the house of Bourbon, which had only returned to France five months ago, and France herself, who had been conquered five months previously, found themselves already restored to their proper place in Europe, and had again regained that influence that belonged to them in the most important deliberations of the congress. And three months later, these same powers, who had done nothing to save the unfortunate Louis XVI., were called upon by me, to render a tardy, but solemn, homage to his memory. That homage was further a means of linking together the chain of events, and a new consecration of the legitimate rights of the house of Bourbon. I should have said, that the Emperor and Empress of Austria powerfully seconded me in the pious and noble ceremony, celebrated at Vienna, January 21, 1815, at which all the sovereigns, and notable personages then in the capital of the Austrian Empire were present.

The first object with which the commission of the eight powers occupied itself, was the future lot of the king and realm of Saxony, and then that of the duchy of Warsaw. Prussia had, for some time, coveted the possession of the kingdom of Saxony. In acquiring it, she would not only have obtained possession of a rich and beautiful country, but one which would greatly strengthen her former territory. In the course of the war which had been terminated by the peace of Paris, the allies of Prussia had promised her, that, in the forthcoming arrangements, Saxony should be assured her. Prussia, consequently, counted with certainty upon that important acquisition, and already regarding herself as sovereign of that beautiful state which her troops occupied, held the King of Saxony prisoner in a Prussian fortress. But when the proposal was made in the committee of the eight

powers to give it to her, I declared I could not consent to it
I admitted that Prussia, deprived by Napoleon of vast and
numberless possessions that she could not wholly recover, had
a right to be indemnified, but, I asked, was that a reason that
Prussia in her turn should plunder the King of Saxony? Did not
that mean substituting for a right founded upon justice, the right
of the strongest, of which Prussia had so nearly become the
victim? And, by making use of this right, renouncing as a
matter of fact the interest her position inspired? Did not, moreover, the territories that the congress had to dispose of offer
ample means of indemnity? France wished to show herself
complying in all the arrangements that concerned the King of
Prussia, provided they were not contrary to justice; and I
repeated that she could neither participate in, nor consent to,
any that constituted an usurpation; while without mentioning
the interest that was attached to the person of the King of
Saxony, commanding, as he did, respect by his misfortunes, as
well as by the virtues that had shed such lustre on his reign, I
invoked in his favour the sacred principle of legitimacy alone.

Prussia considered that all the requirements of this principle
would be satisfied by assigning to the King of Saxony some
indemnity in the way of unoccupied territory, and that, whether
that prince thought so or not, the possession of Saxony would
be sufficiently legitimate for her, if judged so by the allied
sovereigns. Thereupon, I observed to Prince von Hardenberg
that a recognition of that kind made by people who have no
right to a thing themselves can scarcely confer it on another
who has equally no right to it.

This deplorable disregard for all principle must be attributed
to the disorganization and agitation that Europe had experienced
during twenty-five years. So many sovereigns had been despoiled, so many countries had changed masters, that public
law, tainted by a sort of corruption, no longer reproved usurpation. The sovereigns of Europe had been gradually forced by the
sway of irresistible circumstances to recognize usurpers, to treat
and even to ally themselves with them. They had thus, little by
little, been led to sacrifice their scruples to their safety; and, in
order to satisfy their ambition, when they, in their turn, found

the opportunity, they were ready to become usurpers themselves. Respect for legitimate rights had become so weak in them, that, after the first victory over Napoleon, it was not the sovereigns who thought of the rights of the house of Bourbon ; they had even several other projects upon France. And if she recovered her kings, it was, that, as soon as she could express her wish, she threw herself into the arms of that august family, that brought her wisely restricted liberties and the remembrance of a glorious past. At first, the restoration had been, for the powers who, I repeat, were present indeed, but whose work it was not, in any respect, far more a matter of fact than of right.

When the ministers of France openly constituted themselves at the congress the defenders of the principle of legitimacy, no disposition was shown to admit the consequences of it, except in so far as they did not contradict in any way the respective conveniences before which it was intended that the principle should yield. Thus, to secure the triumph of that principle, I was obliged to surmount every obstacle that ambition, thus foiled at the very moment of satisaction, might raise.

As for Prussia, she sustained her pretensions on Saxony with vehemence and tenacity. Russia, either on account of the attachment that her sovereign bore towards the King of Prussia, or because the price of that concession would be the possession of the duchy of Warsaw for the Czar Alexander, supported it with all her power. Her ministers spoke in this vein, without the least embarrassment.

"Arrangement is everything in politics," said one of them to me. "Naples is your first interest ; give up Saxony, and Russia will support you for Naples."

"You speak to me now of a bargain," I replied. "I cannot do so. I am so fortunate as not to be quite so much at my ease as yourself; it is your will and your interest that decide you, while as to me, I am obliged to follow principles, and principles do not allow of compromise."

The principal object of England, in concurring in the views of Prussia and Russia on Saxony, appeared to be that of fortifying by a second line of defence on the Elbe, the one that Prussia already had on the Oder, so that this power might oppose a more solid barrier to enterprises which in the end Russia might form against Germany. But that idea, even from a strategic point of view, was a pure illusion.

Austria had scarcely any other determinate motive in supporting the pretensions of Prussia, than that of maintaining arrangements which had previously been precipitately and lightly projected in the tumult of camps. She had not been debarred even by the danger to herself in allowing Prussia to establish herself on the mountains of Bohemia, a danger that she scarcely seemed to see until France informed her of it. I found a direct means of making the Emperor Francis understand, without it passing through one of his ministers, that he had a grave interest in Saxony being preserved. The reasons I developed to the intermediary [1] whom I employed made a great impression on his mind.

England very soon understood that it would be imprudent to throw a new element of enmity and discord between the two powers which defended the borders of Germany against Russia. Moreover for Prussia, Saxony would have been for some time a precarious possession, and one not sufficiently submissive, but always ready to seize opportunities for escaping from her, and recovering her independence. It would therefore have been, for Prussia, an acquisition that was more likely to weaken than to strengthen her.

The question of the disposal of Saxony was thus freed from the particular considerations which had been the motive for the first determination of England, and, being presented to Austria under the real point of view, under which her interest should bring her to consider it, France found these two powers at last disposed to listen without prejudice to the strong reasons that she had for winning consent to her principles. When these two powers saw that their own convenience lay in accordance with the principles of legitimacy they willingly recognized that the same principle applied to the convenience of others. They were thus led to become its defenders also, and things very soon reached such a point that a secret and contingent alliance was

---

[1] This intermediary was Count von Sickingen, of a noble German family which was descended from the famous Captain Franz von Sickingen (1481-1523).

formed between France, Austria, and England, against Russia and Prussia.[1] Thus France, by the sheer force of reason and the power of principles, broke an alliance which was only directed against herself. (Fortunate would she have been, if the fatal catastrophe of the 20th of March had not happened to renew its bonds ! !)

The allies thus found themselves divided, whilst we had just formed a new alliance in which France was the principal party. The first alliance, viz.: that against Napoleon, which the allies desired to prolong beyond the object for which it had been contracted, could only bring them the means of satisfying their private ambitions and views, whilst the aim of the new alliance could be no other than that of maintaining the principles of order, of the preservation of kingdoms and of peace. In this way, France, who had but just ceased to be an object of dread to all Europe, became, in a measure, her arbitrator and moderator.

After England and Austria had once come to a decision, Prussia was of course obliged to yield and ended by consenting to Saxony's continued existence as a kingdom, and declaring herself satisfied with the promise of a portion of it, subject to the condition that it be voluntarily ceded by the sovereign of that country. This important point once obtained, it was necessary to induce the King of Saxony to make the sacrifice. I myself, the Duke of Wellington, and Prince Metternich, were bidden to present ourselves to the king, and endeavour to get his consent to it. The news of the arrival of Napoleon in France had just circulated through Vienna. It caused the utmost excitement at the congress. We were given twenty-four hours only in which to fulfil our painful mission. I started immediately for Petersburg, where the King of Saxony had finally been allowed to reside.

The Comtesse de Brionne,[2] who dwelt in that town, whither

---

[1] January 3, 1815. By this treaty France, Austria and England promised to make common cause against the ambition of Prussia and Russia, and promised each other an army of one hundred and fifty thousand men.

[2] Louise-Julie-Constance de Rohan, the wife of Charles-Louis de Lorraine, Comte de Brionne. (See Voi. I., Part i.)

she had retired on emigrating . . . Madame de Brionne !! . . . who had had for so many years as great an affection for me as though I had been her child, and who believed I had done her wrong . . . oh! politics must wait. On arriving at Presburg, I hurried to throw myself at her feet. She allowed me to stay there long enough to feel her tears falling on my face.

"It is you at last," she said; "I always knew I should see you again. I may have been dissatisfied with you, but I have never for a moment ceased to love you. My heart has followed you everywhere. . . ."

I could not say a word, I wept. She sought to recompose me by asking all sorts of questions.

"You have a fine position?" she said.

"Oh yes, it is well enough," I replied. But my tears choked me. The feeling I experienced was so profound, that I was obliged to leave her for a few minutes; feeling faint, I went to breathe the air on the banks of the Danube. Having recovered myself a little, I returned to Madame de Brionne. She recommenced her questioning; this time I was better able to answer her. She just mentioned the king, and spoke at some length of *Monsieur*. She named the King of Saxony to me, knowing that I had defended his cause; she felt interest in him herself. A few days after this interview, death deprived me of the friend I had been so happy to find again.

In the evening, I went to the palace, and acquitted myself of the commission with which I had been entrusted. The King of Saxony, whose ardent desire was to be able to confide in me, had asked me to see him alone. In this interview, in which he spoke of his gratitude to me without the slightest embarrassment, I showed him the necessity of making some sacrifice, and endeavoured to convince him that, at the point which things had now reached, it was the only means of guaranteeing the independence of his country. The king detained me nearly two hours. He as yet engaged himself to nothing, simply saying that he was about to retire within with his family. A few hours after, Prince Metternich, the Duke of Wellington, and myself received an invitation to present ourselves at the palace. Prince Metternich, whom we had chosen to be our spokesman, explained to the king with considerable discretion, the wishes of the powers. The king, in noble and touching language, told us of his affection for his people, though letting us see in advance that he would place no obstacle in the way of whatever, be it only in· accordance with the honour of his crown, might contribute to the final settlement of the affairs of Europe ; he however reserved to himself the right to send to the congress a minister invested with full powers to treat of his interests.

We set out for Vienna, without being the bearers of the king's adhesion, but persuaded nevertheless, that he was decided, and that it was through Herr von Einsiedel, his plenipotentiary, that his consent would reach the congress.

After several conferences to which Herr von Einsiedel had been admitted, the points at issue between Saxony and Prussia were settled, not to their mutual satisfaction but by common accord.[1] Thus the principle of legitimacy was not made to suffer in that important circumstance.

From these arrangements it resulted that Russia, who had laid claim to the possession of the entire duchy of Warsaw, was obliged to desist, Prussia recovered a considerable portion of it, and Austria, who had not ceased to possess a portion of Galicia, took up again a few of the districts that she had ceded in 1809.

This arrangement, which, at first glance, may seem to have had no importance except for those two powers, was of general interest. Poland almost entirely in the possession of Russia would probably have been a cause of continual anxiety to Europe. It was of importance for the security of the latter, that two powers rather than one if exposed to see themselves deprived of all they possessed, should be, by a sentiment of common danger, disposed to combine on every occasion against the ambitious enterprises of Prussia. Mutual interest became for them the strongest link, and it is for that

[1] Prussia acquired all the upper and lower Lusatia, nearly the whole of Misnia and Thuringia, with the towns of Torgau and Wittemberg (treaty of May 18, 1815).

reason that France sustained the pretensions of Prussia and Austria.

The Russian minister sought to foil me with my own arguments. He pretended that if the principle of legitimacy required the preservation of the realm of Saxony, it ought to exact also the restoration of Poland. He added that the Czar Alexander wished to have the totality of the duchy of Warsaw to erect it into a kingdom, and that I could not thus, without being inconsistent, refuse to subscribe to its being placed in his possession. I replied with vivacity that one could really and honestly regard as a question of principle the re-establishment, as a national body and under an independent government, of a numerous people, formerly powerful, occupying a vast and continuous tract of territory, and who, though it had allowed the bonds of its unity to be broken, had nevertheless remained homogeneous by a community of manners, language, and hopes ; that if that were what was desired, France would be the first not only to give her adhesion to the restoration of Poland, but even to wish for it sincerely, on the condition that Poland should be restored such as it was formerly, such as Europe wished that it should be. But, I added, there is nothing in common between the principle of legitimacy and the more or less great extent that would be given to the state Russia pretends to form with a small portion of Poland, and without even evincing the intention of uniting, later, with it the beautiful provinces which, since the last division, have been annexed to that vast empire. The ministers of Russia, after several conferences understood that they would not succeed to conceal, under the veil of the principle of legitimacy, the interested views that they had been instructed to enforce, and they confined themselves to negotiating, in order to obtain a more or less great portion of the territory which, for some years, had composed the grand duchy of Warsaw.

By rendering homage to the principle of legitimacy in the decision taken with regard to the kingdom of Saxony, the fate of Naples had been implicitly pronounced upon. The principle once adopted, no one could refuse to admit the consequences of it. Therefore France, after having rejected the pretensions founded upon the right of conquest, exacted the assurance that Ferdinand IV. should be recognized King of Naples. It was necessary to overcome the real difficulty of several cabinets who were bound to Murat, and especially of Austria, who had made a treaty with him. I was far from refusing to adopt, all that leading to the same end, could be reconciled with the dignity of the powers. Murat came to my aid. He was in a state of continual agitation ; he wrote letters upon letters, making declarations, ordering his troops to make marches and counter-marches, and furnishing me with a thousand opportunities for exposing his bad faith. An unfortunate move of his army in Lombardy was regarded as an aggression, and that aggression became the signal of his ruin.[1] The Austrians marched against him, beat him, followed him up, and a few days after, abandoned by his army, he left the kingdom of Naples as a fugitive, and that country soon returned to its allegiance to its legitimate king. The restitution of the realm of Naples to Ferdinand IV. consecrated anew, by a striking instance the principle of legitimacy, and besides, it was useful to France, because it gave her for ally in Italy, the most powerful state of that country.[2]

---

[1] They were agreed at Vienna to overthrow Murat, but no pretext could be found when he himself furnished it. He had as agent at Vienna, the Duke de Campo-Chiaro, who had been refused admission to the congress. Though he had thus no official position, Murat sent him, towards the end of February, 1815, a note, with orders to communicate it to the powers ; in it, the king demanded explanations from the sovereigns, concerning their intentions towards him, declaring that, if necessary, he was ready to fight, and warning them that he would then be forced to pass over the territories of several of the Italian states newly created. Austria seized that opportunity, and, under the pretext of protecting the Austrian princes in Italy, had one hundred and fifty thousand men marched against Murat.

[2] Were it not my duty to my family to mention here the honourable decree which King Ferdinand IV. rendered in my favour when bestowing on me the duke-dom of Dino, gratitude alone would induce me to do so.—(*Prince Talleyrand.*)

The King and Queen of the Two Sicilies had entrusted to Prince de Talleyrand the defence of their interests at the Congress. The following are the letters they wrote to him on the subject. We shall here transcribe them from the originals, as they are to be found among the papers of the Prince.

Letter from the King of the Two Sicilies.

"MONSIEUR LE PRINCE,

"My unsteady hand compels me to borrow the aid of another, whom I know however to be faithful, in order to express my feelings to you ; for having been

The arrangements made with regard to several other parts of Italy had in view the establishment in that peninsula of a strong counter-poise, capable of checking Austrian power, if its ambitious views carried it some day in that direction. Thus the realm of Sardinia acquired all the state of Genoa. The branch of the house of Savoy, then reigning at Turin, being ready to die out, and Austria being enabled by her family

informed by my proved and devoted minister, *Commandatore* Ruffo, of the favourable disposition you bear to my interests, and of the trouble you are taking to get my kingdom of Naples restored to me, I felt I could no longer defer expressing to you my recognition of your services, nor delay putting my just cause at once into the hands of a minister whose extraordinary abilities in conducting negotiations can alone assure me a fortunate issue ; and this it would be my greatest pleasure to owe to a Périgord. I charge *Commandatore* Ruffo to express to you, in my name, every acknowledgment that confidence in the interest you take in my cause, to be now furthered by you at the Congress, cannot fail to inspire ; and it is in such a spirit that I ask you to receive the anticipated expression of the gratitude of

" Yours very affectionately,

" FERDINAND.

" Palermo, *Oct.* 1, 1814."

Letter of the Queen of the Two Sicilies.

" PRINCE DE BÉNÉVENT,

" The rights you have just acquired to the recognition of all the members of the House of Bourbon, compel me to make use of my old and constant friend, the Baronne de Tailerand, your relation, to assure you of the high regard and esteem that the signal services you have just rendered, in these latter most fortunate events, to a family to which I belong by all possible ties, have inspired me. I join my acknowledgments to those of the King my husband, and of all my family, and am proud to be the exponent of them. The astonishing and rapid events that have just restored to the oldest branch of the Bourbons and to Spain the rank and thrones of their ancestors, have not yet influenced in any way that of the two Sicilies, in spite of the fact that its misfortunes and, above all, its constancy, have won for it sacred rights to the esteem and equity of its allies : but the influence that France is with justice about to re-assume in Europe, is a sure guarantee, that owing to her interest in us, she will support our lawful rights with the noble-mindedness and energy that characterize the nation, the sovereign, and the minister who has had the wisdom and the talent to distinguish clearly, and to choose wisely. It is in these that I put my confidence to-day, as also the hope of the future good-fortune and glory of my family ; the misfortunes of the whole family of the Bourbons, and their cruel experience, teaches us that our different branches must be united for ever, to attain their own prosperity and glory, as well as that of the peoples they are called upon to govern, and that it is to the head of the whole family, to which they must all attach themselves. Such are the sentiments of the King, my husband ; such are the sentiments of my whole family : and they will doubtless form the basis for the future conduct of our government in its political relations. Accept, again, I pray your Highness, the tribute of admiration and acknowledgment, that I, with genuine satisfaction, offer to your talents and services, both in my own name, and that of all my family.

" Yours affectionately,

" CHARLOTTE.

" Vienna, *June* 27, 1814."

alliances to raise pretensions to that fine inheritance, this effect was prevented by the recognition of the rights of the house of Carignan, to which was assured the inheritance of that crown.

Switzerland, the central point of Europe, on which rest three great countries, France, Germany and Italy, was solemnly declared neutral for ever. By this decision, the means of defence for each one of these countries were increased, and the means of aggression diminished. That provision is especially favourable to France, who, surrounded by fortresses on all other points of her frontiers, is deprived of any on those bordering on Switzerland. The neutrality of that country thus gives her, on the only point where she is weak and unarmed, an inexpugnable position.

To preserve the Helvetic people from internal dissensions, which, by disturbing their tranquillity, might have compromised the maintenance of their neutrality, we applied ourselves to conciliate the respective pretensions of the cantons, and to arrange the differences which had existed for a long time between them. The union threatened by the conflict of former interests and of the interests resulting from the new organization made under the mediation of Napoleon, was strengthened by an act combining all the provisions, which appeared most likely to lead to their agreement.

The erection of the new realm of the Netherlands, agreed upon before the peace, was evidently a hostile measure against France ; and that project had been conceived with the view of creating about her a state which should be her enemy, and which the need of protection made the natural ally of England and of Prussia. The result of that combination however, appeared to me less dangerous for France than it was believed, for the new kingdom would have enough to do for some time, in consolidating itself.[1] In fact, formed from two countries opposed in interests and sentiments, it is doomed to remain weak and without stability for many years. That kind of pro-

[1] It had no time to do so. The Revolution of 1830-1832 divided Belgium from Holland.

tective intimacy that England believes she will succeed in establishing between herself and the new state, seems to me destined to be, for a long time to come, a political dream. A kingdom composed of a commercial and of a manufacturing country, must undoubtedly become a rival to England, or be ruined by her, and consequently be discontented.

The organization of the German confederation was to be one of the most important factors in the equilibrium of Europe. I cannot say whether the congress would have succeeded in founding that organization on bases which would have made it serve effectually as support to that equilibrium. The fatal events of 1815, which forced the congress to hurry its deliberations, were the cause that the final act had to be drafted in a somewhat embryonic state, that, until the present, it has not been able to take shape, and that it is still being worked upon, in order to be developed.

The part played by France in that memorable circumstance I will leave to be appreciated. Notwithstanding the disadvantages of the position in which she found herself at the opening of the congress, she succeeded in taking in the deliberations such a leading part, that the most important questions were decided according to her views and after the principles that she had established and sustained, all opposed though they were to the intentions of the powers, to whom the fate of arms had given the power to dictate, without hindrance, the law to Europe. And although, in the midst of the discussions of the congress, the spirit of revolt and usurpation came again to subjugate France, the king, having returned to Ghent, exercised the same influence at Vienna, as from the palace of the Tuileries. At my request, and I should say it, to the honour of the sovereigns, without insistance, Europe issued a crushing declaration against the *usurper.*[1]   I speak of him thus, for after his

---

[1] On the 25th of March, 1815, at the news of the arrival of Napoleon at Paris, England, Austria, Russia and Prussia renewed their alliance. All the other states of Europe adhered to that treaty. At the same time, the powers issued the following declaration :—"In breaking thus the convention that sent him to Elba,

return from Elba, Napoleon was but an usurper. Until then he had been a conqueror, his brothers alone had been usurpers.

I again secured at that time the reward of my fidelity to upright principles. In the king's name I had invoked them for the preservation of other people's rights, and they had become the guarantee of his own.

All the powers, seeing themselves again threatened by the revival of revolution in France, armed with all speed. The negotiations at Vienna were hastily concluded in order to apply all one's energies to cares then becoming more pressing ; and the final act of the congress although only roughly sketched in some of its parts, was signed by the plenipotentiaries who parted afterwards.

Affairs being thus terminated, the king, and consequently France, having been received in that alliance against Napoleon and his supporters, I left Vienna, where nothing any longer detained me, and I started on my way to Ghent, far from imagining that, on arriving at Brussels, I should learn the result of the battle of Waterloo. His Highness the Prince de Condé was kind enough to furnish me all the details of it. He spoke, with a grace that I shall never forget, of the success France had had at the Congress of Vienna.

After this succinct account of the deliberations of the Vienna Congress, the following correspondence will perhaps be read with more interest.

All this correspondence—that is to say the minutes of the letters written by King Louis XVIII. in his own hand, and the originals of my letters—is deposited in the archives of the Department of Foreign Affairs. The copies which I give here

Buonaparte destroys the only legal title to which his existence had been attached. In reappearing in France with schemes of disturbance and destruction, he has deprived himself of the protection of the law, and manifested to the face of all that there can be neither peace nor truce with him. . . . The powers declare in consequence that Napoleon Buonaparte has placed himself outside all civil and social bonds, and that, as enemy and disturber of the peace, he has delivered himself up to public vengeance."

are taken from the original letters of the king, and from my own minutes.[1]

No. 1. The Prince de Talleyrand to King Louis XVIII.[2]

VIENNA, *September* 25, 1814.

SIRE,

I left Paris on the 16th. I arrived here on the morning of

---

[1] The following correspondence was published a few years ago by M. Pallain (*Correspondence inédite de Louis XVIII. et de M. de Talleyrand*), with the exception however of the letters of the King's Ambassadors to the Minister of Foreign Affairs which are included here. We have noticed between the official text found by M. Pallain in the archives of the Ministry of Foreign Affairs and the text which M. de Talleyrand wished to preserve in his memoirs certain differences, often insignificant, at times to the contrary, curious enough, which at any rate appeared to us interesting to reproduce. The additions and varieties will be found in notes and italics. Besides, there are in our text several passages that are not reproduced in the text of the archives, we have equally underlined and indicated them.

[2] We give here the whole text of this first letter, such as it is found in the work of M. Pallain. The differences are so numerous, that it would have been difficult to otherwise point them out.

VIENNA, *September* 25, 1814.

SIRE,

I left Paris on the 16th. I arrived here on *the 23rd, in the evening. I stopped only at Strasbourg and at Munich.*

The Princess of Wales had just left Strasbourg. She had accepted an invitation to a ball at the residence of Mme. Franck, widow of the banker of that name. She danced all night. At the inn *where I put up, she gave a supper to Talma. Her manners while at Strasbourg explains perfectly why the Prince Regent prefers to know her in Italy instead of in England.* At Munich the king spoke to me of his attachment for your Majesty and of the fears that Prussian ambition gave him ; he told me, *in a most gracious manner :* " I have served France twenty *and one* years, that cannot be forgotten." *Two hours' conversation that I was able to have with M. de Montgelas proved fully to me* that it is only necessary to follow the principles adopted by your Majesty, as the basis of the political system of France, to secure the good-will of and to conciliate the confidence of powers of an inferior *order.*

At Vienna the language of reason and moderation is not yet spoken by the plenipotentiaries.

One of the Russian ministers *said to me yesterday,* " They wished to make us an Asiatic power, *Poland will make Europeans of us.*"

As for Prussia, she asks nothing better than to exchange her old Polish provinces for those which she covets in Germany, and on the banks of the Rhine. Those two powers * should be regarded as intimately linked on that point.

The Russian ministers insist, without having admitted up to the present the least discussion, on a territorial extension that would carry the power of Russia to the banks of the Vistula, by annexing even old Prussia to their empire.

I hope that the Czar, who in different circumstances permitted me to explain to him frankly, what I judged most useful to *his interests and to his glory, will enable me to combat before him the policy of his ministers. The philanthropist La Harpe revolts at the idea of the ancient division of Poland, and pleads her subjection to Russia ; he has been at Vienna for the last ten or twelve days.*

They still dispute the right of the King of Saxony to have a minister at the

* Russia and Prussia.—(*Translator*).

the 24th. The Princess of Wales[1] had just left Strasbourg when I arrived there.[2] She had accepted an invitation to a ball at Mme. Franck's, widow of the banker of that name, where she had danced all night. She had given a supper to Talma the evening before her departure. All this explains to me the motives that led the Prince Regent to prefer to have her on the Continent rather than in England. She purposes setting off for Italy. At Munich, the king[3] spoke to me of his attachment for your Majesty. He said, " I have served France for twenty years. That cannot be forgotten. *If Monsieur, or Monseigneur the Duc de Berry, had come to Strasbourg when I was at Baden, I should have hastened to pay them my respects."* [4]

I foresaw that it would only be necessary to follow the principles laid down by your Majesty as the basis of the policy

congress. *M. de Schulenburg, whom I have known for a long time, told me yesterday that the king had declared* that he would sign no act of cession, of abdication, nor exchange, that could destroy the existence of Saxony, *or modify the rights of his house.* That honourable resistance might make some impression upon those who still *share* the idea of the union of that kingdom to Prussia.

Bavaria has offered to the King of Saxony to support his pretensions if necessary, *by a large body of troops. Herr von Wrede says that he has orders to give as many as forty thousand men.*

The question of Naples is not resolved upon. Austria would like to place Naples and Saxony on the same footing, and Russia would make them serve as compensation.

The Queen of Naples is *not much regretted.* Her death appears to have put Prince Metternich *more* at his ease.

Nothing is determined in regard to the *conduct and the progress of affairs at the congress. The English even, whom I believed more methodical than others, have made no preparatory work on that subject.*

I am inclined to believe that the idea of having two commissions will prevail: the one composed of the six great powers, and dealing with the general affairs of Europe; the other to prepare the affairs of Germany, and being likewise composed of the six first German powers. I would have desired that there should have been seven. The idea of a commission for Italy displeases Austria prodigiously.

The line of conduct which your Majesty has traced for his ministers is so noble, *that it must of necessity, if all reason has not disappeared from the earth, end by giving them some influence.*

I am, with the most profound respect, Sire,
Your Majesty's most humble, obedient servant and subject,
PRINCE DE TALLEYRAND.

P.S.—*The Czar of Russia and the King of Prussia have just arrived. Their entrance was most beautiful. They were on horseback; the Emperor of Austria in the middle. Some disorder, occasioned by the horses, was the cause that for a considerable portion of the ride the King of Prussia was at the right of the Emperor Francis. He did not resume his place until a little before the arrival at the palace.*

[1] This is the princess who caused so much scandal by her conduct, and by her divorce case with King George IV. of England.

[2] Omitted in the text of the archives.

[3] Maximilian I., King of Bavaria. He was colonel in the service of France before the Revolution of 1789. He was known at that time under the name of Max de Deux Ponts (*Max von Zwei Brücken*).

[4] Omitted in the text of the archives.

of France, in order to assure to ourselves the return to, and to conciliate the confidence of, the powers of an inferior rank.

Since my arrival here, I have been able to receive but a few persons. M. de Dalberg, who had preceded me by a day, had for his part picked up a few particulars.[1]

I see, Sire, that the language of reason, and moderation, will not be employed by all the plenipotentiaries. One of the ministers of Russia said a few days ago: "They wanted to make an Asiatic power of us. Poland will make us European."

Prussia, on her part, asks nothing better than to exchange her former Polish provinces for those she covets in Germany and on the banks of the Rhine. These two powers[2] should be considered as intimately united on that point.

The Russian ministers insist, without up to the present having allowed any discussion, on a territorial aggrandizement which shall carry that power to the banks of the Vistula, by uniting even old Prussia to its empire. *They announce, however, that this question still has to be treated by their sovereign, who, alone, can modify their instructions.*

I hope, that upon the arrival of the Czar of Russia, who, in different circumstances, accorded me the right to explain to him frankly what I judged most useful to his real interest and glory, I shall be able to inform him, how much it would be to the advantage of his general philanthropic policy, if he would allow moderation to temper might. Perhaps I may even find in this respect, the only point of contact with M. de la Harpe,[3] who is already here. The Emperor of Russia, and the King of Prussia, are expected to-day.

They still contest the right of the King of Saxony to send a minister to the Congress. He has sent Count von Schulenburg,[4] a clever agent whom I know well. We can take advantage of this. The king has declared that he will sign no act of cession, abdication, or exchange that can destroy the existence of Saxony. This honourable resistance would cause those who still cling to the idea of the union of this kingdom to Prussia to come to their senses.

---

[1] Omitted in the text of the archives.

[2] Russia and Prussia.—(*Tanslator*).

[3] M. de La Harpe, a Swiss statesman, former tutor to the Czar Alexander, who has already been seen playing an important part in the affairs of his country at the time of the Directory.

[4] Frederick-Albert, Count von Schulenburg, born in 1772. He was appointed minister of Saxony at Vienna in 1798, then at Ratisbonne. Attended the congress of Rastadt (1799), and was, a short time after, sent to Copenhagen, then to St. Petersburg (1804). He returned to Vienna in 1810, and attended at the congress of 1814 as Saxony's plenipotentiary. He retired in 1830, and consecrated himself until his death (1853) exclusively to literature.

Bavaria has offered to support the King of Saxony by fifty thousand men if necessary. They do not seem to agree as to the non-admission of a plenipotentiary of Naples, but I regard this question as not being definitively decided.

Austria wants Naples and Saxony to be treated on a par, and Russia to make them serve as compensation. The Queen of Naples is mourned by no one; and her death seems even to have put Prince Metternich more at his ease.

Nothing, moreover, is yet determined with regard to the progress and conduct of the affairs of the congress, and even in the arguments of the English ministers, I thought I could detect that they had not yet matured their plans in this respect.

Two commissions have been proposed, of which, the one is to be composed of the great powers, and the other of the inferior ones. They intend to have the affairs of Germany treated by a special commission.

The part which your Majesty prescribes for your ambassadors is so noble, and so befitting your own dignity, that they will be enabled to aid in all that can bring order to Europe, and re-establish a real and durable equilibrium.

I beg your Majesty to believe that we shall exert ourselves to meet your confidence, and to follow the line traced in the instructions given by your Majesty to your ambassadors at the congress.[1]

I have the honour to be . . . . .

PRINCE DE TALLEYRAND.[2]

No. 1 A.[3] THE KING'S AMBASSADORS AT THE CONGRESS TO THE MINISTER OF FOREIGN AFFAIRS AT PARIS.[4]

VIENNA, *September* 27, 1814.

MONSIEUR LE COMTE,

The despatches of the king's ambassadors at the congress have had as yet but little with which to acquaint the department. The king's ministers keep to the line of conduct set forth in their instructions. In all their conversations, they revert to the article of the treaty of May 30, which gives to the congress the honourable mission of establishing a real and durable equilibrium. That disinterested stand leads them to appeal to the

---

[1] Omitted in the text of the archives.

[2] Prince Talleyrand alone conducted the correspondence with the king.—(*M. de Bacourt.*)

[3] Prince Talleyrand's letters to the French Foreign Minister and to the King, simply bear a number; those of the French Ambassadors bear the letter A besides; and those of the King to Prince Talleyrand the letter B.

[4] The Comte de Jaucourt held the portfolio of Foreign Affairs at Paris during the absence of Prince de Talleyrand.—(*M. de Bacourt.*)

principle of public law which is recognized by all Europe, and from which springs, almost of necessity, the restoration of King Ferdinand IV. on the throne of Naples, as well as the succession of the Carignan branch to the house of Savoy.

The non-abdication, and non-cession, of the King of Saxony, gives to the king's ministers the right to defend his cause. You see, Monsieur le Comte, that we keep to generalities. Nevertheless, we should tell you, that their application appears to be foreseen by the ministers of the courts which, before the peace, we called allies, and that that puts the king's ministers in a position which is very suitable to the grand part he is called upon to play in these circumstances.

Our information authorizes us to say that misfortune and ambition do not yet allow the Prussian ministers to use such language as so pacific an assembly as the congress sitting at Vienna would seem to warrant.

We have the honour . . . . . .

> THE PRINCE DE TALLEYRAND.
> THE DUC DE DALBERG.
> THE MARQUIS DE LA TOUR DU PIN GOUVERNET.
> THE COMTE ALEXIS DE NOAILLES.

No. 2.—THE PRINCE DE TALLEYRAND TO KING LOUIS XVIII.

VIENNA, *September* 29, 1814.

SIRE,

We have, at last, almost finished the round of our visits to the numerous members of the imperial family. It has been very soothing to me to meet everywhere with testimonies of the high regard felt for the person of your Majesty, of the interest shown in you, and of the wishes that are formed for you—all more or less happily expressed, but always with a sincerity that cannot be suspected of being feigned. The empress, who, since our arrival, has been obliged to occupy herself exclusively with the empress of Russia, had appointed us an hour for to-day. She was indisposed, but though she had had her mother, the archduchess, receive several persons for her, she expressed a wish to receive herself the embassy of your Majesty. She questioned me, with an interest that was not simply that of politeness, as to your Majesty's health. "I remember," she said, "having seen the king at Milan, when I was very young. He was full of kindness towards me. I have never forgotten him, under any circumstances."

She spoke in like terms of the Duchesse d'Angoulême, of her virtues, of the love borne her at Vienna, and of the memories that she left there. She also deigned to address some obliging remarks to the minister of Your Majesty. Twice in the conversation she mentioned the name of the Archduchess Marie Louise, the second time with a sort of affectation. She calls her *ma fille Louise.*[1] Notwithstanding the cough which continually[2] interrupted her, and notwithstanding her being so thin, this princess has the gift of pleasing, and possesses graces that I could almost term really French, if, to too fastidious eyes those graces did not seem somewhat affected.

Prince Metternich is exceedingly polite to me. Count von Stadion shows me more confidence. It is true that the latter, dissatisfied with what the other does, intrenched himself in financial matters, the management of which he has, though I strongly doubt whether he understands them. He has left the direction of the cabinet, which perhaps renders him more communicative.

I still have every reason to be satisfied with the frankness of Lord Castlereagh. He had a few days ago, with the Emperor Alexander, a conversation which lasted an hour and a half, and of which he came at once to inform me. He pretends that in that conversation the Czar Alexander displayed all the resources of a most subtle mind ; but that he, Lord Castlereagh, spoke in terms most positive and even sufficiently harsh to be impolite, had he not veiled them by means of zealous protestations for the glory of the Czar. Notwithstanding all that, I fear that Lord Castlereagh has not that spirit of decision that it would be so necessary for him to possess, and that the spectre of parliament that ever haunts him renders him timid. I shall do my very best to inspire him with firmness.

Count Nesselrode told me that the Emperor Alexander desires to see me, and requested me to write to him to solicit an audience.[3] I did so already, several days ago, and have not yet received his reply.[4] Can it be that our principles, of which we make no mystery, are known to the Czar Alexander, and make him feel somewhat uneasy before me ? If, as I am inclined to believe, after all that has been related to me, he does me the

[1] My daughter Louise (Napoleon's wife).—(*Translator*).
[2] Text: *continuellement* (continually). Var. *souvent* (often).
[3] Text : *une audience* (an audience). Var. une audience *particulière* (a *private* audience).
[4] Text : "*Je l'ai fait il y a déjà plusieurs, jours et n'ai pas encore sa réponse.*" " I did so already several days ago and have not yet received his reply." Var. "*Je l'ai fait il y a plusieurs jours, et n'ai pas encore de réponse.*" " I did so several days ago and have not yet received a reply."

honour of talking to me about the affairs of Poland and Saxony, I shall be conciliating but positive, speaking only of principles, and never swerving from them.

I imagine that Russia and Prussia make so much stir and speak with so much haughtiness, only in order to learn the intentions of the other powers. If they should find themselves alone in their opinion, they will think twice before bringing matters to a crisis. That Polish enthusiasm with which the Czar Alexander was filled at Paris has grown cold at St. Petersburg. It has revived at Pulawi ;[1] it may die out again, though we have here M. de la Harpe, and the Czartoryskis are expected ;[2] I can scarcely believe that a simple but unanimous declaration of the great powers will not suffice to stay it.

Unhappily, he who is at the head of affairs in Austria, and who claims to regulate those of Europe regards as the most obvious mark of the superiority of genius a carelessness which, in certain respects, he carries to the point of ridicule, and in others, to a point which, in a minister of a great state, and in circumstances such as these, becomes really calamitous.

In this state of affairs, when so many passions are rampant, and when so many people are bestirring themselves in all directions, rashness and carelessness are two rocks which seem to me to be equally avoided. I therefore endeavour not to depart from that calm dignity which alone befits the ministers of your Majesty, who, thanks to the wise instructions given them, have only principles to defend, and no combination of personal interests to uphold.

Whatever may be the issue of the congress, two opinions must be impressed and enforced, that relative to the justice of your Majesty, and that relative to the strength of his government ; for these are the best, or rather the only guarantees of consideration abroad and of stability at home. Those two opinions having been once impressed, as I hope they may be, we shall, in any case, come out of the congress with honour, whether its results be or not be in conformity with our wishes and the good of Europe.

[1] Mansion of the Princes Czartoryski in Poland. That superb residence has been celebrated by the poet Delille in his poem entitled *Les Jardins.*

[2] The Czartoryskis were one of the most powerful and wealthy families of Poland. Their family was then represented by Prince Adam-Casimir (1731-1823), starost-general of Podolia and *feldzeugmeister* in the Austrian army, as well as by his two sons : Adam-George, born in 1770, former ambassador of Russia and, later, senator of the kingdom of Poland : and Constantine-Adam, born in 1773, who was at the time a colonel of infantry in the Russian army.

No. 2A.—THE AMBASSADORS OF THE KING AT THE CONGRESS TO THE MINISTER OF FOREIGN AFFAIRS AT PARIS.

VIENNA, *September* 29, 1814.

MONSIEUR LE COMTE,

During the last few days we have been introduced to the imperial family of Austria. It seemed to us that the emperor and the archdukes tried to be very obliging. The empress especially received us with much good grace. They expressed to us their attachment to the king, and asked many questions regarding the health of Madame la Duchesse d'Angoulême. The fêtes have commenced.

The affairs of the congress have made but little progress since the last letter that we had the honour of writing you. We continue to follow closely the instructions that have been given us.

By proclaiming the principles they contain, France and the king will influence the affairs of Europe in a manner as noble as it is suitable.

It appears that, hitherto, all that ought to have been agreed upon, with respect to the progress of affairs, has not been decided.

The king's ministers have not yet thought it advisable to interfere, and we are waiting, Monsieur le Comte, till some agreement be come to on those different subjects, before informing you of the results.

We have been informed in the most positive manner that Russia will abandon none of her pretensions on Poland. She declares that the duchy of Warsaw is occupied by her armies, and that they will have to be driven out. Such are the terms she employs.

Prussia has ceded her what she calls her rights on that country, and seeks compensation in the kingdom of Saxony. This state of things leaves great uncertainty as to the issue of the congress.

Information received as to the sentiments of Austria do not leave much hope that that power will employ her numerous armies to back up those principles without which nothing can be stable.

The king's ministers think they have reason to believe that the firm and energetic language that they have adhered to in divers circumstances has produced some effect ; that it has even led to hesitations in plans already almost decided.

Prince Talleyrand has expressed a wish to see the Emperor of Russia. His letter, sent three days ago, has remained unanswered.   It is only after that interview that one can judge of the degree of moderation that that sovereign will bring to bear on the general affairs of Europe.   His ministers do not appear to have complete instructions.   They avoid us because they are afraid of entering into a discussion with us.

The Austrian ministers show signs of suspicion.

The Prussians serve the Russians.   It does not appear that the English ministers take a very decided tone.

The agents of the minor courts seek to make overtures to France, and we encourage them to do so.

We can only send you those few observations ; but they will give you some idea of the state of affairs.

No. 1B.—King Louis XVIII. to the Prince de Talleyrand.

Paris, *October* 3, 1814.[1]

My Cousin,

I received your despatch of September 25, and for the sake of your eyes and of my hand, I have this letter written by some one who is far from being ignorant of my affairs.[2]

The Kings of Naples and Saxony are equally near relations to myself.   The claims of each are equally just ; but not so my interest in them.   The fact of the kingdom of Naples being in the hands of a descendant of Louis XIV., increases the power of France.   Remaining in those of a member of the Corsican's family, *flagitio addit damnum.*   I am scarcely less indignant at the idea that this kingdom and Saxony could serve as compensations.   I need not outline here my reflec- tions on such a neglect of all public morality ; but what I must hasten to tell you is, that if I cannot prevent this iniquity, I will, at least, not sanction it, but, on the contrary, reserve to myself and my successors, the liberty of redressing it, should an opportunity present itself.

In saying this, I am, of course, supposing an extreme case, for I am far from despairing of the success of the cause, if England holds firmly to the principles Lord Castlereagh has manifested here, and if Austria persists in the same resolution as Bavaria.

That which Herr von Schulenburg told you of the determina-

---

[1] This letter is dated October 13, in the text of the archives.

[2] The letters of Louis XVIII. to Prince Talleyrand were copied by the Comte, afterwards Duc de Blacas d'Aulps, but signed by the king.   We have already said that the king's minutes are now in the record office of the Ministry of Foreign Affairs, though no one knows how they came there.—(*M. de Bacourt.*)

tion of the King of Saxony, is perfectly true ; that unhappy prince has himself informed me of it.

You can easily judge with what impatience I await news from the congress, which must already have begun work. Thereupon, I pray God, my cousin, that He preserve you in His safe and holy keeping.

LOUIS.

NO. 3A.—THE KING'S AMBASSADORS AT THE CONGRESS TO THE MINISTER OF FOREIGN AFFAIRS.

VIENNA, *October* 4, 1814.

MONSIEUR LE COMTE,

Since our last letter, we have made one more step. It has not yet, however, brought us within sight of the work of the congress. We will here briefly lay before you the various events that have taken place.

Prince Metternich, in a note, dated the 29th of September, and addressed to Prince Talleyrand, has invited him to a private conference. [Subjoined to No. 1, is a copy of that note.[1]]

The word *assister*, and the plenipotentiaries mentioned in the note, led to the supposition, that the fact of their presence there was to be simply an act of courtesy of the allies towards France. Prince Talleyrand replied to it in the note subjoined to No. 2. You will observe, Monsieur le Comte, that by putting Spain before Prussia, the intention of Prince Metternich was frustrated.

Later on, it eked out, that Prince Metternich had addressed Count de Labrador an invitation couched in the following terms : " Prince Metternich and his colleagues, the ministers of Russia, England, and Prussia, invite . . . ."

Count Labrador, who is on terms of intimate relations with the French embassy, and who seems to approve of the regularity of its conduct and principles, replied as Prince Talleyrand suggested to him.

The conference was held at the residence of Prince Metternich himself. The latter had chosen Herr von Gentz, who is well known for his English and Prussian sympathies, to draw up the reports of the sitting.

A protocol and the draft of a declaration were read.

The protocol began by naming the *allies* at each paragraph,

---

[1] Mention is often made, either in Prince Talleyrand's letters or in those of the ambassadors, of documents subjoined to the correspondence and forwarded to the Department of Foreign Affairs. Those documents were not found with the MS. of the Prince's Memoirs. They could not, therefore, be reproduced here.

and the declaration was made in their name.   It will be found subjoined to No. 3.

Prince Talleyrand, having twice noticed the word *allies*, and declared that it was an insult at a congress like that now assembled, pointed out that the conclusions of this document wounded the respect due to the other powers ; and that it was not for *them alone* to take an initiative which no right justified ; that it would be better to invite all the powers to unite in congress, to have commissions appointed, and thus proceed with that moderation, without which nothing can be legitimately done ; he finally declared that he could recognize no special arrangement that had been made since the signing of the treaty of Paris.

That very evening, Prince Talleyrand addressed the result of his observations to the five ministers who had met that morning. His note is under No. 4.

This note seems to have retarded the summoning of a second conference; and we have heard that the ministers seemed rather perplexed about it.   On the other hand, we have been told that they seemed to think we wished to teach them a lesson, and that they did not appear to do justice to the care which was taken to bring them to principles which alone can re-establish Europe on a secure basis.

Prince Talleyrand, seeing that these ministers had held preliminary conferences, that they had signed a protocol, and had decided upon publishing that document as being in conformity with the agreements they had made, to assume a kind of initiative in the matters that still remained to be settled, decided on also drawing up and sending an official note. Noticing that official measures had been resorted to on the one side, he believed it necessary that similar measures be taken by the other also.

You will see, Monsieur le Comte, in perusing these different documents, that affairs in general are not yet treated with that frankness, and that sentiment of justice and equity, which would bring them to a speedy termination.   You will also see that the position of the embassy of France is a very delicate one, inasmuch as its aim is to induce the other powers to be moderate and reasonable, and that those powers are still bound by previous engagements, and inspired by an intolerable ambition.   The opinion that we express in this respect, is borne out by the conversation that Prince Talleyrand had with his Majesty the Emperor of Russia, with which it is necessary that you, Monsieur le Comte, should be acquainted.

The emperor affectedly inquired of the prince, what was the present internal situation of France, the state of her armies, of her finances, of public opinion ; and emphatically announced his intention of preserving what he held, and laid down as a principle, namely, that, in the arrangements about to be made, he meant to *suit* himself. Prince Talleyrand observed that he ought rather to seek what was *right* therein. The emperor then uttered these words : " *It is war then !* . . . . *It is war that you want* . . . . *?* " Prince Talleyrand, without reply-ing, made a gesture which gave the Czar to understand, that if war broke out, it would be the latter's own doing ; and that he would bear the responsibility of it. Thereupon, the Emperor of Russia explained that he had already made his arrangements with the great powers, which Prince Talleyrand took the liberty to question, seeing that France had not con-curred in those arrangements, and that all the powers proclaimed themselves free from any private engagements at variance with what had been agreed upon at Paris.

Such is the situation of affairs. We hear on all hands that the intermediate and smaller powers are already looking towards France for support ; and we further flatter ourselves that the Russian nation and army, having no interest in the restoration of Poland, and not wishing for war merely to further certain ambitious views, the Emperor of Russia will return to his senses, and consent to Europe regaining rest and tranquillity, by taking his stand on the principles that reason dictates.

We have the honour, Monsieur le Comte, to forward to you a copy of a letter from the minister of Portugal to Lord Castlereagh, in which he protests against his exclusion from the preliminary conferences, as Portuguese minister. Prince Talleyrand thought fit to second his protest.

Be pleased to accept . . . .

No. 3.—The Prince de Talleyrand to King Louis XVIII.

VIENNA *Oct.* 4, 1814.

SIRE,

On September the 30th, between nine and ten o'clock A.M. I received from Prince Metternich a note of some five lines, bearing the date of the preceding evening, in which he proposed to me in his name alone, to call on him at two o'clock, to *attend* a preliminary conference, at which I should only find the ministers of Russia, England, and Prussia assembled. He added that he had made the same request to Count de Labrador, Spanish minister.

The words *attend* and *assembled* were manifestly in-
tentionally employed.   I replied that I should be very pleased to
meet the ministers of Russia, England, Spain, and Prussia at
his house.

The invitation addressed to Count de Labrador, was couched in
the same terms as the one I had received, with the difference
only that it was in the form of a note in the third person, and
was written in the name of Prince Metternich and *his colleagues.*

Count de Labrador having come to show it to me, and to
consult me on the reply to be made, I showed him what I had
written, and he wrote his in identical terms, naming France with,
but before, the other powers.   We thus purposely, Count de
Labrador and myself, united what the others seemed anxious
to divide, and we divided what they seemed especially anxious
to unite.

I was at Prince Metternich's before two o'clock, and the
ministers of the four courts were already sitting in conference
round a long table : at one end Lord Castlereagh was apparently presiding : at the other, a gentleman whom Prince
Metternich introduced to me as filling the office of secretary at
their conferences.   It was Herr von Gentz.   I was shown to a
vacant seat between Lord Castlereagh and Prince Metternich.
I asked why I alone of your Majesty's Embassy had been
invited, which brought about the following dialogue :

" It was wished to bring only the heads of cabinets together,
at the preliminary conferences."

" Count de Labrador is not one of them, and yet has been
invited."

" That is because the Secretary of State of Spain is not in
Vienna."

" But, besides Prince von Hardenberg, I see here Herr von
Humboldt, who is not a Secretary of State."

" This is an exception, necessitated by the infirmity with which
you are aware Prince Hardenberg is afflicted."[1]

" If it be only a question of infirmities, each of us could have
his own, and possesses an equal claim to have them considered
as a valid excuse."

There seemed then a disposition, to allow each Secretary of
State to bring with him one of the plenipotentiaries attached to
him, and for the present, I thought it useless to insist further.

The Portuguese ambassador, Count de Palmella,[2] having
been informed by Lord Castlereagh, that preliminary conferences

---

[1] Prince von Hardenberg was afflicted with little short of complete deafness.
[2] Senhor de Souza-Holstein, Count, then Duke of Palmella (1786-1850), was later
Regent of Portugal (1830).

were to be held, which Count de Labrador and myself were to attend, and of which no intimation had been sent to him, had thought fit to protest against an exclusion which he had considered both unjust and humiliating to the Crown of Portugal. He had therefore written to Lord Castlereagh a letter, which the latter produced at the conference. His arguments were strong, and ably deduced. He asked that the eight powers that had signed the treaty of May 30th, and not six of those powers only, should form the preliminary commission, which was to start the congress for whose summoning they had stipulated. Count de Labrador and myself seconded that request. A certain disposition was shown to acquiesce in it, but a definite decision was deferred until the next sitting. Sweden has not yet any plenipotentiary here, and has consequently not yet been in a position to protest.

"The object of to-day's conference," said Lord Castlereagh to me, "is to acquaint you with what the four courts have done, since we have been here." Then addressing Prince Metternich, he added, "You have the protocol."

Prince Metternich then handed me a document signed by himself, Count Nesselrode, Lord Castlereagh, and Prince von Hardenberg. In this document, the word *allies* occurred in each paragraph.

I objected to that expression. I said it necessitated my asking where we were, whether still at Chaumont, or at Laon?[1] if peace had not been made, whether war had been declared, and if so, against whom? They all replied that they did not attach to the word *allies*, any meaning at variance with our present relations, and that it had only been employed for the sake of brevity; so I pointed out, that however important it might be to abridge work, that importance was not such as to warrant the neglect of accuracy.

As to the contents of the protocol, it was but a tissue of metaphysical deductions intended to justify pretensions based on treaties unknown to us. To discuss these arguments and pretensions would have opened up an area of endless dispute. I felt it necessary to meet all with one peremptory argument. I read several paragraphs and said, "I do not understand." I read them again, posing with the air of a man who seeks to grasp the meaning of a thing, and I said, "I do not understand any better." I added: "There are but two dates, between which there is a gap, in my eyes, that of May 30th, when the formation of a

---

[1] On March 25, 1814, the allied sovereigns, after the rupture of the negotiations at Châtillon, had signed a declaration at Laon whereby they agreed anew to the provisions of the treaty of Chaumont.

congress was stipulated for, and that of the 1st of October, when this congress was to meet.   All that has been done in the meantime I ignore, and it does not exist in my eyes."

To this, the plenipotentiaries replied that they cared little for that document, and that they asked no better than to withdraw it, upon which Count de Labrador remarked that they had nevertheless signed it.   They withdrew it.   Prince Metternich put it aside, and there was no longer any question of it.

After having foregone that document, they produced another. It was a project of declaration which Count de Labrador and myself were to sign with them, if we should adopt it.   After a long preamble, on the necessity of simplifying and abridging the work of the congress, and after repeated assurances that there was no intention of encroaching on the rights of any one, the project stated, that the points to be settled by the congress, should be divided into two series, for each of which a commission should be appointed, to which application could be made by the states concerned, and that when those two commissions had completed their work, the congress should then assemble for the first time, and all questions be submitted for its sanction.

This project was evidently intended to render the four powers who call themselves *allied* absolute masters of all the deliberations of the congress, seeing that on the supposition that the six chief powers should constitute themselves judges of the questions relative to the composition of the congress, to the points that it should settle, to the order in which these should be settled, and should, alone and without control, appoint the commission to prepare all the work, France and Spain, even supposing they always agreed on all questions, would still be but two against four.

I declared that in order to form an opinion on a project of that nature, a first reading would not be sufficient; that it required to be meditated upon; that, above all, it was necessary to ascertain whether it was compatible with the rights that we were all bent on respecting; that we had come to consecrate and secure the rights of each of the powers, and that it would be most unfortunate if we should begin by violating them; that the idea of·arranging everything before assembling the congress was quite new to me; that they proposed to finish with what, as I believed, it was necessary to begin; that, perhaps, the rights it was proposed to confer on the six powers could only be given them by the congress; that there were measures which irresponsible ministers could easily adopt, but that Lord Castlereagh and myself were very differently situated.

Here Lord Castlereagh said that the remarks I had just made had all occurred to him, and that he fully appreciated their force. " But," he added, "what other expedient can we find to avoid involving ourselves in inextricable and dilatory proceedings ? "

I asked why the congress was not there and then assembled ? What difficulties were in the way ? Each plenipotentiary thereupon alleged what he regarded as an obstacle to the adoption of such a measure. A conversation ensued, in the course of which, it being a question of him who reigns at Naples, Count de Labrador expressed himself without reserve.[1] As for myself, I simply remarked : " Of what King of Naples do you speak? We do not know who he is."[2] And Herr von Humboldt having observed that the powers had recognized him and guaranteed to him his states, I firmly replied:[3] " Those who gave him such a guarantee, had no right, and therefore no power, to do so." And, in order not to lay stress on that language, I added : " But there is no question of this at present." Then reverting to the congress, I said that the difficulties which seemed to be apprehended would perhaps be less than was believed, that it was necessary to seek some means of obviating them, and that we should surely find it. Prince von Hardenberg declared that he did not hold to one expedient more than to another, but that some was required in order that the princes of Leyen and of Lichtenstein[4] might not interfere in the general arrangements of Europe. Thereupon we adjourned until the next day, after the other plenipotentiaries had promised to send me, as well as Count de Labrador, copies of the draft of the declaration, and of the letter of Count de Palmella.

(The different documents referred to in the letter I have the honour to write to your Majesty, are enclosed in the despatch I write to-day to the Department of Foreign Affairs.)

After having received them, and thoroughly examined them I thought it best not to wait until the next conference to make

[1] Text : . . ; " une conversation s'en est suivie dans laquelle, à l'occasion de celui qui régne à Naples," . . . (a conversation ensued, . . .). Var. ". . une conversation *générale* s'en est suivie. *Le nom du roi de Naples s'étant présenté à quelqu'un,"* . . (a *general* conversation ensued. *The name of the King of Naples having occurred to some one,* . . .)

[2] Text : " De quel roi de Naples parlez-vous ? nous ne savons qui c'est." (Of what king . . .) Var. : " De quel roi de Naples *parle-t-on ? Nous ne connaissons point l'homme dont il est question."* (Of what king of Naples *do you speak ? We do not know the person you mention.*)

[3] Text : . . , "j'ai reparti d'un ton ferme " (I firmly replied). Var. : . . , "j'ai dit d'un ton ferme *et froid* " (I firmly and coolly said).

[4] Two of the smallest principalities of Germany. That of Lichtenstein, for instance, only contained 7,000 inhabitants.

my opinion known. I drew up a reply, first in the form of a verbal note; then, remembering that the ministers of the four courts had held conferences among themselves in which they had drawn up and signed protocols, it struck me that it was im-portant that there should not be between them and the minister of your Majesty, merely conversations, of which no trace remained, and that an official note would be the most suitable means of opening the negotiations. Therefore, on the 1st of October I addressed to the ministers of the other five powers a note with my signature attached, bearing in substance :—

"That the eight powers who signed the treaty of May 30th, appeared to me, for that simple reason,[1] fully qualified to appoint a commission that should prepare, for the decision of the congress, the points that it was first of all to settle, and to propose to it the formation of the commission that it might have deemed expedient to appoint, as well as the names of the persons who were deemed most fit to sit on them ; but that their competence extended no further; that, not being the congress, but only a fraction of it, the fact of conferring on themselves powers which can only belong to that assembly, would constitute an usurpation which, if called upon to concur in it, I should feel much exercised to conciliate with my responsibility ; that the difficulty found in summoning the congress was not of the nature of those which grow less with time, and that, since it was sometime or other to be overcome, nothing could be gained from delaying ; that minor states had undoubtedly no right to interfere in the general arrangements of Europe, but that such desire would not even occur to them, and that, therefore, they would cause no hindrance ; that all those considerations naturally led to wish that the eight powers should, without delay, examine the pre-liminary points to be decided by the congress, in order that it might soon be opened, and that those points might be submitted to it."

After having sent this note, I betook myself to the special audience that the Emperor Alexander had accorded me. Count Nesselrode came to tell me, on his Majesty's behalf, that he desired to see me alone ; indeed, the Czar himself had reminded me of that wish on his part the evening before, at a court ball, where I had the honour of meeting his Majesty. On seeing me, the emperor took my hand, but his manner was not so affectionate as usual. His tone was curt, his demeanour serious, and perhaps a little solemn. I saw clearly that he was about to play a part.

---

[1] Text: . . , " me paraissaient par cette circonstance seule," . . . (appeared to me . . .). Var. : . . . , " me paraissaient par cette circonstance seule, *et à défaut de médiateur,*" . . . (appeared . . . . . . simple reason, *and for want of a me-diator* . . .).

" First of all," he said to me, " what is the situation of your country ? "

" As well as your Majesty has wished it to be, and better than one would have dared to hope."

" Public opinion ? "

" It is daily improving."

" Liberal ideas ? "

" Nowhere is there more liberal ideas than in France."

" But what about the liberty of the press ? "

" That exists with a few restrictions dictated by circumstances.[1] Those restrictions will disappear in a couple of years, and will not prevent all that is good and useful being published in the meantime."

" And the army ? "

" It is altogether devoted to the king. One hundred and thirty thousand men are now under the colours, and, at the first call, three hundred thousand more could join them."

" What about the marshals ? "

" Which, sire ? "

" Oudinot."

" He is devoted to the king."

" Soult ? "

" He was at first in a bit of humour. He was given the governorship of Vendée ; he behaves there most satisfactorily. He makes himself beloved and respected."

" And Ney ? "

" He regrets a little the endowments of the past ; your Majesty might soothe his regrets."

" The two Chambers ? it seems to me they show signs of opposition ? "

" As in all deliberative assemblies opinions may differ, but affection to the sovereign is unanimous ; and notwithstanding the difference of opinions, the government always secures a large majority."

" But there is no accord."

" Who could have said such a thing to your Majesty ? When after twenty-five years of revolution, the king finds himself in a few months as firmly established on his throne as though he had never left France, what more certain proof could there be that everybody has the same end in view ? "

" Your personal position ? "

" The confidence and kindness of the king are beyond all I could have hoped."

[1] The charter had guaranteed the liberty of the press ; but a law passed in September, 1814, had re-established the censorship for a period of two years.

" Now let us talk business affairs. We must finish them here."

" That depends upon your Majesty. They shall be concluded promptly and happily, if your Majesty displays the same nobleness and magnanimity as when dealing with French affairs."

" But it is important that each of us should obtain what suits him."

" And that each obtain his rights."

" I shall keep what I have."

" Your Majesty would keep only what legitimately belongs to you."

" I have made an agreement with the great powers."

" I am not aware whether your Majesty reckons France as one of those powers."

" Yes, I certainly do.   But if you will not admit that every one of us is to get what suits him best, what do you mean ? " .

" I place right first and interest after."

" The interests of Europe constitute rights."

" This language, sire, is not yours ; it is foreign to your feelings and your heart disapproves it."

" No, I repeat it ; the interests of Europe constitute rights."

I then turned towards the wainscot close to me, I put my head against it, and striking it with my forehead, I exclaimed : " Europe, Europe, unfortunate Europe ! " and turning round to the emperor—" Shall it be said," I asked of him, " that you have brought about her ruin ? "

He replied, " Rather war than to renounce what I possess."

I let my arms fall in the attitude of a man afflicted, but decided, who had the air of saying to him, "the fault shall not be ours." I kept silent. The Czar remained a few minutes without replying, he then repeated, " Yes ; rather war."

My attitude remained unchanged. Then raising his hands and moving them nervously as I had never seen him do before, and in a manner that recalled to my mind the passage that terminates the elegy of Marcus Aurelius, he cried out rather than he said, " It is time for the play, I must go : I promised the emperor that I would do so ; I am expected"—and he moved away.   Having opened the door, he came back to me, clasped me in his arms and said, with a voice that was no longer his own, " Adieu, adieu ! we shall meet again ! "

In all that conversation of which alone I can relate to your Majesty the striking features, Poland and Saxony were not once mentioned, but only indicated by periphrases. Thus that the Czar would designate Saxony in saying, " *Those who have betrayed the cause of Europe*," to which I was in the case of replying, " Sire, that is a question of dates," and, after a slight pause, I might have added, " and the effect of the difficulties into which one may have been thrown by circumstances."

The emperor once spoke of the *allies*. I criticized that expression as I had done at the conference, and he accounted for it by having the habit of using it.

Yesterday, which should have been that of the second conference, M. de Mercy was sent to me by Prince Metternich to inform me that it would not be held.

A friend of Herr von Gentz having gone to see him in the afternoon found him engaged on a work which, he told him, was very pressing. I believe it was a reply to my note.

In the evening at the house of the Prince von Trautmansdorf[1] the plenipotentiaries reproached me for having addressed it to them, and especially for having given it, by signing it, an official character. I told them that as they wrote and signed amongst themselves, I had believed that it was necessary that I should also write and sign. I infer from this that my note rather perplexed them.

To-day Prince Metternich wrote to inform me that a conference would be held this evening at eight o'clock ; later he sent me word that there would be none, because he was expected at the Czar's.

Such is, sire, the present state of affairs.

Your Majesty sees that our position here is intricate : it becomes more so every day. The Czar Alexander gives full swing to his ambition ; in this he is incited by M. de la Harpe and by Prince Czartoryski. Prussia hopes for a large increase ; Austria, pusillanimous as usual, has only a bashful ambition ; but she displays complacency in order to be aided. And these are not the only difficulties : there are others still which proceed from agreements made by the courts, formerly allied, at a time when they did not hope to beat him whose overthrow they have witnessed, and by which they intended to make with him a peace which would enable them to imitate him. To-day, your Majesty replaced on the throne, has exalted justice ; the powers for the benefit of whom those agreements were made, will not renounce them, and those who perhaps regret being bound do not know how to release themselves. It is I believe the case with England.[2] The ministers of your Majesty might thus meet with such obstacles that they would have to renounce all other hope than that of preserving honour. But we have not yet come to that. I have the honour to be, &c.

---

[1] Councillor of State and High Chamberlain of the Emperor of Austria (1749-1817).

[2] Var : . . . . *dont le ministre est faible* (whose minister is weak).

No. 4A.—THE KING'S AMBASSADORS AT THE CONGRESS TO
THE MINISTER OF FOREIGN AFFAIRS AT PARIS.

VIENNA, *October* 8, 1814.

MONSIEUR LE COMTE,

In our despatch of the 4th inst. we had the honour to
inform you that the close logic that we opposed to the four
powers, who still represent themselves as bound together by
secret clauses, embarrasses them very much.

It is in fact natural that these powers, whose aim it is to get
France to sanction the overthrow of all principles founded on
public law, and, at the same time, to consent to the plunder of
Saxony, be singularly inconvenienced when they find that same
France willing to act only in accord with justice.

However difficult be our part to play with persons who
doubt our sincerity and will not allow principles of reason to
modify their views, all we learn confirms us in the belief that
we must strictly adhere to the line we have adopted. We feel
that it is the only one that can form a bulwark to oppose the invading forces that threaten Europe, if serious attention is not
paid to them.

We have the honour of acquainting you with all that has
been done since our last despatch.

Lord Castlereagh has drawn up a project of declaration
which Prince Metternich handed to Prince Talleyrand on the
evening of the 3rd. (No. 1, subjoined documents.)

It was communicated only under the form of a project, but
the reading of it confirms us in our opinion that the four great
allied powers will, conforming to their arrangements, continue
to follow a system of convenience adopted on the supposition
that Bonaparte remain on the throne of France, and that they
do not take into consideration the restoration of the house
of Bourbon, which changes all the state of Europe, and by
means of which everything should be restored on its former
basis.

At first glance, it is plain that great danger must result
from this system, that a real and durable equilibrium becomes
impossible, and that considering the weakness of the cabinet of
Vienna, France alone would no longer be mistress of the events
that the future seems to have in store.

Prince Talleyrand replied by private letter to Lord Castlereagh. Therein he lays special stress on the importance of the
idea that the congress should open, and that the powers could
only prepare and propose—but not decide alone—matters of
general interest.

Though that letter be in the form of a note, it is nevertheless couched in such terms as will serve to enlighten Europe, some day, if necessary, concerning the attitude followed by France in the affairs of the congress. (See No. 2.)

Since then, Prince Metternich has summoned a second conference.

The Prince de Talleyrand and Count de Labrador were invited to it, but the ministers of Sweden and Portugal did not attend it.

That conference has been barren of result. It was felt, however, that it was necessary to acquaint the different powers with the motives that delayed the opening of the congress.

Prince Talleyrand opposed the project of Lord Castlereagh as being contrary to the principle by which the congress is constituted and which Article XXXII. of the treaty of Paris distinctly sets forth.[1] Thereupon the plenipotentiaries agreed to draw up new projects, and the next day Prince Talleyrand sent to Prince Metternich a draft which could serve for the purpose. (See note 3).

This draft, Monsieur le Comte, as you will see on reading it, sets forth, at the same time, the principle by virtue of which the congress assembles, the reasons for delay, the consideration felt for the rights of the powers, and the principle upon which each plenipotentiary shall be admitted.

According to the principle established by the declaration, the King of Saxony would find himself summoned and Murat excluded. Nevertheless the exclusion of the latter offers no less difficulties than the admission of the former, and we suppose that there exists between Russia, England, and Prussia an agreement on the points that our instructions enjoin us not to admit.

Prince Metternich often pleads Murat's cause, and seeks to intimidate the congress with the obstacles that he might offer at the head of eighty thousand men, if, at the news of his exclusion, he marched into the interior of Italy. We point out how little justified is this fear, and that it would only require a landing of French and Spanish troops in Sicily to put an end for ever to that royal comedy in which no one can wish to take part, and which would be more dangerous to Austria than even to France. We see at each step we take that the principal difficulty which opposes our success is that arising from the

---

[1] Art. XXXII.—In the delay of two months all the powers that have been engaged, on one side or the other, in the present war, shall send plenipotentiaries to Vienna to settle at a general congress the arrangements which are to complete the provisions of the present treaty.

timid character of the Austrian ministers, and from the peculiar apathy of the nation; that Russia and Prussia carrying that conviction in their calculations, shall insist upon their unjust pretensions, and that, perhaps nothing will remain for us but to declare that, protesting against such violence, France will take no part in it. We often repeat that it is singular that it should be the French embassy at the congress that takes it upon itself to transact the business of the Austrian cabinet.

Lord Castlereagh equally lacks force and dignity in this circumstance, and we sometimes ask ourselves how he will justify one day before Parliament the heedlessness he displays for the great principles which constitute nations.

The ministers of Bavaria, Denmark, and Sardinia begin to murmur, and we are told that they are concerting themselves for asking the great powers whether the congress is formed, and if so, when it will assemble.

This idea was suggested by us, and we hope that this step shall, if the powers tarry too much, lead to an explanation.

To-day, in the evening, Prince Metternich invited Prince Talleyrand to a new conference, and requested him to arrive at his house an hour before the general meeting in order to discuss some important points.

The result of that conversation induces the hope that Prince Metternich will adopt some of our ideas, and that he will seek to conciliate the pretensions of the powers with the principles that we put forward.

At the general conference, which was attended by the ministers of Portugal and Sweden, no agreement was arrived at concerning our projected declaration. It was decided not to prejudge anything by an inflexible principle too loudly proclaimed, but to adjourn the opening of the congress until November 1st, and to endeavour, in the meantime, to promote business by means of confidential communications between the different powers. It is in this sense that a project of declaration was prepared and presented by the other ministers. After long debates, Prince Talleyrand succeeded in adding the following phrase to it: "That the propositions to be made at the congress should conform to the *public law* and to the just expectation of Europe." The other ministers tried in vain to have that term *public law* omitted. The Prussian ministers demurred for a long time, and it was only after a debate which lasted two hours, that the insertion was carried, so to speak, at the point of the sword. It has been clearly seen that they wished to finish affairs rather by means of their own accord, than by conforming to the principles of reason and justice, upon which is properly founded the public law of Europe.

We have the honour of addressing you a copy of that declaration which, save several corrections, shall be published such as it is. (See No. 4.)

We have not, as you see, Monsieur le Comte, obtained a complete victory, but things are intact, the principles of public law are maintained, and the declaration leaves us a great latitude for watching over all the interests it is our duty to do.

We are told that the minister of Bavaria has sent in a formal protest with regard to his exclusion from the commission summoned to prepare work.

Prince Metternich appeased him by holding out to him the hope that Bavaria will preside over the commission which is to deal with the affairs of Germany, and that, in that capacity, she would have a voice in all the general arrangements.

Be pleased to accept. . . . .

No. 4.—The Prince de Talleyrand to King Louis XVIII.

Vienna, *October* 9, 1814.

Sire,

The ministers of the four courts, being embarrassed by my note of October 1st, and finding no argument with which to combat it, have hit upon no other plan than that of becoming angry. "That note," Herr von Humboldt said, "is a firebrand thrown among us." "They would like to sever us," said Count Nesselrode, "but they will not succeed in doing so." Thus openly avowing what was easy to suspect, that they had formed a league among themselves to become masters of all and to constitute themselves the supreme arbiters of Europe. Lord Castlereagh, with more moderation and in a gentle tone, told me that their intention was that, the conference to which Count de Labrador and myself had been invited, should be quite confidential, and that I had deprived it of that character by addressing them a note, and especially an official one. I replied that it was their fault and not mine ; that they had asked me for my opinion, and that I was forced to give it, and that if I had reduced it to writing and signed it, it was because, having seen that in their conferences among themselves they wrote and signed, I was induced to suppose that it was necessary that I should do the same.

However the contents of my letter having transpired, those gentlemen, in order to allay the effect of it, had recourse to the usual means of the cabinet of Berlin. They replied that the principles I put forth were but a decoy; that we wanted the left bank of the Rhine, had designs on Belgium, and wished for war. That intelligence came to me from all sides ; but I ordered all the members of the legation to explain themselves before all with so much simplicity and candour, and in so positive a manner, that the authors of those absurd rumours reaped only the shame of having spread them.

On the evening of the 3rd of October, Prince Metternich, with whom I was at the house of the Duchess of Sagan,[1] handed me a draft of a declaration arranged by Lord Castlereagh; this second project differed from the first, only inasmuch as it tended to have what the four courts proposed, considered as being but a consequence of the first of the secret articles of the treaty of May 30th.[2] But neither was the principle on which he based his project just (for Lord Castlereagh evidently lent to one of the provisions of the article a sense that it did not have, and that we could not admit), nor, had the principle been just, would the consequence drawn from it have been legitimate ; the attempt was thus doubly unfortunate.

I wrote to Lord Castlereagh. I gave a confidential tone to my letter. I endeavoured to point out all the reasons that militated against the proposed plan. (The copy of my letter is subjoined to the despatch I am writing to-day to the department.) Your Majesty will see that I have especially endeavoured to hint, with all possible deference, that the motive for which the plan had been proposed had not escaped me. I deemed it advisable to declare that it was impossible for me to consent to anything contrary to principles, seeing that unless we remained invariably attached to them, we could not again resume, in the eyes of the nations of Europe, the rank and consideration to which we are entitled since the return of your Majesty, and because, discarding them would cause a revival of the Revolution which only resulted from a long forgetfulness of principles.

I have learned that, when Lord Castlereagh received my

---

[1] Sagan, city of Silesia, chief town of a principality formerly possessed by the famous Wallenstein. It passed afterwards to the family of the Biren, Dukes of Courland. Catherine Wilhelmine, daughter of Pierre, Duke of Courland, succeeded him in 1800, as Duchess of Sagan. She died in 1839. Her sister Pauline succeeded her. In 1844, the duchy reverted to Dorothy, third daughter of Pierre, Duke of Courland, and wife of Edmond, Duke of Dino, and, later, of Talleyrand-Périgord, nephew of Prince Talleyrand.

[2] This is that article : "The disposal of the territories renounced by His Most Christian Majesty according to Article III. of the open treaty, and the relations from which a system of real and durable equilibrium is to result for Europe, *shall be settled at the Congress, on the bases arrived at by the allied powers*, and in conformity to the general provisions contained in the following articles, &c. . . . . . "

letter, he gave it to read to the minister of Portugal, who was at his house, and who confessed to him that in law we were right, but added that it was nevertheless necessary to know if what we proposed was practicable, which was really asking, in other terms, whether the four courts could dispense with arrogating to themselves powers over Europe which the latter had not given them.

On that day we had a conference, which at first was only attended by two or three plenipotentiaries, the other ministers arriving only at intervals of a quarter of an hour ; Lord Castlereagh had brought my letter in order to communicate it. It was passed from hand to hand. Prince Metternich and Count Nesselrode simply glanced at it, as men whose penetration was such that the single inspection of a document sufficed for grasping its entire contents. I had been forewarned that I should be asked to withdraw my note. Indeed, Prince Metternich made that request to me. I replied that I could not. Count de Labrador said it was too late ; that it would do no good, for he had already sent a copy of it to his court.

" It is then necessary that we reply ? " said Prince Metternich.

" If you wish to," I said.

" My opinion is," he replied, " that we should settle our affairs all alone." Meaning by " we " the four courts.

I replied, without hesitation : " If you consider the question from that point of view, I am quite your man ; I am quite ready ; I ask nothing better."

" How do you mean it ? " he said.

" It is very easy," I replied. " I shall no longer attend your conferences. I shall be here only as a member of the congress, and I shall wait until it opens."

Instead of renewing his proposal, Prince Metternich returned, gradually and by the use of various periphrases, to general propositions concerning the inconvenience that the actual opening of the congress would cause.

Count Nesselrode said, rather thoughtlessly, that the Czar Alexander intended to start on the 25th, to which I was obliged to reply in a rather indifferent tone :

" I am sorry for that, for he will not witness the conclusion of affairs."

" How can we summon the congress," said Prince Metternich, " when none of the questions which are to be submitted to it are ready ? "

" Very well," I replied, " to show you that it is not a spirit of contradiction that animates me and that I am disposed to adopt all measures that are not in opposition to principles which I cannot desert, since nothing is yet ready for the opening of the congress, since you desire to adjourn it, let it be delayed a fortnight or three weeks, I consent to it, but on two conditions : the one that you convene it at once for a fixed day, the other, that you state, in the note of convocation, the rule according to which its members shall be admitted."

I wrote on a piece of paper that rule, couched in about the same terms as those contained in the instructions of your Majesty. The paper circulated from hand to hand. There were a few questions and some objections, which, however, did not settle anything, and the ministers, who had come in one after the other, having left in the same way, the conference died out, so to say, instead of running its natural course.

Lord Castlereagh, who had remained among the last, and with whom I went downstairs, tried to win me over to their opinion, by giving me to understand that certain matters, which most interested my court, might be arranged to my satisfaction.

" It is not," I said to him, " of such and such private matters that it is now question, but of the principles which should serve to regulate all. If once the connection is broken, how are we to resume it ? We have to meet the wishes of Europe. What shall we have done for her, if we do not replace in honour the maxims to the disregard of which her misfortunes are due ? The present epoch is one of those which scarcely presents itself once in the course of several centuries. A better occasion could never be offered us. Why not place ourselves in a position to take advantage of it ? "

" Ah," he replied, with a sort of embarrassment, " because there are difficulties that you do not know of."

" No, I do not know of them," I replied, in the tone of a man who had no curiosity to know them.

Thereupon we took leave of each other.

I dined at Prince Windischgraetz.[1] Herr von Gentz was there. We talked a long time on the points discussed in the conferences which we had attended. He seemed to regret that I had not arrived sooner at Vienna ; for he was pleased to believe that the matters with which he seemed dissatisfied might have

---

[1] Alfred, Prince von Windischgraetz, of an old illustrious family of Styria. He was born at Brussels in 1787, entered the army and became general. His name became celebrated only in 1848 : he then commanded at Prague and had to suppress a terrible insurrection. He crushed it and was, in recompense, appointed field-marshal. He afterwards took Vienna, which had fallen in the power of the mob, and was sent to Hungary ; but he failed in the latter task and was recalled. He died in 1862.

taken a different turn. He finished by confessing that they all felt that in the main I was right, but that pride was at stake, and that having made a step forward, the best disposed felt it difficult to retrace it.

Two days passed without a conference being held. A fête one day, a hunt the other, were the causes of this. In the meantime I was introduced to the Duchess of Oldenburg.[1] I expressed to her my regrets that she had not come to Paris with her brother. She replied that that journey was only postponed; she then proceeded at once to put the same questions to me as the emperor concerning your Majesty, the state of public opinion, of our finances, and army; all questions that would have surprised me very much from a woman of twenty-two, had they not seemed to contrast still more with her bearing, her looks, and the sound of her voice. I replied to all in a sense conforming to what we have to do here, and to the interests we have to defend.

She further questioned me about the King of Spain, about his brother and his uncle, speaking of them in terms scarcely becoming, and I replied in a tone that I believed best calculated to give weight to my opinion on the personal merit of those princes.

Herr von Gentz, who came to my house at the moment when I returned from visiting the Duchess of Oldenburg, told me that he had been charged to draw up a project for the convocation of the congress. The day before I had made a draft consonant with what I had proposed at the previous conference, and had sent it to Prince Metternich, begging him to communicate it to the other ministers. Herr von Gentz assured me that he had no knowledge of it. He told me that in his, there was no question of the rule of admission that I had proposed, because Prince Metternich feared that by publishing it they would drive to extremities him who reigns at Naples; his plenipotentiary thus finding himself excluded. We discussed that point, Herr von Gentz and myself, and he seemed persuaded that what Prince Metternich feared would not happen.

I expected a conference for the next day, but three-quarters of the day having slipped away without my having received any intimation, I no longer counted on it, when I received a note from Prince Metternich who informed me that there would be one at eight o'clock, and that if I would come to his house a little before, *he would find means of introducing some*

---

[1] Catherine-Paulowna, sister to the Czar Alexander. Born in 1795; widow in 1812, of Pierre-Frederick-George, Grand Duke of Oldenburg, married again, in 1816, to the King of Wurtemberg.

very important matters. (Such were the terms of his note.) I was at his house at seven o'clock. I was at once introduced. He first spoke of a project of declaration that he had had drawn up, which differed, he said, a little from mine but was on the whole, very similar, and with which he hoped that I would be satisfied. I asked him for it ; he did not have it. "Probably," I said to him, "it is being communicated to the allies?"

"Speak no more of allies," replied he, "there are no longer any."

"There are here people," I said to him, "who should be such in this way that even without concerting themselves, they should hold the same views and desire the same end. How can you have the courage to place Russia as a belt around your principal and most important possessions, Hungary and Bohemia ? How can you suffer that the patrimony of an old and good neighbour [1] in whose family an archduchess is married, be given to your natural enemy ? It is strange that it should be us who object to this and you who do not! . . . ."

He said that I had no confidence in him.

I replied, laughing, that he had not given me many motives for trusting him, and I reminded him of certain circumstances in which he had not kept his word. "Besides," I added, "how can I have confidence in a man whose affairs are all a mystery for those who are the most disposed to arrange matters ? As for myself, I make no mystery, and I have no need to do so; that is the advantage of those who negotiate only with principles. There, I continued, are pens and paper. Will you write that France asks for nothing, and will accept nothing, and I will sign it ?"

"But there is," he said, "the Naples business, which is really your own."

I replied, "No more mine than anybody else's. It is for me only a question of principles. I ask that he who has a right to be at Naples, be at Naples, and nothing more ; and this is what everybody ought to wish as well as myself. Let principles be observed, and I shall be found most easy. I will tell you frankly what I ever can and what I never shall consent to ; I feel that the King of Saxony, in his present position, may be obliged to make a sacrifice. I believe that he will be disposed to make one, because he is wise ; but if they mean to deprive him of all his states, and give the kingdom of Saxony to Russia, I shall never consent to that. I shall never consent

---

[1] Saxony. Prince Anthony, brother of the King Frederick-Augustus, married : (1) Princess Marie-Charlotte-Antoinette, daughter of the Emperor Leopold, who died in 1782 ; (2) in 1787, Marie-Therese-Josephe, another daughter of the Emperor Leopold, born in 1767.

either to Luxemburg or Mayence being given to Prussia. I shall never consent to Russia crossing the Vistula, and having forty-four millions of subjects in Europe, and her frontiers on the Oder. But if Luxemburg be given to Holland, Mayence to Bavaria ; if the king and the kingdom of Saxony be preserved, and if Russia pass not the Vistula, I shall have no objections to make for that part of Europe."

Prince Metternich thereupon took my hand saying, " Our views are not so opposed as you think. I promise you that Prussia shall not have Luxemburg nor Mayence. We desire no more than yourself that Russia be increased beyond measure, and as to Saxony, we shall do our very best to preserve at least a portion of it."

It was only to know his own views regarding these different points that I spoke to him as I did. Reverting then to the convocation of the congress, he insisted upon the necessity of not publishing at present the rule of admission that I had proposed, " because," he said, " it would scare every one ; and, as to myself, it perplexes me at present ; for Murat, on seeing his plenipotentiary excluded, will know his case is hopeless ; he will believe that no one knows what his passionate temper may lead him to do ; that he is ready in Italy, and that we are not."

Having been informed that the ministers had assembled, we repaired to the conference. Prince Metternich opened it by announcing that he would read two projects, the one prepared by myself, the other by him. The Prussians declared themselves for that of Prince Metternich, saying that it prejudged nothing, whereas mine prejudged a great deal. Count Nesselrode was of the same opinion. The minister of Sweden, Herr von Löwenhielm,[1] who was attending the congress for the first time, said that nothing must be prejudged. It was also the opinion of Lord Castlereagh, and I knew it was that of Prince Metternich. That project confined itself to adjourning the opening of the congress to November 1, and said nothing more, which gave rise to Count de Palmella, minister of Portugal, observing that a second declaration to convoke the congress would be necessary, and this was agreed upon. This was only delaying the difficulty but not resolving it. However, as the old pretensions had been abandoned, as it was no longer a question of everything being settled by the eight powers, and of

---

[1] Gustavus von Löwenhielm, born in 1771, was an officer in the Swedish army. He was aide-de-camp to Gustavus III., and later to Bernadotte. In 1815, he left the army for the diplomacy, was sent to the congress at Vienna, and afterwards appointed ambassador at Paris.

leaving to the congress only the faculty of approving; as the plenipotentiaries spoke only of preparing by free and confidential communications with the ministers of the other powers, the questions which the congress should decide, I thought that an act of complacency which would not infringe principles, could be useful to the progress of affairs, and I declared that I consented to the adoption of the project, but on the condition that in the place where it was said that the formal opening of the congress should be adjourned until November 1, they should add, *and shall be made according to the principles of public law.* These words provoked an uproar difficult to conceive. Prince von Hardenberg, standing, leaning his wrists on the table, almost menacing, and shouting as is the wont of those who are afflicted with the same infirmity as himself, uttered these words, interrupted now and again:

"No, Monsieur . . . , the term public law is useless. Why say that we shall act only according to public law? that goes without saying."

I replied, "That if that went without saying, it would go better by saying it."

Herr von Humboldt exclaimed, " What has public law to do here?"

To which I replied, "It has this to do here that it has brought you to this congress."

Lord Castlereagh drew me aside, and asked me if when they had yielded to my desires, I should be more easy.

I inquired in turn whether if I showed myself easy to please, I could expect him to do the same in the Naples business.

He promised to second me with all his influence: "I shall speak of it," he said, "to Metternich; I have the right to give advice on this matter."

"You give me your word of honour," I said.

"I give you it," he replied.

"And," I retorted, "I give you mine to be difficult only on those principles that I ought not to abandon."

Nevertheless Herr von Gentz having approached Prince Metternich represented to him that one could not refuse to speak of public law in an act of such a nature as that being mooted. Prince Metternich had previously proposed to put the point at issue to the vote, thus betraying the use they would have made of the powers they had assumed, had their first project been admitted. They concluded by consenting to the addition I demanded, but there was a no less lively discussion on the question of deciding where it should be placed, and they finally agreed to place it a sentence higher than that where I had proposed to insert it. Herr von Gentz could not help saying even at the conference: " This evening, gentlemen, belongs to the history of the congress. It is not I who shall relate the incidents of it, because my duty forbids me to do so but they will be found there, certainly."

He has since told me that he never saw anything like it.

That is why I look upon it as fortunate to have been able, without abandoning principles, to do something that could be regarded as conducive to the meeting of the congress.

Herr von Löwenhielm is minister of Sweden and Russia, and a Russian at heart. That is probably why he was sent here, the Prince Royal [1] of Sweden wishing for all that the Russians wish.

The princes who were formerly members of the Confederation of the Rhine begin to assemble in order to urge the opening of the congress. They are already drafting projects between themselves for the organization of Germany.

I have the honour to be . . .

No. 5a.—The King's Ambassadors at the Congress to the Minister of Foreign Affairs at Paris.

VIENNA, *October* 12, 1814.

MONSIEUR LE COMTE,

We have the honour of addressing you a printed copy of the declaration made in the name of the powers who signed the treaty of Paris. It is said that we have won a victory by having introduced the words *public law*. That opinion ought to enable you to gauge the spirit which animates the congress.

It may so happen that the adjournment cause uneasiness in people's minds. On the other hand, it is certain that sufficient justice is not yet being rendered to the principles which guide the king in his political relations. For the last twenty years, Europe has only been accustomed to appreciate force, and to fear its abuse. No one yet indulges the hope and shares the conviction that a great power can wish to be moderate.

It has then appeared to us of importance that the publication of this document, the first result of the political work of the congress, be accompanied by a few observations that put the action of France and its actual influence in its true light.

We have the honour, Monsieur le Comte, to address to you those that we believe may be used in the *Moniteur*, and the spirit of which can furnish the right direction to other newspaper articles.

[1] Bernadotte, then Prince Royal, and later, King of Sweden, under the name of Charles XIV.

We have hopes that Austria will support the resistance that we oppose in all circumstances to the cupidity which Russia and Prussia manifest, and the force of our language shall be proportionate to the degree of confidence we shall be able to place in the energy of the cabinet of Vienna.

We believe we may be certain that she will not sanction the destruction of Saxony, and though not everything, it will already be useful that the cabinet of Vienna concur with us to protest against such violence. We observe generally that Russia makes Germany uneasy, and that, without the support of Prussia, her federative system would lack basis.

We have had occasion to speak of the endowments, and we seek to save as many private interests as is possible. But this matter is placed under the influence of the alliance contracted by the allies at Chaumont. A certain power appears to have given its word to another to accord nothing, and thence it is implied that principles can no longer be attacked.

You feel, Monsieur le Comte, that so long as we shall have to negotiate with powers that assume the character of allies, not even the principle that the domains given in the countries which were ceded by the treaties, should be left to the donees, can be made to prevail. That does not, however, prevent us from seeking, on every occasion, to spare the private interests to which it is advisable to afford some support.

The Czar of Russia spoke yesterday to the English ambassador, Lord Stewart,[1] of the restoration of Poland, indicating that he wished to have one of his brothers elected as king thereof. This question cannot fail to be mooted soon. We think that the Emperor of Russia has not yet any set ideas on the subject, and that he is feeling his way to becoming master of that country.

Be pleased to accept . . .

No. 5.—THE PRINCE DE TALLEYRAND TO KING LOUIS XVIII.

VIENNA, *October* 13, 1814.

SIRE,

I have sent in the despatch addressed to the department, the declaration such as it was published yesterday morning.

---

[1] Charles William Stewart, Earl Vane, later Marquis of Londonderry, after the death of his brother, Lord Castlereagh, born in 1778 at Dublin. He entered the army and was colonel in 1803, when he was appointed Under-Secretary of State to the War Office. He served afterwards in Spain as brigadier-general. In 1815, he was appointed ambassador at Vienna, and plenipotentiary at the congress. He retired in 1819, and did not thereafter discharge any public functions until his death in 1854.

It adjourns the opening of the congress to November 1. Some changes, bearing only on the wording, upon which the ministers have agreed without a meeting, and by the medium of Herr von Gentz, were introduced. We have not had a conference since the 8th, nor consequently any of those discussions with which I am afraid I have wearied your Majesty in my last two letters.

The Prussian minister at London, old Count Jacobi Kloest,[1] has been summoned to the aid of Herr von Humboldt. He is one of the lights of Prussian diplomacy. He came to see me —he is an old acquaintance The conversation promptly led him to speak of the great difficulties that presented themselves and of which the greatest, according to him, proceeded from the Czar Alexander, who wished to have the duchy of Warsaw. I told him that if the Czar Alexander wished to have the duchy, he would probably provide himself with a cession from the King of Saxony, and that then we should see.

"Why of the King of Saxony?" he replied, quite astonished.

"Because," I replied, "the duchy belongs to him by virtue of the cessions that you and Austria have made him and of the treaties that you, Austria, and Russia have signed."

"Then"—with the air of a man who has just made a discovery, and to whom something quite unexpected has been revealed—"it is true, Jove!" said he, "the duchy belongs to him." At least, Count Jacobi Kloest is not one of those who believe that sovereignty can be lost and acquired by the single fact of conquest.

I have reason to believe that we shall obtain for the King of Etruria—Parma, Piacenza, and Guastalla, but, in that case, we must no longer think of Tuscany, to which, however, he certainly has some claims. The Emperor of Austria has already hinted to the Archduchess Marie-Louise that he had little hope of preserving Parma.

People within my hearing often wonder, and Lord Castlereagh plainly asked me, whether the treaty of April 11[2] is being put into execution. The silence of the budget in that respect has been remarked by the Czar of Russia. Prince Metternich says that Austria cannot be held to pay off the interest of the moneys invested in the *Mont de Milan*[3] bank, if France does not

---

[1] Baron Jacobi Kloest, a Prussian diplomatist, born in 1745, ambassador of Prussia at Vienna in 1790, then at London, 1792, where he remained until 1816. In 1799, he represented Prussia at the Congress of Rastadt and denounced loudly the assassination of the French plenipotentiaries by the Austrian hussars. He died in 1817.

[2] The treaty of April 11, 1814, signed between Prussia, Austria, and Russia, with the accession of England on the one part, and of Napoleon, on the other, was intended to determine the situation of the emperor and his family (see vol. ii. p. 126). It will be remembered that an endowment of 2,500,000 francs was promised him.

[3] A state-bank founded at Milan by Napoleon under the name of *Mont Napoléon.*

execute the clauses of the treaty which are incumbent on her. On every occasion, this matter always reappears under different forms, and almost always in an unpleasant manner. However painful it may be to dwell on such money matters, I can but say to your Majesty that it is desirable that something be done in this respect. A letter from M. de Jaucourt, who by command of your Majesty, should inform me of it, would certainly have a good effect.

An almost unanimous intention is shown here of removing Bonaparte from the island of Elba. No one yet has any fixed notion as to the place where he can be sent. I proposed one of the Azores. It is fifteen hundred miles from any mainland. Lord Castlereagh seems to believe it possible that the Portuguese might be induced to lend themselves to that arrangement ; but, in this discussion the money question would re-appear. The son of Bonaparte is no longer treated as he was at the time of his arrival at Vienna. He is treated with less pomp and more simplicity. They have taken the grand ribbon of the Legion of Honour from him, and have substituted that of St. Stephen.

The Czar Alexander, as is his wont, only speaks of liberal ideas. I do not know whether it is these that persuaded him, that in order to pay his court to his hosts, he should go to Wagram, there to visit the scene of their defeat. What is certain is, that he had M. de Czernicheff send for officers who, having been present in that battle, could inform him of the positions and movements of the two armies, which he was pleased to study on the field. It was replied to the Archduke Johan [1] the day before yesterday, who asked where the emperor was : "Your Highness, His Majesty is at Wagram."

It appears that he is to go in a few days to Pesth, where he has requested a ball for the 19th. His plan is to appear there in a Hungarian costume. Before, or after, the ball he will probably go to mourn over his sister's tomb.[2] At that ceremony, there will

The emperor and the members of his family had funds deposited there, and Austria, in accordance with Article XIII. of the treaty of April 11, had agreed to pay the arrears of that institution.

[1] The Archduke Johan was the seventh son of the Emperor Leopold ; he was born in 1782. He commanded in chief the Austrian army at Hohenlinden. In 1801, he became director-general of the fortifications. He had equally important commands in 1805 and 1809. Fallen into disgrace, he played no military part in the last campaign of 1813 and 1814, and lived in retreat until 1848. The parliament united at Frankfort there named him vicar of the German Empire. At the same time the emperor had appointed him as lieutenant-general in Austria. He governed some time in quality of vicar of the empire, but the events which took place forced him to retire. He died in 1859.

The grand-duchess Alexandra Polowna, born in 1783, married in 1799 to the Archduke Joseph-Anthony, brother of the Emperor Francis, palatine of the kingdom of Hungary. She died in 1801.

be a crowd of Greeks whom he has had informed of his intention, and who will hasten to come to see the only monarch who is of their creed. I do not know to what extent that pleases this court, but I fancy it does not please it very much.

Lord Stewart, brother of Lord Castlereagh and ambassador at the court of Vienna, arrived several days ago. He has been presented to the Czar Alexander who said to him (according to his account), "We are about to do a grand and noble thing—restore Poland by giving her one of my brothers, or my sister's [1] (Duchess of Oldenburg) husband for king."

Lord Stewart said frankly to him, "I see in this no independence for Poland, and I don't believe that England, though less interested than the other powers, can accommodate herself to that arrangement."

If I am not very much mistaken, either the union between the four courts is more apparent than real, and proceeds solely from the circumstance that some do not wish to suppose that we have the means of acting, and that the others fancy that we have not the wish to do so. Those who know us to be opposed to their pretensions, think we have only arguments to oppose them. The Czar Alexander said, a few days ago, "Talleyrand acts the minister of Louis XIV. here." Herr von Humboldt, seeking to win, and at the same time to intimidate, Count von Schulenburg, minister of Saxony, said, "The minister of France comes here with words noble enough ; but they either conceal an afterthought, or they have nothing to back them up. Woe be to those who believe in them."

The means of putting an end to all these remarks and dispelling all irresolution would be for your Majesty to address a declaration to your people, and after having disclosed the principles that you have ordered us to follow, and your firm resolution not to deviate from them, simply leave others to gather from it that the just cause would not remain unsupported. Such a declaration, as I conceive it and as I intend submitting to your Majesty, would not lead to war—which no one wants—but would induce those who have pretensions to moderate them, and would give to the others the courage to defend their interests and those of Europe. But as that declaration would be at present premature, I ask your Majesty's permission to speak to you about it later, if subsequent circumstances seemed to me to necessitate it.

Our language is beginning to make an impression. I much regret that an accident met with by Count von Münster pre-

---

[1] There is an error here. The prince Pierre-Frederick-George, Duke of Oldenburg, husband of the grand-duchess Catherine, sister of Alexander, died in 1812.

vented him from coming to the aid of Lord Castlereagh who has really need of support. He will be, so we are told, in a couple of days in a condition to attend the sittings.

I have the honour to be, &c.

No. 2B.—KING LOUIS XVIII. TO THE PRINCE DE TALLEYRAND.

PARIS, *October* 14, 1814.

MY COUSIN,

I have received your despatches of September 29th and October 4th. It will be well for the future to number them as I do this. Consequently those of which I acknowledge the receipt should bear the numbers 2 and 3.

I will begin by telling you with genuine satisfaction that I am perfectly satisfied with the stand you have taken, and the language that you used as well with the plenipotentiaries as in your painful conference with the Czar Alexander. You undoubtedly know that he has summoned General Pozzo di Borgo. God grant that that wise man bring back his sovereign to more sensible views ; but it is on the contrary hypothesis that we must reason.

To prevent the success of the ambitious projects of Russia and Prussia is the end towards which we should tend. Buonaparte[1] unaided might perhaps have succeeded in this, but he employed means that are not and never shall be mine. I must then have aid. That which the small states could offer me would never be sufficient. I must then have that of at least one great power. We should have Austria and England, if they really understood their interests ; but I fear that they are already engaged. I particularly fear a system which prevails with many English, and with which the Duke of Wellington himself seems to be imbued, namely, to entirely separate the interests of Great Britain from those of Hanover. In that case, I cannot employ force to cause the triumph of right, but I can still refuse to be guarantee for iniquity ; we shall see if they will dare to attack me on that ground. What I say here applies only to Poland and Saxony —for, as to Naples, I shall always rely on the fine reply you made to Herr von Humboldt.[2]

I suppose things at their worst, because I find that it is the best manner of reasoning—but I look for much better things— from your ability and firmness. Whereupon I pray God, my cousin, that He may have you in His safe and holy keeping.

LOUIS.

---

[1] Var.: " *Pozzo di Borgo* might perhaps . . . . . ."
[2] See Prince Talleyrand's letter dated October 4, p. 229.

Vienna, *October* 16, 1814.

Monsieur le Comte,

Since our last despatch of the 12th, no conference has been held, and all the work of the congress reduces itself to a few steps between the powers and to some insignificant intrigues, which serve nevertheless to disclose the real state of minds here, the excitement of some, the cupidity of others, the bewilderment of all.

The great difficulties which oppose the progress of affairs result from the idea conceived by the Emperor of Russia, who will re-establish a sham Poland under Russian influence, and aggrandize Prussia by Saxony. That prince, if one may dare to say so, has not one sane idea in that respect, and confuses at the same time principles of justice and the wildest conceptions.

Lord Castlereagh, on whom he called in order to insinuate his projects with regard to Poland, combated them. He even handed him a methodical memorandum, in which he presented the question such as we conceived it ; the situation requires either the restoration of ancient Poland, or that that source of trouble and contention be for ever withdrawn from the discussions of Europe.

Lord Castlereagh had his memorandum read to Prince Talleyrand and to Prince Metternich, and he seconds in that respect the true interests of Europe. But, whilst combating exaggerated views, he concludes nothing and appears even to avoid concluding. With respect to the King of Saxony, whose fate is not discussed, Lord Castlereagh continues to indulge the falsest views, and being ruled by the thought that what he terms the treason of the King of Saxony, would serve as an example to Germany and to Europe, he interests himself very little in the preservation of his dynasty, or of the country itself, and he abandons all principle in that direction. The consequences that this measure would entail are too serious for France to permit of consent being given to them, and we hope that Austria will, in the end, become fully alive to what honour dictates, and to her own interest. We have several data on this subject which cause us to believe that our measures will be seconded by the cabinet of Vienna ; but they will only be so, when the confidence of that cabinet in the disposition of France shall be complete.

Austria is bound by the promise given to procure Prussia a population of ten million inhabitants ; but nothing is stipulated with regard to Saxony, and Austria desires to save her.

Prince Metternich, though guided by a timid and uncertain policy, nevertheless judges the opinion of his country, and the interests of her monarchy well enough, to see that the dominions of Austria, encircled by Prussia, Russia, and a Poland entirely in the hands of the latter, would be constantly menaced, and that France alone could aid her in that difficult position. Bavaria having offered her aid, Prince Metternich sounded Marshal von Wrede [1] on the intention of his government to enter into a military league with Austria and France, in order to prevent the execution of the projects of Poland and Saxony. Marshal von Wrede replied that his governmeut intended to join them.

On the other hand, Prince Metternich preserves a defiant attitude, not only with regard to the king's wish to effectually second the policy of the preservation of Saxony, but also with regard to the means to be put at his disposal. This has been confirmed by the story of a gentleman attached to Prince Metternich's staff, who, explaining himself to the Duc de Dalberg, said to him : "You appear to us like the dogs which bark cleverly, but do not bite, and we shall not bite alone." The same individual told him also, that if they could feel sure of the firmness of France, the language of Austria would become stronger, and Russia would not risk war. But she persists in her plans because she does not admit the possibility of Austria and France combining in an armed resistance against the projects sustained by both Russia and Prussia at once. The Duc de Dalberg replied, that the King of France would never sanction such a disregard of public morality as that involved in the destruction of Saxony, and that he had not been the last to order his plenipotentiaries, to pronounce themselves in favour of what honour and the great principles of public order dictated.

The Emperor of Russia has given no decision for the last three days ; he is trying to gain over the English and Austrian ministers before pronouncing his last word in the matter.

It may happen that he will insist on the restoration of Poland, after his own wishes, or, that by renouncing it, he will put a higher price on his sacrifice than the other powers would admit. Relations would then become strained, and we should have to be ready for any event that might result from it. Perhaps Austria would formulate the idea of a league, formed by the powers of the south against those of the north, and it would be as well to be prepared to reply to that proposal.

---

[1] Charles-Philippe, Prince von Wrede, born at Heidelberg in 1767 ; was from 1805 to 1813 at the head of the Bavarian auxiliary troops of France, and was appointed by Napoleon Comte of the Empire. He betrayed Napoleon in 1813, but was crushed at Hanau. After the campaign of France, he became field-marshal. He represented Bavaria at the congress of Vienna. He died in 1838.

We believe that the dignity of the king, the interests of France, and the force of opinion, require that the king do not refuse to concur in the defence of the grand principles which constitute order in Europe, and it would be well and useful that he should be willing to give the necessary authorization for forming, if matters became urgent, a military league with a view to checking the projects of Russia and Prussia.

We think that even were Russia in a condition to take the field, Prussia would not compromise herself, and the firmness of France seconded by Austria really understanding her interest, would save Europe without disturbing the peace.

There is another consideration that determines us to advise the king to refuse his sanction and to offer effectual aid to prevent the destruction of the House of Saxony, and the union of that country with Prussia. That consideration is derived from the revolutionary spirit that we observe in Germany, and that bears a character quite special.

It is not the struggle of the third estate with the privileged classes which gives rise to fermentation in that country. It is the pretensions and pride of a military, and formerly very independent nobility, which preparing the field and the elements for a revolution, would prefer to secure existence in a large state, and not to belong to parcelled out countries and to sovereigns whom she regards as her equals.

At the head of this party are found all the mediatised princes and nobles; their aim is to blend Germany into one single monarchy, in order to play in it the part of a great aristocratic element. Prussia, who has very cleverly flattered all that party, has attached it to herself by holding out to it the prospect of sharing the old privileges which it enjoyed.

One can thus be persuaded that if Prussia succeeded in annexing Saxony, and appropriating for herself isolated territories on one side and another, she would form, in a very few years, a military monarchy very dangerous for her neighbours; and nothing, in this supposition, would serve her better than a great number of enthusiasts, who, under the pretext of seeking a mother-country, would create one by the most fatal upheavals.

It is of the highest importance to prevent these projects and to second Austria in order to be able to cope with them successfully. This determination on the king's part shall aid again to sever the bonds that link Austria and Bavaria to the coalition, and that consideration is very serious in the actual situation of France.

On the occasion of the inquiry that Prince Metternich indirectly made from Marshal von Wrede, if Bavaria should be disposed to ally herself with France and Austria, the military situation of the two parties was mooted, and it was acknowledged that the military position of the powers of the south of Europe was greatly superior to those of the north, and that an offensive operation, made by the outlets of Franconia on the Elbe, would cut off the Prussian armies from their troops on the Rhine, and from a great portion of their resources.

Austria displayed anxiety concerning the Neapolitan armies and the agitation of Italy, where she fears lest Bonaparte should prepare an uprising.

Murat had proposed an alliance to Bavaria, who refused, but if events should lead to war, it would be necessary to carry an army corps into Sicily to engage the attention of Murat. Spain being entrusted with that operation, the French contingent need not be very large.

Austria has at present nearly three hundred thousand men under arms, and, from sufficiently reliable data, these forces are distributed as follows :—

80,000 men in Bohemia ; 90,000 in Moravia and Hungary ; 36,000 in Galicia ; 20,000 in Transylvania ; 30,000 in Austria ; 50,000 in Italy.

Russia may have as many troops. Here is the list of them : 50,000 men in Holstein; 80,000 in Saxony: 150,000 in Poland.

Prussia 150,000, of which 50,000 on the lower Rhine, amongst whom 15,000 Saxons, whose chief, General Thielmann,[1] has taken the side opposed to his former sovereigns and would prove unfaithful—he is not to be relied on.

What would seem to prove that the Czar of Russia does not believe in terminating affairs this year, is, that he has delayed the ratification of the treaty with Denmark and Sweden [2]—of which he is to be the voucher, and that he has not given orders to withdraw his army which occupies and ruins Holstein. The King of Denmark has failed to obtain anything in that respect.

Be pleased to accept. . . . .

No. 6.—THE PRINCE DE TALLEYRAND TO KING LOUIS XVIII.

VIENNA, *Oct.* 17, 1814.

SIRE,

I received the letter with which your Majesty has deigned

---

[1] Johan-Adolfus, Baron von Thielmann, born at Dresden in 1765, took, though a Saxon, service in the Prussian army, fought against France the campaigns of 1792-1795, and 1806. Appointed a general in 1809, he re-entered the service of Saxony, whose cavalry he commanded during the campaign of Russia. In 1813, he joined the allies and took the command of a body of partisans. In 1815, he again took service, and was in command of a Prussian division at Ligny. He died in 1824.

[2] The treaty of peace between Russia and Denmark, signed at Hanover, February 8, 1814. Article 6 of this treaty decided that the Russian troops could not levy any contribution on Holstein.

to honour me. I am happy to find that the line of conduct that I have followed tallies with the intentions that your Majesty is good enough to express to me. I shall exert every effort never to depart from them.

I have to acquaint your Majesty with the state of affairs since my last letter.

Lord Castlereagh, wishing to bring a new effort to bear upon the mind of the Czar Alexander, so as to induce him to relinquish his ideas on Poland, which disturb and lead to upset everything, had requested an audience from him. The Czar wished to make a sort of mystery of it, and paid him the honour of going to his house, and, knowing well what subject Lord Castlereagh wished to discuss, he himself entered upon the matter by complaining of the opposition that he found to his views. He did not, nor could not, understand how France and England could be opposed to the restoration of a kingdom of Poland. Such restoration, he said, would be an atonement for the breach of public morality that the division had outraged—a sort of expiation. In truth, to entirely restore Poland was now out of question, but nothing would prevent that being done one day, if Europe desired it. For the present it would be premature : the country itself had need of being prepared for it ; it could not be so better than by the erection of a kingdom formed of a portion only of Poland, to which could be given institutions of a nature likely to promote the rise and progress of all the principles of civilization, that would spread through the entire nation when once it had been deemed advisable to restore unity to it. The execution of his plan was to involve sacrifices only for himself since the new kingdom would be formed only of portions of Poland over which conquest gave him incontestable rights, and to which he would moreover add those that he had acquired previous to the last war, and since the division (Byalistock and Tarnopol). No one could thus complain of his wishing to make those sacrifices ; he made them with pleasure, for conscience' sake, to console an unhappy nation, to advance civilization ; he staked his honour and reputation on it. Lord Castlereagh, who had all his arguments ready, deduced them in a conversation that was very long, but without persuading or convincing the Czar Alexander, who retired, leaving Lord Castlereagh indeed very little satisfied with his intentions ; but as the Czar did not consider himself defeated, he put his arguments into writing, and presented them the same evening to His Majesty, under the title of *Memoranda*.

After giving me, in a very long conversation, the preceding details, Lord Castlereagh gave me this document to read, at which, by the way, Prince Metternich, on hearing of it, testified a surprise that he would not have shown, had there not been among the ministers of the four courts a general determination not to communicate to the others what they were severally doing.

The *memorandum* commences by reproducing the articles of the treaties concluded by the àllies in 1813, which decided that : *Poland should remain divided between the three powers in proportions that they shall amicably agree upon, without the interference of France.* (Lord Castlereagh hastened to tell me that this referred to the France of 1813, and not to the France of to-day.) It then reports, word for word, the discourses held, promises made, and assurances given, by the Emperor Alexander at different epochs, in different places, especially at Paris which are all in direct opposition to the policy that he is now pursuing. This is succeeded by the enumeration of services rendered by England to the Emperor Alexander.

To secure him the undisturbed possession of Finland, she agreed to bring Norway under the dominion of Sweden ;[1] by so doing, making a sacrifice of her own wishes, perhaps even of her interests as well.

By her mediation she had obtained for him concessions from the Ottoman Porte and other advantages ;[2] and from Persia, the cession of a considerable portion of territory.[3] She believes herself therefore to have the right to speak to the Czar Alexander with more frankness than the other powers, who do not happen to have rendered him the same services.

Passing thence to the examination of the actual policy of the emperor, Lord Castlereagh declared that the entire restoration of Poland as a completely independent state would obtain the assent of everybody ; but that to create a kingdom out of a fourth of Poland, would be but to create regrets for the three other fourths, and just cause for anxiety for those who might be possessed of any portion of it whatever, and who, from the moment that there existed a kingdom of Poland, could no longer count for a single moment on the fidelity of their subjects ; that thus, instead of a focus of civilization, they would only have established one of insurrection and trouble, whereas peace and tranquillity are the wish, as they are the need, of all. While admitting that conquest has given certain

---

[1] Norway, before 1814, belonged to Denmark. Now Denmark had, in 1813, an alliance concluded with Napoleon, by which the latter was to give her certain subsidies, whereas Sweden had taken the part of the allies, and had signed with England a treaty (March 3, 1813). Sweden thereupon invaded Norway. The treaty of August 14, 1814, suspended hostilities, and on the 4th of the following November, the Norwegian Diet proclaimed the King of Sweden, King of Norway.

[2] Peace of Bucharest in 1812, by which Turkey ceded to Russia Bessarabia and a part of Moldavia, and recognized the Russian protectorate over Wallachia.

[3] Treaty of Peace between Russia and Persia (October 12, 1813).

rights to the emperor, it maintains that the limits of those rights is that line that cannot be passed without trespassing on the security of his neighbours. It conjures him by all he holds dear, by his humanity, by his reputation, not to go beyond it, and concludes by saying that it entreats him to weigh, all the more carefully, all the reflections that are being submitted to him, that should he persist in his views, England would regret to find herself unable to assent to them.

The Czar Alexander has not yet replied.

Lord Castlereagh's attitude is as good in the question of Poland as it is bad in that of Saxony. He speaks of nothing but treason ; of the necessity of an example. Principles do not appear to be his forte. Count von Münster, whose health is improving, has tried to convince him that the equilibrium, perhaps even the very existence, of Germany depended upon the preservation of Saxony ; but all he succeeded in effecting was to raise in him some doubts. However, he has promised me, not to pronounce himself of the same opinion as ourselves on this question (he seems indeed to have, with regard to that, engagements with the Prussians, that bind him), but at least to offer no objections.

His attitude towards the Emperor Alexander has been assumed, not only by the advice, but even at the request of Prince Metternich. I should not have doubted it, had neither the one nor the other told me of it. Austria foresees all the consequences of Russia's projects, but, not daring to come forward herself, she has made England do so.

If the Czar Alexander persists, Austria, having too great an interest in not giving way, will not, I believe, give way, but her timidity will cause her to protract things indefinitely. This resolution, however, offers dangers that become daily greater, that might become very serious, and to which I must all the more call the attention of your Majesty, that their cause might prolong itself far beyond the present time, in such a manner, as even to demand all your attention for the rest of your reign.

The seeds of revolution are sown broadcast in Germany. Jacobinism predominates there, not, as in France twenty years ago in the middle and lower classes, but among the highest and wealthiest nobility ; a difference sufficiently great to make it impossible to estimate the progress of a revolution, should one break out there, by that of our own. The men whom the dissolution of the German Empire, and the Act of the Confederation of the Rhine have reduced from the rank of petty sovereigns to that of subjects, impatiently submitting to masters whose equals they were, or believed themselves to be, aim at changing an order of things, at which their pride revolts, and at replacing all the governments of that country by a single one. With these, university men and the youth imbued with their theories conspire, as well as those who attribute to the division of Germany into small states, the calamities rained upon her by so many wars of which she has been the continual scene. German unity—that is their cry, their doctrine, their religion, carried even to fanaticism, and this fanaticism is shared even by princes actually reigning. Now this unity, from which France had nothing to fear when she possessed the left bank of the Rhine and Belgium, would now be a serious question for her. Besides, who could predict the consequences of the eventual outbreak of a mass like Germany, when her heterogeneous parts bestir and blend themselves as a whole? Who knows where the impulse thus given would stop? The present position of Germany, of which a great portion does not in the least know who is to be her master, the military pursuits, the vexations ordinarily attendant upon them, the fresh sacrifices demanded, after so many previous sacrifices, the present wrongs, the uncertainty of the future, all these favour a possible change in her political condition. It is but too evident that if the congress adjourns, if it decides nothing, it will aggravate this state of things, and it is greatly to be feared, that in aggravating it, the result will be an upheaval. It is therefore most urgent that it should accelerate and conclude its labours. But how conclude? By granting what Russia and Prussia demand? Neither the safety nor the honour of Europe permit it. By opposing force to force? It would require for that, that Austria, who has, I believe, the desire, should also have the will. She has immense forces under arms; but fears an uprising in Italy, and dares not match herself alone against Russia and Prussia. She can rely upon Bavaria, who declares her intentions quite frankly, and has offered her fifty thousand men to defend Saxony: Wurtemberg would furnish her ten thousand: other German States would join her, but that does not sufficiently reassure her. She would like to be able to count upon our aid, and does not believe she can do so. The Prussians have spread the report that your Majesty's ministers have received double instructions, which prescribe for them, the one the language that they are to adopt, the others, that they are to promise nothing. Prince Metternich heard Marshal von Wrede tell him that this was his own impression. One of his most intimate acquaintances said a few days ago to M. de Dalberg, "Your legation speaks very cleverly, but you will not act, and we shall not act alone."

Your Majesty will easily believe that I like and desire war no more than yourself. But in my opinion, it would suffice to show our readiness for it, and there would be no need to wage it. It is my opinion again, that the fear of war should not prevail over that of a greater evil which war alone could prevent.

I cannot believe that Russia and Prussia would run the risk of a war against Austria, France, Sardinia, Bavaria, and a large portion of Germany ; or if they had no fear of doing so, so much the more unlikely is it that they would recede before Austria alone, supposing, what is not the fact, that she would engage in the struggle alone.

Thus Austria deprived of our support, would have no other resource than either to postpone the congress indefinitely, or to dissolve it, which would open up the way for revolutions ; or, to yield and consent to what your Majesty has resolved never to sanction.

In that case, no other course would remain for your Majesty's ministers but to retire from the congress, reconciling ourselves to getting nothing of what you most desire. Nevertheless the state of things which would thus be established in Europe would render inevitable in a very few years the war we now sought to avoid, and we might then find ourselves in a situation in which we should have less means of waging it.

I believe it not only possible, but probable, that if the reply of the Czar Alexander should leave no hope of seeing him yield to persuasion, Prince Metternich will ask me if, and to what extent, Austria can count upon our co-operation.

The instructions which your Majesty has given state, that the dominion of Russia over all Poland would threaten Europe with so great dangers, that, if it could not be removed, except by force of arms, resort must be had to them without hesitation, which, I think, may authorize me to promise in general terms, and for this cause alone, the help of your Majesty's troops.

But in order to reply positively to a definite demand, and and to promise determinate help, I need special authorization and instructions. I take the liberty of begging your Majesty to grant me them, and to be assured that I shall make use of them only in cases of manifest and extreme necessity. But I persist in believing that the case I am presupposing will not present itself.

In order, however, to be ready for any emergency, I ask your Majesty to deign to honour me, as speedily as possible, with your orders.

Since the declaration that I have had the honour of sending

to your Majesty, the ministers of the eight powers have not met.

A commission composed of Austrian, Prussian, Bavarian, Würtembergese, and Hanoverian ministers are working at the federal constitution of Germany. They have already held a conference. It is doubtful, considering the diversity of the interests of those whom they represent, and of their individual characters, whether they will arrive at an agreement.

I have the honour to be, &c.

No. 7.—The Prince de Talleyrand to King Louis XVIII.

Vienna, *Oct.* 19, 1814.

Sire,

Count de Labrador, for having expressed the same opinion as myself in the conferences to which we have both been summoned, and perhaps also for having come rather frequently to my house, where Lord Castlereagh found him once, was subjected to the keenest reproaches by the ministers of the four courts. They taunted him with having deserted them, with deserting the men to whom Spain is indebted for the recovery of her independence, and, what is most worthy of remark, it was Prince Metternich who displayed most violence in the matter. Notwithstanding this Count de Labrador has not altered his opinion, but has thought it advisable to call on me less frequently than he formerly did. From this, can be seen how far ministers, less independent by their position or personal character are, or believe themselves, free to entertain close relations with your Majesty's legation.

The five ministers who met to examine the federal constitution have been required to give their word of honour that they would abstain from communicating to any one whatsoever the proposals that might be laid before them. It is especially against the legation of France that this rather useless precaution has been taken. Having failed to induce her to play in the negotiations the part they had intended her to take, they now seek to isolate her.

A ray of light has nevertheless pierced the darkness, with which it is sought to surround her, and which it is intended to thicken as time wears on. Perhaps we hold the thread that is to guide us through the maze of intrigue in which it was, at first, hoped we should lose our way. This is what we have learned from a man whose position enables him to be well informed.

The four courts have not ceased to be allied, in this sense that, the sentiments which animated them during the war have outlived hostilities, and that they display, in the arrangements of Europe, a spirit similar to that in which they fought. Their intention was to proceed alone with these arrangements. But they saw that the only means of imparting a certain character of legitimacy to them was to have them invested with some sanction or other. That is why the congress has been called together. They would have liked to exclude France from it, but could not do so after the fortunate change for the better that has taken place in our country, and from this point of view that change has displeased them. At all events, they had flattered themselves that France, being for a long time to come solely engaged with her internal difficulties, would attend the congress only for the sake of form. Seeing that she presented herself with principles that they could not oppose, and were yet unwilling to follow, they have made up their mind to put her aside *de facto*, without excluding her, and to concentrate all power in their own hands, in order to proceed without hindrance in the execution of their plan. This plan is, in the main, but that of England. It is she that is the soul of everything. Her want of regard for principles is not surprising : her interests constitute her principles. Her aim is simple. She is anxious to preserve her naval superiority, and, with that, the trade of the world. To effect this, she wants the French navy never to become strong enough to cause her any fear, either combined with others, or alone. She has already taken care to isolate France from the other naval powers, by the treaties she has imposed on them. The restoration of the house of Bourbon having caused her to fear the renewal of the "Family Compact," [1] she hastened to conclude with Spain the treaty of July 5th, whereby that power bound herself never to renew that compact. She has still so to situate France, as a continental power, that she may be able to devote only a very small portion of her forces to naval service. With this object in view, she seeks to unite Austria and Prussia, rendering the latter as strong as possible, and setting them both up as the rivals of France. It is to carry out this plan that Lord Stewart was appointed ambassador to Vienna. His sympathies are entirely Prussian ; that is the reason why he was chosen. Care will likewise be taken to appoint in Berlin a man whose sympathies lean towards Austria. Nothing would strengthen Prussia more than to give

[1] The "Family Compact," a treaty concluded August, 1761, between France and Spain, and by which all the branches of the House of Bourbon mutually agreed to assist one another.—(*Translator.*)

her Saxony; that is why England wishes that country to be sacrificed, and given to Prussia. Lord Castlereagh and Mr. Cook [1] are so determined on this point, that they are bold enough to say that the sacrifice of Saxony without any abdication, without any cession on the part of her king, would not offend principles. Austria ought naturally to discard such a doctrine. Justice, propriety, her security even, everything urges her to do so. How has her resistance been overcome? Nothing was easier. She has been confronted with two difficulties, one of which she was helped to surmount, on the condition that she would give way on the other. The Emperor of Russia very opportunely expresses the desire to have the whole duchy of Warsaw, and to form what can but be the shadow of the kingdom of Poland. Lord Castlereagh is opposed to this project, and is drawing up a memorandum that he will produce before his parliament, in order to make his countrymen believe that he experienced so much trouble in arranging the affairs of Poland, that he cannot be blamed for not having saved Saxony, and, as the reward of his exertions, he urges Austria to consent to the partition of that kingdom. Who knows but that the desire of forming a sham kingdom of Poland was not suggested to the Emperor Alexander by the very men who are opposed to it, or who knows if this desire be sincere? Whether the emperor, in order to make himself agreeable to the Poles, has not made them promises which he would be very sorry to keep? Whether the resistance offered him is not what he most wishes, and whether he would not be very much puzzled if people assented to what seems to be his wish? Be this as it may, Prince Metternich, who prides himself on giving the impulse to everything, himself receives the impulse in this case, and, without being aware of it, is the sport of the intrigues he thinks he is plotting, and is being deceived like a child.

Although I cannot vouch for the exact truth of the foregoing particulars, I must say that they do not seem to me at all improbable.

A few days ago, certain persons, whom Prince Metternich is in the habit of consulting, were summoned by him. They all were of the opinion that Saxony should not be abandoned. Nothing was concluded, and the evening before last I learned

---

[1] Edward Cook, or Cooke, an English statesman, was at first chief clerk of the Irish House of Commons, then secretary of the War Office in that country, and member of Parliament. He promoted, by his writings, the union of the English and Irish Parliaments, was afterwards appointed Home and Foreign Secretary of State by Lord Castlereagh, whom he accompanied to the Congress of Vienna as plenipotentiary. He retired from public life in 1817, and died in 1820.

from a reliable source that Prince Metternich, personally, had abandoned Saxony, but that the Austrian Emperor was still hesitating.

One of the commissioners for the drawing up of the federal constitution said that the proposals made to them were made on the supposition that Saxony no longer existed.

Yesterday was entirely devoted to two fêtes : one of which was a military one, commemorative of the battle of Leipzig : the legation of your Majesty could not attend it; I was present at the other, which was given by Prince Metternich, in honour of the peace. I was anxious to find an opportunity of saying a word to the Emperor of Austria. I was not fortunate enough to do so. I had been more fortunate at the preceding ball, when I had been able to say to him, on the questions at issue, a few words calculated to produce some effect on his mind ; he seemed then to me to quite share the views I expressed. Lord Castlereagh talked with him for nearly twenty minutes, and I have been told that Saxony was the subject of the conversation.

The arrangement that would give this country to Prussia, would be considered in Austria, even by the members of the cabinet, as a misfortune for the Austrian monarchy, and in Germany as a calamity. It would there be looked upon as an infallible indication that, sooner or later, Germany was doomed to be divided as Poland was.

The King of Bavaria again yesterday, ordered his minister to take new steps in favour of Saxony, and said to him : " That project is most unjust, and quite upsets me."

If Austria wishes to preserve Saxony for herself, it is probable that she will, at any rate, secure our co-operation, and, in order to be in a position to give an affirmative reply to any request of that nature, I have begged your Majesty to honour me with your orders. At the same time, as I have had the honour of informing your Majesty, I hold it for certain that Russia and Prussia will not open hostilities.

Should Austria yield without having asked for our support, it would be because she had decided to dispense with it. She would thus take from your Majesty all hope of saving Saxony, but she could not deprive you of the glory of defending the principles that constitute the security of every throne.

Besides, so long as Austria has not definitely yielded, I will not despair, and I even believe I have found a means which, though it may not prevent the sacrifice of Saxony, will, at least perplex those who wish for it : it is to inform the Emperor of Russia that we do not object to his possessing, under any denomination [1] whatever, the portion of Poland that may fall to his share, provided that does not extend his frontiers in such a way as to disturb his neighbours, and provided, at the same time, Saxony be preserved as an independent kingdom.

If the emperor has no real wish to make a kingdom of Poland, and merely seeks for an excuse to give to the Poles, this declaration of ours will cross his projects. He will not be able to tell the Poles, nor will they believe, that France is opposed to the accomplishment of their dearest wishes. In his turn, Lord Castlereagh will be puzzled to explain to parliament how he could have objected to what is desired by many people in England, when France did not object to it.

If, on the other hand, the Emperor Alexander really holds to the idea of this kingdom of Poland, the consent of France would be one more reason for him to persist in it; Austria, being thus again confronted by the difficulty from which she had thought to have extricated herself by abandoning Saxony, will be forced to reconsider her decision, and be brought over to us.

In no case can this declaration do us harm. What is important to us is, that Russia have as small a portion of Poland as possible, and that Saxony be saved. It is of less importance to us, or rather it is of no importance at all, whether Russia gain possession in one way or another of that which ought to be hers, and which she ought to possess. That is a matter that concerns Austria alone. Therefore when she sacrifices unnecessarily what she knows to be of interest to us, and that in which she ought to feel far more interest herself, why should we hesitate to replace her in the situation from which she sought to extricate herself, especially when it depends upon her to settle at once both her difficulties and our own ; and when for that she needs only to march hand in hand with us.

I am informed that, within the last few days, the Emperor Alexander repeatedly expressed the intention of sending for me. If he does sò, I shall try the plan I have just had the honour of submitting to your Majesty.

General Pozzo, who has been here for some days, speaks of France in a most becoming manner.

The Elector of Hanover, who can no longer bear that title, since there is no longer a German Empire, or an emperor elect, and being unwilling to rank below the sovereign of Wurtemberg, over whom he formerly took precedence, has just assumed the title of king. Count von Münster (who has nearly recovered

---

[1] Text : . . . , "sous quelque dénomination" (under any denomination whatever.) Var. : "sous quelque *domination*" (under any *rule* whatever).

from the effects of his fall) has notified this decision of his sovereign.

Before replying to him and recognizing the new title assumed by his master, I await the authorization which your Majesty will no doubt think advisable to give me.

I have the honour to be. . . . .

No. 7A.—The King's Ambassadors at the Congress to the Minister of Foreign Affairs at Paris.

Vienna, *October* 20, 1814.

Monsieur le Comte,

In one of our preceding despatches we had the honour of informing you that the four allied powers, conformably to their arrangements, continue to follow a system of convenience, agreed upon for the case in which Bonaparte should have remained on the throne of France; that they ignore the restoration of the House of Bourbon, which changes the state of Europe, and which should have necessitated the restoration of the system existing in 1792. But as the might of France still alarms them, it is with a singular blindness that Prince Metternich continues to second the projects of the three powers; that he facilitates for Russia the means fo taking possession of the duchy of Warsaw, for Prussia, the occupation of Saxony, and for England, the exercise of the most absolute influence over what was and may still be called, the coalition. This state of things produces a very strange effect; all the friends of the Austrian monarchy are favourably disposed towards us; on the other hand, the friends of the ministry, assume a hostile attitude.

There has been no other conference after that of which we have had the honour of informing you. The ministers of the four powers meet together, talk, project, change, and nothing is finished. Nevertheless the moment of decision approaches. We are strictly informed of all the minor political movements, though they have given their word of honour to each other to inform us of none of their intentions.

The policy of the powers arises from the consternation in which they still are. They wish to execute the engagement made on the 13th of June, 1813, and to finish the affairs of Poland, without France interfering. Their aim is finally to isolate France, and they repent of the peace which they have signed.

The effects of the English policy are to be seen everywhere. Again alarmed at the effect that the continental policy has produced on England, the English ministers wish, that in the north, and on the Baltic, there should be powers strong enough to prevent France from being able at any time to fetter the commerce of England with the interior of the Continent.   For this reason, they lend themselves to all that Prussia demands, and support her pretensions with all their power.

This combination resulted in the aggrandizement of Holland by the Low Countries, as well as in that of Hanover and of Prussia.   It is in the same spirit that England has exacted that Spain should never renew the stipulations of the "Family Compact."   She fears lest the king should, by means of alliances add fresh power to that already possessed by France.   This negotiation was the object of the hurried journey of Lord Wellington from Paris to Madrid.

Lord Castlereagh further proves by this same policy that he knows how to judge, neither the situation of the Continent, nor that of France ; and that he does not see that they have both been the victims of this policy, and would fear it more than England herself.

In this state of things, situated between passions on the one side, and the ambition of the powers on the other, the king's ministers have to sustain with the greatest firmness the conservative principles of the law of nations, not to stoop to any complacency which may overthrow these principles, to oppose to this act of violence all the dignity and calmness possible, and then await until reason and time enlighten the different powers as to their real interests.

At a ball given yesterday by Prince Metternich, Count von Schulenburg went up to Marshal von Wrede, and asked him what he could tell him regarding Saxony.   The marshal replied : " Go up to the master of this house, and see if he dares raise his eyes to you."

At that same ball, the King of Bavaria asked Count de Labrador if he ever saw Prince Talleyrand.

The Spanish minister said " Yes."

" I should like to see him, too," said the King, " but I dare not.   At any rate, I give you my word of honour that I am a devoted friend of the House of Bourbon."

We wait until these feelings shall be notified officially to us to explain ourselves ; and we shall, while waiting, lose no opportunity of repeating, that this disregard of all moderation prolongs the revolution, and must necessarily lead to fresh agitations.   Time will enlighten us as to the final decisions we shall have to take.

The king must now be convinced, that the policy he has adopted, which he has outlined in his instructions, and from which we swerve in nothing, assures him the consideration and the gratitude of all those who are not blinded by passions and a most fatal delusion.

Be pleased to accept . . . .

No. 3B.—KING LOUIS XVIII. TO THE PRINCE DE TALLEYRAND.

PARIS, *October* 21, 1814.

MY COUSIN,

I have received your reports numbered 4 and 5.

The most certain proof that that of October 1st was good is, that it displeased the plenipotentiaries of the formerly allied courts, and that it has, at the same time, compelled them in some measure to retrace their steps ; but we shall not go to sleep on this success. The existence of the league you spoke of in your No. 4, has been unveiled to me, as well as the determination to revenge on France the humiliations to which the Directory, and far more, Buonaparte,[1] have subjected Europe. I shall never allow myself to be reduced to such a point as that ; therefore I strongly favour the idea of the declaration, and wish you to send me a draft of it at your earliest convenience. But this is not all ; you must prove the existence of *purposes behind those which they reveal,* and, for this, it seems to me to be necessary to make preparations for putting the army, if need be, on a footing of greater efficiency than it is at present.

I will certainly get M. de Jaucourt to write the letter you require ; but, between ourselves, I would go beyond the stipulations of April 11,[2] if the excellent idea of the Azores were put into execution.

I shall be quite satisfied if they give Parma, Piacenza, and Guastalla to the young prince.[3] It is his patrimony. Tuscany was a territory that was hardly acquired justly.

The unfortunate Gustavus IV.[4] has announced his intention of coming here in a few days. If it is spoken of in Vienna, you might boldly assert that this journey conceals no political

---

[1] Var. : "*Bonaparte.*"

[2] The treaty of April 11, which determines the destination of Napoleon, and certain members of his family.

[3] The young King of Etruria, son of the late Duke of Parma, dispossessed of Parma in 1801, as he was of Tuscany, in 1807.

[4] Gustavus IV., King of Sweden, son of Gustavus III., born in 1778, succeeded his father in 1792, under the tutelage of his uncle, the Duke de Sudermania. Conquered by Russia and France, having made his nobles and people discontented, he excited a revolution and abdicated in 1809. The Diet sent him into perpetual exile, and proclaimed the Duke of Sudermania king, under the title of Charles XIII. As to King Gustavus, he lived henceforth in foreign lands under the title of Colonel Gustavson, and died in 1837.

stipulation, but that my door shall never be closed to him who always opened his to me.

I shall not close this letter without expressing to you my satisfaction at your conduct ; whereupon I pray God, my cousin, that He may always have you in His safe and holy keeping.

LOUIS.

No. 1.—The Comte de Blacas d'Aulps to the Prince de Talleyrand.

PARIS, *October* 21, 1814.

M. de Jaucourt doubtless informs your Highness of the arrival of Mina [1] at Paris, of his arrest, of the quite inconceivable conduct of the Spanish *chargé d'affaires,* [2] or to express it better, of him who takes that title, and of the measure that has been adopted in consequence.

For the rest, I have nothing new or special to acquaint Your Highness with to-day ; but I would not close this letter without remembering myself to you and expressing anew the most sincere assurances of my most *sincere* attachment.

BLACAS.

No. 8A.—The King's Ambassadors at the Congress to the Minister of Foreign Affairs at Paris.

VIENNA, *October* 24, 1814.

MONSIEUR LE COMTE,

Prospects have not improved. Since our last despatch all is intrigue, mystery, and incoherence, in the general policy.

The Emperor of Russia persists in occupying the grand duchy of Warsaw. He will only give up a few portions of it, and pretends to be regenerating Poland in it.

Prussia persists in retrieving her losses by the incorporation of Saxony. The Emperor of Russia announces that he has consented to it. He declares that he has entered into a personal engagement with the King of Prussia about it.

Austria offers but a weak resistance ; she proceeds cautiously, seeking to gain time to strengthen herself against the bad impression that this act of injustice is producing on men's minds.

---

[1] A celebrated partisan chief during the war of independence in Spain, who, after the restoration of Ferdinand VII., had been obliged to flee from Spain and had taken refuge in Paris.

[2] The Marquis de Casa Florès, who on his own authority alone, had had Mina arrested and kept him imprisoned at his residence. The French government obliged the marquis to set his prisoner at liberty, and ordered Casa Florès to quit Paris immediately.

She does not yet make overtures to us, and believes the case lost, though still wishing to connect it to the discussion which is to take place on the delimitation of boundaries in Poland.

The only good faith England has shown is in seeking to obtain for Prussia all that this power demands. Prussia is to become the guarantee for all English relations with Germany which tend towards an intimate union between Austria and Prussia ; England would add to these Hanover and Holland.

The 1st of November is drawing near, and nothing will have been decided. No conference has taken place. People wonder whether the congress will be opened at all, or whether before it sits, Europe will know the causes which have delayed it. Several ministers are of opinion that it would be preferable to dissolve it for the time being, and then to summon it again when greater readiness shall be shown to shed light upon the true needs of Europe.

Prince Metternich has replied to the note of the Prussian ministers demanding Saxony, to make up the ten millions of population which composed the Prussian monarchy of 1805. This reply decides nothing, and agrees to nothing. It rather discusses, and leads to the idea that the question of Saxony cannot be treated in an isolated fashion, and must be mooted with the arrangements to be made for the new limits of Poland.

In this state of things, Prussia will temporarily occupy Saxony with her armies, and this concession on the part of the Court of Vienna, is already very unfortunate. It leaves Russia the opportunity of doing as she likes in the duchy of Warsaw, and furnishes Prussia with means for strengthening her position in Saxony.

It will be seen that the calculations made as to the character of the Emperor of Russia, and the King of Prussia, are at fault; and we fear that false ideas of glory and *camaraderie*, if one may thus express oneself, will render them deaf to all remonstrances ; that England will applaud them, because she finds these projects in accordance with her own interests, and that Austria will be found unwilling to run the risks of another war.

Prince Metternich, in order to cloak his shame a little, makes a great deal of the advantage gained in the Russian armies leaving Germany ; and does not see that they are concentrating themselves at a short distance from the Oder, and that sixty thousand men are still in Holstein. Lord Castlereagh, on his part, is only alarmed by the idea of not seeing his projects exe-cuted to such an extent as he had hoped. His only desire is to try and moderate the pretensions which the Emperor of Russia has on the duchy of Warsaw; but he protests that the good faith he is compelled to put into his communications with Prussia does not allow him to oppose her keeping Saxony for her own aggrandisement.

We are therefore persuaded that the religion professed by the King of Saxony and his family[1] influences the arrangements of England, and that she is only too glad to see this country fall back into the hands of Protestant princes. This observation is confirmed by the habitual language of the English embassy.

Prince Talleyrand had an interview with the Emperor of Russia yesterday, which has produced no satisfactory result, and which has confirmed the fears that we had that this prince is running blindly into principles of expediency and ambition, such as must needs alarm Europe. Before his departure for Hungary, where he was to stay four days, he had a conversation with the Prince Metternich, in which he expressed his views in the most unbecoming manner.

It may now be wondered what means are at our disposal for opposing the disorder which is threatening us anew, since England and Austria will not second our efforts? Lord Castlereagh admits now that he had presumed too much of his influence over the Emperor of Russia, that he regretted not having opposed all Europe to him, united, as had been proposed at Paris, and that this means might yet be tried. If it proved barren of result, as we ourselves think, it will still be easy for the king to sanction nothing; and this will be the last step to be taken, if no other means present itself of modifying this state of affairs.

The conferences for the arrangement of German affairs continue. There has been a contest between the King of Wurtemberg, and the new King of Hanover, for precedence; and the question as to who will be head of the new Germanic league, has not yet been decided.

The court of Vienna might not be opposed to the idea of its sovereign reassuming the German imperial dignity, provided it were agreed that that dignity should be made hereditary to the throne of Austria. England would apparently second the idea, and Prince Metternich seeks here perhaps a means of gaining consideration for his policy, and covering its weakness. In doing so, he follows the mistakes of Count von Cobenzl, who, when his sovereign abandoned the title of Emperor of Germany, consoled him and his country, by stipulating that it be replaced by that of Emperor of Austria.

In one of the conferences the Prussian ministers proposed

---

[1] The younger branch of the house of Saxony, that is the royal branch, was Catholic.

and carried that, for the security of the German league, the confederate states should forego the right of legation and of making war and peace. The Bavarian ministers are sternly opposed to this policy, which reduces the states to the position of simple vassals of Prussia.

Be pleased to accept . . . .

No. 8.—The Prince de Talleyrand to King Louis. XVIII.

Vienna, *October* 25, 1814.

Sire,

I was much pleased to receive the letter dated October 14, with which your Majesty deigned to honour me. It has strengthened and consoled me. Your Majesty will see by the account of an interview with the Emperor Alexander, held two hours before the arrival of the messenger, how much I stood in need of it.

I had, as I have had the honour of informing your Majesty, already heard that he had on more than one occasion expressed an intention of seeing me ; and this intimation, coming, as it did, from three members of his more confidential circle, was credited by me as being made by his own command ; while I understood at the same time that he desired me to prefer a request for an interview myself. He had not yet replied to Lord Castlereagh. Instead of that, he had expressed to Austria his intention of withdrawing his troops from Saxony, and handing over the administration of that country to Prussia. The rumour ran that Austria had consented to this, albeit with regret. (The Prussians themselves had given credit to the rumour.) Finally, the Emperor Alexander was on the point of setting out for Hungary. For all these reasons I had determined to ask an audience, and had received notice that the emperor would see me the day before yesterday at 6 P.M.

Four days ago, Prince Adam Czartoryski, for whom Poland constitutes the whole world, came to visit me, and excusing himself for not having come sooner, declared that what had kept him away more than anything else, was that he had heard that I took such a very unfriendly attitude on the Polish question.

"Why, we are more friendly than any one else," I replied ; "we wish her united and independent."

"That would be very fine," he answered, "but it is a chimera ; the great powers would never consent to it."

"Then again," I said, "Poland is no longer the subject of

T 2

greatest interest to us in the north.   The preservation of Saxony is of far more importance to us.   We consider this question as being paramount to us, while we only hold as being subsidiary that of Poland, when it becomes a mere question of boundaries.   It is for Austria and Prussia to fix their frontiers.[1] We wish them to be satisfied on that point ; but, once set at ease as to your neighbours, we shall put no obstacle in the way of the Emperor of Russia's giving what form of government he pleases to the country handed over to him.   For our compliance in this respect, I ask for the preservation of the kingdom of Saxony."

This insinuation on my part, pleased Prince Adam sufficiently well, to make him seek, immediately on leaving me, an interview with the emperor, with whom he was closeted three hours. The result was that Count Nesselrode, whom I had not seen at my residence since the first moments of my arrival, called on me on the morrow evening for some explanations which I gave him, without at the same time going beyond what I had already told Prince Adam, but directing all my efforts to convincing him that the preservation of the kingdom of Saxony was a point which it was impossible for your Majesty to forego.

The emperor, thus knowing beforehand in what he could, and in what he could not, expect me to meet him, I reaped this advantage, that on his first approach I could tell his intentions, and judge whether his end in the conversation granted me, was to propose means of conciliation, or to notify his wishes.

He evinced some embarrassment at seeing me.   I expressed my regret at having only seen him once since my arrival.

"He was formerly good enough to spare me a privation of this nature," I told him, "when I had the good fortune to be in the same part of the world as himself."

His reply was that he would always be pleased to see me, that it was my fault if I had not seen him since ; why had I not come ? adding this singular phrase: " I am a public character, and can always be seen ;" whereas I must tell you that his ministers and most intimate servants are sometimes compelled to wait several days before they can see him.   Then " Let us to business," he said.

---

[1] Text : "nous ne sommes qu'en seconde sur celle de la Pologne, quand elle devient une question de limites.   C'est à l'Autriche et à la Prusse à assurer leurs frontières"—(as translated in the text).   Var. : "nous ne sommes qu'en seconde sur celle de la Pologne.   Quand elle devient une question de limites, c'est à l'Autriche et à la Prusse à assurer leurs frontières."   "We consider that of Poland as being subsidiary.   When it becomes a question of boundaries, it is for Austria and Prussia to fix their own frontiers."

I will no longer weary your Majesty with the tedious details of a conversation which lasted an hour and a half; and what will still more deprive me of any fear in limiting myself to what is essential, is that, however careful I may be in abridging what I have to tell you, as having been uttered by the emperor's own lips, your Majesty will yet perhaps find it beyond all credence.

"At Paris," he said, "you were for a kingdom of Poland. How comes it that you have changed your opinion?"

"My opinion, sire, is still the same. At Paris, it was a question of the restoration of the whole of Poland. I wished then, as I do to-day, her independence. But we have a different matter in hand now. The question is limited to the fixing of such boundaries as may put Austria and Prussia in security."

"They need not be anxious. Besides, I have two hundred thousand men in the duchy of Warsaw. Let them drive me out if they can! I have given Saxony to Prussia; and Austria consents."

"I do not know that," I replied. "I should find it difficult to believe, it is so decidedly against her own interests. But can the consent of Austria give to Prussia what belongs to the King of Saxony?"

"If the King of Saxony refuses to abdicate, he shall be led to Russia; where he will die. One king has already died there." [1]

"Your Majesty must permit me to disbelieve it. The congress has not assembled to witness such an outrage."

"How outrage? Why? Did not Stanislas go to Russia? Why should not the King of Saxony go? The case of both is the same. There is no difference in my opinion."

Words failed me. I declare to your Majesty that I knew not how to restrain my indignation.

The emperor continued to speak very fast; one of his sentences was: "I thought France considered herself indebted to me. You are always speaking to me of principles. Your public law is nothing to me: I don't understand all that. What do you think are all your parchments and treaties to me?" (I had reminded him of the treaty by which the allies had agreed that the duchy of Warsaw should be shared by the three courts.) There is one thing which in my eyes outweighs everything else —my word of honour. I have given it, and I will keep it. I

---

[1] Stanislas II., Poniatowski, the last King of Poland. He abdicated in the year 1795, retired to Grodno, where he lived on a pension served by the co-dividing powers, and died two years afterwards at St. Petersburg.

promised Saxony to the King of Prussia when we joined each other."

" Your Majesty has promised to the King of Prussia from nine to ten million souls ; and can give them without destroying Saxony." (I had a list of the countries which could be given to Prussia, and which, without overthrowing Saxony, would give her the number of subjects that the treaties had guaranteed. The emperor took it and kept it.)

" The King of Saxony is a traitor."

" Sire, the term traitor can never be applied to a king ; and it is of the greatest importance that it never should be."

I put perhaps a little heat into the last phrase. After a moment's silence,

" The King of Prussia," he said, " shall be King of Prussia and Saxony, just as I shall be Emperor of Russia and King of Poland. The spirit in which I shall consider all questions that may interest France, will depend upon that which she now shows me on these two points."

In the course of this conversation, the emperor had not, as in the first that I had had with him, moments of generosity and nobler feelings ; he was imperious, and showed traces of great irritation.

After having said that he would see me again, he repaired to the private court ball, whither I followed him, having had the honour to be invited. I found Lord Castlereagh there, and began to chat with him, when the Emperor Alexander perceived us in the recess of a window and beckoned to him. He led him to another room, and spoke with him for about twenty minutes. Lord Castlereagh then returned to me. He told me that he was very little satisfied with what he had just heard.

Lord Castlereagh, I cannot doubt, either formed for himself, or received from his government, the order to follow the plan which I had the honour of laying before your Majesty in my letter of the 19th inst. It consists in isolating France, in reducing her to her own strength alone by depriving her of all alliance, and by hindering her from getting a powerful navy. Thus, while your Majesty only brings to the congress views of justice and friendliness, England brings nothing but a spirit of jealousy and entirely personal interest. But Lord Castlereagh finds in the execution of his plan difficulties that he had not foreseen. Wishing to avoid the reproach of having left Europe a prey to Russia, he would like to detach certain powers from the latter, and at the same time put them in opposition with France. While what he would like more than all, would be that Prussia should become, like Holland, a power, which, with subsidies,

England could dispose of as she pleased. But as, to accomplish this, Prussia must be strong, he would wish to aggrandise her, and have, in her eyes the merit of doing so, all to himself. But the ardour that the Emperor Alexander brings to the interests of Prussia forbids this. Lord Castlereagh's aim is to unite, if possible, Prussia to Austria, and the kind of aggrandisement that he wishes to procure for Prussia, is of itself an obstacle to this union. He would like to break the bonds which exist between the King of Prussia and the Emperor Alexander, and seeks to form others repellent to customs, tradition, and a rivalry, suspended indeed, but not yet extinct, and which a crowd of personal interests must infallibly re-ignite. Besides, before uniting Prussia and Austria, he would have to protect the interests of this latter monarchy and provide for its safety, a matter obstructed, as Lord Castlereagh finds, by the pretensions of Russia.

Thus the problem which he has set himself, and which I hope he may never succeed in solving to the damage of France, at least to such an extent as he seems to wish, presents difficulties sufficient to stay a mightier genius than his. He himself sees no obstacles save those that arise from the Emperor Alexander, for he does not hesitate to sacrifice Saxony.

I therefore told Lord Castlereagh that the dilemma in which he found himself was the direct consequence of his conduct, and of that of Prince Metternich; that they had only themselves to thank for making the Emperor of Russia what he was; that if from the beginning, instead of rejecting my proposal to convene the congress, they had supported it, nothing of all this would have happened; that they had wished to match themselves alone against Russia and Prussia, and they had found themselves too weak: whereas, if the Emperor of Russia had from the first day been brought face to face with the congress, that is to say, with the express wish of all Europe, he would never have dared to hold the language that he holds to-day. Lord Castlereagh admitted the truth of what I said, regretted that the congress had not been called together sooner, and, expressing a wish that it should meet as soon as possible, proposed to me to draw up with him a formal summons, such as could not possibly give cause for any objection, and should defer any difficulties which might arise, to be settled by the great powers.

Herr von Zeugwitz, a Saxon officer, who has just come from London, and who, before his departure, had an interview with the Prince Regent, reports that that prince spoke to him with expressions of the liveliest interest of the King of Saxony, and said that he had ordered his ministers at the congress to defend conservative principles, and not to depart from them at all. The Prince Regent had held the same language to the Duke Leopold of Saxe-Coburg,[1] who told it to me himself two days ago. This leads me to think that the attitude here assumed by the English mission, is diametrically opposed to the wishes and personal views of the Prince Regent.

Austria has not yet consented, as the Emperor of Russia affirmed, to Saxony being handed over to Prussia. She has said on the contrary that the question of Saxony was essentially subordinate to that of Poland, and that she could not reply to the former until the latter were settled. But although she has spoken in her report of the cession of Saxony as infinitely painful and odious in all respects, she has yet allowed to appear too prominently a disposition to yield on this point if she were first satisfied on the other.

It is even asserted that the Emperor of Austria told his brother-in-law, Prince Anthony (of Saxony), that the cause of Saxony was lost. What is certain is, that Austria consents to Saxony being occupied by Prussian troops, and governed in the interests of the King of Prussia.

Meanwhile public opinion declares itself more and more each day in favour of the cause of the King of Saxony, and of those who defend it. It is, I think, to this that I owe the flattering reception which the archdukes and the Empress of Austria herself were so good as to give me three days ago at a ball at Count Zichy's,[2] and the day before yesterday at the court ball.

The Emperor of Austria started yesterday morning for Ofen,[3] preceding the Emperor of Russia, who started in the evening. He is going to weep over the tomb of his sister, the grand-duchess, who had been married to the archduke palatine; after which the ball and fêtes prepared for him will engross his whole attention. He expects to return to Vienna on the 29th.

As, on his departure, he left neither authority nor instructions with any one, nothing can be discussed, and nothing of any importance can well take place in his absence.

I saw Prince Metternich this evening, who is gradually re-gaining a little courage, and spoke to him in the strongest terms. The Austrian generals, many of whom I have seen, declare for the preservation of Saxony. They bring forward on the

---

[1] The future King of the Belgians. It is known that in 1816 he married the Princess Charlotte, granddaughter of King George III.

[2] Count Zichy of Vasonykio, issue of an old and eminent Hungarian family. Born in 1753, he was president of the Aulic Court of Hungary (1788) and became later Minister of War (1803). He died in 1826.

[3] German name of Buda-Pesth.

subject certain military arguments, which are beginning to make an impression.

I have the honour to be, Sire, ...

No. 4B.—KING LOUIS XVIII. TO THE PRINCE DE TALLEYRAND.

PARIS, *October* 27, 1814.

MY COUSIN,

I have received your despatch (No. 6), and hastened as much as possible to forward you by the messenger who left here on Tuesday, the additional instructions you asked for. I hope your measures may prove sufficient, but, as I informed you (No. 3B), you must let them see *that there is something else behind*, and I am going to give orders for the army to be held in readiness to take the field. God is my witness that, far from wishing for war, my desire is to have some years quiet, in order to dress the wounds of the State; but I must, before everything, preserve intact the honour of France, and prevent principles, and an order of things as contrary to morality as prejudicial to tranquillity, from being established. Also (and this is not less necessary), I wish that my personal character be respected, and cannot allow it to be said, as was the case with the affair of the Spanish *chargé d'affaires*, that I am firm only when pitted against the weak. My life, my crown itself, are nothing to me beside interests so great as these.

It would nevertheless be very painful for me to be forced to ally myself for these reasons with Austria, and Austria only. I cannot understand how Lord Castlereagh, who expressed such correct opinions on Poland, can be of a different opinion with regard to Saxony. I should very much rely on the efforts of Count von Münster to bring him back, had not the language of the Duke of Wellington on this same subject given me cause to fear that this was not the policy of the minister but of the ministry. There is certainly no lack of arguments with which to refute him, but examples sometimes carry more weight, and I can conceive a very striking one in the case of Charles XII. The execution of Patkul[1] proves sufficiently how vindictive this prince was, and how little he cared for the law of nations; and yet master, as one may say, of all the states

---

[1] Patkul (1660-1707) was a Livonian gentleman. Livonia was at that time subject to Sweden. Patkul tried on several occasions to unite his country to Russia, and excited several revolts against the Swedes. Peter the Great sent him as ambassador to Augustus III., King of Poland, who in order to get on good terms with Charles XII. handed him over to this prince. Patkul was immediately brought before a court-martial, which condemned him to be drawn and quartered.

of King Augustus, he contented himself with robbing him of Poland, not feeling justified in touching Saxony.

It seems to me that in comparing the two circumstances, viz., that of the duchy of Warsaw with that of the kingdom of Poland, and that of Saxony with herself on a former occasion, the analogy is sufficiently plain. Whereupon, my cousin, I pray God may have you in His safe and holy keeping.

LOUIS.

P.S.—Your No. 7 just received. It confirms me in my resolution to take up a warlike position to enforce respect.

I approve of the declaration you are about to make to the Emperor of Russia, and could wish that your conference had already taken place.

I authorize you to recognize in my name the King of Great Britain as King of Hanover.

L.

No. 9A.—THE AMBASSADORS OF THE KING AT THE CONGRESS TO THE MINISTERS OF FOREIGN AFFAIRS AT PARIS.

VIENNA, *October* 31, 1814.

MONSIEUR LE COMTE,

The date fixed for the opening of the congress was approaching, and yet it was only this evening that Prince Metternich has thought fit to call a conference to which all the plenipotentiaries of the eight powers that signed the treaty of Paris were invited.

Prince Talleyrand came and presented the Duc de Dalberg and the Comte de la Tour du Pin as French plenipotentiaries.

The Portuguese ambassador brought four plenipotentiaries, and Prince Metternich Baron von Wessemberg.[1]

Prince Talleyrand had, in order to facilitate business, drawn up a rough draft, arranging the work of the congress. (See subjoined documents, 1–5.)

He had had an interview the evening before with Lord Castlereagh, who, while approving the arrangement, had insinuated that it would be necessary for him to talk it over with Prince Metternich, and that every proposition emanating from France would always inspire a feeling of distrust.

Prince Talleyrand showed it before the sitting to Prince Metternich and some other plenipotentiaries.

---

[1] Johan-Philippe, Baron von Wessemberg-Ampfingen, born in the year 1773, was an Austrian diplomatist. He represented Austria at the Diet, at the time of the affair of the Secularizations (1802), was afterwards ambassador at Berlin, then at Munich, and London. He assisted Prince Metternich at the Congress of Vienna. In 1848 he was for a while Minister of Foreign Affairs, and died in 1858.

At the opening of the conference, Prince Metternich made a very diffuse speech, of which the object was to show that the confidential communications which had passed with regard to the affairs of Poland, had as yet been barren of result, but that they were on the eve of solution ; that the German Conferences were hastening forward the work of a plan of federation which would give to Europe a fresh guarantee of tranquillity ; that, such being the state of affairs, he would not advise that the congress be adjourned, but that they should seek a plan affording the time to discuss those questions foreign to the other powers. He insisted that the actual congress could not be so called, and that the *form of resolutions* could not be admitted there.

Hereupon Prince Talleyrand remarked how very extraordinary it seemed, to change the intention, nay, the very meaning of the words themselves, from one conference to another. That at Paris a congress had been requested, that now, they said, this congress which they had requested, ought not to be held, and ought not to be a congress ; that they ought to reassemble immediately on the first of November, but that the *summons* had not been made with the necessary *formalities*, that the *opening* ought not to be an *opening.* . . . .

Prince Metternich finished by proposing a new delay of ten to twelve days for the verification of powers, which all the plenipotentiaries would be invited to send to an office appointed for the purpose. And speaking of the influence which could be brought to bear upon the congress, he said, with some show of malice, that it could be of two kinds : (1) that of the difficulties ; and (2) that of the facilities, which could be put in the way of the work.

Prince Talleyrand took up this phrase, and said that when every one's interests lay the same way, there was no other "influence" than that of cleverness and stupidity.

Prince Metternich then communicated to us his own project of declaration, which is subjoined to No. 6. Discussions, insipid and without interest, occupied two hours, showing nothing but the levity and want of reflection which had been given to such important matters.

At last it was agreed :—

1. Not to adjourn the congress ;

2. To appoint a commission for examining credentials ;

3. To reassemble on the morrow to hear a new scheme of convocation read ; to determine whether the work could not be done by commissions appointed by the congress, to be re-examined by a general commission, and to determine the form of discussion to be admitted.

It was also agreed that the drafts presented by the French commissioners should serve as the basis for the morrow's discussion.

The commission for examining credentials was appointed by lot. Russia, England, and Prussia were selected. A report will be drawn up by this commission after the credentials have been handed in.

These conclusions would lead to the idea that one step more had been effected ; but on examining the state of affairs, it will be seen :—

1. That the four powers have not renounced the idea of establishing that system of the balance of power which they have worked out to their own advantage.

2. That they would allow France no voice in the matter.

3. That their momentary embarrassment is the consequence of the unexpected and exaggerated claims of the Emperor of Russia.

4. That, in order to free themselves from this dilemma, they are willing to sacrifice Saxony, and to present an appearance of unanimity on the question of Poland.

5. That the principles set forth by the King of France have reminded Europe of her proper dignity, and that the voice which he has raised, if it has not yet rallied all the wiser minds, will yet finish by being listened to one day.

In all this the weakness of the Austrian government, the ignoring of all principle on the part of the cabinets of Russia and Prussia, and the suspicions of the cabinet of London against France, are plainly to be seen. And it is impossible to stand firm against such powerful intrigues save by marching in the path pointed out by Reason alone, and by taking one's stand on the wise teachings she gives with regard to the existence and mutual relations of separate bodies of society.

If the powers directly interested in the settlement of Poland could, on the question of boundaries, come to some understanding that did not disturb the balance of power in that part of Europe, we shall have the hope that things in general will arrange themselves, and we shall await with patience, news of the same. By a secret agreement Russia, Prussia, and Austria, have determined to effect the partition of the grand-duchy of Warsaw without France being allowed to interfere, and we believe we shall have no cause to regret this.

If they can come to some such understanding, Europe will remain undisturbed. If they cannot, the coalition is *ipso facto* dissolved, and France will find herself called upon to undertake the most honourable intervention that she has ever had the opportunity of doing in state matters.

It is not yet possible to foresee the last move of the Emperor of Russia, who alone, by his presumption and unpractical ideas, is on the eve of rekindling wars and disturbing Europe for some time to come.

He returned the day before yesterday, in the evening, from his visit to Hungary, which he had made in company with the Emperor of Austria and the King of Prussia.

This journey, which he had himself proposed, was further marked by intrigue. He wished to cajole the Hungarian people, and to surround his person with the head clergy of the Greek Church, a class very numerous in Hungary. We hear from Lord Castlereagh himself, that the Greeks are already fomenting war against Turkey ; that the Servians have just taken up arms, and that a Russian army is on its way to the frontier. And while giving himself to such disturbing projects on that side, the Emperor of Russia is telling the Swiss ministers here that he will not leave Vienna till he has finished their business. He has nominated, according to what we have heard, Baron von Stein to negotiate with them.[1]

Before his departure for Hungary, he had given orders that a reply on the question of Poland should be prepared for Lord Castlereagh, and that memoranda on the restoration and organization of that country should be drafted.

If he persists, this draft will infallibly have a decided influence over future events in Europe, and one perhaps, not altogether to the advantage of Russia.

It is believed that the reply will be forwarded to Lord Castlereagh after the Emperor Alexander has corrected and approved it. It is thought to lay claims to creating a new Poland in the duchy of Warsaw, and giving Saxony to Prussia.

The Grand-Duchess of Oldenburg declared, the day before

---

[1] Charles, Baron von Stein, born in 1757 at Nassau, of a noble and ancient family. He entered the Prussian service in 1779, and in 1784 was appointed minister at Aschaffenburg, and entered the cabinet in 1804. Immediately afterwards, he was made first president of all the Fiscal Chambers of Westphalia at Münster, and Minister of Customs and Manufactories in 1804. He was one of the most inveterate enemies of France in the Prussian cabinet, and took an active part in the resistance in 1806. After the defeat he was obliged to retire. Recalled in 1807, his efforts at reorganizing the finances and the army roused the jealousy of Napoleon, who demanded his dismissal (1808). He fled to Austria. In 1812, he went to Russia, where he was eagerly welcomed by the emperor, who attached him to his person, and made him one of his most trusty councillors. During the years 1813 and 1814, he excited the passions of Germany against France by every means in his power, and followed the allied sovereigns to Paris. He then went to the Congress of Vienna, where he again met the Emperor Alexander, who made use of him on several occasions, but on this new scene of action he played but a secondary part. Plenipotentiary at the Congress of Aix-la-Chapelle in 1818, he was appointed state councillor in 1827, and died in 1831.

yesterday, that it seemed to her that *her brother* had decided these two questions.

We have often repeated our opinion, that in order to prevent this, there is no other means than that of opposing the public opinion of Europe against the abuse of her strength that Russia would make, and that it is for this reason that it was necessary to convene the congress and give it as much dignity as possible. If Russia grew too aggressive, France must all the more play the part of protectress.

Were it not for the weakmindedness of Prince Metternich and the prejudice of Lord Castlereagh against any influence whatever on the part of France in the affairs of Europe, the matter would soon be settled. Meanwhile, this condition of affairs is protracted, and so long, one may almost say, as this fear of France exists, men will remain blind to all other dangers.

In the midst of all these efforts to bring the Emperor of Russia back to more moderate ideas on the subject of Poland, the German conferences present some interest, on account of the conduct of Bavaria with respect to them.

Prussia's plan was to form a very close league, and share the leadership of it with Austria. Bavaria frustrated this, by demanding that each should take full powers of leadership in turn. She saw that Prussia's object was to use this league as a support in her usurpation of Saxony. And as she will not consent to this, she will make known her intentions, when the occupation of Saxony has been officially notified to her ; and she must now declare her intentions of never consenting to this. In order to be able to sustain this independent attitude, Bavaria has just ordered a strong levy of recruits, and raised her army to the number of seventy thousand men.

You therefore see, Monsieur le Comte, that if, in our last despatches, we induced the king to assume an attitude suitable both to his own dignity and to the exigencies of the moment, we so acted that he need have no fear of being compromised in a coalition aimed against France ; but that, on the contrary, he should find himself at the head of those who will unite to defend the liberties of Europe whenever threatened.

The article in the *Moniteur*,[1] which so boldly gives utterance

---

[1] The following is the Article :

"The preceding declaration," (that namely of the plenipotentiaries who would adjourn the opening of the congress till November 1, see p. 248 and following)—"by exposing the motives which led to the prorogation of the Congress of Vienna, is the first guarantee of that spirit of wisdom which will direct the work of the assembled plenipotentiaries. It is in fact by maturity of views, in the absence of all passion, that

to the principles which direct the policy of the king, has caused a great sensation here, and has been almost universally approved. We have observed that while spreading the rumour that, chagrined by the loss of conquests, the French army would drag the government into a fresh war, and that it was necessary to remain still under arms, this same government had sufficient force, and a sufficiently firm hold upon public opinion, to declare that France was content with her boundaries, because she possessed within herself all the elements of strength and prosperity which she needs for her happiness.

It is in this way that the hate and suspicion still surrounding us on all sides will best be allayed, and confidence restored, which is the principal aim of our policy, and which will give the king that force and dignity which are his due in his relations with Europe.

Be pleased to accept . . . .

No. 10A.—The Ambassadors of the King at the Congress to the Minister of Foreign Affairs in Paris.

VIENNA, *October* 31, 1814.

MONSIEUR LE COMTE,

The conference mentioned in our letter of to-day has been held this evening, before the departure of the messenger; we therefore have the honour of informing you of its result.

After reading the protocol of the conference of the 30th, the

the authority that is to protect the principles of public law, invoked and recognized in the last treaty of Paris, must rise again.

"Thus the legitimate expectations of our contemporaries will be met, and in the following negotiations a result conformable to what the universal law of nations, and the universal law of justice, prescribe to nations in their mutual intercourse, will be obtained.

"At a time when the great powers are leagued together for the express purpose of introducing into the relations of states respect for property and safety for crowned heads, no other political transactions except those stamped with this equitable character ought to be expected.

"Europe is already accepting this happy omen, and France, who envies no other states the advantages they may reasonably expect, only aspires to the adjustment of a fair equilibrium. Having in herself all the elements of strength and prosperity, she does not seek them beyond her own territories; she lends an ear to no insinuation of simple expediency; and assuming again the part which has hitherto won her the esteem and acknowledgment of peoples, she seeks no other fame than that which rests upon the alliance of force with moderation and justice; she desires to become again the supporter of the weak and defender of the oppressed.

"It is in this spirit that France will concur in arrangements tending to consolidate the general peace; and the sovereigns, who have so nobly proclaimed these same principles, will sanction this lasting treaty which is to assure the peace of the world."—*Moniteur*, October 22, 1814.

declaration, of which a copy is subjoined, was passed.   It will be printed some time to-morrow.

The projects proposed by Prince Talleyrand have been approved, and have found their place in the documents bearing in the correspondence the Nos. 2 and 3.   Prince Metternich introduced a proposal to discuss the questions Nos. 4 and 5.   Count Nesselrode asked that this discussion might be put off till to-morrow, as he had not had time for receiving the orders of the emperor.   This was also agreed to.   In a conversation between the two emperors in Hungary, when they discussed the question which would seem likely to put them at variance, the Emperor of Russia said, " I have not yet said my last word."

At the meeting of to-day, Lord Castlereagh, was attended by Lords Stewart, Cathcart,[1] and Clancarty.[2]

We are told that Counts Rasumoffski[3] and von Stackelberg[4] would be present at the next conference to represent Russia.

Be pleased to accept . . . .

No. 9.—The Prince de Talleyrand to King Louis XVIII.

Vienna, October 31, 1814.

Sire,
The state of things does not seem modified at first sight; but there are not wanting symptoms of a change, which have already begun to show themselves, and may gain in importance according to the conduct and language of the Emperor of Russia.

On the morning of the day on which he set out for Hungary, he had an interview with Prince Metternich, in which it is agreed on all hands that he treated this minister with a pride and violence of language, which would have been thought extra-

---

[1] Lord William Cathcart, born in 1755, entered the army, served in the campaign in America, became brigadier-general in 1793, and served in this capacity in Holland. He was peer of Scotland in 1807, member of the Privy Council and vice-admiral. In 1809 he directed the expedition against Copenhagen.   In 1812 he went to St. Petersburg as ambassador, followed the Emperor Alexander during the campaigns of 1813 and 1814, and signed the treaty of Paris, May 30.   He was sent to Vienna as plenipotentiary at the congress.   In 1815, he was created peer of England, and died 1843.

[2] Richard Power-Trench, Earl of Clancarty, Privy Councillor, Chairman of the Committee of the Privy Council for the Colonies and Commerce, Postmaster-General.   In 1814 he was accredited to the Court of Vienna as plenipotentiary.

[3] André, Count, afterwards Prince, Rasumoffski, was born in the year 1752. Russian diplomatist ; was successively ambassador at Stockholm, Naples, and finally, at Vienna, where he took part in the congress.   He died in 1836.

[4] Gustavus, Count von Stackelberg, private counsellor and Chamberlain of the Czar.   He was at the time we speak of, ambassador of Russia at Vienna, and, as such, attended the Congress.

ordinary, even towards one of his servants. *The story runs*[1] that Prince Metternich having said on the subject of Poland, that, if it were a question of making one, they also could do so, he had not only termed this expression gross and improper, but had allowed himself to be carried so far as to say that Prince Metternich was the only man in Austria who could have taken such a *rebellious* tone: and they add that matters reached such a pitch that Prince Metternich told him he would ask his master to appoint another minister to represent him at the congress. Prince Metternich came away from this interview in a state of mind such as his friends say they have never known him in before. He who, a few days ago, had told Count von Schulenburg that he would retrench himself in Time, and make an arm of Patience, has shown that he could very well lose it, if it had to undergo many such trials as that.

This is not likely to dispose him to come to friendly terms with the Emperor of Russia, and the opinion of the Austrian generals and archdukes ought to render him equally disinclined to abandon Saxony. I have reasons for believing that the Emperor of Austria is now bent on offering some resistance.

There is a certain Count von Sickingen here, who is admitted to the intimacy of this sovereign, and whose acquaintance I have formed. After the departure for Hungary, he went to Marshal von Wrede, and then came to me, to bid us on the part of the emperor to suspend all business until his return.

There is a current report that during the journey to Buda-Pesth, whence the sovereigns returned at noon of the day before yesterday, the Emperor Alexander having complained of Prince Metternich, the Emperor Francis replied that he thought it better that the business should be transacted by ministers, that there was thus more liberty and more progress: that he never transacted his own affairs himself, but that, at the same time, his ministers did nothing without his orders; that finally, in the course of the conversation he said, among other things, that when his people, who had never abandoned him, who had done everything for him, and given everything to him, were disturbed, as they were at the present time, his duty was to do all that he could to tranquillize them; that on this, the Emperor Alexander, asking if his character and loyalty ought not to be sufficient to prevent and remove all uneasiness, the Emperor Francis replied that secure frontiers were the surest safeguard for peace.

This conversation has come to my ears in almost precisely the same words from Count von Sickingen and Prince Metternich.

---

[1] Suppressed in the text of the archives.

It seems that the emperor, little accustomed to showing fight, returned very well pleased with himself.

All the precautions taken to prevent our knowing what is passing in the commission of the political organization of Germany have failed.

At the first sitting, it was proposed by Prussia, that all the princes whose states were completely included in the confederation, should renounce the right of making war, peace, and of sending embassies. Marshal von Wrede having refused to agree to this, Herr von Humboldt exclaimed that it was easy to see that Bavaria had still at heart an alliance with France, and that this was a fresh reason for pressing the proposal still more urgently. But at the second sitting, the marshal, having received his orders from the king, peremptorily rejected the proposal, and it was withdrawn, with the substitution that half the military forces of the confederation should be under the control of Austria, and half under that of Prussia. Marshal von Wrede proposed that the number of controlling powers be increased and that their authority alternate among them. It was further proposed to establish between all the confederate states an intimate bond, for the purpose of keeping the possessions of each one in the state in which they will have been settled by the arrangements now about to be made. The King of Bavaria, who easily understood, that Prussia had in view by this to secure to herself the possession of Saxony as against the opposition of those powers whose wish is to preserve this kingdom intact ; who fully perceives that he would have everything to fear himself, if Saxony were once sacrificed, and who is ready to defend it, if only he be not abandoned to rely upon his own resources alone, has ordered in his dominions a fresh levy of twenty thousand men, which will raise the number of his forces to seventy thousand. Far from wishing to enter the proposed league, his intention, at least at present, is that, as soon as the Prussians have seized on Saxony, his minister retire from the commission, declaring that he refuses to be an accomplice, and far less a guarantee, for such an usurpation.

The Prussians do not know of this intention of the king, but they are quite aware of his armaments, and probably suspect him of wishing to unite his forces with those of the powers who might wish to defend Saxony. They feel besides, that without the consent of France, Saxony will never be *for them*[1] a solid acquisition. It is also said that the ministry, which does not share the blind devotion of the king to the Emperor Alexander, is not without fears of trouble from Russia, and that it would *willingly*[2] renounce all claims to Saxony provided it found means

---

[1] Suppressed.   [2] Text : Volontiers (as translated) = Var. : *peut-être* (perhaps.)

elsewhere of completing the number of subjects which Prussia has a right to claim by the treaties. Whatever may be her sentiments and views, the Prussian ministers appear very anxious to meet us, and send us invitation after invitation.

Lord Castlereagh, who has thought of the plan of fortifying Prussia on this side of the Elbe, under the pretext of making her serve as a barrier against the encroachments of Russia, has this project still greatly at heart. In a conversation that he had with me a few days ago, he reproached me for making the question of Saxony one of the first importance, whereas, according to him, this was as nothing, while that of Poland was everything. I replied that the question of Poland would be one of the first importance in my eyes if he himself had not reduced it to a simple question of boundaries. Did he wish to establish Poland in a position of complete independence? I should be entirely with him. But when the discussion was one of boundaries, it was for Austria and Prussia, who were the parties chiefly concerned, to step to the front. My part was then reduced to supporting them, and that I meant to do. As to his project of uniting Prussia and Austria, I made use of arguments to which he could not reply, and cited to him facts in the policy of Prussia throughout the last sixty years, which he was compelled to admit ; but while condemning the old wrongs done by this ministry, he retrenched himself in the hope of a better future.

Meanwhile, I know that several people have brought forward objections which have struck him. For instance, it is asked, how he could consent to put one of the greatest commercial towns of Germany (Leipzig), where one of the greatest fairs of Europe is held, under the dominion of Prussia, with whom England had no guarantee of being always at peace, instead of leaving it in the hands of a prince with whom England could never have occasion to pick a quarrel? He was struck with a kind of astonishment and fear of his policy compromising in any way the mercantile interests of England.

He had invited me to draw up with him a plan for summoning the congress. I had sent him one with which he had expressed himself satisfied.

I also drew up some drafts for the first meeting of ministers, for the verifying of credentials, and for the commissions which were to be appointed at the first sitting of the congress. (These several projects are all subjoined to my despatch addressed to the department, and that M. de Jaucourt will submit to your Majesty.) As M. de Dalberg and myself both owed a visit to Lord Castlereagh, we went together to carry those drafts to him the day before yesterday in the evening. He found nothing to find fault with in them, but observed that the fear that the Prussians had of us would surely cause them to suspect some veiled intention. The fears, real or pretended of the Prussians, led the conversation naturally back to the eternal question of Poland and Saxony. He had some maps on the table, by means of which I showed him that Saxony being once in the same hands as Silesia, Bohemia could be taken in a few weeks, and that Bohemia once taken, the heart of the Austrian monarchy was left open and defenceless. He appeared astounded. He had spoken to us as if he had rested his expectations on Prussia from its being impossible to rest them on Austria. He seemed surprised when we told him that the latter only needed money in order to assemble her troops, that she would, in that case, have very imposing forces, and that for this a million sterling would now be sufficient. This roused his spirit, and he seemed disposed to support Poland to the very end. He knew that in the Russian cabinet, they were at work at a reply to his report but no longer apparently expected it to be satisfactory. He had received information that Servia was under arms, and told us that a Russian contingent, commanded by one of the best generals of the country, was on its way to the frontiers of the Ottoman Empire. Nothing therefore was in his eyes more urgent or necessary than to put a barrier against the ambition of of Russia. But he wanted this to be done without war ; if this were impossible, war at least without the aid of France. From his estimation of our strength, he almost gives the idea of its being France that he fears the most. " You have," he told us, " twenty-five million inhabitants, really equivalent to forty millions." Once he let escape him : " If only you no longer had any designs on the left bank of the Rhine ! "...It was easy for me to prove to him, from the state of affairs, both in France, and in Europe generally, which was all under arms, that to give France credit for ambitious views now, was to give her credit for being mad. " That may be," he replied, " but a French army traversing Germany now under any pretext, would make too great an impression, would awaken too many bitter memories." I represented to him that war would not be necessary, that it would amply suffice to set Russia face to face with Europe united under a single purpose, and this brought us back to the opening of the congress. But he, speaking continually of difficulties, without ever saying in what these difficulties consisted, advised me to see Prince Metternich ; from which I came to the conclusion that they had concerted together some plan, which he would frankly have communicated to me, had he not feared some objection on my part. In conclusion, he naively admitted, in accusing us of having retarded matters, that, without us, everything would by this time have been arranged, as they had been of one mind at first, an admission which shows how much influence, in their opinion, your Majesty must have in the affairs of Europe.

To sum up, Lord Castlereagh's attitude, without being very favourable, seemed to me to be in a fair way to become so, and perhaps the reply which he is awaiting from the Emperor Alexander will contribute to this also.

Yesterday morning, I received a note from Prince Metternich, inviting me to a conference at eight o'clock in the evening.

I will not weary your Majesty with the details of this meeting, prolific indeed of words, but barren of result. They are to be found elsewhere[1] in my letter to the department.

The end of it all has been, that a commission for verifying credentials has been formed, composed of three members, appointed by lot, that the credentials will be sent to them for verification, and that after this the congress will meet.

This evening, we have had another meeting. The rough draft of the declaration relative to the verification of credentials has been read and passed, and will be printed to-morrow. I am sending off[2] a copy of it this evening in my report to the department. I thought that your Majesty would prefer that all documents should be adjoined to the letter addressed to M. de Jaucourt, in order that the department may have and preserve them in their proper sequence.

For the last eight months the situation of France has been of such a character, that, no sooner has she obtained one end, than she has had a second before her, equally necessary to attain, without, in the majority of cases, being left the power to choose her means of reaching it. Scarcely has the tyrant been hurled down, scarcely has it been rendered possible to openly express the desires, which, in the depths of the heart, have, from all parts and for a long time, been demanding the recall of your Majesty to his kingdom, than it was necessary to provide for the disarmament of France, covered as she was, at the time of your return, with five hundred thousand foreigners, which could only be effected by bringing about a cessation of hostilities by means of an armistice obtained at any price. Therefore, to obtain the immediate release of the kingdom from the armies which were devouring its substance, it was necessary, to the exclusion of all other considerations, to aim at a prompt conclusion of peace. Your Majesty had then apparently nothing else to do but bask in the love of your people and the reward of your own wisdom, when a fresh demand was made upon your constancy

---

[1] Suppressed in the text of the archives.

[2] Text: "J'en envoie ce soir la copie dans ma dépêche au département," = as translated. Var.: "et j'en envoie ce soir la copie dans *une* dépêche," = "and I am sending off this evening the copy in *a* report."

and energy ; that of saving Europe if possible, from the perils with which the ambition and passions of some powers, and the blindness and pusillanimity of others were threatening her. The difficulties of the enterprise have never seemed to me sufficiently great to render hope of success impossible.

The letter with which your Majesty deigned to honour me on the 21st October raises my hopes, at the same time that the expressions of satisfaction you were pleased to accord to my zeal, give me fresh courage to proceed.

I have the honour to be......

No. 5B.—King Louis XVIII. to the Prince de Talleyrand.

PARIS, *November* 4, 1814.

My Cousin,

I have received your letter No. 8. I have read it with great interest, and with great indignation. The tone and the principles for which Buonaparte[1] has so greatly and so justly been blamed, were different in no respect from those of the Emperor of Russia.

I am pleased to flatter myself that the views of the army and of the imperial family will bring back Prince Metternich to more healthy opinions ; that Lord Castlereagh will share, more than he has done at present, those of the Prince Regent, and that you will then employ to advantage the arms I have placed in your hands. But, however that may be, continue to deserve the well-merited praises that I am pleased to repeat to-day, by holding firm to the course you have laid out, and be quite sure that my name[2] shall never be found at the bottom of an instrument sanctioning the most revolting immorality. Whereupon, my cousin, I pray God that He may always have you in His safe and holy keeping.

Louis.

No. 11A.—The Ambassadors of the King at the Congress to the Minister of Foreign Affairs at Paris.

VIENNA, *November* 6, 1814.

Monsieur le Comte,

We have the honour of forwarding to you copies of the reports of the first two sittings which have taken place.

The memoranda mentioned in it, are those which underwent

---

[1] Var.: Bonaparte.

[2] Text: "que mon nom ne se trouvera jamais." Var.: "que jamais mon nom," = "that never shall my name," &c. (More emphatic.)

discussion, and were presented by the embassy of France; they have been forwarded in the last despatch to the department.

A third conference was held on the 1st of November, at which the Comte de Noailles, who arrived the same morning, was present.

The result was unimportant; it has not yet even been decided, up to the present, to draft a report of it.

Prince Metternich, in his quality of president, laid down in a remarkably diffuse and disjointed speech: "That before proceeding to the formation of committees and commissions, it was necessary to understand each other; that it was necessary for each power to have settled with the others what interested it directly."

He told us further:

"That every question treated had two sides; that this congress was not a congress; that its opening was not, properly speaking, an opening at all; that the commissions were not commissions; that in the assembly of the powers at Vienna, the only advantage they had to note was that of *an Europe without distances :* that they could agree, or they could not."

Prince Metternich has shown in this sitting the full extent of his mediocrity, of his taste for petty intrigues and an uncertain and tortuous course, as also of his marvellous command of words that are vague and void of meaning.

To take one example out of a thousand; he terms the commissions "*chances of negotiation.*" It would be useless to point out the irrelevance of such a way of talking.

We had been told that the negotiations relative to the principal questions had taken a turn for the better, and while awaiting the confirmation of this, carefully avoided increasing difficulties which might trammel the course of affairs.

The majority at this meeting agreed in their wish to gain time, and to debate subsequently the possibility and the forms of a general convocation of the congress.

The question of Poland, and, as a natural consequence, that of Saxony, are however now boldly attacked.

The Emperor of Russia, we are informed, has sent his reply to the English ministers. The report, drafted by Baron von Anstedt,[1] has not been of a satisfactory nature, and must be understood to show but little conciliatory spirit.

---

[1] Johan, Baron Anstedt, a Russian diplomatist, was born at Strasbourg in the year 1760. In 1789, he went to Russia and was given a post in the Foreign Department. He was several times appointed envoy at Vienna. In 1811, he was made director of the diplomatic cabinet of Prince Koutousoff. He represented Russia at the Congress of Prague (1813), went thence to Vienna (1814), and was till his death, Russian plenipotentiary at the Diet of Frankfort. He died in 1835.

Lord Castlereagh replied yesterday. We are told that he insists, in the name of England, and for the safety of Europe, that Russia pass not the Vistula.

Prince Metternich has been obliged to take up this question, as the emperor, his master, has submitted the subject for the consideration of a state council, and this, in its conclusions, determined: " That Russia could not advance further without menacing the military positions of Austria, and that it was yet more important for Germany to prevent *the defiles of the Saale*[1] falling into the hands of Prussia."

The supplementary instructions of the king, which had been brought by M. de Noailles, enabled the plenipotentiaries to throw out hints as to the active part which France would take in order to bring about a real and lasting balance of power and to hinder Russia from obtaining possession of the Grand Duchy of Warsaw, Prussia, and Saxony.

The minister of Bavaria had been apprised of this, and notice of it had also been sent to the Emperor of Austria. We believe that this will sustain Prince Metternich in the resistance which he must offer to the claims of Russia and Prussia. Already the firm and decided tone taken by the embassy from the beginning has forced him to second with more energy the great interests of Europe. We are generally assured that the two powers, Russia and Prussia, are getting enlightened as to the difficulties which they may expect to meet with before they can succeed in their various projects. The influence which the English ministers also exercise on these questions gives us grounds for hoping that they will be modified, and that the king will have the glory of having stopped the execution of schemes which would have been disastrous for Europe and her future tranquillity.

Lord Castlereagh indeed always shows an inclination to procure Saxony for Prussia, but this latter power will reflect that she cannot hold it in peace without the concurrence of France, and will prefer perhaps to arrange matters by other combinations.

Prince von Hardenberg has admitted to one of his friends that he believes that this incorporation of Saxony is very distasteful to Germany, and that Prussia would perhaps consent to leave a nucleus of it.

Austria appears to wish that this nucleus be composed of the *three-fourths* of Saxony, if the Russian boundary be definitely fixed at the Vistula. Saxony would then retain from fifteen

---

[1] The Saale takes its rise in Bavaria, traverses the whole of Saxony and empties itself in the Elbe. It was through the defiles of the Saale that Napoleon passed in the campaign of 1806.

to sixteen hundred thousand inhabitants, and would still be larger than Wurtemberg or Hanover

This outcome would indeed be beyond all that could possibly have been expected when the French plenipotentiaries arrived at the congress, and the king would have attained a really remarkable success, should things turn out in this way.

The arrangements of the German Federation continue to be treated with much secrecy. Bavaria resists Prussia, and refuses to sacrifice any rights of sovereignty, save what may be absolutely necessary for the formation of the league.

It has hitherto been impossible to treat of the exchange of territory, because everything depends upon the fixation of the Prussian boundaries.

There remain now two other political subjects of interest to settle, which will apparently soon be taken into consideration. They are the affairs of the Helvetian corporation, and those of Italy.

Prince Metternich thought fit yesterday to invite Prince Talleyrand to a conference at which Lord Castlereagh and Count Nesselrode were present ; and these two subjects were there broached.

These gentlemen informed Prince Talleyrand that a commission had been appointed to arrange with the Swiss deputies present at Vienna the affairs of the Helvetian corporation. Prince Talleyrand said that he had appointed M. de Dalberg to debate as to the course that France had to pursue in this matter.

With regard to Italian affairs, the embarrassment of Prince Metternich was very plain when we were on the subject of Naples. It must be attributed, I suppose, to the fear with which public spirit, as well as the little taste the Italians have for the Austrian government inspire him, and to the influence that Murat exercises over the Jacobins of Italy, particularly over those of the former kingdom of Italy, of which he was some time governor.

In order to paralyse this influence, Prince Talleyrand proposed to abstain from touching on the fate of Murat till after the other Italian questions had been settled, and when provisory rule should have been brought to an end, and the country organized in a geographical order commencing with the northern states.

Prince Metternich admitted that it was not possible in treating the affairs of Italy, to discard the claims of the kingdom of Etruria, but that he desired one or two legations[1] for the Archduchess Marie Louise and her son. The other ministers, holding that these possessions were a property left unappropriated by the

---

[1] Legation = the name of the six administrative divisions of the Papal States.

treaty of Tolentino, thought it equitable to compensate the loss of Parma by an equivalent.

Seeing that, in the affairs of Italy, France seeks to get three points, namely, the succession of the house of Carignan to the throne of Sardinia, the establishing of the house of Parma and the expulsion of Murat, we must not raise too many difficulties. Prince Talleyrand has not yet turned his attention to this question. But it may be taken for granted that the Italian question will be arranged with these points as a basis.

Prince Talleyrand has appointed M. de Noailles, to whom he has disclosed the purposes of the king, for the commission which will be formed for treating this subject in detail.

With regard to the affairs of Switzerland, Lord Castlereagh would have liked to have been able to dispense with the interference of France, but the deputy from Bern[1] declared that his instructions demanded it imperatively ; and that his government, as also that of Soleure and Fribourg, believed it impossible for Swiss interests to be satisfactorily settled without the intervention of France. The Russian minister, Count Capo d'Istria,[2] and Sir Stratford Canning[3] appear to hold

---

[1] Louis Zerdeler (1772-1840), member of the upper council in the canton of Bern, was made, after the Decree of Mediation, minister at St. Petersburg and plenipotentiary at the Congress of Vienna. He resigned his functions in 1815.

[2] Jean, Comte Capo d'Istria, was born at Corfu in the year 1776. At twenty-seven years of age, he was chosen to be Secretary of State by the imperial commissioner of Russia in the Ionian Isles. When the peace of Tilsit brought these islands under the rule of France, Capo d'Istria laid down his functions and went to St. Petersburg, where he obtained a post in the cabinet of the Foreign Secretary. He followed the Emperor Alexander in the campaigns of 1813 and 1814, and was charged to Switzerland with a secret mission, the object of which was to get the neutrality of this country declared and respected. In 1814, Capo d'Istria was sent to the Congress of Vienna as plenipotentiary, and, the year following, was made Foreign Secretary of State. Greece was already beginning to rise, and the situation of Capo d'Istria, a Greek by birth and minister of the Czar, became full of difficulties. He was in fact dismissed in 1819, at the time of the insurrection of Ypsilanti. He then retired to Geneva, where he lived eight years, after which he was appointed President of Greece by his countrymen in 1827. He accepted these functions and held them for four years in the midst of war and civil strife, and was assassinated in the year 1831.

[3] Sir Stratford Canning, born in 1786, was an English diplomatist and a relation of the celebrated minister of that name. In 1814, he was plenipotentiary minister to Switzerland, and was sent in the same capacity to the Congress of Vienna. In 1824 he was made ambassador at St. Petersburg, and afterwards (1827) at Constantinople. In 1832 he entered the House of Commons, returned to Constantinople in 1842, and, with some intervals, resided there until 1858. He then returned to England, where he lived until his death in the year 1880.*

* This footnote is incomplete and inaccurate in some respects. It may therefore be as well to subjoin here the following abstract of the long and reliable notice devoted to the English diplomatist in the *Dictionary of National Biography* :—

Stratford Canning, first Viscount Stratford de Redcliffe (this title being derived from the name of a seat of his family, near Bristol), was first cousin of George Canning, the famous statesman, and youngest son of Stratford Canning, who, having been disinherited for marrying beneath his rank, settled down as a merchant in Clement's Lane, London, where the future diplomatist was born, November 4, 1786. He was still an infant when he lost his father, whose business had to be given up. His mother, Mehetabel, being left with scanty means, retired to Hackney, where young Canning was sent to school. In time, he went to Eton, and afterwards entered the Cambridge University.

At Eton he had been the pupil of Sumner, afterwards Archbishop of Canterbury. There, he

the same opinion. The suspicion and jealousy of the other powers will then be overcome on this point, and we hope that the settlement of the Swiss question will not present many difficulties.

The canton of Bern desires to recover that part of the canton of Aargau which belonged to it before. The canton of Zurich, urged on by former motives of jealousy, will only consent on condition of receiving itself a portion of it. Legitimate rights struggling against a system of expediency, such as is to be seen in Germany in the question of Saxony, may here also be observed. The authorities seem disposed to give the bishopric of Basel to the canton of Bern. On this point a question presents itself which ought to be immediately submitted to the decision of the king.

The canton of Geneva asks for ten or twelve thousand souls of

published, in conjunction with Richard Wellesley and others, a collection of essays. Fox, Sheridan, and others, were great friends of his mother, and powerfully contributed to developing his natural gifts.

In 1807, his cousin, who had been appointed Foreign Secretary, nominated him prècis writer. In the same year, young Stratford was sent to Copenhagen as secretary to the special but fruitless mission sent to Danemarck to adjust pending difficulties. In June, 1808, he was appointed first secretary to the English embassy at Constantinople. In July, 1810, on the retirement of his chief, he was raised to the rank of minister plenipotentiary and *chargé d'affaires* to Turkey. In 1812, he succeeded in obtaining the signature of Turkey to the treaty of Bucharest with Russia, which enabled the latter to make use of the army she kept in the Danubian principalities, to check the progress of Napoleon. On his return to England, he received, as reward of his services, a yearly pension of £1,200. He stayed at home for about eighteen months, devoting his leisure to literature. It was then that, with some friends, he founded the *Quarterly Review*, to which he contributed several political essays. In May, 1814, Lord Castlereagh having succeeded G. Canning at the Foreign Office, sent Stratford as minister plenipotentiary to Switzerland, where he was instrumental in effecting the federation of the cantons as a neutral state. After having arrived at a decision with Count Capo d'Istria, the Russian envoy to Switzerland, he went to submit it to the commission appointed by the Congress of Vienna to settle Swiss affairs. On his return home, in 1817, he was appointed member of the Privy Council. In 1820, he was sent to Washington to arrange certain difficulties pending between the government of the United States and the Cabinet of St. James. He succeeded in arranging a treaty which, however, was rejected by the American Senate. After some years spent in inactivity, he was sent to St. Petersburg, in November, 1824, on a short mission to induce the Czar to support the independence of Greece conjointly with England and France. In the following year, he returned to Constantinople in order to promote the independence of Greece, but the unexpected battle of Navarino momentarily put an end to his mission, and he had to leave Constantinople for Corfu with the other ambassadors. In 1829, the negotiations were renewed, and Turkey yielded partly. On his return to England, Stratford was made G.C.B., and, owing to the enmity of Lord Aberdeen, failing to obtain the post he desired, he resigned and devoted himself to parliamentary debates. In 1828, he had been elected a member for Old Sarum (the rottenest borough on the list), and sat for various other constituencies until 1841, when he was again appointed ambassador to Turkey. In 1832, he went on a short mission to Portugal. In 1835, he had been appointed ambassador to the Court of St. Petersburg, but the Czar Nicholas refused positively to receive him. He retained his post at Constantinople during the whole of the Crimean War, and succeeded so fully in winning the confidence of and, so to say, in fascinating the Sultan, that what the late Mr. Kinglake says of him, in his admirable history of the Crimean war, hardly seems exaggerated. Stratford Canning fully deserved the title of "Great Elchi" (full ambassador). At the conclusion of the war in 1858, he returned to London. In recognition of his services, he had, in 1852, been raised to the peerage with the title of Viscount Stratford de Redcliffe.

Since then, he lived in retirement until his death, taking part in political debates only when the Eastern question again came to the front. He contributed several papers to the *Times* and to the *Nineteenth Century*. In 1813, he had written on Bonaparte a poem which won the praises of Byron, his former school-fellow at Eton. In 1866, he published *Shadows of the Past*. Among his other literary contributions, may be cited *The Exile of Calauria* and *Alfred the Great in Athelney*, an historical play of three thousand lines of blank verse, published in 1876. He was a profoundly devout Christian, and during the latter years of his life, he wrote several religious essays. He died, without surviving male issue, August 14, 1880. His political papers were collected and published in 1881, under the title of *The Eastern Question*, with a memorial preface by the late Dean Stanley. Mr. Gladstone created him Knight of the Garter.

The fact that during all his career he was the bitterest enemy of the traditional enemy of England, and that to his energy and ability England was indebted for the paramount influence she, until recently, enjoyed, commercially and politically, in Turkey and the Levant generally, may justify this long rectifying note.—*(Translator.)*

the country of Gex,[1] so as to be contiguous to the canton of Vaud. In exchange, she would offer France twice the number of population taken on the bishopric of Basel, and the military frontier between Huningen, Vesoul and Besançon would be improved.

France would lose nothing but the point situated on the lake of Geneva, and she could stipulate that the right of navigation and commerce be reserved to her.

This exchange, which we consider advantageous, would necessitate however the restoration of a part of the canton of Aargau[2] to the canton of Bern, the bishopric of Basel being then much reduced. But every advantage that can be gained for the canton of Bern is, so to speak, an advantage given to France, because of the strong sentiments of attachment and devotion which bind this canton to the House of Bourbon.

We notice at the same time that the Emperor of Russia will, if this exchange does not take place, surround the canton of Geneva by a part of Savoy which hems the lake towards Valais. That exchange would consequently serve to dismiss this plan.

Would you therefore have the goodness, Monsieur le Comte, to transmit to us the orders of the king as soon as possible, with any modifications it may please his Majesty to make. If his Majesty consents to the exchange, he will signify the desire on the part of France of doing all in her power for the advantage of the Helvetian corporation ; and, according to the words of the Swiss deputies, nay, of the deputy of Bern himself, she would thus gain for herself a preponderating influence. Prince Talleyrand thinks the exchange would be advantageous ; but we need an authorization to make it.

Be pleased to accept, &c.

No. 10.—THE PRINCE DE TALLEYRAND TO KING LOUIS XVIII.

VIENNA, *November* 6, 1814.

SIRE,

The Comte de Noailles, who arrived here Wednesday morning (November 2nd), has brought me the additional instructions, which your Majesty was so good as to address to me. Your Majesty's resolutions are now known to the Austrian cabinet, to the Emperor of Austria himself, and to Bavaria. I thought it useless to speak of them to Lord Castlereagh, always so ready to take alarm at the intervention of France, and I could not speak of them to Count von Münster, who, having

---

[1] France then possessed the portion of the Gex country situated on the lake of Geneva, with the town of Versoix. This was the territory coveted by the canton of Geneva.

[2] Aarau, Brugg, Lenzburg, and Zofingen with adjacent territory.

just left the hands of his doctors, is engaged in preparations for his marriage with the Countess von Lippe, sister of the Prince Regent of Buckeburg.

The Comte de Noailles, the day after his arrival, was present at a conference that led to no result whatever. It was a question of deciding, whether the verification of credentials once terminated, commissions should be appointed for preparing the work, how many should be appointed, and with what formalities and by whom they should be appointed. Prince Metternich made a long speech, in order to prove that the name "*Commission*" was unsuitable, because it supposed a delegation of authority, which in its turn supposed a deliberating assembly, and this the congress could not be. He proposed various expressions in place of that which displeased him, and, unable to satisfy himself with any of them, concluded that it would be necessary to seek others in the next conference, which has not yet been held. These scruples as to the name *Commissions*, were without doubt strange, and out of place, when no difficulty had been made of applying it to the three ministers charged with the verification of credentials, and to the five who were drawing up the political organization of Germany. But, if I had supposed that Prince Metternich had any other object in view than that of gaining time, he would himself have undeceived me.

After the meeting, he asked me to his study, and told me that he and Lord Castlereagh had determined not to allow Russia to pass the Vistula ; that they were doing their utmost to get Prussia to make common cause with them on this question, and that they hoped to succeed. He conjured me to leave them time for this and not to press them. I wanted to know on what conditions they flattered themselves that they would receive the consent of Prussia ? He replied, by promising her a portion of Saxony, that is to say, from four to five hundred thousand souls of that country, with especially the town and district of Wittemberg, which may be considered as necessary to protect Berlin, all this arranged in such a manner as to leave Saxony still from fifteen to sixteen hundred thousand souls, Torgau, Kœnigstein, and the course of the Elbe, from the district of Wittemberg to Bohemia.

I have been informed that, in a Council of State, presided over by the emperor himself, and composed of Count von Stadion, Prince von Schwarzenberg and Prince Metternich, as well as of Count von Zichy and General Duka,[1] it was decided as a principle that the question of Saxony was of a greater interest for Austria even than that of Poland, and that the safety of the

---

[1] Peter, Count Duka, born in the year 1756, was made *feldzeugmeister* and Privy Councillor of the Empire of Austria, and died in 1822.

monarchy demanded that the defiles of Thuringen and of the Saale should not fall into the hands of Prussia. (I enter into more minute details on this subject in my letter of to-day, addressed to the department.)

This circumstance has caused me to put a little more confidence in what Prince Metternich has said to me on the subject, than I should have done otherwise. If we succeed in preserving the kingdom of Saxony intact, with from four-fifths to three-fourths of its population, we shall have done a great deal for justice, for the general good, and a great deal also for the glory of your Majesty.

The Emperor of Russia has answered the report of Lord Castlereagh. I shall see his reply, and shall have the honour of describing matters more pertinently, than by *hearsay* in my next despatch. At present, I only know with certainty, that the emperor complains of the injustice which he pretends has been done him, in supposing in him an ambition which he has not. He represents himself as in some way ill-treated, and then, without too marked a transition, declares that he will desist from none of his former pretensions. This reply roused Lord Castlereagh's ire, and he sent an answer to the emperor, which is to be taken by Lord Stewart this evening. His brother has charged him with this commission, because throughout the war, he had and still retains, the confidence of the emperor.

Herr von Gentz, who translated this answer for the benefit of the Austrian cabinet, to whom it has been forwarded, says it is very firm and very good.

The affairs of Switzerland are now being considered. I have chosen M. de Dalberg to take part in the conferences in which they will be discussed. I will not repeat to your Majesty all that has passed on this question, for my report to the department gives a full account of it.

Yesterday at four o'clock, I paid a visit to Prince Metternich, who had asked me to call on him. I found Count Nesselrode and Lord Castlereagh there. Prince Metternich began with fine protestations of his desire to be in my confidence, to be on good terms with France, and to do nothing without us.[1]

"What they desired," he said, "was that, putting aside all susceptibility, I should do all in my power to aid them in advancing matters, and in getting out of the dilemma, in which he affirmed they found themselves."

I replied that their situation with respect to me, was very different from mine with regard to them ; that I neither wished, did, nor knew anything with which they were unacquainted ;

---

[1] Text: "sans nous" = "without us." Var.: "sans *elle*" = "without *her*," (France).

while they, on the contrary, had been doing, and were daily doing a mass of things of which I was ignorant, or, if I did get to hear of some of them, it was only by hearsay from the town, that it was only in this way, that I knew of the existence of a reply from the Emperor Alexander to Lord Castlereagh. (Here,[1] I saw I embarrassed him, and understood that he was unwilling to be convicted of having been indiscreet in this respect, before Count Nesselrode.) I hastened to add that I was quite ignorant of the contents of that reply, nor did I in fact know definitely, if there had been one at all. Then, I remarked, that as to the difficulties of which they complained, I could only attribute them to one cause, and that was their refusal to assemble the congress.

"You will," I told them, "have to assemble it one day or other. The more you delay, the more grounds will you give for the suspicion that you have views which you dare not show in broad daylight. So much hesitation seems to indicate an uneasy conscience; why do you object to declare, without waiting for the verification of credentials, which may take a considerable time, that all those who have sent theirs to the seal-office, must meet at some specified place? The commissions will be reported there; it will be declared that each can carry his demands thither, and they each will go his own way. The commissions will then do their work, and business will progress with a certain amount of regularity."

Lord Castlereagh approved of this plan, which had for him the merit of clearing out of the way the difficulty relative to the contested credentials. But he remarked that the word "*Congress*" alone was sufficient to frighten the Prussians, and that Prince von Hardenberg had an especial horror of it. Prince Metternich repeated the greater number of the arguments he had laid before us at the last conference. He thought it preferable to summon the congress only when they had come to some agreement, at least on all the more important questions.

"There is one," he said, "that is demanding our attention now."

He meant that of Poland, but refused to mention it by name, and passed swiftly to the affairs of Germany, properly so called.

"There is," he said, "great unanimity on these questions (*i.e.* of Germany) amongst all who are directly concerned in them. The affairs of Switzerland are now coming to the front, and ought not," he added, "to be settled without the intervention of France."

I told him, I had thought it impossible for them to have any other opinion, and had therefore selected M. de Dalberg to

---

[1] Suppressed in the text of the archives.

take part in the conferences which would be held on the subject. Passing thence to the affairs of Italy, the word "*Complications,*" which Prince Metternich is perpetually making use of, for the purpose of expressing himself vaguely—a resource of which his feeble policy is in constant need—was employed for the affairs of Genoa and Turin, and those of Naples and Sicily. He wanted to prove that the tranquillity of Italy, and therefore of Europe, depended on the Naples business, not being arranged at the congress, but on its being deferred to some subsequent date.

"The force of things," he said, "will necessarily place the House of Bourbon on the throne of Naples."

"The force of things," I replied, "is now to be seen in all its might. It is at the congress that this question ought to be settled. In the geographical order, this question is the last of those of Italy, and I am quite content to follow the geographical order ; *but* my compliance can go no further."

Prince Metternich then proceeded to speak of the supporters Murat had in Italy.

"Organize Italy, and there will be none left him. Put an end to an odious temporary arrangement ; strengthen the right of possession in upper and middle Italy ; from the Alps to the frontiers of Naples, let there be not a single spot of ground under military occupation ; let there be rightful sovereigns, and a regular government ; fix the succession of Sardinia ; send an archduke to rule Milan ; recognize the rights of the Queen of Etruria ; give back to the Pope what belongs to him, and which you detain ; Murat [1] will not have any hold left on the affections of the people and will be no more for Italy than a brigand."

This geographical line for treating Italian affairs seemed to answer, and it was decided to call the Marquis de Saint-Marsan [2] to the next conference, in order to settle with him the affairs of Sardinia, in accordance with this plan. M. de Brignolles,[3] deputy

---

[1] Var.: "*et alors* Murat," = "*and then* Murat."

[2] Antony Asinari, Marquis of St. Marsan, was born at Turin in 1761 of an old family of Languedoc. He entered when still quite young into the diplomatic service, and was entrusted with various missions. In 1796, he was made Minister of War and of Marine. When Piedmont was incorporated with France, M. de St. Marsan was appointed state-councillor by Napoleon and French minister at Berlin. In 1813, he returned to Paris and was made a senator. In 1814, M. de St. Marsan was placed by the allied sovereigns at the head of the temporary government of Turin. King Victor Emmanuel, on his return, appointed him Minister of War and plenipotentiary at the Congress of Vienna. In 1816, he was Foreign Secretary, and President of the Council in 1818. He retired in 1821 and died in 1828.

[3] Antony, Marquis de Brignolles-Sales, descended from an ancient and illustrious Genoa family. Born in 1786, he was at first *auditeur* at the imperial Council of State, and, later, prefect of Savona. In 1814, he was sent to the Congress as plenipotentiary by the city of Genoa. He took allegiance to the House of Savoy, became head of the royal University (1816), ambassador at Rome (1839), and later at Paris. He was appointed Minister of State and Senator, and died in 1863.

of the town of Genoa, is also to be heard on all that concerns the commercial interests of this town. Lord Castlereagh insists on Genoa being a free port, and, on this occasion, spoke with disapprobation and bitterness, of the franchise of the port of Marseilles.

We should have been justified in believing that our position was improving, were it not that I hardly dare to rely on appearances here, having too great reason to distrust the sincerity of Prince Metternich ; and further, I know not what may be the meaning of the unexpected departure of the Grand Duke Constantine, who leaves Vienna to-morrow direct for Warsaw.

An expected journey of the Emperor Alexander to Gratz, *in Styria*,[1] is much spoken of. It is said that he intends to go as far as Trieste. One of the archdukes must do him the honours of this part of the Austrian monarchy. The journey is announced for the 20th instant.

The court of Vienna continues to show its guests a hospitality, which, considering the state of its finances, must burden it considerably. Kings, emperors, empresses, queens, hereditary princes, prince-regents, are to be seen everywhere. The court defrays the expenses of all. It is estimated, that the expense for each day must amount to two hundred and twenty thousand florins in paper money. Royalty certainly loses some of the grandeur which befits it in such assemblies. It seems to me rather unbecoming to find three or four kings, and more princes, at the balls and teas of private citizens.[2] It is necessary to come to France to see in royalty that brilliancy and dignity which render it at once august and dear in the eyes of the people.

I have the honour to be, ...

No. 6B.—KING LOUIS XVIII. TO THE PRINCE DE TALLEYRAND.

PARIS, *November* 9, 1814.

MY COUSIN,

I have received your report, No. 9.

I see with satisfaction, the approaching opening of the congress, but still foresee many difficulties.

I have charged the Comte de Blacas to report to you :

1st. An interview which he has had with the Duke of Wellington.[3] You will see that this latter speaks in far plainer terms than Lord Castlereagh. Which of the two gives the true

---

[1] Omitted in the text of the archives.

[2] Var.: " de simples particuliers *de Vienne*," = " at the houses of private citizens *of Vienna*."

[3] The Duke of Wellington was at that time ambassador at Paris. He was then appointed plenipotentiary at the congress from February 1 to March 26, 1815.

intention of his court? I do not know; but what Lord Wellington says will, in any case, be a good weapon in your hands.[1]

2nd. A document which this ambassador declares to be authentic; nothing can astonish me that Prince Metternich does, but I should be surprised, if on October 31st, you had not yet been acquainted with such a fact. However that may be, it was in any case necessary for you to be informed of it.

You will learn with pleasure that my brother arrived on Sunday in very good health. And now, may God have you, my cousin, in His safe and holy keeping.

LOUIS.

No. II.—THE COMTE DE BLACAS D'AULPS TO THE PRINCE DE TALLEYRAND.

PARIS, *November* 9, 1814.

I AM but following out, your Highness, an order of the king, in hastening to transmit to you, from his Majesty, important information, and instructions which he considers no less essential.

Your late interview with the Emperor of Russia, and yet more, your fears as to the compliance of Austria and England, have begotten in the king a lively desire to gather any information serving to enlighten him as to the real disposition of this latter power. That which has been reported to you of the language held by the Prince Regent, besides what his Majesty already knew in this respect, caused him to see the necessity of sounding the intentions of the British Cabinet.

A conversation which I have just had with the Duke of Wellington, has accomplished this, or at least has furnished the king with the opportunity of claiming the co-operation of England, more strongly still, on all the more thorny points of the negotiation. Lord Wellington, after assuring me that the instructions given to Lord Castlereagh, and *with which he was well acquainted*, were absolutely opposed to the designs of the Emperor Alexander on Poland, and consequently on Saxony, since the fate of Saxony depends absolutely on the determination come to with regard to Poland, told me that it was by devoting attention solely to this great question, and by neglecting all secondary interests, that an understanding would be most easily arrived at. According to him, Austria will never lend support to a project rejected by France, and Prussia herself, who takes Saxony *for want of something better*, would

---

[1] Text: "mais le dire de *Lord Wellington* sera dans tous les cas," as translated. Var.: "mais *le Duc de Wellington* sera en tous cas," = "but *the Duke of Wellington* will be in any case."

be extremely pleased to find herself again possessed of the Duchy of Warsaw. Finding the Duke of Wellington [1] so explicit on this point, I thought that, according to the commands of the king, I ought to try and take steps which, although quite deprived of any official character, might yet more and more engage him in the admission of the only views likely to be avowed by the court of London. I represented to him, that if the views of his government were such as he told me, and if the only obstacle to a prompt and happy issue of the negotiations lay in the difficulty of reducing to one uniform resistance various oppositions of different natures, it seemed to me that a compact concluded between France, England, Spain, and Holland, and which should have no other aim than the public expression of the views held by them conjointly on this question, would soon obtain the assent of the other courts. This means, by presenting an imposing concurrence of opinion, would dissolve at once the charm which was beguiling so many states into a direction contrary to their interests, and the king, having no other ambition than the enforcement of the principles of public law, and of a just balance of power in Europe, could flatter himself that there would be no cause which would drive from his side those who, animated by the same sentiments, would be invited to rally there.

This proposal, whose advantages the Duke of Wellington was obliged to admit, was rejected by him, on the grounds of its being superfluous ; but he protested to me with more emphasis than ever, the just intentions of his government on the question of Poland and Saxony, and even on that of Naples, and he reiterated that an exclusive attention given to these great interests would soon bring the plenipotentiaries to the end from which the court of St. Petersburg was swerving.

Your Highness therefore sees that (whatever may be the reticence of her minister at the Congress) England is very sensible here of the instructions with which she has entrusted her envoy, instructions which in connecting,[2] as the Duke of Wellington has done, the question of Saxony with that of Poland,[3] offer the king the most important support. In this state of affairs, his Majesty thinks that you could to some advantage make use of the information which I have the honour

---

[1] Text: "trouvant le Duc de Wellington tellement explicite," = "finding the Duke of Wellington so explicit." Var.: "*Le* trouvant tellement explicite," = "finding *him* so explicit."

[2] Text : "en liant" = "in connecting." Var. : "*lorsqu'on lie*" = "*when one connects.*"

[3] Text: "la question de la Saxe à celle de la Pologne," = "the question of Saxony with that of Poland." Var.: "la question de la Pologne à celle de la Saxe," = "the question of Poland with that of Saxony." (Mere inversion of words.)

to give you.   By challenging the instructions of Lord Castle-reagh, you are thus empowered to put him to the necessity of giving you some reply, which it would be difficult for him to make entirely indefinite, since one day he will be compelled to prove that his policy has been consistent with that of his government, and with the best interests of his country.

The independence of Poland, which would be very popular in England if carried out, would certainly not[1] be so if Russia is allowed to do as she proposes.

Your Highness will therefore doubtless see, that in your intercourse with the English minister it will be very important to keep these two suppositions distinct.   The king is of opinion that the stronger the views you express in favour of a real and complete independence of the Polish people, if that should be practicable, the more you will deprive Lord Castlereagh of all means of justifying in the eyes of England[2] the abandoning of the Grand Duchy of Warsaw to the Emperor Alexander.

The king has informed you of the orders which his Majesty has given[3] to the Minister of War, and which are to place the army on a footing of peace.[4]

The document which I here subjoin by order of the king, and which has been given to me as authentic, proves how necessary this measure was, in the midst of the breakers that surround us. Nothing can cause surprise that comes from Prince Metternich, yet it would all the same be very singular should such a fact not have been known to you on October 31st.   Be so good, I beg of you, never to mention from whom I obtained the document which I am forwarding to you.

I am glad you are satisfied with the services of the Chevalier de Vernègues.   I have known for a long time the enlightened zeal he has for the cause we ourselves serve, as well as his character, which deserves the highest esteem.

I have given M. d'André a situation on the estates of the king ; it was necessary at first to give him means of support ; but I think that he will, in the end, be able to serve the king to far more advantage than in an administration of which the revenue is of small importance.

---

[1] Text : "ne le serait," = " would not be so."   Var.: "ne le sera," = "*will not* be so."

[2] Text : "aux yeux de l'Angleterre," = "in the eyes of England."   Var.: "aux yeux de *la nation Anglaise*," = "in the eyes of *the English nation*."

[3] Text : "vous a fait connaître les ordres que sa Majesté a donnés," = "has informed you of the orders which his Majesty has given."   Var.: "vous a *instruit des* ordres que *S.M. avait* donnés," = "has *acquainted* you *with* the orders which *H.M.* had given."

[4] Add.: "*Je me flatte que cette détermination, dictée par les considérations dont vous sentez toute la force, ne tardera pas à devenir superflue,*" = "I flatter myself that this resolve, dictated by considerations of which you fully feel the force, will not be long in becoming superfluous."

*Be pleased to accept the renewed assurance of my unalterable
attachment and of my high regard.*

BLACAS D'AULPS.

*P.S.—This letter was partly written before the arrival of your
No. 9, which only proves more and more the necessity of establishing
good terms between ourselves and England on the questions which
divide the negotiating parties.*[1]

No. 12 A.—THE AMBASSADORS OF THE KING AT THE CONGRESS
TO THE MINISTER OF FOREIGN AFFAIRS AT PARIS.

VIENNA, November 12, 1814.

MONSIEUR LE COMTE,

All the private information that reaches us causes us to
fear that the questions of Poland and Saxony are still in an
unsatisfactory stage, and that what hinders progress is the blind
obstinacy of the Emperor of Russia and of the King of Prussia,
as well as a fatal inertia on the part of Austria.

A messenger from the King of Saxony, who left Berlin on
the 5th instant, has brought with him an emphatic protest which
he has communicated to us. This declaration says that the
king will not consent to any exchange, and refuses absolutely to
abdicate. His intention is that this expression of his opinions
should be published. We think that it can only produce a
very good effect, and shall probably forward it to you by the
next messenger for insertion in the *Moniteur* The King of
Saxony, since the temporary establishment of a Prussian administration, refuses all the proposals which have been offered
him, and has told the Prussian government as much.

Meanwhile, the Grand Duke Constantine has left for Warsaw.
He carries, as we hear, instructions for organizing this new
Poland, which, insignificant as it is in itself, will yet prove a
source of trouble for its neighbours. Austria has taken alarm
at this ; her cabinet apparently is quite willing to exhaust
all means for turning the Emperor of Russia from his designs,
and severing him from the King of Prussia. Feeling, however,
uncertain of success, she has chosen to march nearly twenty
to twenty-five thousand men to Galicia. These troops are to
reinforce the line which she already has on that frontier ; but
Austria shows no desire to oppose the invasion of Saxony by
means of arms.

Prince Metternich has despatched a messenger to London.
He probably carries an order to Count von Meerveldt to
represent to the British cabinet the extreme importance of

---

[1] The latter part of this letter and the postscript are not found in the text of the
record-office of the ministry of Foreign Affairs.

stoutly seconding the advice given by Lord Castlereagh in his notes to the Emperor of Russia. This minister wishes the Grand Duchy of Warsaw to remain independent, or at least that the Vistula be the boundary line between Russia, Prussia, and Austria. It is on this point that the three powers are still negotiating. The Emperor Alexander, however, has determined to make one step further in pursuit of his aim, and is beguiling the King of Prussia, whom he has advised to commence the organization of Saxony, as he himself has that of Warsaw.

This conduct sows in Europe the seeds of war, which, at the present moment, it would be impossible to remove. It will also furnish elements for long disturbances, and render very difficult the settling of German affairs.

The result of the last private conference has been to resume the discussion of Italian affairs.

The Austrian ministry is the more resolved to bring them to some conclusion, that the Jacobin agitation, making itself felt in that part of Europe, under the open protection of Murat, perplexes her. This agitation is backed by Russia and by the English. Lord William Bentinck [1] has sown, in those parts, the seeds of revolutionary ideas which were intended to thwart Bonaparte's designs, but, as things now stand, they do more harm than good.

The incorporation of Genoa with Piedmont will be made, we believe, by virtue of a capitulation. The Genoese had drawn up a proposal for a constitution, but of so democratic a character that it could not be allowed. But the capitulation is so much the more needed, that the Genoese have a strong repugnance to this act of submission, and that it is advisable to put down, as far as possible, the germs of bitterness and discord which crop up on all sides whenever the union of Belgians and Dutch, Saxons and Prussians, Italians and Austrians, is introduced.

We have good hopes of being able to restore Parma to the Spanish succession, and to get *one of the legations* given to the Archduchess Marie-Louise. If this exchange can be brought about, its return to the Holy See will be proposed in the case of the prince dying without male issue. The fate of Murat has not yet been broached ; but the embassy of the king will regard no arrangement as final if the retirement of Murat is not stipulated for.

Swiss affairs also have not yet been touched upon. It is believed that the allies propose connecting Switzerland with the military system of Germany, in order to oppose stronger barriers to France. The nomination of Herr von Stein, on the part of

---

[1] It will be remembered that Lord William Bentinck had for several years commanded a body of English troops in Sicily.

Russia, as commissioner appointed for this purpose, may perhaps lead one to suspect some concealed intentions. But this arrangement would be so strongly opposed to the interests of the Swiss, that it may be left to them to overthrow it, when it comes within the range of practical politics.

You will therefore see, Monsieur le Comte, by this brief description of what is occupying the congress, that no very great results have as yet been attained, but that private intrigues have been sufficiently active. On the side of the great powers these intrigues proceed from two causes : the fear with which revolutionary France still inspires them, and the secret desire which they harbour of seeing France restrained within such limits, that she be rendered unable to regain that influence which she exerted at certain epochs of her history.

The policy adopted by the king will restore to the country the confidence which the measures of her last government lost her, and with that the interference of France will be more sought after than dreaded.

The Comte de Noailles, who was presented to the sovereigns on his arrival, has collected the observations and sayings which have come in his way, and which seemed to him worthy of interest. We have the honour to inclose herewith the report containing them. They present nothing but what can give satisfaction.

Be pleased to accept, &c.

No. 11.—THE PRINCE DE TALLEYRAND TO KING LOUIS XVIII.

VIENNA, *November* 12, 1814.

SIRE,
Prince Metternich and Lord Castlereagh have persuaded the Prussian ministry to make common cause with them on the question of Poland. But the hopes built on the concurrence of Prussia have not been of long duration. The Emperor of Russia, having engaged the King of Prussia to dine with him a few days ago, he had with him a long conversation, of which I have gleaned a few details from Prince Adam Czartoryski. He reminded him of the friendship which united them, of the high value he attached to it, of all that he had done to make it lasting. Their age being almost the same, it was pleasant to think that they might, for a long time to come, witness the happiness which their people would enjoy from their close intimacy. He had always bound his hopes of fame to the restoration of a kingdom of Poland. When he was almost able to touch the goal of his wishes, was he to have the mortification of having to count among his opponents his dearest friend, and the

only prince upon whose sentiments he had relied? The king made him a thousand protestations, and swore to support the Polish question. "It is not sufficient," continued the emperor, "for you alone to be of this disposition, your ministers must also conform to it." And he made the king summon Prince von Hardenberg. He having arrived, the emperor repeated to him all that he had said, and the promise that the king had given. Prince von Hardenberg was about to make some objections, but pressed by the Emperor Alexander, who asked him if he refused to obey the orders of his king, and these orders being absolute, there was nothing left him but to promise to carry them out faithfully. This is all that I have been able to gather of the scene; but there were probably many other particulars, of which I am in ignorance, if it is true as Herr von Gentz has assured me, that Prince von Hardenberg declared "he had never seen the like."

This change on the part of Prussia has disconcerted greatly Prince Metternich and Lord Castlereagh. They would have liked Prince von Hardenberg to have tendered his resignation, and certainly this could have gravely embarrassed [1] the king and the emperor, but he does not appear to have even thought of it. [2]

As to myself, believing as I do that Prince Metternich obtained the concurrence of the Prussians by more concessions than he avowed, I am inclined to think this defection as good for us, and your Majesty will see that my presentiments were only too well founded.

The Grand Duke Constantine, who left two days ago, went to organize the army of the Duchy of Warsaw. He was also charged with drawing up a civil organization for the country. The tenor of his instructions, according to Herr von Anstedt, [3] who prepared them, is that the Emperor Alexander will never withdraw any of his pretensions. The emperor has also probably engaged the King of Prussia to give likewise a military and civil organization to Saxony. He is reported to have said: "From civil organization to ownership is not far." In a letter which I received from M. de Caraman, [4] I find that the brother of the Minister of Finances and several generals have left Berlin in order to organize Saxony. [5] M. de Caraman

---

[1] Text: "que cela aurait pu embarrasser," = "that this *could* have embarrassed." Var.: "que cela *aurait* embarrasé," = "this *would* have embarrassed."

[2] Text: "mais il ne parait pas y avoir même pensé" = "but he does not appear to have even thought of it." Var.: "mais il ne parait pas *même* y avoir pensé" = "but he does not appear *even* to have thought of it."

[3] Var.: Herr von Anstetten.

[4] Victor Ricquet, Marquis, afterwards Duc de Caraman, was born in 1762. In 1814, Louis XVIII. appointed him ambassador at Berlin, and, in the year following, at Vienna. He was present as plenipotentiary at the different congresses of the Holy Alliance, and created Duc in 1828. He died in 1829.

[5] Var.: add. *civilement et militairement* = civilly and militarily.

adds that, nevertheless, the occupation of Saxony is at present only represented as temporary, and not definite, at Berlin.

There is yet a further tale, that the Emperor Alexander, after speaking of the opposition of Austria to his views, and bitterly complaining of Prince Metternich, said : " Austria believes herself assured of Italy, but there is there a Napoleon, who might be found useful "—a saying which I could not guarantee, but which circulates, and which, if true, would enable one to form an idea of him who uttered it.

Lord Castlereagh has not yet received a reply to his last note : some even believe that the emperor will not deign to answer it.

While the affairs of Poland and Saxony thus remain in suspense, the ideas, which, in the conference which I had the honour of describing to your Majesty, I had put forward on the organization of Italy, have borne fruit. The day before yesterday, I was with Lord Castlereagh, and found him full of it. Prince Metternich, who dined yesterday with us at the house of M. de Rasumowski, was no less so. To-day, he summoned Lord Castlereagh, Count Nesselrode, and myself in order to consider this question. On my coming he told me that it would only be question of this to-day ; that the day after to-morrow, to-morrow, perhaps in an hour, he would be in a position to speak to me of Poland and Saxony, but that for the moment he could not do so. I did not press the point. The discussion centred round the country of Genoa alone. It was proposed not to incorporate it with Piedmont, but to give it to the King of Sardinia by a capitulation which would insure [1] it certain privileges and private institutions. Lord Castlereagh had brought some memoranda and projects which had been addressed to him on the subject, and read them to us. He very strongly insisted on the establishment of a free port, of a bonded warehouse, and of a transit with defined rights across Piedmont. It was decided to meet again to-morrow, and summon MM. de Saint-Marsan and de Brignoles to the meeting.

After the conference, being alone with Prince Metternich, and desiring to know how he stood with regard to Poland and Saxony, and what he proposed to do on this subject, in place of putting him direct questions which he would only have eluded, I spoke to him of himself, and, assuming the tone of an old friend, I told him that, while occupied in business affairs, it was yet necessary to think of oneself, and that it seemed to me he did not do so sufficiently : that there were matters to which one was forced by necessity, but that it was indispensable that this necessity be made

---

[1] Text : "qui lui assurât" = "which would insure it." Var. : " qui lui *assurera* " = " which *will* insure it."

plain to every one ; that one might be actuated, as he probably was, by the most disinterested motives ; but that, if these motives were unknown to the public, one was yet calumniated, because in that case, the public could only judge by results ; that he was exposed to reproaches of all kinds, as, for instance, of having sacrificed Saxony ; that I sincerely hoped he had not done so ; but why give pretext for such rumours ? Why not give his friends the means of defending or justifying him ? A slight unbending on his part was the result of the frankness with which I spoke to him. He read me his letter to Prussia on the question of Saxony, and some affectionate thanks [1] on my part led him to confide it to me. I promised him it should remain secret. I enclose a copy of it with the letter that I have the honour to write to your Majesty. I beg of your Majesty to take great care of it, and to permit me to ask for it again on my return.

Your Majesty will see in this letter that Prince Metternich had promised the Prussians not, as he had assured me a portion of Saxony, but the whole of it, a promise which he had fortunately made dependent on a condition which rendered its accomplishment impossible.[2] Your Majesty will see further by this note that Prince Metternich abandons Luxemburg to the Prussians, after having assured me on more than one occasion that he would not give it to them. This same note reveals further the project, formed now for some time, of putting Germany under what they are pleased to call the influence, and which would really be the absolute dominion, of Prussia and Austria.

Prince Metternich protests now that he will never abandon Saxony. As to Poland, he has given me to understand that he would sacrifice much, which signifies that he would sacrifice everything, if the Emperor Alexander refused to yield an inch.

I was still with him when a report of the state of the Austrian army was brought to him. He allowed me to see it. The actual forces of this army are 374,000 men, of whom 52,000 are cavalry, and 800 pieces of cannon. It is while possessing such an army as this that he thinks the best thing for Austria to do is to submit to and suffer everything. Your Majesty will be pleased to remark that the number of the troops is the effective strength of the army.

[1] Text: "affectueux" = "affectionate." Var. : "assez affectueux" = "*sufficiently* affectionate."

[2] Prince Metternich gave Saxony to Prussia on two conditions : (1) that Prussia should abandon Russia on the Polish question ; (2) that on the side of the Rhine, the Mein on one side and the Moselle on the other should be the boundaries between the states of North and the states of South Germany, an arrangement which compelled Prussia to give up Mayence. Now it is well known that Frederick William and the Emperor Alexander were very closely united in their views on Poland, and that, on the other hand, Prussia eagerly coveted Mayence.

I shall not seal the letter which I have the honour to write to your Majesty till after my return from a conference, to which I am going this morning.

I have just left the conference. I found myself in company with Count Nesselrode, Prince Metternich, and Lord Castlereagh. M. de Saint-Marsan, to whom notice of the meeting had been sent, was also admitted. The only question under discussion was that of the incorporation of Genoa with Piedmont. A kind of authority,[1] given by the provisory government formed some months ago by Lord William Bentinck, caused some difficulties to arise. They will be removed by trying to establish, that Genoa is a vacant country. It was determined that the eight powers should reassemble to-morrow to make a declaration to this effect, and to give to M. de Brignoles, the envoy from Genoa, a copy of the protocol which shall contain this declaration. There will only remain to decide upon the method of the incorporation. I availed myself of the conference of to-day to speak of the succession of Sardinia. M. de Saint-Marsan, as I had suspected, had received from his court instructions agreeable to the rights of the house of Carignan. I proposed a wording which acknowledges these rights. M. de Saint-Marsan adopted and seconded it, and I have every reason for believing that it will be adopted.

The discussion relative to the affairs of Switzerland will not be long now in commencing.

I have the honour to be. . . .

No. 7B.—KING LOUIS XVIII. TO THE PRINCE DE TALLEYRAND.

PARIS, *November* 15, 1814.

MY COUSIN,

I have received your letter No. 10, and await with impatience the further details which you promise.

I seize eagerly the hope that you hold out to me for Saxony, and I believe I can give myself up to it with some confidence, seeing that Prince Metternich speaks no longer his own opinion, but that of a council. I should certainly prefer that the kingdom should remain intact, but I think that its unhappy king may deem himself fortunate if two-thirds or three-fourths of it are left him.

With regard to the proposed exchange, I do not like, as a general rule, giving up what belongs to me, still less do I like

---

[1] Text: "Une espèce de pouvoirs donnés" = "a kind of authority given." Var. : "une espèce de *pouvoir donné*" = "a kind of *authority given*" (singular instead of plural).

robbing another ; and after all, the rights of the Bishop-Prince of Basel, less important doubtless though they be to the tranquillity of Europe, are yet no less sacred than those of the King of Saxony. If, however, the spoliation of the former of these princes is inevitable, moved by the twofold consideration of pre serving a portion of his estates to the King of Sardinia, and of rendering a great service to the canton of Bern, I will consent to the exchange and now send you an authority *ad hoc*.[1]

Whereupon, my cousin, I pray God that He may have you in His safe and holy keeping.

LOUIS.

No. 13A.—THE AMBASSADORS OF THE KING AT THE CONGRESS TO THE MINISTER OF FOREIGN AFFAIRS AT PARIS.

VIENNA, *November* 17, 1814.

MONSIEUR LE COMTE,

Since the sending off of our last despatch another conference has been held. It has fixed the fate of Genoa agreeably to the secret article which incorporates that country in Piedmont.

A commission has been appointed to settle the conditions under which this incorporation shall be effected. Austria, France, and England have been chosen as members of it. It will be composed of Count Wessemberg, the Comte de Noailles and Lord Clancarty.

Lord Castlereagh has been put to some embarrassment by the conduct of Lord W. Bentinck at Genoa. This latter had flattered the Genoese with hopes of a complete independence. Lord Castlereagh has rather weakly maintained that this admiral went beyond his powers, and said that it was necessary by all means to soften to the Genoese the sacrifice which is imposed upon them. He assured the Deputy of Genoa that he would procure for his country, all the advantages enjoyed by his own country, Ireland, and we are curious to see how he will compensate the State of Genoa for the right of nominating members for the House of Commons and for the House of Lords, a prerogative which Ireland enjoys by its incorporation with Great Britain, and which cannot be given to the Genoese, since Piedmont possesses no parliament. This fact, and many others,

---

[1] Add. : . . . of which you will make use in the five following cases, of which the first is only a rule of conduct for us :—(1) the impossibility of saving the principality of Basel ; (2) the guarantee to the King of Sardinia of what remains to him of the kingdom of Savoy ; (3) restitution of its share of Aargau to the canton of Bern ; (4) the free exercise of the Catholic religion in the portion of the Gex district given up to the canton of Geneva ; (5) free navigation for France on the lake of Geneva. On these conditions you may agree to the exchange and sign.

prove that the noble lord has less studied the complications of European politics, than he has been struck with the danger to which a new system of continental blockade would expose his country.

In this conference, the plenipotentiary of Spain, Count de Labrador, maintained that it was necessary to leave to the Genoese the right of forming their own constitution, and that the secret article gave no right to the King of Sardinia, which had not signed the treaty of Paris. This minister wished doubtless to try, if the desire the Genoese had evinced to become subjects of the Queen of Etruria could not be realised.

The desire not to change the provisions made by the treaty of Paris has caused the majority to decide that the *incorporation* of Genoa with Piedmont ought to be effected ; and that the act of submission on the part of this republic to France, and the cession which was made of it by the treaty of Paris, protected the principles of the law of nations. We supported this view.

As soon as the report of this conference has been sent to us we shall have the honour, Monsieur le Comte, to transmit it to you.

We address you meanwhile a document [1] which is far more curious, and which would severely denounce the principles of the coalition if we had not been witnesses of the embarrassment it causes, and of the desire which the ministers of the four powers have of declaring it either apocryphal, or published by a culpable precipitation on the part of Prince Repnin,[2] Governor of Saxony.

This document deserves peculiar attention. It proves that in spite of all the trouble taken, since our arrival at the congress, to conceal from us the secret machinations of Russia and Prussia, in spite of the weakness of Prince Metternich and the incapacity of Lord Castlereagh, we have penetrated from the very first the deceitful combinations and tortuous path which the ministers of the four powers have followed, and which, without the intervention of France, would have destroyed even the possibility of coming to an agreement on some system of political equilibrium, a system which, badly conceived perhaps, will yet be under the ægis of the general principles which ruled Europe before the Revolution.

---

[1] Prince Repnin, Governor of Saxony, had issued a proclamation, which declared that that country ought to be given up to Prussia.

[2] Nicolas, Prince Repnin-Wolkonski, a Russian general and diplomatist, was a grandson of the famous field-marshal of that name. Born in 1778, he was a colonel at Austerlitz, and was taken prisoner in that battle. In 1809, he was appointed ambassador at Cassel by King Jérôme Napoleon. Lieutenant-general in 1813, he was, after the battle of Leipzig, made Governor-general of Saxony for the allies, King Frederick Augustus being considered a prisoner of war. In 1814, he was accredited with plenipotentiary powers at the Congress of Vienna ; after the peace he was appointed Governor of Little Russia (1816) and entered later (1835) into the Council of the Empire. He died in 1845.

The publication of this circular in the German papers has caused a great deal of vexation to Herr von Stein, who, by his system of organization in Germany, has made himself the champion of the union of Saxony and Prussia.

The English and Austrian ministers reproach him for having spoken of their consent, which they pretend they never gave, and which, as a matter of fact, they had subjected to very unimportant conditions. Refutations therefore in several of the gazettes will soon appear. But it is well that this scandalous transaction, which lays bare the plots that have been woven here, should be disclosed.

The minister of Saxony has not yet thought fit to publish the protest of the king, and will limit himself at present to announcing it only.

We have the honour to address to you a copy of the circular, and you will be so kind, Monsieur le Comte, as to get it inserted in the *Moniteur*, just as it is here subjoined, addressed to the ministry of Foreign Affairs. The occupation of Saxony by the Prussians is beyond all doubt a very grave fault on the part of the Austrian ministry, and an ignoring of all principles on the part of Lord Castlereagh ; but it does not yet decide the question, and we see with satisfaction, that public opinion is very strong indeed against this measure. Bavaria has declared that she will never consent to the destruction of the House and people of Saxony, and that a German League could not be formed out of such elements. She has renewed her offers to Austria, if this power will resort to all her forces and adopt a more honest and candid policy. Wurtemberg seems to be moving in the same direction.

Public opinion in Austria expresses without reserve, its disapproval of the execution of this measure, and Prince Metternich is greatly blamed, as neglecting the most important interests of the monarchy.

Prince Talleyrand has had a third conversation with the Emperor of Russia, a full account of which he gives in his special report to the king. He has left no doubt in the emperor's mind as to the part the king will take in the matter. The emperor himself was more affable and less autocratic than he had been at former interviews.

Prussia, for her own part, cannot remain blind to the fact that this union, carried out in the face of so many difficulties, might become a source of embarrassment and danger for herself. The Prussian ministers are therefore trying the effect of negotiation. They appear to be willing to reserve to the King of Saxony an equivalent, or a part of Saxony enclosing one half of the population ; but nothing has been agreed to in this respect on their part. They have even announced, that it would be sufficient if a Duke of Saxony only were retained.

Prince Talleyrand has proved to the Emperor of Russia, that 1,600,000 inhabitants must be kept for Saxony, because Saxony comprises rather more than two million souls, that she ought to retain all that she has on the left bank of the Elbe, and that her territories on the right bank have a smaller number of inhabitants, not rising above 500,000 to 600,000 souls. A little less than 1,600,000 souls might perhaps be agreed to ; and as England and Austria have not yet abandoned their demand for fixed limits in Poland, all is still intact, and the final result of a negotiation which, without the firmness of the ambassadors of the king, would have been entirely abandoned, cannot yet be given.

In any case, it will be less important for France to see a part of Poland sacrificed to Russia, than to see all Saxony destroyed, and some Austrian ministers are of opinion that if a sacrifice must be made on one point or another, Austria ought to be more compliant on the question of Poland's boundaries, on condition that Prussia does not gain the advantage of uniting Saxony to her monarchy.

It is by the combined action of these several interests, and by a course more conformable to true principle on the part of England, that we hope that this cause may be definitely settled.

The news from Italy speaks of the intrigues of the King of Naples and of his armaments. We observe here, the fear with which this inspires Prince Metternich. We are informed also that the court of Russia has recalled the officer whom she had accredited at Murat's court, and that the credentials, despatched to the minister of Russia at Palermo, expressly state that he is accredited to the *King of the Two Sicilies.*

A pamphlet, drafted by a certain Filangieri,[1] aide-de-camp of Murat, is circulating here ; it is of a revolutionary and threatening character. The police have bought it up. Prince Metternich makes use of the alarm roused, in order to mislead public opinion with regard to the preservation of Murat on the throne of Naples. But he is the only one, even of the Emperor of Austria's ministers, who supports a cause which Europe will soon treat as it deserves.

The Emperor of Russia has signed the ratifications of the treaty made between himself and the King of Denmark, and

---

[1] Charles Filangieri, Prince of Satriano, Duke of Taormina, was born in 1785, was a Neapolitan general, and one of the most devoted officers of Murat. He was badly wounded in 1815, at the moment of the renewal of hostilities with Austria. He kept his rank after the restoration of the Bourbons. In 1848, King Ferdinand charged him with the subduing of Sicily. He succeeded after bloody battles, was appointed lieutenant-general and governor of the province, but retired shortly afterwards, and lived in retirement till his death.

they were exchanged yesterday. The Russian troops are now to evacuate Holstein.

No conclusion has yet been come to on Swiss affairs, and those of the German federation are not very far advanced. Prince Metternich and Prince von Hardenberg have communicated the general line of policy to be followed to Count Nesselrode, that he may submit it to the emperor. In a reply dated November 11, Count Nesselrode announces to the cabinets of Austria and Prussia that Russia approves of the proposed basis of the federal compact.

We have the honour to address to you this project, as it was communicated confidentially to us, and such as it is used at the deliberations of the German Commission. Many changes have been made in it, chiefly the division into districts, the right of war and peace. . . . . We hope to be shown the note of Count Nesselrode, and shall acquaint the ministry with its contents.

Be pleased to accept, &c.

No. 12.—The Prince de Talleyrand to King Louis XVIII.

VIENNA, *November* 17, 1814.

SIRE,

Before the Emperor of Russia secured the support of the King of Prussia, certain persons [1] who were in his confidence having advised him to turn to the side of France, to come to some understanding with her, and to see me, he had replied that he would willingly see me, and that in future, in demanding an audience of him, I should have to apply, not to Count Nesselrode, but to Prince Wolkonski, his first aide-de-camp. I told the person by whom the message had been brought that if I demanded an audience of the emperor, Austria and England could not ignore it, that they would take umbrage at it and build besides all sorts of conjectures on it, and that, in demanding an audience by the unusual channel of an aide-de-camp, I should give an air of intrigue to any relations with the emperor, which would suit neither him nor me. Some days after, having asked why I had not been to see him, he was told my reasons, and approved of them, adding: "Then it is I who must attack him first." Having often the occasion of finding myself with him at the same meetings, I made it a rule to come across him as little as possible, or even to abstain from going near him, shunning him, in fact, as much as was compatible with propriety. I was proceeding after this fashion on Saturday at the house of Count Zichy, where he

---

[1] Text: "des personnes" = "certain persons who were in his confidence.'
Var. : "*les* personnes" = "*those* persons who were in his confidence."

was. I had passed almost all the time in the gambling-room, and, profiting by the moment when every one was advancing to the tables, I prepared to retire, and had already reached the door of the antechamber, when, feeling a hand resting on my shoulder, I turned round, and saw it was that of the Emperor Alexander. He asked me why I had not gone to see him? when he should see me? what was I doing on Monday? He told me to go to him on that day at 11 a.m.; to go there in evening dress; to resume the custom of wearing evening dress with him; and, while saying this, he took my arms and pressed them in a friendly way.

I was careful to inform Prince Metternich and Lord Castlereagh of what had passed, in order to remove all idea of mystery, and to prevent all suspicion on their part.

I went to the emperor at the hour indicated.

" I am very pleased to see you," he said; "and you also wished to see me, did you not?"

I replied that it was with regret that I found myself in the same town as himself, and yet saw him so seldom. After which the conversation began.

" How are affairs now, and what is your position in them?"

" Always the same, sire. If your Majesty is willing to put Poland in a state of complete independence, we are ready to second you."

" I desired at Paris the restoration of Poland, and you approved of it. I desire it still, as a man, and as being always faithful to liberal ideas, which I will never abandon. But in my position, the desires I have as a man cannot guide me as a sovereign. Perhaps the day will come when Poland will be set again on a footing of complete independence. At present it cannot be thought of."

" If it is only a question of the partition of the Duchy of Warsaw, that concerns Austria and Prussia far more than ourselves. These two powers once satisfied on this point, we shall be satisfied too: so long as they are not satisfied, it is for us to support them, and it is our duty to do it, because Austria has allowed difficulties to spring up which could easily have been prevented."

" How so?"

" In demanding, at the time of her alliance with you, that the part of the Duchy of Warsaw which had belonged to her might [1] be occupied by her troops. You would certainly not

---

[1] Text: " En demandant, lors de son alliance avec vous, à faire occuper" = as translated. Var. : "En *demandant à faire, lors de son* alliance avec vous, *occuper*" = order of words different; no alteration in sense.

have refused it, and if she had occupied this district, you would never have thought of ousting her from it."

" Austria and I are in agreement now."

" That is not what is publicly believed."

" We are agreed on the principal points : it is only a question of a few villages now."

" France takes only a second place in this question : in that of Saxony she takes the first."

" As a matter of fact, the question of Saxony is for the house of Bourbon—a family question."

" By no means, sire.   In the affair of Saxony there is no question of any private individual, or of a private family : it is a question in which all the kings have an interest ; it is a question of the first interest for your Majesty as well ; for your first interest is to take care of the personal glory which your Majesty has acquired, and whose brilliance flashes across your empire. Your Majesty owes it this consideration not only for yourself, but yet more for your country, whose patrimony it has now become.   You will put a sanction on it by protecting it, and by making those principles respected which are the foundation of public order and of the security of all men.   I speak to you, sire, not as minister for France, but as a man who is sincerely attached to your person."

" You speak of principles, and one of the first principles is that a man should keep his word of honour, and I have given mine."

" Obligations are of various kinds, and that which your Majesty took towards Europe in passing the Niemen ought to be of far more weight than any other.   Permit me, sire, to add that the intervention of Russia in the affairs of Europe is generally looked upon with an eye of jealousy and suspicion, and that if this has lately in some degree been allowed, it is solely owing to the personal character of your Majesty.   It is therefore necessary that this character should remain what it has always been."

" That is an affair which concerns me alone, and of which I am the sole judge."

" Pardon, sire, but when one is a historic personage,[1] one has the whole world for judge."

" The King of Saxony is a man of unworthy character : he has broken his pledge more than once."

" He never gave any to your Majesty : he never gave any except to Austria.   She alone therefore has the right to reproach him ; and, on the contrary, I know that the projects formed on

---

[1] Text : " quand on est homme de l'histoire " = " when one is a historic person-age."   Var. : " quand on est *l'homme* de l'histoire " = " when one is *the* historic personage."

Saxony have caused the Emperor of Austria the most genuine grief—a thing which your Majesty ignores most certainly : otherwise, living, as your family and yourself do, with him and even in his palace for the last two months, you would never have caused him that grief. These very projects also grieve and alarm the people of Vienna : I have fresh proofs of this every day."

" But Austria is abandoning Saxony."

" Prince Metternich, whom I saw yesterday evening, showed me inclinations of a different nature from that which your Majesty does me the honour to mention."

"And you yourself? It is said that you would agree to yielding up a part ? "

"We shall only do it with the greatest regret. But if, in order that Prussia may have a population equal to that which she had in 1806, and which amounted to some 9,200,000 souls, it is necessary to give from 300 to 400 thousand Saxons, it is a sacrifice which we will make for the sake of peace."

"And that is just what the Saxons fear the most. They demand nothing better than to belong to the King of Prussia : all that they desire is not to be divided."

"We are within range for knowing [1] what is going on in Saxony, and we know that the Saxons are driven to despair at the idea of becoming Prussians."

"No ; all that they fear is being divided, and that is, as a matter of fact, the most unfortunate thing that can befall a nation."

"Sire, suppose we apply this mode of reasoning to Poland ! "

" The division of Poland is not my doing. It is not my fault if the evil be not repaired : I have told you that perhaps it will be so one day.—The giving up of the two Lusatias would not, properly speaking, be a division of Saxony ; they were never incorporated with it ; they were till quite recent times a fief dependent on the crown of Bohemia ; they had nothing in common with Saxony, save the bare fact of having been possessed by the same sovereign.[2] Tell me is it true that armies are being prepared in France ? " (In putting this question the emperor came so close to me, that his face almost touched mine.)

---

[1] Text: "de *savoir*" = "for knowing." Var. : "de *connaître*" = "for being *acquainted.*"

[2] Lusatia is a province of Germany situated between the Elbe and the Oder, to the north of Bohemia and to the south of Brandenburg. It was divided into upper and lower Lusatia, each one governed by a margrave. The Lusatias formed originally part of the kingdom of Bohemia, from which they were detached in 1231 by King Ottokar, who gave them as a dowry to his daughter at her marriage with the Margrave of Brandenburg. They nevertheless reverted to the King of Bohemia in the following century. In 1635, the Emperor Ferdinand II. detached this province afresh from Bohemia, and gave it definitely to the Duke of Saxony, Johan-Georg.

"Yes, sire."

"How many troops has the king?"

"One hundred and thirty thousand men under arms, and three hundred thousand, dismissed to their homes, but ready to be called out on the first necessity."

"How many of them are being mustered now?

"As many as are necessary to maintain peace. We have by turns felt the need of having no army at all and the need of having one. Of having no army at all when it was Bonaparte's,[1] and of having one when it was the king's. For this it was necessary to disband and recompose, to disarm at first, and then to arm again, and that is what at this moment we have just finished doing. Such is the aim of our actual armaments. They menace no one, but when all Europe is under arms, it was thought fit that France should be so too in a fitting proportion."

"That is well. I hope that these matters may lead to a closer union between France and Russia. What are the desires of the king in this respect?"

"The king will never forget the services which your Majesty has rendered him, and will always be ready to acknowledge them, but he has his duties as sovereign of a great country, and as head of one of the most powerful and ancient houses of Europe. He could not abandon the House of Saxony. In case of necessity he wishes us to protest; Spain, Bavaria, and other states as well, would protest also."

"Listen. Let us strike a bargain. Give way to me on the question of Saxony, and I will do the same for you on that of Naples. I have given no promise there."

"Your Majesty knows that such a bargain is not feasible. There is no similitude between the the two questions. It is impossible for your Majesty not to have the same wants with regard to Naples as ourselves."

"Ah! well, then persuade the Prussians to give me back my word."

"I see very few Prussians,[2] and should certainly fail to persuade them. Your Majesty can do so. You have every influence over the mind of the king; besides you can give him satisfaction."

"How?"

"By leaving him a little more of Poland."

"It is a singular proposal you make me: you wish me to take something from my own property, in order to give it to them!"

---

[1] Text: "Bonaparte." Var.: "Buonaparte."

[2] Text: "fort peu de Prussiens" = "very few Prussians." Var.: "fort peu *les* Prussiens" = "I see *the* Prussians but very little."

The interview was here interrupted by the Empress of Russia, who came to visit the emperor. She was pleased to make some polite remarks to me. She only remained a few minutes, and then the emperor said, " Let us continue."

I recapitulated briefly the points on which I could, and those on which I could not, come to an agreement with him, and concluded by saying that I must insist on the kingdom of Saxony being preserved with sixteen hundred thousand inhabitants.

" Yes," said the emperor, " you insist a good deal on a question which has been already *decided*." But he did not pronounce this last word in a tone which showed an unalterable determination.

His aim in summoning me before him had been to know:

1. What the armaments were which he had heard were being prepared in France, and with what views they were being prepared. I believe I answered him in such a manner as to free him from all suspicion of being threatened by them himself, and yet [1] so as not to leave him too great a feeling of security.

2. Whether your Majesty would be disposed to form an alliance with him one day. Unless he renounce his lust of conquest, which is most improbable, I do not see how it will be possible for your Majesty, animated by the conservative spirit to ally yourself with him, except in an extraordinary case, and for a temporary end. But it was not advisable, if he desired this, to deprive him of the hope of it, and I had to avoid doing so.

3. What was our exact intention with regard to Saxony. In this respect I left him so few doubts, that he said to Count Nesselrode, from whom I learnt it: "The French have made up their minds on the question of Saxony; but let them arrange with Prussia if they can. They would like to take some of my possessions and give them to her; but that is what I will never agree to."

I have reported this interview with so many details in order to show your Majesty how his tone has changed since the last interview I had with him. Throughout the whole interview he did not give a single sign of irritation or bad humour, all was calm and pleasant.

He has certainly the interests of Prussia less at heart, and is less tied by his friendship to the king, than embarrassed by the promises he has made ; and I really believe that, in spite of the chivalrous character he affects, and slave as he wishes to be thought to his word, he would be delighted, at the bottom of his heart, could he find an honest pretext for releasing

---

[1] Text : " cependant, à ne pas laisser " = " yet so as not to leave him." Var. : " *de façon* à ne pas laisser " = " *in such a manner* as not to leave him."

himself. I am the more led to this opinion by a conversation he had with Prince von Schwarzenberg, and which I believe contributed no little to the desire he had to see me. He asked him how their affairs[1] stood, whether they could come to an understanding, and pressed him to give him his opinion, not as Austrian minister, but as a friend. After defending himself from replying[2] for some time, Prince Schwarzenberg said bluntly that his conduct towards Austria had been neither frank nor even loyal, that his claims tended to putting the Austrian monarchy into considerable danger, and matters into a position which would render war inevitable. That if war should not break out now (either from respect for the recent[3] alliance, or from fear of showing themselves to Europe in the character of fools who could foresee nothing, and who had put themselves by a blind confidence at the mercy of events), it would infallibly come in a period varying from eighteen months to two years hence. Thereupon it escaped the emperor to say :—

" If only I had not gone so far ! But," he added, " how can I free myself ? You see in what a position I am ; it is impossible for me to retract."

At the same time that Prince von Schwarzenberg was representing war as inevitable sooner or later, a body of troops, despatched by Austria to Galicia, apparently seemed to indicate that it might soon be declared. The cabinet of Vienna means to rouse itself from its lethargy. Prince Metternich has spoken to Prince von Wrede of an alliance, asking if, from the present time, Bavaria would not join twenty-five thousand men to the Austrian forces, to which Prince von Wrede replied that Bavaria would willingly join seventy-five thousand men, but on the following conditions :—

1st. That the alliance be concluded with France ;

2nd. That Bavaria should furnish twenty-five thousand men and no more, for every hundred thousand that Austria should put into the field ;

3rd. That if England granted subsidies to Austria, Bavaria should receive a part proportionate to their respective forces.

I believe that at bottom these are only simple projects ; but it is already much that England[4] should determine to make them, and must naturally have caused in the Emperor Alexander the desire to ascertain what he has to fear, or to hope for, from us.

---

[1] Text : "leurs affaires" = "their affairs." Var. : "*les* affaires" = "affairs."

[2] Text : "de répondre" = "from replying." Var. : "de *rompre*" = "from *breaking off.*"

[3] Text : "alliance récente" = "recent alliance." Var. : "alliance *naissante*" = "*dawning* alliance."

[4] Text : "Angleterre" = "England." Var. : "*Autriche*" = "*Austria.*"

Knowing his custom, when speaking to those who are opposed to his wishes, of affirming that he has come to some agreement with others, and not wishing that my conversation with him should be made known under a false light, I profited by an interview paid me by Herr von Sickingen to inform the Emperor Alexander of my views through him. The emperor has revealed them to Prince Metternich, and by what he told him, I see that Herr von Sickingen has been a faithful mediator. This confidence has produced the best effect. The widespread sentiments of suspicion of which we have been the mark during the first days of our stay here, is weakening every day, and the contrary feeling increasing.

On my return from the Emperor Alexander, I found the minister of Saxony in my rooms, who came to inform me of :—

1st. A protest of the King of Saxony, which this Prince had sent to him, with the command to lay it before the council ; but only after having consulted [1] Prince Metternich, to whose advice he was to conform ;

2nd. A circular of Prince Repnin, who was governor-general of Saxony for the Russians. This paper, of which I inclose a copy in my despatch to the department, that it may be printed in the *Moniteur*, was the cause of the king's protest, which can only be printed after having been laid before congress. I shall then only have a copy of it.[2]

This circular, by which Prince Repnin announces to the Saxon authorities that in consequence of a convention concluded on September 27, the Emperor Alexander, according to the expressed wish of England and Austria, had ordered the adminis-

[1] Text : "après avoir consulté" = "after having consulted." Var. : "après avoir *communiqué*" = "after having *communicated*."

[2] The following is the circular :—" A letter of the Minister, Baron von Stein, dated October 21, has informed me of a convention concluded September 28 at Vienna, by virtue of which his Majesty the Emperor of Russia, in concert with England and Austria will put the administration of the kingdom of Saxony into the hands of the King of Prussia. I am ordered to hand over the government of that country to the representatives of his Majesty the King of Prussia, and to replace the imperial Russian troops by those of Prussia, in order to effect the union of Saxony and Prussia, which will shortly take place in a more positive and solemn manner, and to establish a closer fraternity between the two nations. . . . After the preliminary deliberations, of which the aim is the well-being of the two parties, their Majesties have declared the following : King Frederick William, in his quality of future sovereign of the country, has declared that he will not incorporate Saxony as a province of his states, but will unite it to Prussia under the title of kingdom of Saxony, will preserve it always in its integrity, will leave it the enjoyment of its rights, privileges, and advantages which the constitution of Germany will decree for those parts of Germany which form a portion of the Prussian monarchy, and so far will change nothing of its actual constitution. And his Majesty the Emperor Alexander has testified the special satisfaction he feels on account of this declaration." (*Moniteur*, November 15, 1814. See also on the ceremony of the delegation of the powers of Prince Repnin to the Prussian authorities, the issue of the *Moniteur* of November 24.)

tration of Saxony to be handed over to the delegates of the King of Prussia, who must in the future be in possession of that country, not as a province of his kingdom, but as a separate kingdom which he has promised to maintain in its integrity, has put Prince Metternich and Lord Castlereagh in the greatest embarrassment, and roused the most lively complaints on their parts.

It is quite true that their consent has been abused in the most odious manner, being misrepresented, and declared absolute, when it was purely conditional ; and this justifies their complaints.   But it is not less true, that they have given a consent which they bitterly repent having given.

Your Majesty already has the note of Prince Metternich.

I have to-day the honour of forwarding you that of Lord Castlereagh, which I only received two days ago, and then only on condition of my promising to keep it in the utmost secrecy. This is why I address it immediately to your Majesty.   I am told that Lord Castlereagh is trying to get it back from the Prussians.

This note confirms all with which I have had the honour of informing your Majesty for the past six weeks, and reveals more than I could possibly have believed, if it did not in itself represent incontestable proofs of its assertions.

However strange the letter of Prince Metternich may have been, as soon as one compares it with that of Lord Castlereagh, the differences that exist between the two are all in favour of the former.

Prince Metternich tries to persuade Prussia to give up her views on Saxony.   He explains the moral and political reasons which make it repugnant to him to give his consent, and while giving it, declares it to be necessity which wrenches it from him.

Lord Castlereagh, on the contrary, after expressing a lively and perfectly barren pity for the royal family of Saxony, declares that he has no *moral* or *political* repugnance to giving Saxony to Prussia.[1]

---

[1] The following is what Lord Castlereagh, in a note addressed to Prince von Hardenberg, says of Saxony :—" As to the question of Saxony, I declare to you that if the incorporation of the whole of that country in the Prussian monarchy be necessary to secure sufficiently great advantages for Europe, whatever grief I might personally experience at seeing such an old family in such misfortunes, I could nourish no moral or political repugnance to the measure itself.   If ever sovereign has placed himself in a position in which it was necessary for the future tranquillity of Europe that he should be sacrificed, I believe it is the King of Saxony, by his perpetual shuffling, and because he has been not only the most devoted, but also the most favoured vassal of Bonaparte, contributing with all his power, and with the greatest eagerness in his two-fold position, of head of the German and Polish states, to spreading general thraldom into the very heart of Russia." [*Lord Castlereagh to Prince von Hardenberg* (*October* 11, 1814).]

Prince Metternich only consents on the ground that Prussia will have suffered losses for which it will be impossible to compensate her in any other manner.

Lord Castlereagh, on the contrary, only consents so long as Prussia preserves that, for the loss of which Prince Metternich would compensate her. He wishes Saxony to be so much increase of power for her, and not an equivalent for something she is to give up.

Thus they both subordinate the question of Saxony to that of Poland, but in senses absolutely different, which shows how little agreement one with another these closely united allies have, and this after crying out so loudly that France wanted to divide them.

Meanwhile they have agreed to disavow the circular of Prince Repnin, and I believe it will not be recognized even by the Prussians themselves.

For the rest, it seems to me to be difficult for forgetfulness— if it is not contempt—of the most common principles and notions of healthy politics to be carried further than it has been in this note of Lord Castlereagh.

He came yesterday to invite me to dinner, and to appoint an interview for to-day. I was expecting some confidence or important disclosure; he merely spoke of his dilemma. Deceived in the hopes he had built on Prussia, and seeing his policy for this reason overthrown from its basis, he has fallen into a kind of depression. He came to consult me as to the means of giving a spur to affairs, to make them advance more speedily. told him that the Emperor Alexander pretended to be at one with Austria on the Polish question, and that there only remained some details to settle; that if this were so, the best thing to do in my opinion, was to get Austria to terminate this arrangement as soon as possible; that they had wished to subordinate[1] the question of Poland to that of Saxony, and it had not succeeded; that it was therefore necessary to separate them, and terminate that of Poland first; that Austria, tranquil on this side, and no longer obliged to trouble herself about the two questions, would devote her entire attention to that of Saxony, which all the Austrian generals considered to be by far the most important of the two; that Russia, once satisfied on the question which interested her directly, would probably trouble herself very little about the other, and that Prussia, finding herself alone face to face with England, Austria, France and Spain, the affair would be easily and quickly arranged.

---

[1] Text: "qu'ils avaient voulu subordonner" = "that they had wished to subordinate." Var.: "qu'ils *avaient subordonné*" = "that they *had subordinated*."

The circular of Prince Repnin has been the signal awaited by Bavaria for declaring that she would consent to no arrangement, and would enter no German league, were the preservation of the kingdom of Saxony not first vouched for. This is what Prince von Wrede positively declared to Prince von Hardenberg, who, though saying that he could take no responsibility on himself and must refer to the king on the matter, has yet given it to be understood that the King of Saxony could be retained with a million subjects.

Thus all is yet in suspense. But the chances of saving a great part of Saxony have increased.

I had proceeded so far in my letter, when I received that with which your Majesty has deigned to honour me dated November 9, and that which you were so kind as to get the Comte de Blacas to write me.

Your Majesty will judge by Lord Castlereagh's letter which I have the honour to inclose, either, that this minister has instructions of which the Duke of Wellington is ignorant, or that he does not believe himself bound by those which have been given him, and that if he made the question of Saxony depend on that of Poland, it is in precisely the opposite sense to that which the Duke supposed.

As to what concerns Naples, I have described to your Majesty the proposal which Prince Metternich brought forward, in one of those conferences at which only himself, Lord Castlereagh, Count Nesselrode and myself were present, viz., that of only discussing this affair after the congress, and my reply. (It is in No. 10 of my correspondence that you will find this detail.) The threats contained in the letter of which M. de Blacas has sent an extract, are found, it is said, in a pamphlet published by an aide-de-camp of Murat named Filangieri, who was quite recently still at Vienna. (This pamphlet has been suppressed by the police.) But I hope that if Italy is once organised from the Alps to the frontier of Naples, as I have proposed, these threats will cease to excite fear.

I waited before closing my letter till I had returned from a conference which had been appointed for this evening at eight o'clock. But nothing was done except to read and sign the protocol of the last sitting.

The Emperor of Russia is sufficiently unwell to be obliged to keep his bed, but it is nothing more serious than an indisposition.

I have the honour to be, &c.

PARIS, *November* 22, 1814.

MY COUSIN,

I have received your despatch, No. 11. It would furnish
me with ample matter for reflection, if I had not forbidden
myself this indulgence when it can only serve my own satisfaction.

The conversation which the Comte Alexis de Noailles has
heard from the mouth of the princes with whom he has con-
versed, has afforded me great pleasure. I was especially struck
with that of the King of Bavaria : but what good would[1] these
dispositions work, if they were not backed by Austria and
England ? Now, I am very much afraid that, in spite of the
marvellously clever manner in which you have spoken to Prince
Metternich, in spite of the conditions mentioned in the note of
October 22 having been carried out, both Poland and Saxony
will be abandoned. In this misfortune, there would always
remain to my unlucky cousin, his constancy in adversity, and to
me (for I am more resolved on it than ever) the comfort of
never having participated by any consent whatever in such
iniquitous spoliations.

I put great faith in the proposal attributed to the Emperor
Alexander on the subject of Italy ; it is, in that case, of the
highest importance that Austria and England be well convinced
of the truth of the adage, trivial perhaps, but full of sense, and
above all eminently applicable to the situation :

"Sublata causa, tollitur effectus."

I am more satisfied with the turn of affairs in Italy : the
union of Genoa, and the male succession of the House of Savoy,[2]
are two important points, but what is more important than all,
is, that in spite of the boasting, perhaps in reality too well
founded, by Murat in his gazettes, the kingdom of Naples
should return to its legitimate sovereign.

Whereupon, my cousin, I pray God may have you in His
safe and holy keeping.

LOUIS.

---

[1] Text : "que serviraient" = "what good would they work." Var. : "que
serviront" = "what good *will* they work."
[2] Text : "de la maison" = "of the House." Var. : "*dans* la maison" = "*in*
the House."

No. 14 A.—THE AMBASSADORS OF THE KING AT THE CONGRESS TO THE MINISTER OF FOREIGN AFFAIRS AT PARIS.

VIENNA, *November* 23, 1814.

MONSIEUR LE COMTE,

We have the honour to forward you a copy of the report of the last sitting. We have met since, to adjust and sign it, but have transacted no further business.

Count de Labrador on this occasion further called attention to the rights of the Queen of Etruria, and asked that, when the arrangement of affairs in Italy should be treated, this should have some attention. Prince Metternich told him that he was prepared to discuss the matter, and waited for Count de Labrador to read him his memorandum. The ambassador of Spain will forward it one of these days.

If the words of Prince Metternich could inspire the least confidence, one would be justified in believing that he found the Archduchess Marie-Louise sufficiently provided for by having obtained the State of Lucca, which brings in a revenue of from five to six hundred thousand francs,[1] and that, for the time being, the Legations could be restored to the Pope, and Parma to the Queen of Etruria. But we are informed that while he gives utterance to this opinion, the Archduchess Marie-Louise, following the invitation of the emperor, her father, has had the arms of her carriages and seals changed, and is effacing the imperial arms of Bonaparte, in order to substitute those of Parma.

The Comte de Noailles, whose business it is to follow the Italian negotiations, has received an order from Prince Talleyrand not to admit any arrangements which may be determined on, except as provisory dispositions, which will only be sanctioned by a formal guarantee, when all present a general and satisfactory policy. This precaution was the more necessary, because we see Prince Metternich second with every day more and more heat and obstinacy, the cause of Murat. He does it under pretext of the danger that would accrue from provoking Murat to a revolutionary war. Prince Metternich, by himself proclaiming him head of the Jacobins in Italy, exaggerates his influence, and will not allow that in order to paralyse the danger which this agitation presents, it will be sufficient to get rid of the principal mover in it. The fact is, he is unwilling to do violence to his affections for Madame Murat, and believes that in preserving this family on the throne, he will be able to arrange as he likes all his designs on Italy. It is therefore necessary for the Comte de Noailles to use this reserve, when the signing of the articles for

---

[1] From £20,000 to £24,000.

the incorporation of Genoa and Piedmont, shall be introduced. For the rest, the succession of the House of Carignan has been stipulated for, and is no longer likely to give rise to any objection.

Things are in this state, and the important questions concerning Poland and Saxony are hindering the progress of affairs, and we do not believe that their solution has made much progress during the last eight days. The circular of Prince Repnin has given rise to Lord Castlereagh and the cabinet of Vienna writing rather firm letters to the Prussian cabinet, in which they declared that the union of Saxony will only be admitted conditionally, as stated in the letters sent on the occasion of the temporary occupation of Saxony by Prussian troops, and that if Prussia would not co-operate in establishing Poland's limits in the interests of the three powers, the concession made with regard to Saxony would have to be regarded as null and void.

Lord Castlereagh and Prince Metternich have gone further still. They are persuaded that if the Emperor of Russia and the King of Prussia refuse these overtures, it will be necessary to make preparations for enforcing more moderation on them.

We are, in fact, assured that military measures have been concerted, and a plan of campaign discussed between the Austrian and Bavarian leaders. The co-operation of France is considered necessary for this. But neither Prince Metternich, nor Lord Castlereagh, have thought fit to speak of it, nor to have it mentioned to the plenipotentiaries of the king at the congress.

One might well be astonished at this silence, could one once be convinced that all these military measures bore a character other than that of simple demonstrations, after the kind of measures by which Prince Metternich so often aids his policy. There are even some people, who have the reputation of being well informed, who believe that Lord Castlereagh and Prince Metternich have not yet decided upon any definite policy on this subject, and that they are afraid of being compelled to mix in such matters.

Meanwhile Lord Castlereagh, whether it is that he feels it necessary to oppose some barrier to the Russian and Prussian intrigues, or that public opinion in England and throughout Germany has made him change his policy and system, appears to have decided on provoking war with Russia, if she does not moderate her pretensions, and he has spoken of it to some persons, affirming that England would furnish the necessary subsidies. This minister and Prince Metternich himself, owing to suspicions so gratuitously levelled at France, and the fears nourished that an alliance with this power would compromise the situation of Belgium and the left bank of the Rhine, will not appeal to France save in the last extremity. We even think that, if it is possible for them to avoid it, they will do so, and you may be quite sure, Monsieur le Comte, that we shall not provoke them to it.

Besides, experience has already taught these powers that they cannot dismiss the intervention of France, and that she does them more good than harm in settling the affairs of Europe.

On our arrival here, the desire of ousting France from all share in the deliberations was manifest. She now takes a part in all that concerns Italy and Switzerland ; she will intervene to great advantage in the territorial divisions of Germany, and we should not be astonished if the arrangements relative to Poland were only made with her consent. To hinder her from so doing, and to contradict us, the enemies of France have for some days been spreading the most absurd reports as to her interior situation ; and what has astonished us greatly is, that these rumours are repeated in the diplomatic correspondence of the English and Austrian legations at Paris. Amongst these assertions maintained with some cleverness, we mention one, to the effect that the king would not be in a position to make use of his army. We have been able to combat it by the communication of a letter from the Comte Dupont,[1] who speaks of the state of the army in most satisfactory and positive terms, and does so too without leaving the slightest opportunity for reply. The other assertions will all fall into oblivion, when time shall have exposed the intrigue.

The affairs of Germany suffer in the same way as all the others, from the delays caused by the decisions of the Emperor of Russia, and here, as elsewhere, he seeks to interfere, in order to further his main views.

We have had the honour of informing you that the project of federation in twelve articles, which we have addressed to you in our last despatch of the 16th, has been modified in its principal provisions. The Austrian and Prussian cabinets had communicated it in its rough draft to the cabinet of Russia. This communication remained without reply. But in order to flatter the Czar, and mislead public opinion in Germany, which pronounced itself so strongly against the union of Prussia and Saxony, the Russian cabinet thought fit to take up the possibility of intervention in German affairs, and Count Nesselrode gave a reply

[1] General Dupon who was then Minister of War.

of which we here subjoin the copy. If the great alliance is broken in consequence of the affairs of Poland, this letter will of course be considered as null and void.

It cannot, in general, escape us that the real embarrassment of the allied powers at the congress is owing to the illusion they entertain, in thinking that they can regulate the affairs of Europe on *bases* which they have declared settled, but which are not so as yet.

Be pleased to accept, &c

No. 15 A.—THE AMBASSADORS OF THE KING AT THE CONGRESS TO THE MINISTER OF FOREIGN AFFAIRS AT PARIS.

VIENNA, *November* 24, 1814.

MONSIEUR LE COMTE,

We inclose with the despatch dated yesterday, a letter, which one of the principal heads of the Foreign Office of this country addressed to the Duc de Dalberg, pointing out to him an article in the *Gazette de France* which has caused a great sensation, and whose admission by the censorship is difficult to explain, if, as the author of the letter remarks, it was wished to reconcile public opinion with the persecutors and spoilers of Saxony.[1]

---

[1] The following is the article :—" After long indecision, the fate of Saxony seems to be definitely fixed. King Frederick-Augustus descends from the throne ; his territories are shared between Austria, Prussia, and the Duke of Saxe-Weimar. Many a voice will be raised to deplore the instability of human affairs. Some reflective minds will meditate on the impenetrable decrees of that eternal Providence which, according to the expression borrowed from Scripture by one of our greatest poets (Racine, *Athalie*, acte iii.) : ' Frappe et guérit, perd et ressuscite.'* Some will see in the fall of the reigning house nothing less than a revolution ; others will see in it a return to order. It is for the first of these that a glance on the origin and division of this illustrious family will not be without interest.

" The second elector, Frederick the Courteous, or the Peaceful, who died in 1464, left two sons, of whom the eldest, Ernest, was the head of the Ernestine branch, and the younger Albert, of the Albertine branch. By virtue of the recognized right of primogeniture, Johan-Frederick, sixth elector, reigned, without having his rights contested, when the troubles excited by the famous league of Smalcalde broke over the empire. Charles V., with a powerful army, commanded by the celebrated Duke of Alba, marched against the confederates. The battle of Muhlberg, fought in 1547, was decisive. Johan-Frederick, the soul of the league, fell into the power of the emperor, who used his victory cruelly. A court-martial, presided over by the inflexible Spanish general, dared to condemn to death the Elector of Saxony as a rebel to the imperial power. This introduced an entirely new legislation into the German empire. The illustrious prisoner, after having heard the reading of his arrest, continued quietly his game of chess with Prince Ernest of Brunswick : ' It is less my life, than my electorate, that they covet,' he said. The event showed that he was not deceived : Charles V. gave him his life, but at the Diet of Augsburg in 1548, he deprived him of his electoral dignity, in order to confer it on the Duke Maurice of Saxony, head of the younger or Albertine branch. The unhappy Johan-Frederick was

* Strikes and heals, blights and restores to life again.

In a situation so ominous as that in which the fate of this sovereign is placed, in the midst of most difficult debates on such a question, how is it that the heads of journals were

left only the little town of Gotha, where he was-kept in honourable captivity.   More deserving of pity even than he, his son, accused of having tried to re-enter the palace of his fathers, at Dresden, was arrested and conveyed to Vienna as a common culprit.

"Although indebted for his renewed political existence to the protection of Charles V., the usurper Maurice greedily seized the occasion of showing in favour of Lutheranism that zeal which had served him as a pretext in the spoliation of the legitimate elector.   He aided the Protestants, concluded a secret alliance with Henry III., King of France, fell upon the emperor, and was on the point of taking possession of his person by force in the defiles of Tyrol.   He forced the treaty of Passau from him in 1552.

"Since that time, the Albertine branch has preserved the electorate, whilst the eldest or Ernestine branch, reduced to very straitened circumstances, split up into a a great number of branches.   As many as fourteen have been counted.   There are only six extant now.   The first is that of Weimar ; the duke of this name is therefore the direct and natural heir of the Elector Johan-Frederick, who was so violently and unjustly robbed by Charles V.

"In spite of the lapse of time, the titles of his descendants have never sunk into oblivion.   On the short appearance he put in at Rastadt, Buonaparte said one day to the minister of the Elector of Saxony, with that bluntness that was habitual to him : 'When then does your master intend restoring the electorate to the Ernestine branch ?' *

"It was however the same man who wished this prince later on to take the title of king.

"From that day date all the misfortunes of Frederick-Augustus ; surrounded, enmeshed, he was obliged to forget that he was a German, and had to make common cause with the oppressor of Germany.   The insensate expedition of Moscow permitted princes and people to foresee the moment of their deliverance.   The King of Saxony retired to Bohemia, and there on neutral territory at length rejoiced in his liberty, and is said to have solemnly promised to unite his efforts with those of the liberators of Europe.   Motives, which we will not here discuss, induced him to change his resolution.

"Napoleon, a fugitive, abandoned him, without any resources to fall back upon, to the vengeance of the allies.   Frederick-Augustus demanded to see them ; if we are to believe the unanimous report of the public papers, his request was refused.

"Public opinion, unanimous as it was on the subject of the private virtues of this prince, is singularly divided as to his public conduct.   One party accuses him of having committed an indelible crime by being constant to his alliance with the enemy of the human race ; others are tempted to see in him the instrument used by Providence for prolonging the blindness of Napoleon.   As a matter of fact, by putting his fortresses and troops at his disposal, the King of Saxony inspired him with the foolish hope of preserving the Elbe as a boundary.   Whilst he was pleasing his fancy with the absurd possession of Dresden, whilst he was sacrificing armies, so long invincible, in keeping and protecting this useless city, everything was being prepared for the downfall of this insensate conqueror.   If he had not been master of places on the Elbe, he would have been constrained to take up a position behind the Rhine, and there, supported by numerous fortresses, assured besides of communication with France, there would have remained to him means of still treating honourably with his conquerors.

"Thus the invisible and powerful Hand abases that which it has exalted, and exalts that which It has abased ; thus, after three centuries the Albertine branch fell from the throne which it had usurped, and the Ernestine branch recovers a part of what had been ravished from it.   The French in lamenting the fate of Frederick-Augustus, will respect in him a prince issued from the same blood as the august princess who gave birth to our well-beloved sovereigns, Louis XVI. and Louis XVIII."

* Some say that it was to the elector himself after the battle of Jena that he addressed this singular compliment.

informed of the sense and spirit in which the government believes it necessary to direct public opinion, as much for the glory,
as for the true interests, of the king and of France?

It is important that the origin and the author of this article,
which was inserted in No. 315, November 11, of the *Gazette de
France* be known. It is equally important that the *Moniteur*
should publish a well-reasoned article, which without being
official, would discuss the same question under the aspects of law
and utility. The memorandum joined to the report of the 23rd will
furnish M. de Rheinhard[1] with the materials for such an article.

We have had it secretly circulated, and have observed that it
has created some impression. It is necessary to change it so
that the insertion in the *Moniteur* may not seem to have been
inspired by this memorandum, though its principles and arguments may be employed.

We forward you at the same time an article from the *Gazette
Universelle*, which has apparently issued from the Austrian
cabinet, and is meant as a reply to the famous circular of Prince
Repnin.

It will be well when inserting it in the *Moniteur*, to add that
the editor is pleased to communicate it to the public as worthy
of attention, and as representing the best possible principles.
We think that the little rap given to France might be omitted.

Our papers have, for outsiders, a far stronger authority than
those of other countries, because they are known to be under the
supervision and control of the government.

We beg of you, Monsieur le Comte, to forward us the
information we require.

The importance of the question of Saxony cannot escape
your notice. The principles we must sustain in it are identical
with those that we must employ for putting a barrier to the
march of revolution, and for consecrating anew the principles of
the law of nations, without which the whole social edifice of
Europe would be shaken.

Be pleased to accept, &c.

No. 13.—The Prince de Talleyrand to King Louis XVIII.

VIENNA, *November* 24, 1814.[2]

SIRE,

No sooner had we uttered the word *principles* here, and
asked for the immediate sitting of the congress, than the rumour

---

[1] M. de Rheinhard was at that time head of the Seal Office at the Ministry of
Foreign Affairs.

[2] Var. : November 25, 1814.

spread abroad on all sides that France still regretted the left bank of the Rhine, and Belgium, and would never rest until she had recovered them, that the government of your Majesty most probably shared this wish of the army and the nation, or that [1] if it did not share it, it was not sufficiently strong to resist it; that, on both hypotheses, the peril was the same, that one could not therefore keep too strict a guard against France; that it was necessary to oppose to her, barriers which she could not cross, to make the arrangements of Europe subordinate to this aim, and to be well on one's guard against her negotiators who would leave nothing undone to hinder it. We found ourselves all at once treated with the very prejudices against which we have had to struggle for two months. We have succeeded in triumphing over the most painful of these suspicions, and it is no longer said of us that we have received double instructions (as Prince Metternich told Prince von Wrede) that we were bidden speak in one sense and act in another, and that we had been sent to sow discord. The public does your Majesty justice. It believes no longer in any after-thoughts on your part. It applauds your disinterestedness; it praises you for having embraced the defence of principles. It avows that no other power is playing a part so honourable as yours. But those whose interest it is that France should continue to be an object of suspicion and fear, when unable to excite them by one pretext, do so by another. They represent her internal condition under an alarming light. Unfortunately they base their assertions on news sent from Paris, by those whose names, functions, and reputations enforce belief. The Duke of Wellington, who keeps up a very active correspondence with Lord Castlereagh, speaks only of conspiracies, secret discontent, and ominous murmurings, precursors of storms ready to burst. The Emperor Alexander says that his letters from Paris foretell trouble. Herr von Vincent,[2] on the other hand, tells his court that he is expecting a change in the ministry, and that he is sure of it. Men pretend to regard a change of ministers as a certain index of a change of policy, both at home and abroad. The conclusion is, that France cannot be relied on, and that no agreement with her ought to be arranged.

We may refute such news as much as we please, cite dates and facts which prove its inaccuracy, oppose to it the news that we receive ourselves, indicate the source whence I believe the Duke of Wellington gets his information, even show how suspicious a source this is, they none the less persist in asserting that, at a

---

[1] Text: " Ou que " = " or that." Var.: " vu que " = " seeing that."
[2] Herr von Vincent was at that time Austrian ambassador at Paris.

distance from Paris, we cannot know what is going on there, or that we have some interest in concocting it, and that the Duke of Wellington and Herr von Vincent being on the spot, are better informed, or more sincere.

I do not wish to accuse Lord Castlereagh of having propagated the prejudices which we have had to combat, but, whether he has imagined them himself, or whether they have been suggested to him, he is certainly imbued with them more than anyone else. The long war which England has had to sustain almost alone, and the peril she was in on account of it, have produced[1] so lively an impression on him, that it deprives him, so to speak, of the power of judging to what extent times are changed. Of all the fears, the least reasonable, nowadays, is certainly that of a return to the continental system. Meanwhile, those who enjoy more intimate relations with him, assure me that he is always possessed by this fear, and that he thinks he cannot accumulate too many precautions against this imaginary danger. He thinks he is still at Châtillon, treating, and writing treaties of peace, with Bonaparte. It is easy to guess what effect the intelligence sent by the Duke of Wellington must have on a mind filled with these ideas, the Duke himself thus becoming an obstacle to that good understanding which he seems to think so easy to establish between Lord Castlereagh and ourselves.

I have sought this mutual understanding by all the means in my power both before Lord Castlereagh left London, at the time of his passage to Paris, and since we have been at Vienna. If it has not yet been attained, it is not only owing to the prejudices of Lord Castlereagh, but because there has been a real and absolute opposition between his views and ours. Your Majesty ordered me to defend principles. The note of October 11,[2] which I have the honour of forwarding your Majesty, shows what respect he has for them. We must strain our utmost to preserve the King and kingdom of Saxony. Lord Castlereagh wishes with all his heart to treat the one as a condemned culprit, of whom he has constituted himself the judge, and to sacrifice the other. We wish Prussia to acquire and retain a great part of the Duchy of Warsaw, and Lord Castlereagh wishes it also ; but from such different motives, that he employs the same means for destroying Saxony, as we for saving her. He would thus turn against us the support which we would have given

---

[1] Text : "et le péril que cette guerre lui a fait courir, ont produit " = "and the peril that this war made her run, produced. . . ." Var. : "et le péril *dans lequel cette guerre l'a mise, ont fait* " = "and the peril *in which this war placed her, made.*"

[2] See page 328.

him on the question of Poland. Purposes so different cannot possibly be reconciled.

I have often spoken, even to the Emperor Alexander himself, of the restoration of Poland as a thing that France desired, and which she was prepared to support. But I have never demanded this restoration without giving an alternative, because Lord Castlereagh has not asked it himself, because I should have been the only one to make the demand, and because in so doing, I should have irritated the Emperor Alexander without gaining any merit in the eyes of others, and also because I should have wounded Austria, who, up to the present time at least, has not wished for this restoration.

It is hardly two days since Lord Castlereagh, whom I reproached for the manner in which he had conducted affairs during the past two months, replied to me : " I have always thought that when one was a member of a league, one ought not to separate one's self from it." He then believes himself in a league. This league is certainly only a continuation of their alliance previous to the peace. Now, how can he be expected to come to an understanding with those against whom he declares himself in league ?

The other members of the league or coalition against France are in a similar position. Russia and Prussia are only expecting for opposition from our part. Austria may desire our support on the question of Poland and Saxony ;[1] but her minister desires it far less for these two objects, than he fears our interference in others. He knows how much we have the affairs of Naples at heart, and he has it scarcely less at heart himself, but in a very different sense from that in which we have it. On Sunday last I went to see him, after dining with Prince Trautmansdorf. I had, the evening before, received a letter from Italy, stating that Murat had an army of seventy thousand men, most of them armed, thanks to the Austrians, who had sold him twenty-five thousand rifles. I wished to come to some explanation with Prince Metternich, or at least to show him that I knew of it. I drew him on to the Naples business, and, as we were in a drawing-room, with a great many people, I offered to follow him to his study and show him the letter I had received. He said there was no hurry, and that this question would come on later. I then asked, if therefore he was not decided ? He replied that he was, but that he was unwilling to kindle fire everywhere at once. And as he was alleging, as he always does, his

---

[1] Text : "dans les questions de la Pologne et de la Saxe " = "in the questions of Poland and Saxony." Var. : "dans la question de la Pologne et dans celle de la Saxe" = "in the question of Poland and in that of Saxony."

fear lest Murat should bring about a rising in Italy, " Why then,'' I retorted, " did you furnish him with arms if you fear him ? Why have you sold him twenty-five thousand rifles ? " He denied the fact, as I had expected ; but I did not leave him the satisfaction of believing that I was the dupe of his denial. After I left him, he returned to the dancing-room, for it is at balls and fêtes that he wastes three-quarters of his time, and his head was so full of the Naples business, that having come across a lady whom he knew, he told her, that people were worrying him with this Naples business, but that he would never consent to it, that he respected the situation of a man who made himself beloved in the country he governed ; that he besides passionately loved the queen, and was in continual communication with her. All this, and perhaps a little more on the same subject, was said masked. We must expect that he will put in motion every imaginable expedient for preventing the affair of Naples being treated at the congress, according to the insinuation he dropped some time ago at a meeting, and which I had the honour to report to your Majesty.

The four allied courts, each having some reason for fearing the influence which France might have in the congress, have naturally united, and fear to become reconciled with us when divided, because every step made in that direction would draw from them concessions which they do not wish to make.

Self-love, as is natural, is also mixed in this reluctance. Lord Castlereagh thought he was in a condition to bend the Emperor of Russia, and only succeeded in irritating him.

Finally, all these motives are always enhanced by a feeling of jealousy against France. The allies thought they had crushed her more ; they did not expect to see her in possession of both the best finances and the best army in Europe. Now they believe it and admit it, and have even gone so far as to regret having made the treaty of Paris, to reproach each other with it, and to acknowledge their powerlessness to understand how they could have had the folly to make it, and to say all this, even at the conferences and in our presence.

We can therefore reasonably expect England and Austria to make real and sincere overtures to us, only in a case of the most urgent necessity, such as in that of their discussions with Russia ending in an open rupture.

All the same, in spite of these feelings, in spite of the diffi-culties they persist in causing us, and those which the letters from Paris also produce, the powers are here, with regard to us, in an attitude of respect and complacency, such as we could never have dared to expect six weeks ago, and which I may also say they are greatly astonished to see themselves.

Hitherto the Emperor Alexander has not budged an inch.

Lord Castlereagh, personally piqued, although he has lately received a letter from Russia, couched in very conciliatory terms, says, though not to us, that if the emperor will not stop at the Vistula, he must be forced to do so by war ; that England could only furnish very few troops on account of her war with America;[1] but that she would furnish subsidies, and that Hanoverian and Dutch troops could be employed on the Lower Rhine.

Prince von Schwarzenberg is for war, saying that it could be fought with greater advantage now than some years hence.

A plan of campaign has even been drawn up at the War Office, and Prince von Wrede has drawn up one on his own account.

Austria, Bavaria, and other German States, would put three hundred and twenty thousand men in the field.

Two hundred thousand under Prince von Schwarzenberg would be led through Moravia and Galicia to the Vistula.

One hundred and twenty thousand commanded by Prince von Wrede would be led from Bohemia to Saxony where they would raise a revolt ; and thence to the district lying between the Oder and the Elbe. Glatz and Neiss would at the same time be besieged.

The campaign would not commence before the end of March.

But this plan necessitates the co-operation of one hundred thousand Frenchmen, of whom one-half would be taken to Franconia to keep the Prussians from turning back the army of Bohemia, and the other half would engage them on the lower Rhine.

It is therefore necessary to await till this co-operation, on the absolute necessity of which all the generals are agreed, be demanded of us, if war must take place.

But at present neither Lord Castlereagh nor Prince Metternich speak to us of war, and we are even assured that it has not yet been broached between them. It is only to Bavaria that they have separately made overtures on this subject.

Whether they still put some hope in negotiation or whether they wish to gain time, they are still negotiating. Lord Castlereagh's project having miscarried, they tried to reintroduce Prince von Hardenberg on the scene. But he was unable either the

---

[1] England had been at war with the United States for more than two years. The declaration of war by the government of Washington (June 19, 1812) had been provoked by England's pretensions of getting American vessels to respect the pretended blockade of the frontiers of the French Empire from Hamburg to San Sebastian on the Atlantic, and from Port-Vendres to Cattaro on the shores of the Mediterranean ; and further by the rights which the English claimed of confiscating the wares of enemies found on neutral vessels.

day before yesterday or to-day, to see the Emperor Alexander, who, although much better, still keeps his room, and I do not think he has seen him to-day.

The arrangements with respect to Genoa are agreed upon in the Italian Commission. They are being drafted now, and the commissions have charged the Comte de Noailles with this work. The rights of the House of Carignan have been acknowledged. The Comte de Noailles has been instructed by me to accept the arrangements made for Piedmont, only as an integrant part of the arrangements to be made with the concurrence of France for the whole of Italy. It is a reservation which I thought fit to make for the sake of Naples.

The affairs of Switzerland are going to be treated by a committee of which the Duc de Dalberg is a member, as I have had the honour of informing your Majesty.

Those of Germany are suspended by the refusal of Bavaria and Wurtemberg to take part in the discussions, till the fate of Saxony be settled.

There are a thousand reasons why I should like to be near your Majesty now. But I feel retained here by the notion that I can be of more service to you, and by the hope that in spite of all obstacles, we shall end by getting at least a good deal of what you wished.

I have the honour to be, ...

No. 9 b.—KING LOUIS XVIII. TO THE PRINCE DE TALLEYRAND.

PARIS, *November* 26, 1814.

MY COUSIN,

I have received your letter No. 12, and I can say with truth that it is the first which has satisfied me, not that I have not always been so, with your line of policy and manner of informing me of the condition of affairs, but, because for the first time, I see justice emerging. The Emperor of Russia has gone back a step, and in politics, as in everything else, the first step was never the last. This prince was deceived however if he thought to draw me into an alliance (political of course) with him. You know my plan is, general alliance, but no private ones. The latter are the causes of wars, the former the guarantee of peace ; and without fearing war, peace is the aim of all my wishes. It is to get peace, that I have increased my army, and that I have authorised you to give my support to Austria and Bavaria. These measures are beginning to succeed. I believe I can expect *otium cum dignitate*, and that is quite sufficient to cause me satisfaction.

You have said all that I could have said on Lord Castlereagh's letter. I explain the diversities of his language and that of the Duke of Wellington, by their respective positions : the one follows instructions, the other gives them.

I should like to have seen the affairs of Italy from the Alps to Terracina already settled : for I anticipate great results from that settlement. Whereupon, my cousin, may God have you in His safe and holy keeping.

LOUIS.

No. 16 a.—The Ambassadors of the King at the Congress to the Minister for Foreign Affairs at Paris.

VIENNA, November 30, 1814.

MONSIEUR LE COMTE,

No general conference has been held since our last dispatch. Prince Metternich and Prince von Hardenberg have both been obliged to keep their beds from colds.

The affair of Genoa meanwhile has been adjusted and ended. The acts are about to be signed, and the next messenger will carry copies of them to the department. Signor de Corsini has been charged with answering the memorandum of Count de Labrador, who claimed Tuscany for the Queen of Etruria. The debate on this question is about to take place, and we are afraid that it will be only with the greatest difficulty that the queen will recover this ancient patrimony of her family. Lord Castlereagh has expressed an opinion to this effect. A meeting to arrange the affairs of Switzerland has been held, and the French plenipotentiary invited to it.

The demands of the canton of Bern have been heard, but nothing is concluded. There appears to be general goodwill towards Bern, but there is also no wish to overthrow the existence of the remaining nineteen cantons, which was guaranteed by the act of Federal Union. The results of these conferences according as they emerge will be reported to the king.

The authorisation that the king has given for the exchange of a portion of the district of Gex will be of great use. We observe however that in this matter, it is no longer a question of the spoliation of the Prince-Bishop of Basel, who had already in 1803, at the time of the recess of the German Empire, lost his rights of sovereignty, and received a grant of a hundred and twenty thousand francs,[1] and has exercised spiritual powers ever since.[2]

The German conferences have been suspended, Wurtemberg and Bavaria would not assist in riveting the fetters prepared for them. A reply made by the Austrian and Prussian cabinets to the Wurtemberg plenipotentiaries, increased their suspicion in this respect. We subjoin here a copy and a French translation.

The minor and medium States of Germany, have meanwhile formed a second league, and the Grand Duke of Baden has joined it, owing to some advice given him to this effect by the Empress of Russia, his sister.

As to Polish and Saxon affairs, they are in the same state, and at no period of the congress have the allied powers given to France a more complete proof of their disunion than they have done at this time, when England, Austria, Russia, and Prussia agree on no single point which ought to be a basis for the general arrangement of Europe.

The attitude that France has assumed, places her in a position to await quietly the result of these intrigues, and only to appear on the scene for the purpose of getting the voice of reason heard. It is in this spirit that we think it would be useful to write some newspaper articles, against the teachings of the *Correspondant of Nuremberg*, and the *Rhine Mercury*, which both delight in falsifying facts and in fostering the animus which reigns in Germany against France.

Be pleased to accept. . . . .

No. 14.—THE PRINCE DE TALLEYRAND TO KING LOUIS XVIII.

VIENNA, *November* 30, 1814.

I have received the letter with which your Majesty has deigned to honour me, dated the 15th inst., and, by the same

---

[1] About £4,800.

[2] The bishopric of Basel was at one time a partly independent state. The Bishop, Prince of the Holy Empire since 1356, possessed, as vassal of the Empire, the towns of Porrentruy, Delemont, and Laufen with their territories, the whole being incorporated within the district of the Upper Rhine. He was besides independent sovereign of the towns of Bienne, Neuveville, the seigniories of Tessemberg, Erguel, and Illfingen. In 1792, the Revolution transformed the bishopric into the republic of Rauracia, which only lasted a few months; in 1793, the districts of Delemont and Porrentruy were annexed to France; and in 1797, Erguel and Val-Moutiers underwent the same fate. The Bishop of Basel thus deprived of his states the remainder of which were secularized in 1803, received a grant of 10,000 florins. In 1815, the old bishopric of Basel was adjudged by the Congress of Vienna to the canton of Bern, with the exception of twelve parishes which were given to the canton of Basel, and of one district which was given to Neuchâtel.

messenger, the authorisation which your Majesty has been pleased to give me for the exchange of a small portion of the country of Gex for a portion of Porrentruy.

The former Prince-Bishop of Basel has already resumed, as bishop, the spiritual administration of Porrentruy, but he cannot, as prince, recover the possession he lost, not by the simple fact of conquest, but by the general secularization of the ecclesiastical states of Germany in 1803. As prince, he enjoys a grant of sixty thousand florins, and does not lay claim to more. He can therefore be no obstacle to the project of exchange which we have had the honour to lay before your Majesty. But this exchange may be rendered difficult by one of the conditions upon which your Majesty has made it contingent: namely, the restitution of Bernese Aargau to the canton of Bern, for according to all appearances, this restitution will cause great, and, perhaps insurmountable difficulties. I suppose however that if one were limited to restoring some bailiwicks of Aargau to the canton of Bern, and to giving it as compensation the parts of the bishopric of Basel comprised in the ancient boundaries of Switzerland, that Bern would be content with this arrangement. Your Majesty would be content with it yourself.

The commission charged with settling Swiss affairs has, up to the present, done nothing else but to convince itself that the multiplicity and divergence of the several claims render them very thorny to deal with. Those who, in the beginning, wished to regulate them alone, and who contested our rights to interfere, have been the first to demand our concurrence, one may almost say, our help and advice. It is true that the Swiss envoys who are here, and who, from the beginning of our sojourn at Vienna, have allied themselves with us, have declared that if the powers thought that they could establish a settled order of things in Switzerland, without the intervention, or even the assistance[1] of France, they have rocked themselves in the vainest of vain hopes.

When the allies were treating of peace and were wishing to make it with Bonaparte,[2] they had addressed themselves to the cantons which had suffered most from the Swiss revolutions, rousing in them the recollection and feeling of their losses, and holding out to them the prospect of repairing them. Their aim was to detach Switzerland from France, and this seemed to them to be an infallible means. But it was found that these cantons were precisely those which were the most attached to the House of Bourbon. Then the allies troubled themselves no further

---

[1] Text: "l'assistance" = "the help." Var.: "*l'assentiment*" = "*the assent.*"
[2] Text: "Bonaparte." Var.: "*Buonaparte.*"

with a means which no longer suited their aim, and which was even contrary to their main purpose, and have gathered from their overtures nothing but embarrassment as to how to back out and quiet affairs. Some formed the idea of uniting Germany and Switzerland in one and the same league.[1] This is another idea which was abandoned.[2] There appears now to be a perfectly genuine wish to terminate matters, by satisfying the chief and most just claims, and by making besides as few changes as is possible. There is therefore some reason to hope that there will be an arrangement for Switzerland, which if not the best in itself, will yet be the best that circumstances allow; that the independence of the country and, what is not less important for us, its neutrality, will be declared.

The commission for Italian affairs has, with regard to that of Genoa, drawn up a report and a proposal consisting of certain articles which will be signed to-morrow, and addressed to the eight powers. I shall have the honour of sending to your Majesty by the next messenger, a copy of this proposal. After the affairs of Genoa, come those of Parma which present more difficulties, if it is true, as is said, that the Emperor of Austria and Prince Metternich have recently given positive assurance to the Archduchess Marie-Louise, that she should preserve Parma. What is certain is, that the archduchess, who hitherto had the arms of her husband on her carriages, has had the arms of the Duchy of Parma painted on one of them. I hope nevertheless that it may be restored to the Queen of Etruria.

It is to Venice that the twenty-five thousand rifles sold to Murat have been taken. It appears that in spite of the protection of Prince Metternich, he does not feel very sure, for he has just written a long letter to the Archduchess Marie-Louise, in which he tells her among other things that if Austria will lend him her support, so as to enable him to remain at Naples, " he will raise her again to the rank from which she ought never to have fallen." (These were the very words of the letter.) Such an extravagance, even in a man of his country and character, can only be explained as an excessive fear which betrays itself.

The conferences of the German commission are still suspended. Wurtemberg has declared that she could give no opinion whatever on the portions of a whole, which were only shown her one after the other, and isolated, and that she would deliberate on

---

[1] Text: " d'unir dans une même ligue " = " to unite in one and the same league," Var. : " de réunir dans *la* même ligue " = " to unite in *the* same league."

[2] Text: " C'est *encore* une idée abandonnée " = " This is *another* idea which was abandoned." Var. : " C'est une idée abandonnée = " This is an idea which was abandoned."

none of them, before she had been informed of the whole. This has drawn forth, on the part of Austria and Prussia, a letter by the tenour of which these two powers show sufficiently plainly the kind of sway which, in sharing her between them, they would like to exercise over Germany.

Persuaded that the influence thus exercised would soon develop into dominion and sovereignty, all the states of the former Rhenish confederation, with the exception of Bavaria and Wurtemberg, have assembled to express their wish for the re-establishment of the old German Empire, in the person of him who was the head of it.

These states are on the point of forming a league, of which the object will be to oppose a resistance of non-consent and inertia to the policy which Austria and Prussia would like to see prevail. The Grand Duke of Baden, who at first held himself aloof, has now joined the others, by the advice of the Empress of Russia, his sister, who has only been the instrument of the Emperor Alexander.

The affairs of Poland and Saxony remain still in the same condition; the step which Prince Metternich had Prince von Hardenberg take, and which did not meet with the approval of Lord Castlereagh, having been without result, as well as the interview that Lord Castlereagh had with the Emperor Alexander.

I have the honour to forward to your Majesty the draft of this discussion in six articles. It still lacks one letter, which I shall have later, and which I have already read. It is the last letter of the Emperor Alexander, in which he tells Lord Castlereagh, that it is sufficient, and invites him henceforth to proceed in his official capacity.

Those who have read these papers do not understand how Lord Castlereagh, after having advanced as far as he has done, could draw back; he himself does not understand how, or in what direction, he could advance another step.

Besides, your Majesty will see that Lord Castlereagh has only occupied himself with Poland, having made up his mind to sacrifice Saxony; and all this in consequence of that policy which only views matters in the bulk, without troubling itself of the elements which go to form them. It is a policy of schoolboys and allies.

I must make the same petition to your Majesty with regard to these papers that I have for those which I have already had the honour to forward you. I have received these in the same manner as the others and under the same conditions.

The Emperor Alexander shows signs of making overtures to

us. He complains of those, who, since we have been here, and especially at first, have, as it were, interposed themselves between him and us, and names Prince Metternich and Count Nesselrode. The intermediary he employs with me is Prince Adam Czartoryski who enjoys most of his confidence at the present time, and whom he has admitted to his council, to which Prince Nesselrode is no longer invited, and which is composed of Prince Adam, Count Capo d'Istria and Herr von Stein.

The emperor has quite recovered and goes out. Prince Metternich is ill; he went out neither yesterday nor to-day,[1] which prevents him from holding a meeting with the ministers of the eight powers.

Lord Castlereagh came this morning to propose to me to make use of this time of forced inaction for turning our attention to the question of the blacks. But while joking on his proposal and on the motives [2] which led him to it, I told him so positively that this must be the last question of all, and that the affairs of Europe must be settled before those of Africa, that I hope he will not give me occasion to repeat it to him a second time.

I have the honour to be, &c.

No. 10 B.—King Louis XVIII. to the Prince de Talleyrand.

PARIS, *December* 4, 1814.

My Cousin,

I am in receipt of your letter, No. 13. Always satisfied with your conduct, I am, as you may readily believe, very little satisfied with the state of affairs, which seems to me far removed from that in which they were when you sent off your letter No. 12. God alone is master of human wills; men can do nothing, and however [3] things may turn, by holding firmly on to principles, by perhaps deserving that the verse: *Justum et tenacem propositi virum*, may be applied to me, honour will remain to me, which is what I am most ambitious of.

I am not surprised at the rumours which are current, of the news that is handed on, and of the seeming consistency given to it by evil-minded people; were I to worry about these,

---

[1] Text: "il n'est sorti ni hier ni aujourd'hui" = "he went out neither yesterday nor to-day." Var.: "*et ne s'est point levé* ni hier ni aujourd'hui" = "and *has not left his bed* either yesterday or to-day."

[2] Text "les motifs" = "the motives." Var.: "les motifs *personnels*" = "the *personal* motives."

[3] Text: "et quoiqu'il en puisse être" = "and however things may turn." Var.: "*mais* quoiqu'il" = "*but* however things may turn."

I should not have a moment's repose, whereas now, my sleep is as peaceful as it was in my youth. The reason is simple : I have never for a moment thought that, after the first moments of the Restoration, the mixture of so many heterogeneous elements, would produce no agitation. I know well that there is some; but I am not disturbed by it. Resolved never to leave the path Equity prescribes me, within the constitution I have given my people, never to relax the exercise of my legitimate authority, I fear nothing, and sooner or later, I shall see these clouds disperse, clouds whose gathering I had foreseen.

You have heard speak of a change in the ministry, and I now announce it to you. I am ready to do all justice to the zeal and good qualities of the Comte Dupont : but I cannot equally praise his administration. Consequently, I have just deprived him of his office, which I entrust to Marshal Soult. I am giving that of the navy to the Comte Beugnot ;[1] and the general superintendence of police to M. d'André.[2] But these partial changes in confidential posts, and of which I could wish you had been first informed, change in no respect the policy, which is *mine :* you must take great care in clearly stating this to all the persons who speak to you of what is taking place to-day.

I shall be very pleased to see you again when the time comes ; but the reasons which determined me to deprive myself of your services near my person, exist in increased measure by the very difficulties which you are experiencing. It is therefore necessary that you continue to represent me at the congress as well as you are now doing, to its close. Whereupon, my Cousin, may God have you in His safe and holy keeping.

Louis.

No. III.—The Comte de Blacas d'Aulps to the Prince de Talleyrand.

Paris, *December* 4, 1814.

Your Highness,

The letter which the King has received from you by the messenger, who had been unable to bring me the reply to that which I had the honour of writing to you, on the 9th ultimo,

---

[1] The office of Minister of the Navy had been vacant since the death of its titular, M. de Malouet (September 7).

[2] Antoine-Balthazar-Joseph d'André was born at Aix in 1759, member of the *parlement* of Provence in 1778, deputy of the nobility at the States-General, president of the Constituent Assembly (August, 1790) ; he took a seat in the ranks of the Constitutionals. In 1792, prosecuted as a monopolist, he took refuge in England, was appointed general director of police, and *Intendant* of the king's household. He died in 1825.

had already thrown important light upon the principal subjects treated in the letters, which you were so good as to forward me on the 23rd. His Majesty has had the goodness to communicate your despatch to me as well as Lord Castlereagh's letter, and it is impossible, as you observe, not to be struck with the difference existing between the style of this note, and the language of the Duke of Wellington.

I cannot, however, I confess, yet decide what are the real causes of this difference. The king dislikes attributing it to a plot merely, of which the aim would be to discredit France. Lord Wellington, by official communications, such as that of which I have spoken to you on the subject of the relations of Naples to Paris, and by his late conduct on the occasion of a correspondence seized on the person of Lord Oxford,[1] has shown a disposition, whose motive could scarcely have been that[2] of the desire to spread chimerical fears alone. It might also be possible that, exaggerating in his own mind perils, rumours of which too generally welcomed, cease not to frighten timid minds, he often thwarted, without meaning it, the policy of the king, or perhaps favoured thereby intentions less loyal than his own. What is certain is, that several circumstances independent of the views of England, furnished only too many pretexts for suspicion likely to encourage vexatious opinions, such as those whose effect you fear. Your Highness knows, and has often deplored with me, the little credit obtained by his Majesty's government, through want of vigour and of unity in the action[3] of the ministry. This weakness, which for some time was only known to the cabinet, could not fail in time to acquire an unfortunate publicity. Add to this, the discontent of the army, whose complaints constantly filled the ears of the princes, in their journeys to the departments ; the feeling of insecurity, to which all the protests against the inefficiency of the police gave rise; finally the informations of all kinds laid to the charge of men, marked out by their intentions or speeches, perhaps utterly without

---

[1] Edward Marley, Earl of Oxford, born in 1773, died in 1849, issue of the family of the English statesman of that name (1661-1724). The title is to-day extinct. Lord Oxford was, at the time, residing at Naples, without any official title. He was in constant communication with Murat and his court, and this aroused the suspicions of the French government. Thus, as the earl was passing through Paris, on his return to England, he was, on some pretext or other arrested. Several letters from the King of Naples were found among his papers : but, proofs of a conspiracy between Murat and Napoleon were looked for in vain.

[2] Text : "motiver le projet unique de répandre " = "the mere project of spreading . . . . could hardly be the motive." Var. : "motiver *uniquement* le projet de répandre" = "the project of spreading . . . . could *solely* be the motive."

[3] Text : "d'ensemble des opérations" = "unity in the action." Var.: "d'ensemble *dans les* opérations" = "unity *in the* action."

foundation, but not without probability, as the instigators of most dangerous plots ; everything, to the very measures of safety which the zeal of the military commanders has rendered too plain, must produce an impression of which foreigners can profit without having contributed to it.

This state of things will explain to your Highness the imperious necessity to which the king felt he must give way, by making some change in his ministry. It was only yesterday his Majesty signified his intention in this respect. Whilst fully admitting the great and good qualities of the Comte Dupont, the King recognized that the army, imputing to this minister mistakes which perhaps the exigencies of the moment rendered inevitable,[1] longed for quite a different policy, and therefore turned his attention to Marshal Soult,[2] whom he has entrusted with the direction of the War Office. This choice which has been dictated to his Majesty by the desire to quiet the troops, and to give them confidence and zeal, so necessary to the maintenance of national power, will without doubt be acknowledged by you, as being in conformity with the principles His Majesty has always followed.

The office of the Ministry of Marine given to the Comte Beugnot and the direction[3] of the police given to M. d'André, are other changes by which the king has sought to meet the wishes of the public.

Your Highness will doubtless consider that this change, inconsiderable as it is, when looked at in comparison with the formation of a cabinet, must none the less lead to important results. As a matter of fact, the spirit of the army and the security of the police, have become so important factors in the loyalty of public opinion that, from this point of view, the resolution of the king possesses the greatest importance. It is to you that his Majesty looks for presenting this change in its true light at Vienna, and to get it looked upon, not as a change of ministry, but rather as affording additional power and enlightenment to the government.

The king regrets keenly that instead of having to entrust this task to your care, he cannot see you near him, so as to offer one more proof of the favourable opinion he wishes to win for his

---

[1] Text : "imputant des torts que peut-être, à ce ministre, les embarras du moment rendaient inévitables " = " imputing mistakes which perhaps the difficulties of the moment rendered inevitable to this minister." Var. : "imputant peut-être à ce ministre des torts que les embarras du moment rendaient inévitable " = "imputing perhaps to this minister mistakes which the difficulties of the moment rendered inevitable." . . . (Same meaning ; order of words simply altered.)

[2] Var : " sur Monsieur le Duc de Dalmatie " = " to the Duc de Dalmatie."

[3] Text : " direction " = " direction." Var. : " direction générale " = " general direction."

ministry.[1] But his Majesty is too fully conscious of the advantageous effects produced by your unremitting efforts.[2] Besides, it is possible that, affairs taking a quicker turn, you may be retained less time than you give us occasion to fear, which I heartily desire.[3]

The last news from Spain is not good. The Comte de Jaucourt will certainly inform you of the report which M. d'Agoult[4] *has just addressed him.*

Nothing has yet been decided here as to the time of the adjournment of the Chambers.[5]

I beg your Highness to kindly accept renewed assurances of my most sincere and invariable attachment.

BLÁCAS D'AULPS.

No. 17A. — The Ambassadors of the King at the Congress to the Minister of Foreign Affairs at Paris.

VIENNA, *December* 7, 1814.

MONSIEUR LE COMTE,

We have the honour to forward to you the report of the commission upon the formation of the kingdom of Sardinia ; it has been drafted by the Comte de Noailles.

It is probable that in the next conference which will bring together the plenipotentiaries of the eight powers who signed the treaty of Paris, all that yet remains to be decided on this question will be definitely settled, to wit :—

1st. The formal recognition that the succession of the House of Sardinia lies in the family of Savoy-Carignan.

2nd. The title of King of Sardinia on taking possession of the State of Genoa ;

3rd. The award of the imperial fiefs.

We have also the honour to forward to the department two German letters, one of which is that written by the court of

---

[1] Text: "qu'il veut" = "which he wants." Var. : "qu'il *désire*" = "which he *desires.*"

[2] Text : "Mais sa Majesté sent les effets avantageux qu'ont produits vos continuels efforts" = as translated. Var.: "*Sa Majesté sent néanmoins toute la vérité des observations que vous lui faites sur l'effet avantageux qu'ont produits vos continuels efforts*" = "*His Majesty nevertheless is too fully conscious of the truth of the observations made by you to him as to the advantageous effects of your unremitting efforts.*"

[3] Text: "et je le désire vivement" = "and I heartily desire it." Var. : "*et pour moi je désire fort que votre retour soit plus prochain que vous ne semblez l'espérer*" = "*and for my part, I hope that your return may be nearer than you appear to expect.*"

[4] Hector d'Agoult, secretary of the embassy at Madrid.

[5] The end of this letter is not found in the text of the archives.

Wurtemberg to the German commission. It provoked the reply of the cabinets of Prussia and Austria, of which our former despatch enclosed a copy. The second letter is that which the court of Wurtemberg drew up as an explanation of the former. Otherwise, German affairs are still suspended, and await the decision of the Saxony question which is still hovering in a state of uncertainty. There appear to be no overtures from either side.

The Swiss conferences have commenced. M. de Dalberg defends to the best of his abilities the interests of the canton of Bern, and although the powers have decided on keeping the nineteen cantons intact, some advantages can yet be won for this canton, at least from the bishopric of Basel. M. de Dalberg will give a general report when some definite arrangement has been arrived at.

Be pleased to accept. . . .

No. 15.—The Prince de Talleyrand to King Louis XVIII.

Vienna, *December* 7, 1814.

Sire,

The present letter which I have the honour to write to your Majesty will be short. I have only this moment learnt the facts which I am going to report. I substitute them for others less important and more vague which I had gathered together.

I am told, and I have every reason to believe it, that a messenger, who arrived this evening, has brought to Lord Castlereagh and to Count von Münster the order to back up Saxony. (I am ignorant as yet to what extent, and whether it is to be done in all cases, or only on certain conditions.) It is added that Lord Castlereagh addressed a letter to Prince Metternich this very morning, informing the Prince of this command, and also that Count von Münster, who has always been of our opinion though rather timidly, is going to express himself on this question with considerable force. Prince von Wrede has in all probability read the letter of Lord Castlereagh at the house of Prince Metternich.

On the morning of the day before yesterday, Prince Metternich had an interview with the Emperor Alexander in which the most ingenious subtleties and artifices were employed on both sides; but it led to nothing. But as Prince Metternich declared that his master would never consent to Saxony being handed over to Prussia, the Emperor Alexander wishing to know if he had told him the truth, attacked the Emperor Francis in the evening after the banquet, and said to him :

" At the present time, we sovereigns are obliged to conform to and obey the wish of the people. The wish of the Saxon people is not to be divided. They prefer to belong to Prussia, rather than be divided, or parcelled out."

To this the Emperor Francis replied :

" I do not understand that doctrine at all. This is mine : a Prince can, if he wishes, surrender a portion of his dominions ; he cannot give up all his country or all his people. If he abdicates his right passes to his legitimate heirs. He cannot deprive them of it ; Europe herself has not the right to do so."

" That is not consonant with modern ideas," said the Emperor Alexander.

" It is my opinion," replied the Emperor Francis, " that it ought to be that of all sovereigns, and consequently yours. As for me, I will never depart from it."

This conversation which was reported to me to the same tenour by two different people, may be relied upon, as a fact. One is therefore justified in saying that the Emperor of Austria's opinion on the question of Saxony does not leave Prince Metternich the choice of defending or abandoning it, and it was not without good grounds that the Saxon minister flattered himself that it would never be abandoned.

It is said that the Emperor Alexander declares that one conversation with the Emperor Francis is worth ten with Prince Metternich, because the former always expresses himself clearly and one knows what to expect from him.

The princes of Germany, who have met for the purpose of considering some means for defending their rights against the projects which they know or guess the commission charged with German affairs has formed against them, are going, I hope, to publish a declaration in favour of the preservation of Saxony. Marshal von Wrede, to whom the majority have addressed themselves, has advised them to press on, saying the moment was favourable. He has promised that Bavaria would join them.

Wurtemberg, for the time being, is ranged on the side of Prussia. It is the Prince Royal, who is in love with the Archduchess Catherine who has influenced the cabinet in this. The court of Stuttgart has done a dirty trick in this, which will do her no good, and will scarcely harm any one else. This conduct so ignoble and disloyal, to say no more, of the King of Wurtemberg, does not seem to me to be calculated to promote the desire of becoming his nephew.[1] I shall ask your Majesty to allow me

---

[1] If the Duc de Berry had married the Grand-Duchess Anne, he would thus have become the nephew of the King of Wurtemberg. The latter, in fact, was the brother of Sophie-Dorothea, Princess of Wurtemberg, who had married the Emperor Paul.

to speak again one day at greater length of this subject which I only mention here.

The Emperor of Russia had expressed a wish to see me ; afterwards, he preferred first to clear up some confused ideas, with which, he informed me through Prince Adam Czartoryski, his mind was perplexed. In my intercourse with him, I have not been able to make use of General Pozzo, who is not now on the best of terms with him. His servants themselves only see him with difficulty. The Duc de Richelieu[1] had to wait a whole month to get an audience. Prince Adam, although an interested party in our discussions, is my most useful mediator. I have not yet seen the emperor. I am told that he is shaken but still undecided. I do not know when, or on what, he will determine.

I have the honour to forward to your Majesty copies of the two papers, which (to use his own expression) " constitute the conclusion of his correspondence " with Lord Castlereagh. He has been generally blamed for having engaged, so to speak, in a hand-to-hand fight, little worthy of his rank, even had he proved victorious in it, whereas the contrary is the fact. Thus, instead of triumphing, which he doubtless contemplated, his vanity carries off nothing from the strife but wounds.

Your Majesty will see from all this discussion, that Lord Castlereagh has only looked at the question of Poland from one point of view, and that he has isolated this subject from all others. Not only has he not demanded the independence of Poland, but he has not even expressed a wish for it : and he has even spoken of the Polish people in terms that rather dissuade than call for this arrangement. He has taken especial care to keep the Polish question perfectly separate from that of Saxony, a country which he had completely abandoned and which he is henceforth going to support.

I have also the honour of forwarding to your Majesty a

The Grand-Duchess Anne was the youngest daughter of Paul I. This princess, after having been on the point of becoming the wife of the Emperor Napoleon in 1810, and of the Duc de Berry in 1814, was married, in 1815, to the Prince of Orange, who became, later, King of the Netherlands, under the name of William II.

[1] Armand du Plessis, Duc de Richelieu, grandson of the marshal of this name. He was born in 1766, and was in 1789 first gentleman of the bedchamber. He emigrated the same year, repaired first to Vienna, and then entered the Russian army, and received from the Empress Catherine the rank of lieutenant-general (1790). He came back to France for a brief period in 1802, but returned to Russia in 1803, and was appointed by the Emperor Alexander Governor of Odessa, and afterwards of all New Russia. Having gone back again to France, he re-assumed his office at the court, and became in September 1815 Minister of Foreign Affairs and President of the Council. He retired in 1818, but retained his dignity of state minister, to which was added that of master of the hounds. He returned to power in February 1820, but only retained office till December, 1821. He died in the following year.

letter of your consul at Leghorn.[1] I have made use here, and
with some success, of the information it contains, which I have
sent to the Emperor of Russia. M. de Saint-Marsan has received
similar intelligence, and Prince Metternich confesses that he has
received the same warnings from Paris. The conclusion which
I draw from it is that it is necessary to rid one's self as soon as
possible of the man at Elba and of Murat. My opinion is
bearing fruit. Count von Münster warmly shares it. He has
written about it to his court. He has spoken of it to Lord
Castlereagh in such terms that the latter in his turn has gone to
rouse Prince Metternich, who is employing all means to get the
contrary opinion to prevail.

His great stratagem is to make us lose time, in the belief that he
thereby gains it. It is already eight days since the commission
for Italian affairs settled those of Genoa. I have already had
the honour of informing your Majesty that they were settled in
accordance with your desires. I subjoin to my letter of to-day
to the department, the work of the commission. Your Majesty
will find in it the clauses, nay even the very terms prescribed in
our instructions. To-morrow the commission of the eight powers
will take cognizance of the report and give its verdict.[2] I doubt
not that the conclusions of the report will be adopted. Tuscany
and Parma will next engage attention. This work, which ought
to be already finished, has been retarded by the slight illness of
Prince Metternich, who, in order to finish nothing, terms his
present state "convalescence."

The time lost to business is wasted in fêtes. The Emperor
Alexander demands and even commands them, as if he were at
his own court. We are invited to those fêtes, shown every regard,
treated with distinction, in order to show the sentiments felt towards your Majesty, whose praises are on everybody's lips ; but
all this does not make me forget that it is now nearly three
months that I have been absent from you.

I have spoken to Lord Castlereagh of the arrest of Lord
Oxford, of which M. de Jaucourt had informed me. Far from
showing any displeasure, he told me he was delighted at it ; and
has depicted Lord Oxford to me as a man who merited no
esteem. I wish that among his papers, some had been found
compromising Murat in the eyes of this court.

The two messengers who have come to me from Paris have
brought me the letters with which your Majesty has deigned to
honour me, dated November 22 and 26.

I have the honour to be. . . .

---

[1] The Chevalier Mariotti, who had been entrusted with watching the intrigues of
Napoleon at Elba. [2] Var.: Add. *sur ce travail = on this work.*

No. 11 b.—King Louis XVIII. to the Prince de Talleyrand.

PARIS, *December* 10, 1814.

My Cousin,

I am in receipt of your letter No. 14.

You have very well interpreted my instructions with regard to the canton of Aargau. I should certainly prefer that Switzerland might again become what she has been hitherto; but I will not wish what is impossible, and provided the canton of Bern be as satisfied as it can expect to be under the circumstances, I shall be so too. With regard to the Prince-Bishop of Basel, I had not remembered the last recess of the Empire; but I see that it solves[1] the question with regard to him. And I have no further objection to make to the projected disposal of Porrentruy.

I have read with interest, and am carefully preserving, the papers you have sent me. Lord Castlereagh speaks very well with regard to Poland, but his letter of October 11, belies his language considerably. If however he has succeeded in persuading the Emperor of Russia, it will be a great advantage for Saxony; but I scarcely see any appearance of it, and we must not swerve from our own line of conduct.

You know Prince Czartoryski, and I know him also; the choice that his Imperial Majesty has made, taking him as mediator, leads me to think that he would rather I should make overtures to him, than he to me. Continue these conferences all the same, while equally continuing to follow out my intentions. No harm can result from them and they may produce some good.

I am pleased to believe that it is from fear that Murat is playing the braggart; all the same, never lose sight for a moment of the fact, that if Buonaparte has any resource left, it is in Italy by means of Murat, and that also, *delenda est Carthago.* Wherefore, my cousin, I pray God may have you in His safe and holy keeping.   LOUIS.

The Ambassadors of the King at the Congress to the Minister of Foreign Affairs at Paris.

VIENNA, *December* 14, 1814.

Monsieur Le Comte,

Our despatch of November 5, to the department pointed out the advantage which might accrue from an exchange

---

[1] Text: "qu'il tranche" = "that it solves." Var.: "qu'il *a tranché*" = "that it *has solved.*"

of a part of the country of Gex for a part of the bishopric of Basel, an exchange which is desired by the Helvetian Confederation, asked by the Genevese and proposed by the great powers.

This sacrifice would have allowed hopes of a greater influence over the Helvetian Confederation, if the return of one of its cantons could have been procured for the canton of Bern.

One would also have been justified in believing that the Genevese recognizing the value of this condescension would endeavour in their turn to get the Vaudois and Aargau people to satisfy the just pecuniary claims which the canton of Bern proffers.

Pressed by the English plenipotentiary to reveal what were the conditions imposed by France for the exchange of a portion of the country of Gex, the French plenipotentiary remitted to him report No. 1, asking him to show it only to the ministers, in order to know if their instructions admitted destroying, in favour of Bern, the principle of the integrity of the nineteen cantons. The English minister, instead of keeping secret this confidential communication, showed it to the Genevese deputies, who drew up a counter project (No. 2).

The conditions which it incloses are all in direct opposition to the orders of the king, who wished that the exchange should be made without depriving the King of Sardinia of any territory, and that Bern should recover the portion of Aargau which this canton (Bern) had possessed before.

During this interval the powers, and especially England, were said to cherish the hope of increasing their influence in Switzerland by this exchange. They were very particular in letting the Helvetian league know what great obligations it was under to them for securing it.

The Genevese, far from recognizing the sacrifice that France had made; pretended they had gained all their advantages from the congress, and maintained that, protected by the allies, nothing could be refused them. To prove this, they assured us, that although the exchange had been made contrary to the expressed wish of France, the king had yet acquiesced in it.

These observations, which were well known, attracted some attention; and in the conferences, the French plenipotentiary took occasion to maintain that England only seconded this exchange so vehemently, to get herself more highly valued; and to be able to realise promises made to the Genevese at the time of the treaty of Chaumont.

Several letters from Paris, addressed to Swiss deputies, announced at the same time that public opinion disapproved of this exchange, and that people were astonished that the French government had consented to it.

It has therefore been thought more to the interests of the king and of France, to dismiss it, and with the more in-sistence, that the internal situation of Switzerland and the obstacles put in the way to all exchange of the new cantons by the Emperor of Russia, has rendered it impossible to obtain the conditions to which the king had attached his consent to the exchange.

The French plenipotentiary sent in consequence a reply (No. 3) to the Genevese project, and declared that the exchange could not be allowed. The English plenipotentiary in express-ing his regrets at this modification of our attitude, announced that his government was intending to make a fresh attempt at Paris, to obtain the execution of the exchange, and proposed to reserve the part of the bishopric of Basel, which was to serve as the make-weight, by leaving it under a provisory government. The other plenipotentiaries refused their consent to this; but allowed this reservation to hold good till the end of the congress, and the projects proposed by England to be furthered.

Although the Austrian and French plenipotentiaries observed that this only prolonged the uncertainty, and was harmful to the real interests of Switzerland, the proposal of England was maintained.

We believe therefore that the Duke of Wellington will receive a fresh command to ask for a fresh decision from the king, in order to know, if, in spite of the recognition of the integrity of the nineteen cantons, the king would consent to this exchange; we think that it is to the interest of the king to refuse it.

1. Because it does not produce the advantages it was believed to give.

2. Because the influence of France in Switzerland can only be increased by means of Bern and her allies.

3. Because that so long as all that concerns the Helvetian Confederation is done under the auspices of the allied powers, France must reserve her means, and only act later, if she wishes to strengthen her influence.

In thus informing you, Monsieur le Comte, of what has passed on this subject, you will be forewarned when the English ambassador presents himself to raise this question. It might also be as well for the French ambassador in London to know of this matter, and we ask you, Monsieur le Comte, to transmit to him the details of it, with which you will also be so good as to acquaint the king.

Prince Talleyrand, in order to thwart the importunities of the English ministers the more easily, has told them that the king has asked the chancellor of France under what form the cessions or exchanges of territory could be made, and that the chancellor had replied that this was not yet sufficiently decided, and that he must decline mixing himself up in such questions : after which the French plenipotentiaries could not furnish a further reply to this question.

It will be well, Monsieur le Comte, to apprise the chancellor of this, that he may avoid giving an explanation on this subject, or, in case the ambassadors of England should speak to him of it, that he may give a reply similar to that which we have given here.

Be pleased to accept. . . . .

No. 19 A.—THE AMBASSADORS OF THE KING AT THE CONGRESS TO THE MINISTER OF FOREIGN AFFAIRS AT PARIS.

VIENNA, *December* 14, 1814.

MONSIEUR LE COMTE,

We have the honour to forward to you the protocol of the last conference. Another has since been held, but the protocol has not yet been drafted. We shall wait to decide, with regard to the proposal of Count de Labrador on the Imperial fiefs, until the time when the fate of the King of Etruria, as well as that of the Archduchesse Marie-Louise . . . . shall be settled. The French plenipotentiaries have proposed, in accordance with the principle of the faithful execution of the dispositions of the treaty of Paris, the formation of three new commissions—

The first to regulate, conformably to article 5, the navigation of rivers.

The second to regulate the rank and precedence of crowns, and all that follows from this ;

The third, to discuss the abolition of the slave-trade.

This last point has caused some difficulties, because the Portuguese plenipotentiary observed that the commission could only be formed by powers interested in it. Count de Labrador has strongly backed the opposition of Portugal. The discussion has been so fierce that the Commission has adjourned its sitting, and the matter has resumed the form of simple negotiations.

We observe again that Portugal has established as a principle that she will not renounce the slave trade for another eight years, and on condition that England regard the mercantile treaty existing between her and Portugal as null and void.

The proposal made by France was in conformity with the

engagement entered into with England to interpose her aid in getting the abolition of the slave-trade pronounced by all the powers, we shall therefore no longer have to occupy ourselves with this.

The other two commissions have been formed.

Prince Talleyrand has appointed as commissioners the Duc de Dalberg over the naval commission, and the Comte de la Tour du Pin over that for fixing the precedence and rank of crowned heads.

Russia has asked to appoint a delegate for the commission of Italy, and has named Count Nesselrode. There has been no difficulty on this subject.

The affairs of Poland and Saxony have been carried a step further without any positive result. Everything has, however, improved with regard to Saxony. Austria has decided to support her; England has changed her tone; all the Russian and Prussian intrigues have been unmasked. The explanations which have taken place have all tended to prove that Prussia can obtain her restoration on the basis of the population which she had in 1805, without depriving Saxony of more than three or four hundred thousand souls.

We have, in this respect, obtained what we wanted, and the king and his policy have got the first advantages. It is possible that Prussia, seconded by Russia, may refuse to yield; but in this case the forces would be very unequal, and Prussia would risk everything. We have some grounds for hoping that she will form a fair estimate of her position, and yield.

Austria still seems determined not to remove Murat. More positive assurance has therefore been desired from England, Russia seeming to be sufficiently well disposed in this respect. Lord Castlereagh is about to ask his court for fresh instructions. He has communicated all the correspondence on the question of Naples to Prince Talleyrand, and has seemed to desire, rather to support what he has written, that our records be searched for all that may prove to the allies that Murat had a double intrigue with Bonaparte. We doubt not that several letters of his, and some despatches which have been preserved, can prove it. You will therefore, Monsieur le Comte, be so good as to transmit them to us in the originals.

Prince Eugène has said that he has some material proofs of this, but he has refused to give them.

Prince Talleyrand gives more details on the general state of affairs in his correspondence, but we can say with confidence that the king and France enjoy at the conference, the position that is their due, and the consideration shown them affords the means of exercising some degree of influence that is honourable for the king, and which assures Europe a sound guarantee.

Be pleased to accept . . .

No. 16.—The Prince de Talleyrand to King Louis XVIII.

VIENNA, *December* 15, 1814.

SIRE,

The note in which the German princes of the second and third rank were to signify their wish for the preservation of Saxony, was on the point of being signed : it has not been signed, and it will not be. The Duke of Coburg[1] was at the head of these princes. His conduct cannot be too highly praised.

One of his sisters[2] is married to the Grand Duke Constantine. His youngest brother is aide-de-camp of the Grand Duke and major-general in the Russian service.[3] He himself served in the Russian army. He enjoys the good graces of the Emperor Alexander, and is an intimate friend of the King of Prussia. Their resentment seemed likely to fear, if he crossed their purposes, and on the other hand, if Saxony were sacrificed there was every reason to hope that he might get some parcels of it. All these motives were insufficient to silence in him the claims of gratitude and of justice, or to make him forget what he owed to his house and country. When in 1807, after the death of the duke his father, his possessions were confiscated, because he was in the Russian camp, and when Bonaparte wanted to proscribe him, he was protected by the intercession of the King of Saxony. Since then, the king had been in a position to extend his sovereignty over all the duchies of Saxony, and he had refused. In his turn, the duke has shown himself the zealous defender of the cause of the king. He had had it pleaded in London by the Duke Leopold his brother, who found the prince regent most favourably disposed

---

[1] Ernest-Anthony of Saxe-Coburg-Saafeld was born in 1784. He served first in the Russian army. After the peace of Tilsit he returned to his estates, which he preserved intact. The Congress of Vienna gave him the principality of Lichtenberg, but he sold it to Prussia in 1834. He promulgated a constitution in 1821, and died in 1844.

[2] Julie-Henriette-Ulrica, Princess of Saxe-Coburg, was born in 1781. She married, in 1796, the Grand Duke Constantine, brother of the Emperor Alexander, who divorced her in 1810.

[3] Ferdinand-Charles-Augustus, Duke of Saxe-Coburg, was born in 1785, and married to the Princess de Kohary. He had by her three sons, one of whom married Dona Maria II., Queen of Portugal, and another the Princess Clementine, daughter of King Louis-Philippe. His daughter Victoria married in 1840 the Duc de Nemours. The Duke Ferdinand died in 1851.

towards him. He has pleaded his cause here among the sovereigns and their ministers. He has gone so far as to remit in his name to Lord Castlereagh a memorial in which he combated his arguments, and which he drew up with us.

Informed by the Duke of Weimar [1] of the note which was being prepared, the Emperor Alexander sent for the Duke of Coburg, and loaded him with reproaches, as much for the memorandum he had forwarded to Lord Castlereagh, as for his more recent doings, accusing him of intrigues, citing to him the conduct of the Duke of Weimar as a model for him to follow, telling him that if he had any representations to make, it was to Prince von Hardenberg that he ought to address them, and saying that he would now receive nothing of what had been promised him.

The duke was noble and firm; he spoke of his rights, as prince of the House of Saxony, of his duties as a German prince, and, as a man of honour he thought he was not free to neglect them. If the Duke of Weimar thought otherwise he could only pity him. As for himself, he had, he said, twice compromised his position by his attachment to his Imperial Majesty. But if to-day it was necessary to sacrifice it for the sake of honour he was ready to do it.

On the other hand,[2] the Prussians, their emissaries, and, especially the Prince Royal of Wurtemberg have frightened a part of the German ministers by declaring that they would consider enemies all those who moved a finger in favour of Saxony.

That is why the note has not been signed. But it is known that it was to be signed, as are also the reasons which prevented it from being so. The wishes it was to express have perhaps acquired more force from the violent attempt to stifle it.

If I have expatiated on this circumstance at greater length than seemed to be necessary, I have done so from the double motive of rendering to the Duke of Coburg the justice that I believe to be his due, and to better acquaint your Majesty with

---

[1] Charles-Augustus, Duke, and afterwards Grand-Duke of Saxe-Weimar, born in 1757, lost his father at the age of eight months, and was proclaimed duke under the regency of his mother, Amelie of Brunswick, who was then only eighteen years of age. He entered the Prussian army, and received an important command in the campaign of 1806. After the battle of Jena, he became member of the Confederation of the Rhine. In 1814, he went to the Congress at Vienna. It was then that the title of grand-duke was conferred on him. He died in 1828. His eldest son, Charles-Frederick, who succeeded him, had married the sister of the Emperor Alexander, the Grand-Duchess Marie Paulowna.

[2] Text: "De leur côté" = "on their part." Var.: "De l'autre côté" = "on the other hand."

the style and variety of the obstacles against which we have to contend.

Whilst these things were taking place, the Prussians received a letter from Prince Metternich, in which he declared to them that the kingdom of Saxony must be preserved intact, establishing by statistics subjoined to his letter, the fact that their population will be the same as in 1805, if in addition to that of the countries which they have retained, and that of the available countries destined for them, three hundred and thirty thousand Saxons only be added.

I hasten to tell your Majesty that Count von Münster has declared that he will renounce the increase promised to Hanover, if it be necessary for the preservation of the kingdom of Saxony. Your Majesty will surely learn this with pleasure, both for the sake of what it facilitates, and the esteem it brings to Count von Münster.

A passage in the letter of Prince Metternich, in which he availed himself of the opposition of France to the views of Prussia or Saxony, having probably caused the Emperor Alexander to fear that there was some agreement already settled, or ready to be settled, between Austria and ourselves, he immediately sent Prince Adam Czartoryski to me.

The prince at once renewed to me the proposal which the Emperor Alexander had made me in the last interview I have had the honour of having with him, namely that we should comply with his desires as to Saxony, he promising us his support in the question of Naples. His proposal seemed the more acceptable that he no longer demanded the abandonment of all Saxony, and consented to the preservation of a portion of that kingdom.

I replied that, as to the question of Naples, I held to the promise that the emperor had made us, that I relied on his word of honour ; that besides, in this question, his interests were the same as ours, and that he could not possibly be of a different opinion from ourselves ; that if the question of Poland, which must be regarded as a personal one for the Emperor Alexander, since he had staked his satisfaction and fame on it, was decided according to his wishes, (it has not yet been entirely settled, but is in a fair way of being so now), he owed it to the persuasion of Austria and Prussia that this was only a question of second-rate importance to us ; that in the question of Saxony, which was really foreign to the interests of the emperor, we had undertaken to persuade the King of Saxony to make some sacrifices, but that the spirit of conciliation could not be carried so far as the emperor seemed to desire.

The prince spoke to me of alliance and marriage. I told him that so many serious matters could not be treated all at once ; that there were, besides, some matters which could not be mixed up with others, because it would be to degrade them to the level of merchandise.

He asked me if we had any engagements with Austria ; I told him no ; if we should come to any, in the case of no terms being settled between us as to Saxony: I replied, *I should be very sorry.* After a moment's silence, we parted, politely, but coldly.

The emperor, who was to have gone in the evening to a fête given by Prince Metternich, did not go. A sudden headache was the cause, or the excuse. He sent the empress and the grand-duchesses.

He requested [1] Prince Metternich to call on him the next morning.

During the ball, Prince Metternich came up to me, and after having thanked me for a little service I had rendered him, complained to me of the perplexity which Lord Castlereagh's letters on Saxony had caused him. I thought that only one of them had been very compromising (that of October 11th); but he spoke to me of another, which I got to-day, and of which I inclose a copy to your Majesty. Although it is headed as being Lord Castlereagh's, I know that it is the work of Mr. Cook, to whom, both in contents and style, it will not do much credit. It has been sent to the three powers who have called themselves allies so long.

Prince Metternich promised me that, on leaving the emperor, he would call on me, were it not too late, to tell me what had passed. This time he kept his word.

The emperor was cold, dry, and severe. He pretended that Prince Metternich told him, in the name of the Prussians, things which they disavowed, and that, on their side, the Prussians told him, as emanating from Prince Metternich, things opposed to what he wrote in his letters, and that he did not know which to believe. He reproached Prince Metternich with having inspired I know not what ideas in Prince von Hardenberg. Prince Metternich had with him,[2] and produced a letter which proved the contrary. The emperor took occasion of this letter to reproach Prince Metternich with having written some unbecoming letters. This reproach had some foundation. The emperor

---

[1] Text: "Il fit engager . . . . le lendemain matin " = as translated.   Var. : "*Le lendemain matin, il fit engager*" = " *The next morning* he requested." Simple inversion in the text.

[2] Var. : "*de M. de Hardenberg*" = " of Herr von Hardenberg."

had in his possession some private and confidential letters which he could only have obtained owing to some very gross indiscretion on the part of the Prussians. The emperor then seemed inclined to doubt that Prince Metternich's note contained the real opinion of the Emperor of Austria, and added that he would like to have an explanation with the Emperor Francis himself. Prince Metternich immediately warned [1] his master, who, should the Emperor Alexander put any questions on the subject, will reply that the letter was written by his orders, and contains nothing that he disavows.

In a conference held between Prince Metternich and Prince Hardenberg, the only difficulties raised referred to the statistics, which were inclosed in the letter of Prince Metternich. They parted without coming to any agreement, a proposal having been made by Prince Metternich to appoint a commission for verifying them.

That is, sire, the present state of affairs.

Austria only calculates that Saxony loses four hundred thousand souls. She is [2] unwilling to give up Upper Lusatia because of the defiles of Gabel, which constitute an inlet into Bohemia. It was by this pass that the French entered in 1813.

The Emperor of Russia consents to the existence of a kingdom of Saxony, which, according to Prince Adam Czartoryski, would only be half the size of that of to-day.

Finally, Prussia seems now to reduce her claims to calculations of population, and consequently to make them turn on the results and verification of the statistics. The question is doubtless not yet decided, but the chances are now more favourable than they have ever been.

Prince Metternich has offered to let me read his note. I thanked him, saying that I knew it, but desired that he should communicate it to me officially ; that it seemed to me he ought to do this, since he had mentioned us in it, for which I could reproach him, as it had been done without telling us ; that it was necessary that we should be in a position to support it and that we could not do so very well except upon an official communication. He has given me his word to do what I asked. My own motive for asking for an official participation, is that it will constitute the true date of the rupture of the coalition.

I proposed some days ago the formation of a commission to treat of the question of the slave-trade. This proposal was

---

[1] Text : "fit prévenir" = "warned." Var. : "*alla* prévenir" = "*went* to warn."

[2] Text : "ne veut point" = "is unwilling." Var. : "ne *voudrait* point" = "*would* be unwilling."

about to be made, and I wished to introduce it to the Congress, in order to do Lord Castlereagh a favour, and to dispose him by this means to meet us on the thorny Italian questions which we are beginning to discuss. I have gained something, for he has, of his own accord, asked me to indicate to him in what manner I proposed to arrange the affairs of Naples, promising to despatch a special messenger to receive the orders he might require. I wrote to him the letter subjoined here. After receiving it, he proposed to show me his correspondence with Lord Bentinck. I have read it, and my impression now is that the English are perfectly free in this question. But certain promises have been made to Murat, which as men, those who made them might feel obliged to keep, if he had himself (Murat) always faithfully kept his own.

"I think I may say," said Lord Castlereagh to me,[1] "that Murat has entered into correspondence with Bonaparte in the months of December 1813, and January and February 1814 ; but I should be very pleased to have the proof of it. That would wonderfully facilitate my action. If you have such proofs among your papers you would be affording me great pleasure if you could let me have them."

In the letter I write to-day to the department, I request that search be made for any that might be found in the archives of the Ministry of Foreign Affairs. It is possible that there may be some traces of an understanding between Murat and Bonaparte at the Office of the Secretary of State.[2]

The Comte de Jaucourt will lay before your Majesty the two letters which I address to-day to the department. I beg your Majesty to be so good as to refuse the proposals which may be made[3] to you concerning the country of Gex. None of the conditions imposed by your Majesty have been kept. We have also many reasons for being discontented with the Genevese who are here. The authority of the chancellor is more than sufficient to justify the abandoning of this question, which has been entered upon rather precipitately.

I have the honour to be. . . .

---

[1] Var. : "*m'a-t-il dit*" = "*said he to me.*"

[2] Var. : "*Du reste, Lord Castlereagh n'a fait aucune objection à la forme que je lui ai proposé de suivre*" = "*At all events, Lord Castlereagh has made no objection to the line of policy I proposed him to follow.*"

[3] Text : "*seraient*" = "*may be made.*" Var. : "*seront*" = "*will be made.*"

No. 12B.—KING LOUIS XVIII. TO THE PRINCE DE
TALLEYRAND.

PARIS, *December* 18, 1814.

MY COUSIN,

I am in receipt of your letter, No. 15, which has caused
me lively satisfaction. If England declares herself frankly in
favour of Saxony, union with Austria and the greater part of
Germany ought to triumph over *modern ideas.* I like the
firmness of the Emperor Francis, and the defection of the King
of Wurtemberg affects me but very little. I await your explanation of the conduct of this prince, but, according to what I know
of him I should advise no one to enter into a very close alliance
with him.

The letters found among the papers of Lord Oxford have
thrown no light on the intrigues of Murat, but the facts found
in the letter of Leghorn, the truth of which cannot be doubted,
since Prince Metternich acknowledges his knowledge of them,
speak for themselves, and it is time [1] that all the powers should
come to an understanding together, to pluck out the last
root of the evil. On this subject, M. de Jaucourt must have
informed you of the unjust, and, I daresay, ungrateful reproach
levelled against the Comte Hector d'Agoult. It would be as
well if you would speak of it to Count de Labrador, in order
that his testimony may enlighten Señor de Cevallos [2] if he is in
error, or confound him if, as I more than suspect, he belies
himself.

I look upon the desire of the emperor to see you as a good
omen. I have nothing to add to what I have told you on the
main questions ; but there is one which I should like to see
brought to a conclusion one way or another, *viz.,* the marriage. [3]
I have given my *ultimatum.* I shall not mind what will take
place in foreign lands, but the Duchesse de Berry, whoever she
may be, shall only cross the frontiers of France on making an
open confession of the Catholic, Apostolic, and Roman faith.
On these conditions I am not only ready but eager to conclude
it. If, however, these conditions do not suit the Emperor
of Russia, let him say so ; we will none the less remain good
friends, and I will take measures for another marriage.

I regret no less than yourself your absence, but in affairs of

---

[1] Text : "et il est temps" = "and it is time." Var. : "et il est *plus que* temps"
= "and it is *more than* time."

[2] Minister of Foreign Affairs for Spain.

[3] The marriage between the Duc de Berry and the Grand-Duchess Anne of
Russia, sister of the Emperor Alexander.

such importance it is necessary to endeavour to do what Lucan said of Cæsar.[1] Whereupon, my cousin, may God have you in His safe and holy keeping.

LOUIS.

No. 20A.—The Ambassadors of the King at the Congress to the Minister of Foreign Affairs at Paris.

VIENNA, *December* 20, 1814.

MONSIEUR LE COMTE,

The questions of Poland and Saxony are not yet solved. Prince Talleyrand gives an account to the king of the communication made him by Prince Metternich of the letter which the latter wrote to the Prussians, and in which he declared that the cabinet of Vienna does not approve of the incorporation of Saxony with Prussia.

Prince Talleyrand has replied by a letter laying special stress on the principles which ought to be followed in arranging the affairs of Europe. We are waiting for the Prussians to give their decision. It was said that they had drawn up a very strong letter, in which they lay as principles that the incorporation of Saxony with Prussia admits of no contradiction. We are told that the Emperor of Russia himself did not wish this letter to be sent.

Lord Castlereagh cannot conceal his embarrassment, but also refuses to explain himself on anything. His embarrassment arises from the fact that he has, on several occasions, abandoned Saxony, even in writing ; and more than that, whenever he has spoken of Poland, he has never spoken of her as *great and independent*, but solely as Poland.

The affairs of Italy, Naples excepted, on which nothing has yet been said, are progressing, and are being managed in the right direction. Nothing, however, is yet terminated.

The conferences on Swiss affairs are advancing, and the report which is to be submitted to the consideration of the eight powers is being drafted. We shall have the honour of forwarding it to the department as soon as it is ready.

Be pleased to accept . . . .

---

[1] Text : "à ce que Lucain dit de César = as translated. Var.: il faut s'appliquer ce que Lucain" = "one must apply to one's self what Lucan." . . . .

No. 17.—The Prince de Talleyrand to King Louis XVIII.

VIENNA, *December* 20, 1814.

SIRE,

I am in receipt of the letter with which your Majesty has deigned to honour me, dated December 10th, and numbered 11.

I have the honour of sending you copies of the letter of Prince Metternich to Prince von Hardenberg, on the subject of Saxony, of the tables which were subjoined[1] to it, and of the official letter which Prince Metternich has written me when communicating these papers to me. He accompanies the whole with a note in his own handwriting, repeating to me, but less explicitly, what he had already told me *vivâ voce*, that this letter would be the last sent by the coalition, and adding that he congratulated himself for being of the same line of policy as the cabinet of your Majesty for the defence of so noble a cause.

I was very eager for this communication for the reason I have had the honour of stating to your Majesty in my preceding letter. I desired it yet more, as probably offering me a quite natural opportunity for making known the decisions, principles, and views, of your Majesty. I have long sought for this opportunity ; I tried various ways for getting it, and now that it has offered itself, I hasten to make use of it, by addressing to Prince Metternich the reply, a copy of which I have the honour to address herewith to your Majesty.

I have shown what the question of Poland might have been for us, if it had been wished : why it has lost its interest, and I added that the fault did not lie with us.

In treating of the question of Saxony, I refuted the revolutionary arguments of the Prussians, and Mr. Cook in his " Saxon point " ; and I believe I have proved what hitherto Lord Castlereagh has been unable or refused to understand, that as a question of the balance of power, that of Saxony is more important than that of Poland, in the condition to which the latter now finds herself reduced. It is evident that Germany, after having lost her own equilibrium, could not help the general equilibrium, and that this would be destroyed were Saxony once sacrificed.

In seeking to convince, I have aimed at not wounding susceptibilities. I have attributed the opinions which I have combated to a sort of fatality, and I have praised those monarchs who sustain them in order to induce them to abandon them.

---

[1] Text: "y joints " = " subjoined." Var. : " annexés " = " annexed "

As to your Majesty, I have not praised you. I have made public the orders you gave us; what could I say more? The facts speak for themselves.

It is said that the Prussians had prepared a note in reply to that of Prince Metternich, and that it was couched in very violent terms; but that the Emperor of Russia to whom it was shown, did not wish it to be sent.

Lord Castlereagh is like a traveller who has lost his way and cannot find it again. Ashamed of having belittled the Polish question, and of having exhausted all his efforts on it, of having been the dupe of Prussia, although we warned him of it, and of having abandoned Saxony to her, he does not know what part to take. Uneasy besides at the state of public opinion in England, he proposes, it is said, to return there, for the re-opening of Parliament and to leave Lord Clancarty here, to continue the negotiations.

The affairs of Italy are proceeding nicely. I have good reasons for hoping that the Queen of Etruria will have the advantage over the Archduchesse Marie-Louise with regard to Parma, and I am trying to arrange matters in such a way that they may be settled without touching the legations.

The commission of precedence, for which I nominated M. de la Tour de Pin, to whom I gave instructions in conformity with your Majesty's resolutions on the subject, will in all probability be in a condition to give its report in from nine to ten days hence.

Your Majesty will perhaps find the letter I have written to Prince Metternich rather long, but I could not make it shorter, It is intended to be one day published and read in England and France. All the words I employ have one special aim, which your Majesty will also find in my voluminous correspondence.

I have the honour to be . . . . .

No. 13B.—King Louis XVIII. to the Prince de Talleyrand.

PARIS, *December* 23, 1814.

My Cousin,

I am in receipt of your No. 16. I have seen the noble and firm conduct of the Duke of Saxe-Coburg and of Count von Münster with great satisfaction. You know my high esteem for the latter, and the duke, besides the bond of relationship between us, is the brother of a princess of whom

I am very fond, the Duchess Alexander of Wurtemberg.[1] But this satisfaction does not prevent me from regretting that the note was not signed : *Verba volant, scripta autem manent.* I am pleased with your interview with Prince Adam Czartoryski ; you will have seen by my last letter that I should like a definite reply with regard to the marriage ; but that I am far from wishing to give it the character of a bargain.

The slave-trade question appears to be in a fair way of being settled. As to that of Naples, which concerns me more closely, an exceedingly vexatious report was current in Vienna, at the time of the departure of the Duc de Richelieu, which was confirmed by private letters, but to which your silence on the point forbids me to give credence : that Austria had strongly declared herself in favour of Murat, and was seeking to entice England to the same opinion. The success of your letter to Lord Castlereagh, and that of the steps I have ordered to be made in consequence, will soon clearly reveal what I have to hope or fear. Nothing can be better than what you propose in this letter, but I am not quite easy on certain promises given to Murat. Should we—a thing of which I am not quite sure, for Bonaparte, after his defeat, destroyed many documents— should we find the most convincing proofs of this, it is yet too well known that an astute politician can deduce whatever he chooses from anything. However that may be, we will pursue our course ; I will never be found to go back one step in it.

It was for the advantage of the canton of Bern that I consented to a portion of the district of Gex being exchanged ; but since the conditions I attached to it do not meet with approval, I will refuse all consent, and I will never more agree to an arrangement which would further rob the king, my brother-in-law,[2] of anything.

Whereupon, my cousin, I pray God may have you in His safe and holy keeping.

LOUIS.

[1] Antoinette-Ernestine-Amelie of Saxe-Coburg Saafeld, born in 1779, married in 1798, Charles-Alexander-Frederick, Duke of Wurtemberg (1771-1833), general in the Russian service, Governor of Livonia and Courland. She had several children, among whom one son, Frederick-William-Alexander, born in 1804, who married the Princesse Marie d'Orléans, daughter of King Louis-Philippe.

[2] The King of Sardinia, Victor-Emanuel I. It is known that King Louis XVIII. had married his sister, the Princess Marie-Josephine-Louise of Savoy. At the same time, the Comte d'Artois had married another daughter of the King Victor-Amadeus (father of the King of Sardinia), the Princess Marie-Therese.

No. 21A.—The Ambassadors of the King at the Congress to the Minister of Foreign Affairs at Paris.

Vienna, *December* 27, 1814.

Monsieur le Comte,

We believe that we can safely say that Austria has been brought back to the policy which the ministers of the king at the congress have been ordered to firmly support.

The embassy of the king, following the line of principles traced in its instructions, has essentially contributed to raising the spirit of the cabinet of Vienna, and with inspiring it with the energy with which it was lacking.

The Prussians, in a letter couched in rather strong terms, have pleaded the cause of the incorporation of Saxony; Prince Metternich has replied to it, and for the first time has dared to relinquish his character of ally, and show us his letter. Prince Talleyrand thought he ought to profit by this circumstance, for laying bare the true principles of the policy of the French Cabinet, and for spreading abroad the knowledge of those which guide it now, and which always will. This last letter has been laid before Lord Castlereagh and Prince von Wrede.

Prince Talleyrand encloses in his letter to the king copies of these several documents.

You will observe, Monsieur le Comte, that the letter to Lord Castlereagh consists of a plain and simple logic, which ought to make this minister see that truth and justice are one, and cannot triumph by means of the arguments he has hitherto made use of.

We are informed that the Emperor Francis has been again attacked by the Emperor Alexander, who asked him if he had read the note of the Prussian cabinet, to which the Emperor Francis replied, *that he had read it attentively: that he had already, before reading it, taken this position, but that he was more determined than ever not to consent to the incorporation of Saxony with Prussia.*

Since then the Emperor Alexander and the King of Prussia have nominated plenipotentiaries to treat the question of the limits of Poland and the affair of Saxony. We notice that the Emperor of Russia has chosen Count Rasumowski, as likely to be agreeable to the court of Vienna. Prince Metternich will treat for Austria, and Prince von Hardenberg for Prussia. Baron von Wessemberg will act as secretary.

This affair is thus at last going to be treated officially; it may encounter some opposition, but will, in all probability, terminate to the greatest advantage of Russia.

In order to conciliate and reconcile the various statistics which the Prussian and the other cabinets submitted for the execution of the agreements entered into in the different treaties, Lord Castlereagh had proposed that a commission should be formed for this purpose. The Prussians consented, on condition that French commissioners be rigorously excluded. Lord Stewart was deputed to announce this insolent arrangement to Prince Talleyrand. The latter, keenly resenting the breach of propriety of this proceeding, declared that a French commissioner should be admitted, or that the French embassy should leave Vienna on the morrow. He added that he wished for a reply the same evening. The reply was given affirmatively and in the most deferential terms.

Prince Metternich, in his capacity of president, proposed for this commission the instructions enclosed under note No. 1. Prince Talleyrand replied by proposing note No. 2, and furnished the French commissioner with instructions conformable to his note.

The commission is composed of :

1. Lord Clancarty ;
2. Count von Münster ;
3. Baron von Wessemberg ;
4. Herr von Jordan, Prussian Councillor of State ;
5. Herr von Hoffmann ; [1]
6. The Duc de Dalberg ;
7. The Baron de Martin, as secretary.

The Prussian commissioners were at the same time accepted as Russian commissioners also ; but, at the second sitting, it was announced that Baron von Anstett was to be adjoined to them on behalf of Russia.

We forward to your department the protocol of the meetings.

This general situation of affairs leads us to entertain the hope that Russia is about to bring the Polish question to a close, and that, after having obtained what she wanted, she will relax her efforts on behalf of Prussia.

The King of Wurtemberg has grown weary of all this delay, and left Vienna yesterday for his own capital.

There is a rumour abroad that he has signed a special agreement, in which he consents to the incorporation of Saxony with Prussia. Count von Winzingerode, his minister, has assured the Duc de Dalberg that the fact was not true, and that the conversations of the Prince Royal of Wurtemberg, who is on the eve

---

[1] Johan Godfried von Hoffmann, economist and German statesman. Born at Breslau in 1765, he was at first professor of political economy at Kœnigsberg. He was appointed Councillor of State in 1808, attended the treaty of Paris and the Congress of Vienna, and accompanied Prince von Hardenberg on several diplomatic missions. He died in 1847.

of his wedding with the Grand Duchess of Oldenburg, could alone have given rise to this report.

The Germans see this marriage with regret, because they begin to detect in Russia intentions which alarm them.

Indeed, the Prince Royal of Wurtemberg, is now on intimate terms with Baron von Stein, whose hero he has become. They are drawing up together constitutions, in which each of them is to play a part; and, it is probable that this intrigue will open the eyes of the other States of Germany, and induce them to prefer a kind of military league to a constitution of which they all might be the dupes.

No decision has yet been taken as regards Italian affairs, and the question of navigation; but the commission appointed to arrange matters of rank and precedence, has sat twice. After a rather long debate on the subject submitted, most articles were eventually agreed on. That relative to salute at sea gave rise to objections on the part of the English commissioner; but, as he only spoke of America, it will be easy, by offering to leave that matter undecided as regards the United States, to ascertain whether England's objections really applied only to America. The principles set forth in the instructions given by his Majesty formed the basis of this decision, which may be regarded as their direct application.

There only remains for us to call the attention of the ministry to various articles of Prussian newspapers, which should not be allowed to pass unnoticed.

The *Correspondant of Nuremberg*, in its issue 355, publishes two such articles, reproduced from the *Gazette of Aix-la-Chapelle;* these articles are most unwarrantable.

It would be well to acquaint the German public with the conduct of Prussia for the last sixty years, and to quote simply facts, in order to explain the motives which should keep France from associating her policy with that of this power.

It is necessary to call attention to the fact that, in her eyes, the end justifies the means, that she stops at no scruple, that the only law she recognizes is her own convenience; that for the last sixty-five years she raised her population from less than four to more than ten million subjects, and that she has succeeded in cutting out for herself, as it were, an immense framework of dominion, by acquiring here and there territories which she intends to swallow by annexing the interlying territories; that the terrible downfall brought upon her by her ambition has been no lesson to her; that if, at this present time, Germany is still in a state of agitation, this is due to Prussia and her insinuations; that she was the first to adopt in Franconia the system of incorporation, the first to withdraw, at Basel, from the policy of resistance to the Revolution, the only one to urge the loss to us of the left bank of the Rhine. . . .

It is necessary to give an energetic answer to the threats proffered by her plenipotentiaries regarding the consequences a new war might have on the tranquillity of France. (You will observe, Monsieur le Comte, that the articles to be written in refutation of the above allegations are only to appear in second-class newspapers).

Be pleased to accept . . . .

No. 18.—The Prince de Talleyrand to King Louis XVIII.

VIENNA, *December* 28, 1814.

SIRE,

Whilst I was writing to Prince Metternich the letter, a copy of which I have had the honour to forward to your Majesty, the Prussians were replying to his letter of December 12 and called his attention to the note addressed to them by him on October 22, and put him in contradiction with himself; they endeavoured to justify their pretensions on Saxony by reference to authorities and precedents, and contested chiefly the correctness of the calculations on which Prince Metternich based his views.

Lord Castlereagh being authorized to communicate to me this reply of the Prussians, called on me, for the purpose of acquainting me with it. (It will be handed to me, and I shall have the honour of sending it to your Majesty by the next messenger.) He read it to me. I said that their arguments were but sophistry. I pointed out that the authorities and precedents to which they referred were devoid of weight and force, the cases and times being no longer the same. In my turn, I showed Lord Castlereagh my letter[1] to Prince Metternich. He read it very quietly, from beginning to end and returned it to me, without saying a word, either of approval or contradiction.

The object of his visit was to acquaint me with his intention of proposing that a commission be appointed to verify the accounts furnished by Austria and Prussia respectively. I replied that I had no objection to such a course being adopted, but that, if in this case, as in many others, we proceeded at random, without rule or fixed principle, we should obtain no result ; that it was thus necessary to begin by adopting principles ; that, before verifying accounts, it was indispensable to acknowledge the rights

---

[1] Var. : *note = note.*

of the King of Saxony, and that, on this subject, we might, he, Prince Metternich and myself, come to some agreement.

"An agreement?" he said, "it is an alliance, then you propose?"

"This agreement," I replied, "may very well take place without alliance, but, if you wish, it can be an alliance, I have no objection."

"But an alliance presupposes war, or may lead to it, and we ought to do everything in our power to avoid it."

"That is also my opinion, every sacrifice should be made to prevent war, every sacrifice, that is, except that of honour, justice and the future of Europe."

"War," he added, "would not be readily accepted by our people."

"A war would be popular with you, whose aim should be really noble, whose object should be for the good of Europe."

"And what might be that aim?"

"The restoration of Poland."

He did not reject this suggestion and simply contented himself with replying: "Not yet." I had only given the conversation this turn, to sound him, and to find out what he would be prepared to do in such and such a case.

"Whether it be," I said, "by an agreement, or by letter that we recognize the rights of the King of Saxony, or by a protocol signed by you, Prince Metternich and myself, the form is indifferent, the recognition itself is all I care about.

"Austria," he replied, "has *officially* recognized the rights of the King of Saxony; you have also recognized them *officially*; as for myself, I recognize them *absolutely*. Is therefore the difference between us such as to demand the act you suggest?"

We separated, after having agreed to his forming a commission, for which each of us should appoint a plenipotentiary.

The next morning he sent Lord Stewart to tell me that every one assented to the commission being formed, and that no objection was made to it except that a French plenipotentiary should sit in it.

"Who objects to that?" I indignantly asked Lord Stewart.

He said, "It is not my brother." [1]

"Who then?" said I.

He hesitated in answering. "But . . . . it is . . . . "

And finished by faltering out the word *allies*.

At this word all my patience forsook me, and without, in my expressions, going further than was fitting, I showed a spirit which was too strong to be merely termed heat or vehemence,

---

[1] Lord Castlereagh.

I traced the only conduct, which, in such circumstances as these, Europe was to expect from the ambassadors of such a nation as England, and, speaking of what Lord Castlereagh had never ceased to do since we had been at Vienna,[1] I said that his conduct would not be overlooked, that it would be judged in England, as it deserved, and I let him foresee the consequences of it. I treated Lord Stewart himself no less severely for his devotion to the Prussians, and concluded by declaring that if they wished always to be what they had shown themselves at Chaumont and to cling to the coalition for ever, France owed it to her dignity to retire from the congress, and that if the proposed commission were formed without a French plenipotentiary being invited to it, his Majesty's embassy would not remain another day at Vienna. Lord Stewart was abashed, and, with an alarmed look, ran to his brother. I followed him a few minutes afterwards, but Lord Castlereagh was not there.

In the evening, I received from him a note in his own hand-writing, in which he told me that, having heard from his brother what I wanted, he had at once acquainted *our* colleagues with my wish, and that all had agreed with pleasure to do what was agreeable to me.

The same evening, Prince Metternich, whom I had seen during the day, made to the powers who were to concur in the formation of the commission, the proposal that the decision arrived at by the said commission should have the force of law. He subjoined two riders to which I readily subscribed : one that the valuation of claims should comprise all the territories taken from France and her allies ; the other that it should be brought to bear solely on population. But I stipulated in addition that the population should be estimated not according to number merely, but according to its wealth. For a Polish peasant without capital, without land, without means of livelihood, ought not to be put in the same rank as an inhabitant of the left bank of the Rhine or of the more fertile and richer districts of Germany.

The commission, for which I chose[2] M. de Dalberg to represent your Majesty, met on the following day. It is working without interruption, and Lord Clancarty displays on this occasion the same zeal, uprightness, and energy as in the commission on Italian affairs, of which he is also a member.

Justice compels me to say that Lord Castlereagh, displayed in this matter less ill will than weakness ; but his weakness was

---

[1] Text: "depuis que nous étions" = "since we had been." Var. : "depuis qu'il était" = " since *he had been.*"
[2] Var. : " *appointed.*"

all the less excusable[1] that the opposition which he expressed proceeded only from the Prussians.

Two points in my note to Prince Metternich pleased the Austrian cabinet : the declaration by which France does not claim anything for herself, and that which concludes my note. After having read the latter, the Emperor of Austria said to Herr von Sickingen : " I share all the opinions expressed therein."

The Emperor of Russia, having asked him if he had read the answer of the Prussians to the note of Prince Metternich, dated December 10, he replied : " Before reading it, I had made up my mind, and my opinion on the subject is still stronger since I read that answer." He is even said to have added : " Let us arrange[2] matters, if possible, but I beg your Majesty not to mention these statements any more."

He said to the King of Bavaria : " I am an Austrian by birth, but I have a Bohemian head.[3] My mind is made up as regards the affairs of Saxony ; I shall not alter it."

Prince Czartoryski, to whom I communicated my note to Prince Metternich, had a copy of it made, which he placed under the eyes of the Emperor Alexander. The latter was pleased with the portion of it concerning himself and his interests.

He admits that France is the only power whose language has not varied, and which has not deceived him. He, however, detected, as he thought, that he was indirectly reproached with not remaining true to his principles, and sent Prince Czartoryski to tell me that his principles had for their object the happiness of nations, to which I replied that these were also at all times the principles of all the leaders of the French Revolution. Besides, a scruple arising from the fear lest the King of Saxony should feel very miserable with the portion of his dominions which your Majesty wishes to preserve to him has arisen in the mind of the Czar. He does not pity the present position of that sovereign, a prisoner and despoiled of his kingdom, but his future prospect when he will have regained possession of his throne, and re-entered the palace of his ancestors. But this scruple no longer bears any evidence of the former staunch resolution on the part of the Czar[4] of sparing the King of Saxony that misfortune.

As for the Prussians, when consenting to the formation of the commission of statistics, and sending their plenipotentiaries to it, they evidently subordinated their claims and hopes on

---

[1] Var. : "*all the more inexcusable.*"
[2] Var. "*Arrangez*" (*arrange*). Second instead of first person of the plural of the imperative.
[3] A German idiomatic expression, meaning to be obstinate.—(*Translator.*)
[4] Text : "resolution." Var. : "*réflexion*" = "*reflection.*"

Saxony to the result of the discussions of the commission, and that result will, in all probability, be favourable to Saxony.

Thus the affairs of Saxony are in a better situation than they ever were.

Those of Poland are not yet concluded ; but their conclusion is being mooted. Counts Rasumowski and Capo d'Istria are to represent Russia. Prince Metternich is to be the Austrian plenipotentiary. He is bent on giving those deliberations a most official character. Baron von Wessemberg is to draw up the protocols. Prince von Hardenberg is to be the Prussian pleni-potentiary. Seeing that these negotiations will only deal with delimitation of territories, this matter will be settled in a few days.

Although I have given my letter to Prince Metternich to Lord Castlereagh to read, I thought fit to send him a copy of it, that it may be found amongst his papers whenever they may be asked for by Parliament, and I have enclosed with it, not merely a letter to present it to him, but the one a copy of which I have the honour to subjoin here. The great problem for the congress to solve, is here put under a new form, and reduced to the most simple terms. The premises are so incontestable, and the consequences follow so necessarily from them, that no objection seems to be possible. I was therefore not much sur-prised when Prince Metternich told me that Lord Castlereagh, who showed[1] him the letter, seemed rather embarrassed by it.

There exists in Italy, as in Germany, a sect of Unionists, that is to say of people who aspire to making Italy one single state. Austria, warned of this, arrested a great number in one night, amongst whom three generals of division were compromised[2] ; and the papers of the party have been seized at the house of a professor named Rosari.[3] It is not known by whom Austria was informed of the plot. Some think it was by Murat, and that he delivered up some of his confederates in order to win favour with the court here.

Your Majesty has seen by the papers I have sent, that I do not allow the affair of Naples to escape my attention. I do not either lose sight of the *delenda Carthago*, but it is not possible to begin with that.

---

[1] Text: "qui lui a montré " = "who showed him." Var. : "qui *lui avait montré* " = "who *had shown* him."

[2] Text : " *Compromis* " = "compromised." Var.: " *compris* " = " *comprised.*"

[3] Giovanni Rosari, born in 1766 at Parma, was a distinguished physician. In 1796, he was one of the first to welcome the new state of things created in Italy by the French. He was Rector of the University of Pavia, and secretary-general to the Minister of the Interior. Compromised in a plot against Austria in 1814, he was arrested and imprisoned. He died in 1837.

I have also the marriage question in my thoughts. Circumstances have so changed that if, a year ago, it was your Majesty who desired this alliance, to-day it is for the Emperor of Russia to seek it. But this point requires developments which I beg your Majesty to allow me to reserve for a special letter which I shall have the honour of writing to your Majesty.

When this letter reaches your Majesty, we shall be in a new year. I shall not have had the pleasure of being near you, sire, on its opening day, and of presenting my respectful congratulations and sincere wishes to your Majesty. I beg your Majesty to allow me now to offer them, and hope that your Majesty will deign to accept the homage.

I have the honour to be . . . .

No. 14B.—King Louis XVIII. to the Prince de Talleyrand.

PARIS, *December* 27, 1814.

My Cousin,

I have just been informed, that a treaty of peace and amity between England and the United States was signed on the 24th inst. You will surely have been aware of it before this despatch reaches you, and I feel satisfied that you will [1] have taken all the steps required by the circumstances. Nevertheless I hasten to charge you, while congratulating Lord Castlereagh on this fortunate event, to bring before his notice all the advantages that Great Britain can derive from it. Free, henceforth, in the disposal of all her means, what nobler employment could she make of them than to assure the tranquillity of Europe, on the basis of equity, the only really firm basis? And can she attain this end better than by allying herself closely to us? The Prince Regent and myself are the only parties disinterested [2] in the affair. Saxony never was the ally of France, Naples has never been in a position to assist her in war, and the same remark applies to England. I am, it is true, the nearest relation of these two kings; but, I am, before everything else, King of France, and father of my people. It is for the honour of my crown, for the welfare of my subjects, that I cannot allow the seeds of an European war to be sown in Germany; that I cannot tolerate in Italy the presence of an usurper whose existence

---

[1] Text : " que vouz *aurez* faites " ... " which you *will* have made." Var. : " que vous *avez* faites " . " which you have made."

[2] Text : " les seuls désintéressés dans cette affaire. La Saxe..." = " the only disinterested parties in this affair. Saxony..." Var. : " *les plus désintéressés dans cette affaire, car la Saxe* " = " the *most* disinterested parties in this affair, *for* Saxony."

constitutes a crying shame for all sovereigns, and threatens the internal tranquillity of all states. The same sentiments animate the Prince Regent, and it is with the liveliest satisfaction that I see him more and more attached to them.

I have just spoken to you as your king, and I cannot refuse to speak to you also as man to man. There is a case which I ought not to foresee, and in which I should consider the ties of blood alone. If the two kings, my cousins, were deprived of their sceptres, as I was for a long time, then I should hasten to welcome them, to supply their wants, care for them in their misfortune, in a word, to imitate with regard to them what several sovereigns, and especially the Prince Regent, have done for me, and like them, in so doing, I should gratify at once, my feelings and my dignity. But that such a case will not happen, I have for warrant the generosity of some, and the true interest [1] of all. Whereupon, my cousin, I pray God that He may have you in His safe and holy keeping.

LOUIS.

No. 15B.—KING LOUIS XVIII. TO THE PRINCE DE TALLEYRAND.

PARIS, December 28, 1814. [2]

MY COUSIN,

I am in receipt of your note under No. 17. Prince Metternich's letter pleased me, because at last Austria has finally pledged herself, but your reply pleased me still more. I do not know if it can be abridged, but I know very well that I should not desire it, first because it says everything, and nothing that is unnecessary ; and secondly because I find there is more of this urbanity so useful, and often so indispensable in business, in developing one's ideas, than in expressing [3] them in terms too laconic.

That which you say of the embarrassment in which Lord Castlereagh finds himself placed, proves to me that I did right in sending you my last despatch. He perhaps does not perceive [4] that the peace with America offers to him a fine opportunity for retracing his steps.

I am very glad that the affairs of the Queen of Etruria are

---

[1] Text : "le véritable intérêt" = "the *true* interest." Var. : "*l'intérêt* = "the interest."

[2] Text : "*Décembre* 28, 1814" = "December 28, 1814." Var. : "*Décembre* 30, 1814" = "December 30, 1814."

[3] Text : "exprimer" = "to express." Var. : "*exposer*" = 'to expose."

[4] Text : "Il est possible qu'il n'apercoive pas" = "he perhaps does not perceive." Var. : "Il est possible qu'il *n'aperçût*" = "he perhaps *did* not perceive."

taking a better turn, but I only consider this as another step achieved towards the attainment of another aim to which I attach a thousandfold more importance.

M. de Jaucourt doubtless informs you of what M. de Butiakin[1] told him ; you are in a better position than I am to know the truth concerning things at Vienna ; but, if it is true, as seems probable, that the Russian nation, which, in spite of its autocracy,[2] counts for something, feels some interest in the subject of the wedding, it must remember that *he who wants the end, wants the means.* As to me, I have given my *ultimatum,* and I shall not modify it. Whereupon, my cousin, I pray God that He may have you in His safe and holy keeping.

LOUIS.

No. 22 a.—The Ambassadors of the King at the Congress, to the Minister of Foreign Affairs at Paris.

VIENNA, *January* 3, 1815.

MONSIEUR LE COMTE,

The situation of affairs is improved, and Austria and England are better disposed towards the policy that the king has defended and sustained hitherto.

The Russian Cabinet at the second conference, which was held to divide the grand-duchy of Warsaw, submitted articles which contained all its own claims as well as those of Prussia.

These are based on the principle that the grand-duchy of Warsaw is Russia's, and that therefrom she detaches portions, which she hands over to Prussia and Austria. The incorporation of Saxony with Prussia is positively settled, and an equivalent of seven hundred thousand souls stipulated for in favour of the King of Saxony, on the left bank of the Rhine. We may hope that by means of *mutual agreement* these proposals will be rejected. The Prussian negotiators requested a counter project, which will soon be drafted.

The discussion of Italian affairs are about to be resumed. After three weeks' waiting, the commission has received the report of Austria on the questions of Tuscany and Parma. . . . .

The report on Swiss affairs will be discussed to-morrow by the commission summoned for the purpose. The proposal relative to the exchange of Gex will be discarded.

The Emperor of Russia is embarrassed by the position he has taken up. He himself had told Prince Talleyrand that he

[1] An attaché to the Russian embassy at Paris.
[2] Var.: "*aristocratie*" = "*aristocracy*."

wished France to share in the discussions which were to take place in the commission summoned on the affairs of Poland and Saxony. On the morrow, his minister, Count Rasumowski, refused permission to Prince Talleyrand to attend the conferences. Such is the inconsistency of this sovereign's proceedings.

There is still, however, some reason to hope that he will forego some of his pretensions. It is expected that the King of Saxony will have to submit to the loss of half his states ; but that the principle of his existence as a sovereign will be secured, and that what can yet be obtained from the portion of the grand-duchy of Warsaw, which Russia wishes to incorporate, will necessarily have to be subtracted from the portion accruing to Prussia by virtue of the different treaties made between the allied Powers.

Be pleased to accept . . . . .

NO. 19.—THE PRINCE DE TALLEYRAND TO KING LOUIS XVIII.

VIENNA, *January* 4, 1815.

SIRE,

I am in receipt of the letter with which your Majesty has deigned to honour me, dated the 23rd of last month.

On the 21st of the present month, the anniversary of the day when was perpetrated that deed [1] to be held up to the execration, and devoted to the tears and mourning of all future generations, a solemn service of expiation will be held in one of the principal churches of Vienna. I have ordered the preparations for it to be made. In ordering them, I have not only followed the impulse of my heart, but I also thought that it was necessary [2] that the ambassadors of your Majesty, as interpreters of the grief of France, should show it in foreign lands and under the eyes of assembled Europe. Everything in this sad ceremony, must be in accordance with the grandeur of its object, the greatness of the crown of France, and the exalted rank of those who will in all probability witness it.

All the members of the congress will be invited to it, and I am informed that they will all come. The Emperor of Austria has told me that he would be present. His example will certainly be followed by the other sovereigns. The most distinguished company of Vienna, of both sexes, will make it a duty to go there. I do not yet know what it will cost, but it is a necessary expense.

---

[1] The execution of Louis XVI.—(*Translator*).

[2] Text : "qu'il fallait " = " that it was necessary." Var.: " qu'il *convenait* " = ' that it was *fitting*."

The news of the signing of the treaty of peace between England and America was announced to me on New Year's day by a letter from Lord Castlereagh. I hastened to send him my congratulations; and I congratulated myself for it, knowing well the influence that this event might have both on the disposition of this minister, and on the resolutions of those whose pretensions we have hitherto had to combat. Lord Castlereagh showed me the treaty. It hurts the honour of neither party, and will consequently satisfy both of them.

This good news was only the forerunner of some better still.

The spirit of the coalition and the coalition itself, had survived the peace of Paris. My correspondence up to the present date offers numerous instances of it. If the projects that I found established here on my arrival, had been put into execution, France would have found herself, for some fifty years, isolated in Europe, without friendly intercourse with a single power. All my efforts were directed to preventing such a misfortune; but my most sanguine hopes never went so far as to lead me to expect complete success.

But now, sire, the coalition is destroyed, and destroyed for ever. Not only is France no longer isolated in Europe; but your Majesty has already a federative system such as fifty years of negotiations held out no prospect of giving.[1]

She is acting in concert with two of the greatest states, three second class powers, and soon will be joined by all the states that follow other principles or other maxims than the principles and maxims of revolution. She will in reality be the chief and soul of this union, formed for the defence of principles which she has been the first to inculcate.

A change so great and so fortunate can be attributed to the protection of that Providence alone which was so visibly manifested in the return[2] of your Majesty.

After God, the efficient causes of this change have been the following:—

My letters to Prince Metternich and Lord Castlereagh and the impression they produced;

The hints dropped to Lord Castlereagh relative to an agreement with France, of which my last letter to your Majesty gave a full account;

The care I have taken to quiet his suspicions, by showing, in the name of France, the most perfect disinterestedness;

[1] Text: "ne semblaient pas pouvoir parvenir à le lui donner = "apparently held out no prospect of giving you." Var.: "ne *sembleraient*" = "*would* apparently hold out no prospect . . . . "

[2] Text: "dans le retour" = "in the return." Var.: "*par* le retour" = "*by* the return."

The peace with America, which, by ridding him of his anxiety on that side, has left him more free to act, and has given him more courage ;

Finally, the claims of Russia and Prussia, set forth in the Russian proposal, of which I here subjoin a copy ; and, above all, the tone in which the claims have been advanced and sustained in a conference between their plenipotentiaries and those of Austria. The arrogant tone taken in this shameful and preposterous document so wounded Lord Castlereagh that, forsaking his habitual calm, he exclaimed that the Russians were claiming to lay down the law, and that England would accept it from no one.

All this had formed his opinion, and I profited by this to insist on the agreement of which I had long been speaking to him. He was sufficiently excited to propose to write me his views on the subject. The day after this conversation he called on me, and I was greatly surprised to find that he had drawn up his ideas in the form of articles.

I had, till now, accustomed him to but little praise from me, which rendered him all the more sensible now to what I said of his project. He asked Prince Metternich and myself to read it attentively. In the evening,[1] and after having made some alterations in the wording, we adopted it under the form of a convention. In some articles the draft ought to have been more carefully made, but with people of weak characters the great thing is to press on to the end, and we signed it to-night. I hasten to forward it to your Majesty.

Your Majesty had authorized me by letter, and especially by the special instructions of October 25, to promise Austria and Bavaria *the most zealous co-operation*, and, consequently, to stipulate in favour of these two powers, the aid which the forces, which would be brought against them in case of war, should render necessary. Your Majesty authorized me to do this, even on the supposition of England remaining neutral. Now England has to-day become an active party, and with her the united provinces of the Netherlands and Hanover, which makes the position of France superb.

General Dupont having written to me on November 9 that your Majesty would have a hundred and eighty thousand men to dispose of on January 1, and one hundred thousand more on March 1, without levying any fresh recruits, I thought that a help of one hundred and fifty thousand men might be stipulated without inconvenience. England engaging herself to furnish the

---

[1] Text : "Dans la soirée" = "in the evening." Var. : "*Je pris heure dans la soirée et après*" = "*I fixed an hour* in the evening, *and afterwards.*"

same number of troops, France could not remain behind her in this respect.

The agreement being made only in case of protection being wanted, the aid would only be furnished in case of attack ; and there is the greatest possible probability that Russia and Prussia will not run this risk.

At the same time, the case might happen, and render a military convention necessary, so I beg your Majesty to be so good as to order that General Ricard[1] be sent to my aid. He enjoys the confidence of the marshal, Duc de Dalmatie : having been for some time in Poland, and especially at Warsaw, he possesses local knowledge which may prove very useful in arrangements of this character, and the opinion he has given me of his merits and ability causes me to prefer him to any other. But he must come *incognito*, and the Minister of War, after having given him the necessary documents, must enjoin on him the most profound secrecy. According to what I have heard of him, he has been well brought up, and your Majesty, if you thought fit, might give him his orders in person.

I beg your Majesty to be so good as to order that the ratifications of the convention be drawn up, and sent to me as promptly as shall be possible.[2] Your Majesty will surely see the necessity of commanding M. de Jaucourt to employ for this work only men of tried discretion.

Austria being unwilling to send[3] messengers to Paris to-day, so as to avoid arousing suspicions, and wishing her minister to be acquainted with the text of the convention desires that M. de Jaucourt may give it to read to Herr von Vincent, telling him[4] it must be kept secret.

I hope your Majesty will likewise be so good as to include these two documents in the collection of all those that I have had the honour to send you up to the present.

The agreement we have just come to is to get the dispositions of the treaty of Paris completed, in a manner most consonant with the true spirit and best interests of Europe.

But if war should break out, we could give it an aim which would render it almost infallible, and procure incalculable advantages for Europe.

---

[1] Étienne Ricard, born in 1771 at Castres, enlisted as a volunteer in 1792. He was afterwards Soult's aide-de-camp, and was promoted to be general of brigade in 1806. He rallied to the Bourbons in 1814, and was made a peer of France. He retired in 1821, and died in 1843.

[2] Text : "le plus promptement qu'il sera possible " = "as promply as shall be possible." Var. : "*le plus promptement possible*" = "as promptly as possible."

[3] Var.: "envoyer *aujourd'hui* (to send *to-day*).

[4] Var. : "*également*" = "at the same time."

France, in a war carried on with noble aims,[1] would succeed in winning back the esteem and confidence of all nations, and such a conquest is worth more than that of one or several provinces, the possession of which is, fortunately necessary neither to her real force nor her prosperity.[2]

I have the honour to be . . . .

APPENDIX I.

We subjoin here the text of the convention of January 3, 1815, although we have found no copy of it in M. de Talleyrand's papers, no more than of the other papers which have been mentioned in his despatches. But this convention was published in the English State papers, whence we reproduce it, and we subjoin to it some details partly ignored, and possibly forgotten by M. de Talleyrand, as to the publicity it received at that time.

SECRET TREATY OF DEFENSIVE ALLIANCE CONCLUDED AT VIENNA, JANUARY 3RD, 1815.

BETWEEN AUSTRIA, FRANCE, AND GREAT BRITAIN.

In the name of the Most Holy and indivisible Trinity.

His Majesty the King of the United Kingdom of Great Britain and Ireland, His Majesty the King of France and Navarre, and His Majesty the Emperor of Austria, King of Hungary and Bohemia, being convinced that the Powers, to whose share it falls to complete the provisions of the Treaty of Paris, ought to be in a position of perfect security and independence, in order to be able to acquit themselves with the fidelity and dignity requisite to so important a duty, and consequently, considering it necessary, in face of pretensions recently put forth, to provide means of repulsing any aggression to which their own possessions, or those of one of their number might be exposed, from a spirit of opposition to the measures they might have thought it their duty to adopt and sustain by common consent, according to the principles of justice and equity ; and having no less at heart the completion of the dispositions of the Treaty of Paris, in a manner that may be most conformable to its true aim and spirit, have for these ends resolved to make a solemn convention and defensive alliance together.

Wherefore, his Majesty the King of the United Kingdom of Great Britain and Ireland, has nominated, as his plenipotentiary in this matter, the most honourable Robert Stewart, Viscount Castlereagh. . . . . .

His Majesty the King of France and Navarre, M. Charles-Maurice de Talleyrand-Périgord, Prince de Talleyrand. . . . .

And His Majesty the Emperor of Austria, King of Hungary and Bohemia, Herr Clement-Wenceslas-Lothaire, Prince of Metternich-Winneburg Ochsenhausen. . . . .

Who, after having exchanged their powers, which were found to be duly drawn up, agreed to the following articles :—

FIRST ARTICLE.—The high contracting Powers mutually agree, individually and collectively, to act in concert, with the most perfect disinterestedness and complete good faith, in order to put into execution the arrangements of the treaty of Paris necessary to complete its dispositions, and to see that they be carried out in a manner that shall be most conformable to the true spirit of the treaty.

If, consequent upon this, and from aversion to proposals that may have been made and sustained by common agreement, the possessions of any of them were attacked,

---

[1] Var.: *"aussi noblement* faite" = "*so nobly* carried on."

[2] See Appendix I. and II. (Part VIII. Vol. II.), containing the text of the treaty of January 3, and a long note of the Marquis de Bacourt.

at such time and in such circumstances, they promise and bind themselves to consider them all three as attacked, to make common cause with the one attacked, and to assist each other in repelling any such aggression with all the forces hereafter specified.

ART. II.—If for the reasons above mentioned, which can only give rise to the present alliance, one of the high contracting powers were to be threatened by one or several powers, the two other signatories shall be bound to do their utmost, by means of a friendly intervention, to prevent hostilities.

ART. III.—In case their efforts to attain that aim failed, the high contracting powers promise to come immediately to the help of the power attacked, each of them with an army of one hundred and fifty thousand men.

ART. IV.—Each aforesaid army will be composed respectively of one hundred and twenty thousand men of infantry, and thirty thousand men of cavalry, with a train of artillery and ammunition proportionate to the number of troops.

In order to contribute more efficiently to the defence of the power attacked or threatened, the auxiliary troops aforesaid will have to be ready to take the field within a delay of six weeks at the latest, after being called upon to do so.

ART. V.—The situation of the countries which might become the seat of war, or other circumstances being likely to prevent England from providing, within the appointed delay, the stipulated contingent of English troops, and keeping it on a war-footing, His Britannic Majesty reserves to himself the right of providing foreign levies as his share of troops to the power requiring his help, the said foreign levies to be in the pay of England, or to pay annually to the power in question a sum of money calculated at the rate of £20 for each infantry soldier, and of £30 for a horseman, until the stipulated help have been completed.

The way in which Great Britain will have to provide her help will be arranged privately between His Britannic Majesty and the power threatened, as soon as the latter shall have claimed the said help.

ART. VI.—The high contracting powers agree, in case war should break out, to arrange privately the mode of co-operation best suited to the nature as well as to the object of the war, and to settle in like manner the plans of campaign, all matters relative to command, respecting which every facility shall be afforded, the lines of operation of the troops respectively employed, the marches of those troops and their provisions in food and forage.

ART. VII.—If it should be found that the help stipulated be not proportionate to the requirements of circumstances, the high contracting powers reserve to themselves the right of making together, within the shortest possible delay, a fresh arrangement fixing the additional help which may be deemed necessary.

ART. VIII.—The high contracting powers mutually agree that in case those who shall have provided the help stipulated above, should, for that reason, be involved in direct war with the power against which their help shall have been provided, the power that shall have claimed help and the powers from whom such help shall have been claimed, waging war as auxiliaries, shall make peace only by mutual consent.

ART. IX.—The stipulations agreed upon in the present treaty shall not alter or modify in any way any provision which the high contracting powers, or any of them, may have previously agreed upon or may subsequently consent to with other powers, inasmuch as those provisions are not or shall not be contrary to the object of the present alliance.

ART. X.—The high contracting powers, having no intention of aggrandizing themselves, and being solely animated by the desire of mutually protecting themselves in the exercise of their rights and in the fulfilling of their duties as independent states, agree, in case, which God forbid, war were to break out, to consider the Treaty of Paris as the legal basis on which, at the time of signing the peace, the nature, extent, and frontiers of their respective dominions should be settled.

ART. XI.—They moreover agree to settle all other matters by mutual consent, whilst adhering, as far as circumstances will permit, to the principles and provisions of the aforesaid Treaty of Paris.

ART. XII.—The high contracting powers reserve to themselves, by the present compact, the right of inviting all other powers to accede to this treaty in such delays and under such conditions as shall have been agreed between them.

ART. XIII.—His Majesty the King of the United Kingdom of Great Britain and

Ireland, having on the Continent no possession which could be attacked in case of war alluded to in the present treaty, the high contracting powers agree that if such war should break out, and the possessions of his Majesty the King of Hanover or those of his Highness the Sovereign Prince of the United Provinces of the Netherlands, as well as those submitted to his rule, were attacked, the said contracting powers shall be obliged to act, in order to repulse that aggression, as though the latter were directed against their own territory.

ART. XIV.—The present convention shall be ratified, and its ratifications exchanged at Vienna, within six weeks, or sooner if possible.

In witness whereof, the respective plenipotentiaries signed it and appended thereto the seals of their arms.

Done at Vienna, on the third day of January, in the year of our Lord one thousand eight hundred and fifteen.

CASTLEREAGH.
METTERNICH.
TALLEYRAND.

SEPARATE AND SECRET ARTICLE.

The high contracting powers specially agree, in the present article, to call upon the King of Bavaria, the King of Hanover, and the Sovereign Prince of the United Provinces of the Netherlands, to assent to the treaty of to-day's date, under reasonable conditions concerning the number of troops they may be called upon to furnish as their share ; in their turn, the high contracting powers bind themselves to enforce the full effect of the respective provisions of the treaties concerning Bavaria, Hanover, and Holland.

It is, however, understood that in case one of the above mentioned powers should decline to assent to the present treaty, after having been called upon to do so, as said above, this power shall be considered as having forfeited its rights to the advantages to which it might have been entitled, in accordance with the stipulations of to-day's convention.

The present separate and secret article shall be as valid and binding as though it were inserted word for word in to-day's convention ; it will be ratified and its ratification will be exchanged at the same time.

In witness whereof the plenipotentiaries signed it and appended thereunto the seals of their arms. Done at Vienna, the third day of January in the year of our Lord one thousand eight hundred and fifteen.

(*The signatures here follow.*)

APPENDIX II.

King Louis XVIII., as seen in M. de Talleyrand's despatch, had received a copy of the convention of January 3 ; the original of this convention, which latter remained secret, had been deposited at the Ministry of Foreign Affairs, in Paris. It is asserted that, on the return of the Emperor Napoleon from Elba, a high official of the French Foreign Office brought him the above convention, with the object of gaining his favour. According to another version, Napoleon himself found the convention in the very desk of Louis XVIII. Be as it may, it is a fact that Napoleon got acquainted with the convention, and lost no time in taking advantage of it.

All the members of the diplomatic corps accredited to Louis XVIII. left Paris soon after the return of the Emperor Napoleon to the capital. M. Butiakin, a member of the Russian legation, whose name is mentioned in one of M. de Talleyrand's despatches, prolonged his stay. The Duc de Vicence, having become Minister of Foreign Affairs, summoned M. Butiakin before him, told him he had an important communication to make to the Emperor of Russia, and asked whether he could rely on him to deliver it, without delay. M. Butiakin, having replied in the affirmative, the Duc de Vicence handed him, some hours afterwards, a parcel containing a copy of the convention, and a letter in which he tried to incense the Emperor Alexander against the treacherous allies who had deceived him. By this means, Napoleon thought he could break the coalition.

M. Butiakin reached Vienna in the early part of April, 1815. Shortly after his arrival, the Emperor Alexander invited Prince Metternich to call on him, and, after showing him the copy of the convention, said : " Do you know this?"—After enjoying a while the confusion of the Austrian Minister, the Czar said gently to him : "But let us forget all this ; the point is now to overthrow our common enemy, and this document, which *he* himself sent me, proves how dangerous and clever *he* is." —Thereupon, the Emperor Alexander threw the document in the fire, and required from Prince Metternich the promise that he would abstain from acquainting M. de Talleyrand with what had just taken place. Considering himself lucky to get so easily out of the trouble in which he had placed himself, Prince Metternich acquiesced in the Czar's request, and never breathed a word of this adventure.

The Emperor Alexander thought he still wanted Prince Metternich, which is why he spared him in this critical circumstance. But he did not display the same indulgence towards M. de Talleyrand, to whom he made no allusion to the convention of January 3, doubtless reserving his vengeance for some other occasion. The fact is that, after the battle of Waterloo and the return of King Louis XVIII. to Paris, the Russian plenipotentiaries, who had been so conciliatory the year before, and who had, on all occasions, endeavoured to lessen the claims their colleagues brought forward against France, became as exacting as they, and supported France, in a certain measure, against the exorbitant pretensions of the other powers, only after the retirement of M. de Talleyrand and the formation of the Duc de Richelieu's Cabinet. —(*M. de Bacourt.*)

END OF THE EIGHTH PART.

RICHARD CLAY AND SONS, LIMITED LONDON AND BUNGAY